"LEAVE ME BE!" SPIKE ROARED. HE PUSHED AND FOUGHT TO BE FREE OF ANGELUS.

"It's the damned spell!" Angelus yelled, holding tight to the grip he had on the younger vampire. "If you were yourself, you wouldn't care one whit about this woman!" But he knew there was a possibility that Spike's feelings were genuine.

Lyanka rolled over on her side to face them. "I put the evil eye upon you, vampires," she croaked in a harsh voice. Her words slurred and were indistinct to a degree because of the broken jaw, the missing teeth, and the smashed mouth. "And I name you. Angelus. William. I curse you, and I curse your get with all the power that I muster. May tragedy and hopelessness follow you to the end of your days. As long as the Seven Founding Stones lie in the hands of my enemies, you will forever more be cursed."

Angelus thought he felt a tingle, then in the next instant dismissed the feeling as being a product of his overstimulated imagination. . . .

D0755075

Buffy the Vampire Slayer™

Buffy the Vampire Slayer
  (movie tie-in)
The Harvest
Halloween Rain
Coyote Moon
Night of the Living Rerun
Blooded
Visitors
Unnatural Selection
The Power of Persuasion
Deep Water
Here Be Monsters
Ghoul Trouble
Doomsday Deck
Sweet Sixteen
Crossings
Little Things
The Angel Chronicles, Vol. 1
The Angel Chronicles, Vol. 2
The Angel Chronicles, Vol. 3
The Xander Years, Vol. 1
The Xander Years, Vol. 2
The Willow Files, Vol. 1
The Willow Files, Vol. 2
How I Survived My Summer Vacation,
  Vol. 1
The Cordelia Collection, Vol. 1
The Faith Trials, Vol. 1
The Journals of Rupert Giles, Vol. 1
Tales of the Slayer, Vol. 1
Tales of the Slayer, Vol. 2
Tales of the Slayer, Vol. 3

The Lost Slayer serial novel
  Part 1: Prophecies
  Part 2: Dark Times
  Part 3: King of the Dead
  Part 4: Original Sins
  Omnibus Edition

Child of the Hunt
Return to Chaos
The Gatekeeper Trilogy
  Book 1: Out of the Madhouse
  Book 2: Ghost Roads
  Book 3: Sons of Entropy
Obsidian Fate
Immortal
Sins of the Father
Resurrecting Ravana
Prime Evil
The Evil That Men Do
Paleo
Spike and Dru: Pretty Maids
  All in a Row
Revenant
The Book of Fours
Tempted Champions
Oz: Into the Wild
The Wisdom of War
These Our Actors
Blood and Fog
Chosen (finale tie-in)
Chaos Bleeds
Mortal Fear

The Watcher's Guide, Vol. 1: The Official Companion to the Hit Show
The Watcher's Guide, Vol. 2: The Official Companion to the Hit Show
The Postcards
The Essential Angel
The Sunnydale High Yearbook
Pop Quiz: Buffy the Vampire Slayer
The Quotable Slayer
The Monster Book
The Script Book, Season One, Vol. 1
The Script Book, Season One, Vol. 2
The Script Book, Season Two, Vol. 1
The Script Book, Season Two, Vol. 2
The Script Book, Season Two, Vol. 3
The Script Book, Season Two, Vol. 4
The Script Book, Season Three, Vol. 1
The Script Book, Season Three, Vol. 2
The Musical Script Book: Once More, With Feeling

Available from POCKET BOOKS

Buffy the Vampire Slayer™ and Angel™ Crossover Titles

The Unseen Trilogy
   Book 1: The Burning
   Book 2: Door to Alternity
   Book 3: Long Way Home
Monster Island
Seven Crows
Cursed

Angel™

City Of (tie-in)
Not Forgotten
Redemption
Close to the Ground
Shakedown
Hollywood Noir
Avatar
Soul Trade
Bruja
The Summoned
Haunted
Image
Stranger to the Sun
Vengeance
Endangered Species
The Longest Night, Vol. 1
Impressions
Sanctuary
Fearless
Solitary Man

Angel: The Casefiles, Volume 1—The Official Companion

Available from Pocket Books

ANGEL™

cursed

By Mel Odom

An original novel based on the hit television series created by Joss Whedon & David Greenwalt

POCKET
BOOKS

New York   London   Toronto   Sydney   Singapore

To Leslie W., a dreamer and a romantic. Enjoy!

Historian's Note: This story takes place in an alternate continuity during *Buffy*'s fifth and *Angel*'s third seasons.

This book is a work of fiction. Any references to historical events, real people, or real locales are used fictitiously. Other names, characters, places, and incidents are the product of the author's imagination, and any resemblance to actual events or locales or persons, living or dead, is entirely coincidental.

First Pocket Books edition November 2003

™ and © 2003 Twentieth Century Fox Film Corporation. All Rights Reserved.

POCKET BOOKS
An imprint of Simon & Schuster
Africa House
64–78 Kingsway
London WC2B 6AH

The text of this book was set in New Caledonia

Printed in Great Britain by
Cox & Wyman Ltd, Reading, Berkshire

2 4 6 8 10 9 7 5 3 1

A CIP catalogue record for this book is available from the British Library

ISBN 0743468201

PROLOGUE

Carpathian Mountains
April 1893

Demons chased the young woman through the blinding rain up the mountainside. The horrid things voiced ululating howls of bloodlust that cut through the clatter of her horse's hooves striking the hard stone in rapid drumbeats as well as the howling wind that whipped at her long cloak.

If the demons caught her, they would kill her.

The pace her pursuers kept along the barren mountain trail was inhuman. That speed, she knew, was killing the horse. In fact, she knew the horse's lungs bled now from the sustained exertion of the chase. Occasional dark specks of crimson stained her bare white hands when the horse expelled great clouds of gray vapor that swirled back over them.

The object she had stolen lay uncomfortably against her middle. The sharp corners of the box that contained the object dug into her flesh with bruising force.

The trail twisted abruptly to the right.

The woman pulled on the reins, but the horse kept its head, driven by the fear and fatigue that filled its small mind. Lightning blazed through the sky. For a split second, the world turned gray. The edge of the trail became sharply defined. Abruptly, the horse sidestepped, throwing its weight away from the edge.

The horse continued on, following the trail now. The stone face alongside the mountain path brushed at the woman's cloak. The saber belted at her hip rattled against the stone, striking sparks that died almost in the same instant they were born.

She glanced back along the trail, watching as the two riders who had followed her from the small town at the foot of the mountains came around the curve. They wore dark cloaks as she did, and the material billowed out behind them like trailing shadows in flight.

In the next instant, the demons appeared around the corner as well. The demons stood five feet tall at the shoulder. Wide-bodied and strong, the demons resembled bears, but they were covered with glittering green-and-brown scales. Elongated jaws flat as a duck's beak held over two hundred serrated teeth in double rows. The demons ran on six limbs in great loping strides that constantly contorted their bodies in arching waves.

The fate of so many people depended on the object she had found and stolen away. The object proved that her people really had a home. Today they were vagabonds or the outcast refuse of other cities, cultures, or societies, accepted nowhere, welcome for their women and their diversion. But they weren't welcome for long.

Around the next turn, she ran headlong into the wind. The rain pelted her face with blistering force and stung her eyes. With her vision blurred and having to fight the instinctive reaction to close her eyes against the pain, she barely saw the bridge in the darkness.

But it was there. The lattice of half-finished timbers, little more than firewood split and laid so the flat sides formed a surface while suspended on a spider's web of rope, gleamed wetly in the downpour.

The bridge ran somewhere between fifty to a hundred feet. In the darkness, with the moon masked by the clouds, she couldn't clearly make out the distance. Rain dripped from the suspension ropes and swept the timbers.

Hollow explosions rang out as the hooves struck the roped timbers. The bridge swayed in wider arcs and shifted treacherously.

The woman drew the sword. Lightning seared the sable sky and reflected from the keen blade. She glanced over her shoulder, thinking of the two men who followed her, wondering if she would trap them on the bridge as she intended to trap the demons.

Instead, they stopped at the bridge's edge.

Her horse stumbled over the split timber planks. One iron-shod foot shot over the side of the bridge. The horse dropped, balancing itself on the other front leg folded beneath it. Only the ropes kept the animal from plunging over the side and taking the woman with it into the whitecapped torrents ripping between the sharp black rocks below.

The woman pushed herself from the saddle. She caught herself on one bended knee and an outthrust hand, then pushed herself back to her feet.

The horse continued to struggle to get to its feet, but the woman knew that wasn't going to happen. The timber planks were too slick, and the animal had been forced past exhaustion. It breathed in great gusts. Its eyes rolled white with fear as it tossed its head to get up.

The woman felt sorry for the horse. When she cut the bridge's ropes, the horse would fall into the river and surely die.

She gripped the sword and raced toward the other end of the bridge. The timber planks vibrated beneath her feet, letting her know the demons pursued her.

Shadows rose up at the other end of the bridge. She recognized the hulking shapes of the demons at once, but it wasn't till lightning flared again to temporarily rip away the darkness that she recognized the man who stood with them.

Tall and aloof, swaddled in woolen garments and a leather cloak, the man held a large revolver in his fist. His long dark hair whipped around his head and clung to his face, blending with the mustache and goatee that framed his features. His swarthy skin showed cruel, hard lines.

He was her worst enemy, and he had tracked her for long months. Or, more precisely, he had tracked the object she had found and now carried.

She stopped her headlong rush and stared at the man.

A sadistic scowl twisted the man's thin lips. "Come here," he commanded.

She stood, transfixed. The planks shivered beneath her, offering concrete testimony that the demons traversed the distance. Behind her, the horse whinnied in fear.

One of the demons launched itself at the horse. Great fangs sank into the animal's throat, and blood matted the hair. Fear strained the horse's whinny.

The rain sank cold talons into the woman and turned her drenched clothing leaden. She pushed away her fear and the paralysis that went with it.

She was dead. She had to accept that. And once that acceptance was there, she was free to act. She swept the sword up in both hands. Lightning flared again as the blade poised at the peak of the arc.

Then thunder pealed, and she brought the blade down. The ropes parted. With the support ropes on that side shorn, the bridge pitched suddenly and twisted toward the surging river below.

The woman toppled with the bridge and fell

toward the river, watching as the horse came free and dropped as well. The man in shadows yelled incoherently.

She went under at once and fought her way back to the heaving surface of the careening water. Cold spray choked her and occasionally blinded her. Then the current seized her and sped her along.

She grew conscious of a great bulk in the water beside her. At first she thought it was one of the demons that had dropped into the river with her, then she recognized the horse. Made buoyant by nature, the horse fought the current, keeping its head up as it swam with awkward grace.

The young woman knotted her hand in the animal's long mane. She held on tightly to the horse, using it to help keep her afloat.

Without warning, she struck something in the water. Her head felt like it had been split open. Her fingers slipped from the horse's mane. She tried to move her limbs and discovered that she couldn't. Unable to swim, she sank, pulled down by the current. When the water closed over her face, she ceased breathing, hoping that she would recover or that the river would again carry her to the surface.

It didn't. She remained underwater. Through the river and the rain, she watched an artery of lightning pulse across the sky. Revealed in the white-hot light, she spotted her tormentor at one end of the bridge.

The river filled her lungs in a wintry rush and drew her more deeply into its deadly embrace.

CHAPTER ONE

Sunnydale, California
Present Day

"Catch you at a bad time, Spike?"

Spike stood in the rancid mess that had, up until a day ago, been a posh—if he had to say so himself—crypt for a vampire.

Now, however, the smell of burned demon eggs cloyed the still air that hung in the crypt. His vampire's keen sense of smell also picked out the almost intangible fragrance of Buffy Summers, who had left hours ago. She had stepped out into the full glare of sunlight, into a place where he couldn't at that time follow.

She had also stepped out of his life and broken his cold, dead heart.

7

Her soft words still rang in his ears. *It's over.* During their years of open warfare, hatred followed by unexpected love, those two words had been the most hurtful things she'd ever said to him. The worst of it was, he knew she was seriously trying not to hurt him at the time. Not at all like the times when she had tried to stake him and end his existence.

Spike had known what she was going to say when she walked into his crypt. He hadn't wanted to know it; he just had. The way she had acted around Riley Finn after her college lover had caught them in bed together had hurt somewhat because Buffy had seemed ashamed. Shame wasn't anything new to Spike, and he didn't put much personal investment in it. But knowing that being caught with him had caused the reaction in her had cut him deeply.

Seeing Buffy's reaction when Finn had told her that Spike was the Doctor, the man they had been hunting for who had the WMDD (Weapon of Mass Demonological Destruction) for sale to a Third World power, had hurt even more. She hadn't believed that at first, but she'd come around quickly enough all the same.

Of course, Finn had been wrong about Spike being the Doctor, but neither he nor Buffy had stuck around long enough to find that out, had they?

"You gone deaf over there, Spike?" the grating voice asked.

Spike took a last glance at the bed where he'd spent so many hours with Buffy while wrapped in each other's arms. He also realized there were a lot of places in Sunnydale he'd never be able to go again without thinking of her. The graveyards where they'd killed together. The Bronze. The Summers house. *God, the list is bloody wearying, it is.*

"No," Spike said quietly to his uninvited guests. "I haven't gone deaf. Just, you know, having one of those putting-my-life-in-order-and-getting-ready-to-kick-someone-else's-ass-for-all-my-troubles moments."

Three demons stood on the threshold. All of the demons were big, towering brutes with broad, horned shoulders, shaggy heads that put Spike in the mind of bison, and blue-gray skin the color of an old corpse. They wore street clothes, large enough to fit professional football players.

The lead demon gazed around the crypt. One of his fuzzy ears flickered.

"I'd fire your redecorator," the demon said.

"Witticisms?" Spike drawled. "Now there's something I wouldn't expect from someone whose head is the size of a five-gallon pail. Or who looked like Mumsy had carved a jack-o'-lantern face of her newborn babe."

"Don't go thinking you're all that clever, Spike." The demon nodded at the fouled crypt. "This mess you made? It isn't exactly an advertisement for feng shui in cleverness."

Spike smiled coldly. He reached into his shirt pocket under his long, leather duster and removed a crumpled pack of cigarettes. He took one out and ran it under his nose, inhaling the tobacco smell. The burned-eggs odor lessened for a moment. He shoved the cigarette between his lips, took out a lighter, and flicked the flame to life. "What do you want?" Spike asked, letting the annoyance he felt creep into his voice.

"Tarl Dannek wants to talk to you," the demon snarled.

Spike recognized the name. Tarl Dannek was a local "investments" broker, which was actually a rather fancy way of not calling the Russian a loan shark. Dannek wasn't the first, or even the only, "investments" broker Spike did business with.

Spike blew out smoke again. "Tell Dannek I'll be by in a day or two to work out an arrangement with my account."

"Mr. Dannek wants to see you now, *vampire*," the demon said. "He heard how your *investment* went belly up on you because of the Slayer."

"You know, mate," Spike replied, "now isn't exactly a good time for me."

The demon who had done all the talking up till now took a stun baton from the back of his belt. He snapped the release button. The metal telescoped out to over two feet. An oily sheen clung to the metal. The other two demons took out similar weapons.

"Mr. Dannek also wants us to throw you a beating," the first demon said.

Without a word, the three demons launched

themselves at Spike. The way they moved made it immediately apparent that they had worked together before. They fanned out, surrounding him on three sides.

Before they got set, Spike was in motion, moving with all his vampire's speed. He felt his features change, marking him with the face of a demon. He flicked his cigarette toward the man on his right. The cigarette smacked into the man's nose, and glowing orange embers cascaded into his eyes. The demon squalled in pain.

Still in motion, Spike watched the lead demon's arm swing forward. He ducked to the side and reached out with his left hand, sweeping the demon's hand away, then spinning on his left foot to come around in a 180-degree turn to drive the knuckles of his clenched right fist against the demon's temple.

Bone cracked with the sound of a pistol shot.

The demon stumbled and dropped to one knee, catching himself on his hands.

The third demon loosed a bloodcurdling yell as he closed in on Spike, swinging the baton. Spike closed his hands and stepped in to meet his opponent's charge. He blocked the swing with his left forearm, then twisted his hips and drove his right hand into the demon's throat.

His fist pulped the blue-gray flesh and crushed the larynx.

The demon froze in his tracks, evidently knowing something more was wrong than just the incredible pain that had to be flaring through his throat. He *hurk-hurked* a couple times, then realized he was choking. All of the fight left him as he collapsed and gripped his ruined throat.

The demon blinded with the cigarette had tears streaming down his face. But the temporary injury didn't stop him from attacking. The baton whipped across Spike's face.

Pain skyrocketed through Spike's head. He stumbled back, partly from his own efforts to avoid the blow too late, and partly from the incredible force delivered by the baton.

Spike went down, catching himself on his hands. His senses spun, but he lashed out with his right foot, catching the demon's ankles. The demon fell, knocked from his feet. Spike rolled and stood. In the next step, he kicked the demon in the face, snapping the big head around and over. Blood burst from the demon's broad nose.

Pain throbbed through Spike's face. He spat blood onto the floor, then wiped his mouth, leaving a stain of crimson across the back of his hand.

The first demon had his feet under him again. He came at Spike with a series of short, hacking slashes. Spike blocked most of them, but all of them hurt. One of them felt like it cracked his forearm. Spike got in three glancing blows to the demon's big head, but none of them seemed to have much effect.

Dodging to his right, Spike caught the demon's baton hand and stopped the swing. Before the demon could draw his hand back, Spike drove his left foot into his opponent's crotch.

Foul breath exploded from the demon's mouth, mixed in with a cry of pain.

Mercilessly, Spike launched a follow-up kick, connecting with the demon's mouth and splitting his lips. Spike felt the demon's hand relax as the big head snapped backward. He plucked the baton from his opponent's hand, spinning the weapon and getting a more secure grip. Using the baton with grim efficiency, Spike broke the demon's right elbow and left knee with lightning-fast blows. The impacts and the cracks trailed on the heels of each other.

Unable to stand on his broken leg, the demon toppled. He covered his head protectively.

"I got a message for you," Spike grated. "Tell Dannek I'll be in touch. Tell him not to send anybody looking for me."

The demon flopped over onto his back, then immediately tried to curl into a fetal ball.

Spike wiped blood from his mouth again, then tossed the baton aside and reached for another cigarette. He lit the cigarette, took in a lungful of smoke, and glanced around the crypt. He hated the idea of cleaning it—not just the work involved, but the fact that once he had the place clean he'd have to just sit with the knowledge that Buffy was gone.

Until she got past whatever moral quandary she'd established for herself, he knew she wouldn't be around. The crypt had been so complete for a time when Spike had first established it. Now it would seem empty, a place for ghosts.

He turned and left, walling off his emotions that swirled within him. More than anything he wanted to go to Buffy's house, to try to talk some sense into her. But he knew he couldn't do that. Buffy wouldn't see him, and a confrontation between them would probably turn into a full-on brawl.

Besides that, he now had Tarl Dannek to worry about. Dannek had loaned Spike the money necessary to buy the demon eggs. Now those eggs were destroyed, and Spike's cash reserves were temporarily wiped out. Something had to happen. Tarl Dannek wasn't the kind of guy who just cut his losses and went away.

Los Angeles

Angel stood in the shadows atop a cargo-holding warehouse in the Los Angeles Port in San Pedro Bay. Local time was shortly after nine P.M. Coming from the north-northwest, the wind stank of brine, fish, and airborne and waterborne chemical and petroleum pollutants.

Ships moved on the dark water out in the harbor. Some sails were in evidence, but most vessels were powered by diesel engines. A helicopter flew overhead, flooding the area with the *whop-whop-whop* of rotor blades. Low, mournful wails of tugboat horns echoed over the bay. PA systems blared down on the docks and rail yards that fronted the water. All of the sounds held the resonant quality of the ocean behind them, and that mixture of noise—the deep vastness of the sea colliding with the cacophonic bleats, whistles, and electronic crackles of the vessels—brought the past and the present to Angel's mind.

The cell phone in his duster pocket vibrated for attention. He punched the Talk button and held the phone to his ear. "What's wrong? Is he okay?"

"Oh, and aren't we the nervous Nellie father?" Cordelia Chase's tone lightly mocked him.

Despite the weeks that had passed since his son's birth, Angel still hadn't quite gotten accustomed to the acquisition of the new term. *Father.* As a vampire, becoming a father was supposed to be impossible. But, as he had learned so many times during his long and event-filled life and posthuman existence, "impossible" happened to him on a daily basis.

"Not nervous," Angel said quickly, trying to cover his concern.

"No?" Cordy asked.

"No."

Her silence offered mute rebuttal.

"So what is it?" Angel asked, trying to ignore her obvious mood.

Ordinarily when Cordelia was irritable, everyone else noticed it but she acted like she didn't have a clue. He peered out over the port, watching the Yusen NYK Line railcars move along the tracks that ran through the Terminal Island Container Transfer Facility.

The TICTF occupied forty-seven acres along the port. Ships brought container cargo up to dockside that were transferred onto waiting train cars while other cargo brought by the Yusen NYK Line and the Evergreen line were loaded back onto the ships. Cargo was constantly incoming and outgoing, and profits were only digital markers kept in computers, credit lines, and banks. Only the warehouse mavens and port authority inspectors kept track of most of the physical goods.

Being a port city, though, L.A. had a large share of black-market cargo that entered and left without ever being marked down in a computer or issued a bill of lading or appearing on a ship's manifest. The port authority discovered some of it, but the black market trade remained brisk and lucrative.

"Is it Connor?" Angel still felt strange using his son's name. He'd thought for a long time before naming his son, but somehow he still didn't feel worthy enough to have named him. How did he know it was the right name? Who knew what Connor would grow up to be? Or what he would think? Or how he would feel about having a vampire for a dad? The whole vampire thing cut down a lot on potential school visits during honor awards, sporting events, and shared lunches in the cafeteria. *Hey Connor, how come we never see your dad at the beach?*

"Connor is fine," Cordelia said. "He's sleeping. And I didn't call so you could check up on me or play Twenty Questions."

Angel waited a beat, watching the large boom lifting cargo containers from a ship's hold and transferring them to a rail car. The ship was *Swift Star*, a cargo vessel out of Germany by way of Singapore. "Why did you call, Cordelia?" Angel asked.

"To find out what you were doing."

"A favor for Giles. Like I told you." Angel propped the phone on his shoulder and took a pair of mini-binoculars from his duster pocket. He zoomed in on the railcars and the ship, dividing his attention. "It's probably nothing."

"Giles wouldn't have called if it was nothing."

"It's nothing so far."

"Oh."

"Where are Gunn and Wesley and Fred?" Angel asked.

"On patrol." Cordelia sounded more irritated. "I could have used a patrol shift."

"You volunteered to stay with Connor."

"I know." Cordelia sighed. "And there's nowhere I'd rather be, Angel. Connor is sweet and cute, and just makes me feel like a step away from momhood—only without the worry lines, the stress, and the recycled baby formula stench. Plus, I get to hand him back to you when I need a break or he needs a diaper change. Most of the time."

Angel considered that, trying to figure out exactly what he was supposed to say to Cordelia. "I appreciate what you're doing."

"I know. And I know you handle most of the day shifts."

That was true. Whenever he had a spare moment, Angel spent time with Connor. He could hold his infant son for hours, just peering at Connor's face and wondering at the miracle that he had been given. Sometimes, Angel even felt a little sad that Darla had not lived to see their son. She had sacrificed herself in an alleyway, staked her own dead heart, and turned to dust so that their son would be born instead of dying from the attack her vampire's body was waging on him as he'd struggled to be born.

"You haven't been listening, have you?" Cordelia accused.

"I was listening," Angel lied. "It's the phone." He shook the handset and slapped it against his thigh.

"Stop hitting the phone. You're going to break it. You can't fool me with that. Remember, I was once a spoiled high school student. I know all about that little scheme."

Cordelia had gone to Sunnydale High three years ago. She'd been one of the in-crowd. Then, when she'd been swept into the troop of monster hunters Buffy Summers had raised to fight the malevolent forces vomited forth and drawn to the Hellmouth under the town, Cordelia had found herself living a double life. By day, she was a high school fashion trendsetter. At night, she was—reluctantly—caught up in the battle against vampires and other semidead things or demons that rose up to feast on the citizens of Sunnydale.

In the last three years, so many things had changed. Angel had relocated to Los Angeles, discovering only a little later that Cordelia had as well.

"You said Giles asked you to scope this out for him?" Cordelia prompted. "So what is it you're looking for?"

"An object."

"Well, that narrows things down. Animal, mineral, or vegetable? I'm entitled to a few clues if we're going to play this game."

"Cordelia, this isn't a game. It's just how it is. I don't know what I'm supposed to find here." Angel watched *Swift Star* through the binoculars. The boom arm swung the large rectangular containers over the ship's side to the docks, then onto the train cars.

"So how are you going to know how to find what you're looking for?"

"Giles told me to expect thieves," Angel said. "Apparently, a Watcher in Hong Kong found out about an object Wolfram and Hart was interested in that came out of Germany. The Black Forest or somewhere. Attorneys from Wolfram and Hart set up a buy through the thieves."

"They wanted this object for themselves?" Cordelia sounded pensive. "Footnote: Objects that

Wolfram and Hart are generally interested in aren't exactly conducive to the welfare of the rest of the world."

"That's one of the reasons I decided to look into this when Giles called to tell me about it. From what I understand, Wolfram and Hart were only acting as the brokers for the object."

"Who's the real buyer?"

"Giles didn't know."

"But he knew about the thieves?"

"They made a try for the object in Hong Kong. Left a lot of dead bodies behind."

She was silent for a moment. "Whoever it is, they're kind of serious about it, huh?"

"Yeah."

An eighteen-wheeler rumbled down the port area beside the Yusen NYK Line. The tractor pulled a long, empty flatbed trailer.

The vehicle drew Angel's attention because it was the first eighteen-wheeler he'd seen pull into the docks not carrying a load. Even back in his days in Galway, Ireland, Angel knew that cargo merchants didn't like to sail anywhere without both buying and selling. A merchant ship always had to do both to manage some kind of profit.

Maximizing the binoculars' magnification, Angel studied the features of the men inside as security lights posted around the docks whipped through the cab. The light briefly illuminated the truck crew. The passengers looked like blocky caricatures of men, as sketchy and as out of proportion as a child's drawing. Their heads were smooth, bullet-shaped without ears. Red-limned eyes in the shape of inverted triangles glowered out at the world.

"Barkuk demons," Angel said.

"Haven't heard of them," Cordelia replied.

The eighteen-wheeler slowed. Ruby brake lights stained the brief wisps of fog drifting in from the harbor. The figures inside the truck cab shifted. Metallic surfaces reflected the light.

"They're usually muscle-for-hire," Angel said.

The eighteen-wheeler moved ever slower, then finally came to a stop near a cargo clearing station where a handful of men stood waiting. The truck's brake lights blinked off at the same time the headlights went out. The doors opened, and the Barkuk demons dropped to the ground. They wore jeans and shirts with three-quarter-length khaki jackets over them. One of them absently caught the cut-down shotgun that briefly flashed into the open and shoved it back under the jacket.

"I've got to go," Angel said.

"What's going on?"

"I'll call you back." Angel punched End, folded the phone, and tucked it back into his duster pocket. He stayed low as he walked to the roof's edge to his right.

Six Barkuk demons emerged from the truck. That fit with what Angel remembered of the demon mercenaries. All of them were stone-cold killers. They killed whomever they were paid to kill, held ground where they were supposed to hold ground, and—when things got really bad and survival was the only coin of the realm—they killed everyone around them that wasn't a Barkuk. When the enemy was overrunning a position, the last place even a non-Barkuk co-combatant wanted to be was in a fighting hole with the demons.

The ground lay fifty feet below. Angel rose and stepped over the roof's edge. He dropped like a stone and landed on his feet in the shadows of the building. He took off at once, closing the distance between himself and the Barkuk demons as they made their way to *Swift Star*.

CHAPTER TWO

Los Angeles

The Barkuks moved in their standard flared pattern that consisted of a point man, two wings, a pivot man that could serve as a secondary point man if the group was broken into two groups, and two men walking slack.

Angel paused at the end of a corridor of containers. He stood masked by the shadows. Security lights gleamed atop tall poles but did little to light the entire area. Still, anyone seeking to steal anything from the docks of the railways and shipyards would be hard pressed to get through the on-site security network.

A huge forklift turned the corner a few rows of

containers farther down. The big boom mounted on the concrete foundation plucked another container from *Swift Star*'s hold and swiveled it over to dry land. The container shifted and swung as it decended from the thick cables. When lowered to the ground, the container bonged loudly. The waiting forklift started forward, hooked the big container, and reversed.

Moving as if with one mind yet without a word between them, the Barkuks slipped through the shadows in pursuit of the container. Looking back the way he was going, the forklift driver never saw them.

The point man of the Barkuks put on a burst of speed, then launched himself twenty feet to the top of a row of containers. He landed running, as if the leap had been effortless, a mere lengthening of stride.

The next leap took the Barkuk warrior to the top of the forklift. He landed with a *clang* that was barely audible over the forklift's noise. The driver halted, evidently fearing he'd dislodged something with his load.

By the time Angel realized what the Barkuk intended, it was already too late. Still, he threw himself forward and yelled, "Look out!"

The Barkuk on top of the forklift maintained his balance on the rocking forklift, bent down in fluid motion, and raked a knife across the forklift operator's throat. Crimson rained down the man's chest.

A shadow stepped from the line of containers to Angel's left. He sensed the movement more than he saw it. Still, he barely got beneath the shotgun blast that cut the air over his head and temporarily rendered him deaf.

On the forklift, the Barkuk demon caught the dying man by the shirtfront as the human tried to stanch the blood flow squirting from his savaged throat. The Barkuk demon hauled the man from the forklift's cockpit with one hand and flung him away as if he'd been a child's toy.

A Barkuk growl ripped through the noisy dock area. Angel didn't speak the language, but he could guess at the meaning. *Run!* or *Kill him!* would have been two assumptions.

The Barkuk warrior that had stepped from the shadows brought his weapon down, trying to point it at Angel for another shot. Reacting swiftly, Angel reached up and caught the shotgun's superheated barrel. If he'd kept his hand in place against the metal, he might have gotten burned.

Instead, he yanked the shotgun with his own immense strength, carefully keeping the barrel pointed away from his head. The Barkuk warrior squeezed the trigger just as Angel shifted directions and thrust the buttstock back into the ovoid face. The recoil from the shotgun blast drove the weapon back even harder. The demon's cheek split beneath the triangular eye and wept yellow blood.

Before the Barkuk warrior could recover, Angel

whirled into him. Angel kept his grip on the shotgun, shoving the weapon away from him. He brought his right elbow back three times in quick succession, driving the hard bone twice into the Barkuk's side to splinter ribs, then into his opponent's face to break his nose. Flesh split above the Barkuk's right eye and blood leaked down to obscure his vision.

The Barkuk squalled in pain and rage, then flailed with his free hand to grapple Angel.

Ducking beneath the big arm, Angel kept hold of the shotgun and stepped behind the Barkuk. The shotgun blasted again, hurtling another swarm of double-aught pellets into the container behind Angel. The ricochets stung his back and shoulders. He didn't worry about the wounds. He was a vampire; eventually those hurts would heal. All he had to do was keep his head—literally.

Drawing his right leg up, Angel brought his foot down hard in a stomp-kick on the Barkuk's elbow. Bone snapped with the brittle intensity of a breadstick but a dozen times louder. Taking advantage of his foe's weakened condition, Angel yanked the shotgun free. He swung the buttstock at the back of the demon's head, driving him down to his knees.

Shadows shifted on the ground.

Always three, Angel reminded himself. *Barkuks always come at you in threes. Until you kill one.*

Angel dodged back, driven more deeply into the narrow corridor between cargo containers. He lifted the shotgun and brought the weapon to his shoulder.

He didn't particularly care for more modern weapons, but his battles over the years had included them. His finger found the shotgun's trigger as he pointed the weapon at the center of the Barkuk. He pulled the trigger while he was giving ground before the ferocious, snarling demon.

The blast of pellets caught the Barkuk in the chest and ripped away his clothing to reveal lightweight Kevlar armor beneath. Even the blunt trauma didn't seem to slow him.

Going with the weapon's recoil, letting the barrel rise instead of fighting it, Angel took quick aim and fired again. The buckshot caught the demon in the face just as he was taking aim with his own shotgun and the corridor behind Angel came to an abrupt end.

Angel squeezed the shotgun's trigger again. Nothing happened. Even as Angel realized the weapon must have fired dry, the Barkuk warrior stumbled forward and fell against him, trapping him against the cargo container behind him.

Amazingly, the Barkuk still lived. Angry fire glinted in the triangular hollows of its remaining eye. Bone shone ivory in the moonlight where the shotgun blast had torn away the right side of its face. The demon struggled to bring the shotgun he held up to Angel's head.

Angel knocked the shotgun away as it blasted into the container beside his head. Something—either a stray pellet or a sliver of metal—nicked his ear. He

27

felt the warmth of his own blood sliding down his neck.

Shoving an arm under the Barkuk's chin and into his throat, Angel levered the demon off him. All the fight left his opponent, and he went down in a slack heap, barely breathing. With all the yellow blood covering his head, Angel didn't know how the demon would survive.

Three, he reminded himself, staggering free. *Always three.*

Angel glanced at the mouth the corridor, searching for the first wounded Barkuk he'd left behind. The demon wasn't there. Angel tossed the empty shotgun away, then made the twenty-foot leap to the top of the containers, seeking the high ground.

He raced across the containers. Whatever was in the container the Barkuks had come for, he knew that whoever had hired them to retrieve it wanted the thing badly. Giles's information had been dead-on.

The rail yards and docks had come alive. Sirens sounded, screeching like banshees. Lights atop security cars and trucks whirled. Out in the harbor, a patrol boat fired to life and swung about, bringing the high-intensity spotlights to bear along the shoreline. Unfortunately, all the security efforts were handicapped by the presence of ships in the docks and transportation vehicles handling various loads. Confusion had also broken out among the longshoremen working the cargoes.

Angel ran in the direction the forklift had been heading. He leaped across the staggered gaps between stacks of containers. Shadows changed shapes and lengths as the light sources around him moved and shifted. Spotlights from the ships in the slips added to the general confusion.

The Barkuk now driving the forklift bearing the target container wound through the stacks of cargo like he'd had a map. His two companions matched pace with him, running alongside while holding their shotguns at the ready.

Angel made the next leap as another forklift came around the next corner. The driver wore a headset and looked startled to see the first forklift bearing down on him. He looked surprised for only a moment, then a shotgun blast erased his features and shattered the revolving yellow hazard light on top of the protective steel cage.

The Barkuk driving the stolen forklift didn't hesitate. He headed into the side of the other vehicle. Metal clanged as the two forklifts slammed against each other like two dinosaurs. Incredibly, both fork-lifts came to a stop.

One of the Barkuks ran forward, yanked the corpse from the second forklift, and drove the vehicle out of the way. He kept the forklift hurtling forward, driving it into the small pickup with security markings that was closing in on the area. The pickup didn't stand a chance against the big forklift and the heavy cargo container.

Driven backward, the pickup smashed against a line of containers behind it. The Barkuk kept the accelerator pinned to the floor. The forklift's front wheels spun but didn't gain any ground.

The forklift bearing the target container careened by the stalled forklift. Metal scraped, and sparks scattered. By the time the stolen forklift raced by, the Barkuk in the wrecked forklift had bailed and set himself into position again.

The stolen forklift driver closed on the eighteen-wheeler the demons had arrived in. He hurtled along the open areas, driving straight for the truck.

Angel ran out of container stacks. Without hesitation, he stepped over the side and hit the ground running.

The sirens shrilled louder. Angel knew the police would be there within minutes. The on-site security teams would be armed as well.

Harsh growls sounded behind Angel. Ahead, Barkuks dodged to either side. Reading the movements, Angel knew that at least one of the two surviving demons he'd left in his back trail had caught up with him. He dove to the left, going flat in a baseball slide that put him up under a white maintenance truck with the familiar Southern California Edison logo on it.

Moving quickly on the other side of the truck now, remembering that the Barkuks showed no reluctance about killing humans, Angel pushed himself to his feet. He rushed forward, opened the door to the maintenance truck, and yanked the driver out. His protective hard hat slammed against the door frame on his way out.

A shotgun blast took out the passenger door window and part of the front windshield. The SCE driver cursed and covered his head with his arms.

Angel shoved the man into motion, watching as he stumbled and fell behind crates marked FARM MACHINERY. He stayed down, getting as far away as he could on his hands and knees.

The maintenance truck sagged as a shotgun blast took out one of the passenger-side tires.

Opening the door, Angel peered in and found the keys swinging from the ignition. He pulled himself up and into the cab. His plan—*It is a plan,* he told himself—formed as he moved. If he could somehow prevent the Barkuks from departing the scene with the container, the police might have a chance at arriving in time to prevent the container's theft. The solution wasn't an optimum choice since it placed the object in police custody, but it beat sitting back and watching the cargo container disappear.

He twisted the ignition. The truck's engine turned over and started easily. The sound also drew a barrage of shotgun fire that spilled safety glass from the blown-out window into his lap.

He let out the clutch, and the big truck surged forward. Unfortunately, the blown tire made it hard to steer. Still, he pulled the wheel in the direction he wanted to go and stayed low behind the dashboard.

Another Barkuk sped for the eighteen-wheeler's cab while the forklift driver clambered from his stolen machine. The third demon leaped to the flatbed.

Before Angel could change gears again, something struck his driver's door. He glanced at the window just in time to see a savage, half-formed Barkuk face fill the window. He couldn't avoid the big three-fingered fist that slammed into his temple.

Pain cascaded through Angel's head, blinding him for a moment. He struggled to hang on to the wheel, grateful that the Barkuk hadn't been physically able to wield the shotgun while he'd swarmed up the maintenance truck's side.

The Barkuk warrior reached through the window and hauled the steering wheel hard left. The truck barely missed the eighteen-wheeler, then crashed into the side of a waiting railroad car packed with new cars.

Giving way before the maintenance truck's speed and bulk, the railcar's side broke. New cars and SUVs dropped from the double-decker. Two of them tumbled down onto the maintenance truck.

Angel barely ducked in time before a SUV slammed hard against the top of the truck's cab and crushed it downward. The explosion of force also ripped the passenger's door free. A red sports car dropped on the Barkuk warrior clinging to the driver's door, smashing him down.

Kicking out, Angel squirmed through the passenger door. He dropped and rolled, coming easily to his feet. Pain wracked his body from the impact as well as the flesh wounds left by the shotgun pellets. He swiveled his head in the direction of the eighteen-wheeler.

The truck surged forward.

Men stepped from the shadows carrying pistols and rifles. They wore flowing dark clothing, broad hats, and boots. Most of them had dark, swarthy faces split by mustaches. Heavy sideburns and beards framed their features. Muzzle flashes lit up their weapons.

The barrage of intense gunfire swept one of the Barkuk demons from the rear of the eighteen-wheeler as the vehicle gained speed. But the truck kept going, smashing against other parked vehicles as it roared out onto the street away from the docks.

The men turned their attention to Angel for a moment. He avoided the sudden hail of gunfire that came his way by diving behind the wreckage of the SCE truck. Bullets tore into the body but didn't penetrate.

Out on the street, the eighteen-wheeler roared through an intersection. Discordant horns blared in response, and a minivan got slammed to one side as the bigger vehicle tore through.

The men in black clothing vanished back into the shadows. A moment later, cars sped in pursuit of the eighteen-wheeler.

Angel's GTX convertible was blocks away. He

hadn't wanted the car found and tied to anything bad that might have happened at the docks. He pushed himself to his feet and ran.

The men who had attacked the Barkuks and the eighteen-wheeler had been gypsies. And gypsies put an entirely different spin on things. He'd never had luck with gypsies.

Sunnydale

"Hello, Dannek," Spike said.

Tarl Dannek stood on the other side of the chef's kitchen in the back of the Blue Note Restaurant. The ex-Russian Mafia mobster was broad and beefy. Evidently, the criminal life in California in general and Sunnydale in particular agreed with him. Gray flecked his dark hair and goatee. He wore a white chef's uniform, a matching apron that already sported sauce stains resembling spilled blood, and a chef's hat. He used a blue-gray marble rolling pin to press out a thin layer of yellow-white dough.

Concentrating on his work, Dannek barely glanced up at Spike. "Ah, Spike. So you found out about my little secret getaway."

"Yeah."

Three bodyguards, two of them demons and one human, started forward, reaching beneath their coats.

Dannek raised a flour-covered hand. "No," he said in a stern voice. He shook his hand, and a little puffy cloud of flour drifted away and sank to the floor. "There will be no gunplay in my kitchen. Not unless it becomes necessary."

The bodyguards stood down with obvious reluctance.

"I'm making blueberry tarts," Dannek said, returning his attention to rolling the dough. "The crust must be very thin. Thick enough to hold the tart together, yes, but thin enough that it seems to melt in your mouth."

"I'll take your word for it. Me, I've always been interested in a different kind of tart." Spike stood in the back doorway to the restaurant. He'd come through the door from the alley with the morning produce while staying in the shade offered by the bulk of nearby buildings. He only had a short while to negotiate his position before the sun claimed the alley and it would be dangerous for him to get out of the building.

Dannek walked to the three-compartment sink and washed his hands. He dried them on a nearby dish towel. "What did you come here for, Spike?"

"To see if we couldn't make a deal."

Leaning against a baker's table, Dannek said, "We already had a deal, yes? I fronted you investment capital to take over the little moneymaking scheme your friend Maurice let you have for a *song*." The mobster made sarcastic "quotes" around *song*.

Spike wanted to smash and break the greedy smile that took shape on Dannek's face. But the chip in his head would prevent that.

"You were too needy when you came to me, Spike," Dannek said. "Too . . . *vulnerable*. For a man like me, vulnerability is a hard thing to refuse. It is like blood in the water for a shark, yes? Surely you understand."

The problem was, Spike did understand. He'd been a patsy twice over. First for Maurice, then for Dannek. And he'd done it all to get money together that he could have used to help Buffy. Not for himself, because money had never been a big issue with him unless he didn't have it when he wanted it. Then he'd simply gone out and gotten it from whatever closest resource existed.

But money had been a considerable worry for Buffy. Since her mom had died, since she'd returned from the grave, Buffy had experienced a lot of financial hardship.

Always a fool for love, Spike told himself. He regretted that side of himself. Of all his qualities that he'd possessed before Drusilla had turned him into a vampire, why did that aspect of his former self keep reappearing?

Maurice, as always, had painted such a great picture of the profits that were going to be made. Okay, so maybe he would have taken Maurice's offer, anyway. He'd really wanted to get his hands on enough money to get Buffy away from thinking about bills and work long enough to fit in more crypt time.

"Why didn't Maurice stick around to make these profits himself?" Dannek asked.

"He's kind of a wanted guy," Spike explained. "He had the deal all set up. Everything was in place. Just had to wait on the buyer. A few days before he asked me to buy into the deal, he saw a couple of guys who have been looking for him. Tracked him all the way from the Netherlands. A man like Maurice, he's always carrying bad baggage." He shrugged. "Said he had to get away, had to make a deal. I believed him. Been through similar circumstances myself."

"As have I," Dannek agreed with a nod.

Thinking quickly, knowing he had to find some way to put them on common ground, Spike said, "Maurice is the one to blame, you know."

"True." Dannek nodded. "I blame him for this very much, yes."

"Then he should be the one you want revenge on."

"I do want revenge on this man. But I want my money back. Vengeance, well—as you know— maybe it will allow you to sleep a little more contentedly at night, but it does not keep the roof over your head, yes?"

"I'll kill Maurice," Spike suggested.

Dannek raised his eyebrows. "You would offer to kill your friend?"

"My *friend* set us both up."

Nodding, Dannek said, "This friend, Maurice, he did inconvenience both of us. Having him killed, that should be worth something, yes?"

"Bloody right," Spike agreed. *Maurice isn't all that great a friend. I've known him what? Eighty, ninety years? And haven't seen him much of those.*

Dannek clapped his hands as a child might in delight. "If you take the time to kill him, and bring me his head, I can knock off"—he paused—"let us say, two thousand dollars from the investment money you owe me."

"Two thousand!" Spike couldn't believe it. "Two thousand is nothing!"

Dannek shook his head. "You drive a hard bargain for the life of your friend."

"This is the guy who screwed you out of a lot of money," Spike said.

"No." Dannek held up a floury finger. "You see, I do believe in you, Spike. I have not been screwed out of my money until you tell me you are not going to pay me, yes?"

Spike stood silently, feeling the jaws of the trap close around him. They weren't on the same side. Dannek wanted his money, and that was all he wanted.

"You are not going to tell me that I am not going to get my money, I hope?" Dannek waited.

The bodyguards stood with their hands under their jackets.

Spike almost erupted at their threatening postures. He was certain he could at least flee the restaurant before they could seriously hurt him. And during that time he also believed he could kill or cripple the demon bodyguards. He could show them how costly pursuing him could be.

Dannek eyed him coldly. "There is always the girl, yes? The one you are involved with? The Slayer?" The mobster's voice was low and neutral, talking like two friends making casual conversation. "Perhaps you might see a short vacation in your future, but this girl—this Buffy Summers—she won't be going anywhere, yes? Sunnydale is her home."

In a burst of superhuman speed, Spike covered the short distance between himself and Dannek. Spike's nostrils flared as his face changed and became that of the demon. He smelled the Russian's blood through his skin.

The bodyguards bared their weapons. Metallic clicks thundered in Spike's ears. He stopped short of the fat Russian dressed in his chef's uniform.

Dannek, only a little taken aback, held his hands up. Flour drifted down from his fingers as they twitched nervously. "No!" he ordered hoarsely. "Do not fire! He will not touch me! He dares not!"

Spike stood, resolute and straining against the edicts of the Initiative chip in his head. His skull pounded as his bloodthirsty instincts warred against the programming. He heard Dannek's heart pounding in its vulnerable flesh-and-blood shell.

"You have the good sense, Spike," Dannek continued. "You have always had the good sense when it comes to things that matter. Things like winning and losing. Living and dying."

"If you say so," Spike grated.

"I do," Dannek said. "I do say so, yes." He took a deep breath, then sneezed, a very human thing to do, once more showing the weakness of the frail form he inhabited that Spike so much despised at the moment.

Spike spoke slowly because he wanted everything clear between them. He stared into Dannek's dark eyes. "If anything were ever to happen to Buffy and I thought you were somehow to blame for it, nothing would save you from me."

Dannek remained quiet for a moment. "She is not part of this as long as you attempt to repay the loan to me."

"I'll get you the damned money," Spike said. He turned and headed for the door, conscious of the bodyguards' guns pointed at his back. Where the hell was he going to get that kind of money on such short notice?

CHAPTER THREE

Los Angeles

Angel sat at the desk in his office and pored over the shipping manifests Cordelia and Fred had put together regarding *Swift Star*'s cargo. Since nearly all the ship's load had been legal, most of the information had been gotten rather easily—although rather illegally.

He sensed Cordelia at the door before he saw her, and before he smelled her perfume. He looked up.

"Got a minute?" Cordelia asked.

Angel glanced into the bassinet beside the desk, where Connor slept with one tiny fist balled up against his mouth. The baby shifted slightly at

Cordelia's voice, obviously recognizing her. Then he relaxed and let out a deep breath, returning to the regular slow pattern he'd had before. "Sure," Angel said.

"Out here." Cordelia pointed toward the hotel's lobby. "Computer stuff."

Angel glanced at Connor.

"He'll sleep," Cordelia said knowledgeably. "You just fed him. He's good for about an hour and a half of serious coma time." She looked at the sleeping baby. "After being up all night looking into this thing, it's really hard to resist the impulse to pick him up and head off to bed. There's nothing like cuddling with a little baby."

Angel silently agreed.

A frown creased Cordelia's forehead. "Ewww! And don't I sound a lot like the old maid baby-sitter?"

"No," Angel said. "I've been thinking the same thing." He turned out the office light. He felt uncomfortable at how quickly the shadows took his son in. They had gathered like they had been lying in wait for him, settled restlessly on razor-blade-thin haunches waiting to claim him. He forced himself to turn his thoughts from that line of thinking. "He'd have been better off with someone else as his father."

"I don't think so." Cordelia took Angel by the arm. "Personally, I think Connor has a terrific dad. I mean, if you overlook the whole vampire shtick. The time-consuming job as champion of the Powers-That-Be. The fact that you've got enemies that stretch back over two hundred and fifty years. And—"

Angel held up a hand in surrender. "I don't think this little Pollyanna speech is coming out exactly the way you intended."

Cordelia wrinkled her nose as she gave consideration to what she had just said. "You're probably right." She squeezed his arm reassuringly.

"The thing that bothers me most," Angel said quietly as he gazed at his son, "is how uncertain the world has become."

Cordelia smiled at him, and he knew that she was trying to lighten his mood. "The *whole* world?"

"My world." Angel hesitated. "*Our* world."

"Because of Connor?"

"Yeah. I know he didn't mean to, but he changed everything."

"What everything?"

Angel paused. He didn't want to answer, almost afraid that if he tried to put the feeling into words he wouldn't do it justice. "He's vulnerable, and he's part of me."

"So he makes you vulnerable?"

"Yeah."

Cordelia peered into Angel's eyes. "Maybe Connor does make you vulnerable."

Good. We're not going to have that argument. But at the same time, Angel felt guilty for even having mentioned that fact now.

"We made you vulnerable, too," Cordelia said.

"Me. Wesley. Gunn. Fred." She paused. "And Doyle."

An image of Doyle's death passed through Angel's mind. He'd seen friends and compatriots die in the past. A few of them he'd killed himself. But that had been when the demon Angelus had walked through his life instead of him. Since that time, there had been others who had touched his life with small kindnesses and ended up leaving him either through violence or just because they hadn't been able to live as long as he had in the hundred years since he'd been reunited with his soul.

"Back in Sunnydale," Cordelia continued, "Buffy made you vulnerable. So did Willow and Xander. You started this investigation because Giles asked you to. As a friend."

"But he also knows when things are about to turn heavy," Angel pointed out. "Anything involving Wolfram and Hart is going to be heavy."

"I know," Cordelia said. "The point I'm trying to make here is that all of us have—in differing degrees—made you more vulnerable. To enemies. To pain. To sorrow. I know that, and sometimes I feel sorry about that. But we've brought you more than weakness, Angel. We've also brought you a strength you've never known before. You've got friends. Family. Roots. Those things aren't all bad." She looked at the sleeping child in the bassinet. "And that little boy? He's going to make you stronger than any of us could."

Angel didn't respond.

"It's the gypsies that have really got you going, isn't it?" Cordelia asked.

Angel nodded. In his life, all two hundred-plus years of it, gypsies had generally been nothing but trouble for him. Even before he'd killed the girl whose family had trapped him and cursed him by reuniting his soul with his vampire body, there had been trouble with gypsies.

"There are a lot of gypsies in the world," Cordelia said.

"I know."

"*If* these were the same gypsies—"

"I know. They'd probably have been more interested in me than they were." Angel followed Cordelia into the ornate lobby of the hotel.

Back in the day, the hotel had been solid, a place to trust for people hoping to grab a handful of Los Angeles's and Hollywood's fame and fortune. Now, the building was pretty much stripped bare of furnishings, and the lobby's overall appearance seemed totally cavernous. Still, people in need of help found their way to him and allowed him to earn his redemption one day at a time.

"What did you find?" Angel asked.

Cordelia stepped behind the hotel desk. A notebook computer sat open on the counter. "Somebody at the docks had a video camera. They sold the film footage to one of the local news stations. I thought maybe you'd like to see it."

"Sure." Angel stared at the screen.

Cordelia tapped keys.

A window opened on the screen. After a brief introduction by a news anchorwoman, the taped footage of the theft at the docks launched.

Due to the night and the distance, the figures were blurry and indistinct. Muzzle flashes revealed some of the strange dress the humans wore, but the darkness kept the demonic appearances of the Barkuk warriors cloaked.

"Nobody identified the gypsies?" Angel asked as the taped footage returned to the anchorwoman.

"No." Cordelia looked at him. "But you don't recognize them either. That's got to be a good thing, right? I mean, if they were part of the same family of gypsies that cursed you and they were here to do something to you, you'd recognize them. Wouldn't you?"

"No," Angel said.

"Oh." Cordelia's brow wrinkled in irritation.

"It was a good thought, Cordy," Angel said. "Just . . . wrong."

Footsteps whispered into Angel's ears. He recognized the length of the stride immediately.

Wesley Wyndam-Pryce looked dapper as ever, though his dark hair was getting longer. He removed his glasses and absently cleaned them with a monogrammed handkerchief. He wore jeans and a button-down shirt, but the sleeves showed creases.

A year and a half ago, the onetime Watcher and mentor to Faith, who was also a slayer, had been ousted from the prestigious organization he had worked for. Being let go by the Watchers Council had nearly broken him. Not all of the things he'd been blamed for had been his fault.

After leaving Sunnydale, Wesley had ended up in L.A. He'd become a self-proclaimed "rogue demon hunter." Dressed in the biker's leathers he'd sported, he was a much different person from the one Angel had known. After Doyle's untimely death, Angel had recognized the need to expand Angel Investigations and had invited Wesley to join the group.

"Where are Gunn and Fred?" Angel asked.

"Still on the streets," Wesley answered. "We're not getting much. I thought I might better serve our efforts by returning here and helping you identify the object they were after."

"Waste of time," Cordelia said.

Wesley looked at her. "You've already identified what it is?"

"No," Angel said. "We still don't know. We found nothing in the paperwork we've been able to turn up."

Wesley sighed. He retreated behind the counter and got a cup of coffee from the pot. "Well then, what is our next move?"

Angel paced restlessly. When thinking on something by himself, he was content to sit. But when surrounded by humans with their respiration and thudding heartbeats audible to his supersharp hearing, pacing felt called for. "The police may have more on the robbery than has been released in the news," Angel answered. "Or we can be more direct and go straight to Wolfram and Hart and find out who their client is."

"The police," Cordelia said, shaking her head, "are not going to be overly generous with the whole help idea."

"She's right," Wesley added. "We haven't ingratiated ourselves with those people. Besides, Wolfram and Hart are going to be influencing the investigation to whatever degree they can."

"Huge," Cordelia said. "Wolfram and Hart never get involved with anything small."

"Wolfram and Hart is our best shot," Angel said. "With them, at least, we don't have to play nice."

Wesley nodded. "You think perhaps a talk with Lilah is in order?"

Lilah Morgan was one of the senior executives at the law firm. Tall and beautiful, her looks hid her cold-blooded efficiency at bending and breaking the law. She also came equipped with a streak of ruthlessness that Angel had seldom seen equaled in any human. During the last two years, Lilah had moved up in the cannibalistic food chain at Wolfram & Hart to become one of Angel Investigations' staunchest enemies.

"Yes," Angel answered.

"I could—"

"No," Angel cut Wesley off. Lately, since Connor's birth, Wolfram & Hart had been at the bottom of too much activity regarding his infant son. "I'll talk to Lilah."

"That could be dangerous for you," Wesley said.

"I know. I'd only consider it at a time when not talking to Lilah would be more dangerous." Angel shrugged. "With everything going on, I think we're there—"

"Wait," Cordelia said, holding a hand up. She stared into the distance. "Vision. I saw a bar. The gypsies, or at least some gypsies, are there."

"What were they doing there?" Angel asked.

"Waiting," she said.

"For what?" Wesley asked.

Irritably, Cordelia said, "I don't know. These things don't exactly come with user directions, remember?"

"Right," Wesley said.

Cordelia narrowed her eyes. "They have something. A device of some kind. I barely saw it in the vision. I think they're there to trade the device to someone else. Or they're holding it there till someone else arrives."

"Is it connected to the thing Giles asked us to look for?" Angel asked.

"I don't know. But maybe it means that the Powers-That-Be are buying into this whole thing too. They give me the visions."

Angel accepted that. If it was true, then even more was riding on the outcome of their current investigation than he'd believed.

"Where is the bar?" Wesley asked.

"I didn't get that," Cordelia replied. "But I saw the name written backward on the window. McCarty's Flesh Fantasy."

"Well now," Wesley said, reaching for the phone book under the hotel counter, "the name certainly sounds unique. If it's listed, we'll have the address soon enough."

Angel moved to the weapons locker as Wesley flipped through the directory's yellow pages. He quickly took out a short-hafted double-bitted battle-ax, a few throwing stars, and a short sword that would fit upside down under his duster on his back.

There was no question about not going.

Spike had been seated at a bar for the last nine hours while wrestling with the cash problem that loomed all around him. However, he hadn't been seated all that time at the same bar. He'd lost count of how many drinking establishments he'd been in, and he knew for certain that he'd been in two of them twice.

Making his way to Willy's Alibi at dusk had been a conscious decision. Buffy often came to the tavern a number of times while searching for information. And if she had relented—or simply couldn't stay away another night—and decided to come looking for him, the Alibi would be one of the places she'd know to look. She knew several of his favorite haunts.

Spike had gone there hoping for a little companionable aloneness and to blow the foam off a few beers. The demon that rushed him from behind was totally unexpected but not unwelcome as a diversion.

Peering into the space where his reflection would have been if he'd been human, Spike saw the creature get up from a table near the back of the bar. At dusk, the Alibi catered to mostly demons and humans who were junkies for whatever illegal treat demons had to offer.

The demon was a Vanguint. The race wasn't overly endowed with brains, despite their bulbous foreheads that were big as two cabbages sitting side by side with a pulsing gray green membrane stretched tight between them. Covered in loose gray skin and built lean, Vanguint usually looked like poster children for famine with a head full of ideas on how to change that. As most of his kind, the demon had a ferocious underbite and a short nose that made him look like a sad-faced Pomeranian. Wide, flaring ears that drooped pathetically and a chronic protruding tongue added to that appearance.

The Vanguint didn't work alone. Four other demons, all built along similar lines, rose up from the bar crowd.

Moving with speed and precision, two traits the Vanguint did possess, the demon pulled a short-hafted wooden spear from beneath his jacket. The weapon was little more than two feet long but possessed a broadly fluted blade that looked like a whaler's harpoon.

Even though he was ready and had expected the Vanguint's speed, Spike barely dodged to the left and rolled around. His back slammed into the bar, and he kept his arms straight out at his sides at shoulder height.

The spear thudded into the bar, piercing the surface. Patrons on either side of the bar moved away quickly.

"Missed," Spike announced, grinning.

The Vanguint pulled at his weapon without a word. As a race, although there were exceptions, the Vanguint weren't big on talking.

The other demons advanced in a pack, like wolves bearding a lone ram. They pulled axes and knives from beneath their clothing.

Looking forward to the coming fight, Spike stepped forward into a martial arts L-stance, right hand forward, then twisted his hips and shoulders to bring his open left hand into sharp contact with the Vanguint demon's chest. Ribs broke beneath the contact, and the sternum might have been fractured. The blow would have driven bone shards through a normal human's heart.

The Vanguint slammed backward in a loose heap. Flailing his pipe-stem arms and legs, he slid beneath a table of large Qorqoth demons sharing from a pitcher of drowned-rat tea. The pitcher slid from the table and smashed against the floor. A handful of rats that had still been kicking futilely against the glass walls of the pitcher streaked away as their lungs filled with fresh air.

The Qorqoth demons weren't happy. One of them raised a huge, hobnailed boot and brought it down on the Vanguint demon's head. The head splattered like a rotten pumpkin and left green-and-purple gore streaked in all directions.

The four other Vanguint never broke their attack. For all their huge heads, they had the single-minded purpose of a Pavlovian-trained dog.

Spike dodged an inhumanly quick two-handed horizontal strike that would have severed his head from his shoulders. He slapped out with his right hand, catching the elbow of his attacker and spinning him into the next demon. Breaking from the bar, Spike took two strides, planted his left foot, and delivered a right roundhouse kick that caught another Vanguint in the back of his neck.

The demon's spine shattered with a series of audible snaps. Nearby patrons cringed and groaned at the sound. Already dying, unable to control his body, the Vanguint dropped to the bar's dirty floor.

The three surviving demons turned to face Spike, struggling to come to terms with almost half their number decimated in only a handful of seconds. They raised their weapons.

Unleashing the demon inside him, Spike felt his face morph, taking on the harsh and brutal lines that he wore with cold delight. He threw his arms wide, catching all three and throwing them all over the bar counter. They landed in a heap on the other side of the bar. Coming up to his feet in a crouch, Spike reached for one of the demons, put a hand behind his opponent's head, and cupped his chin with the other, then spun his head.

The demon's skull separated from his spine with a crack. Spasms quivered through the Vanguint demon, but his brain had already gotten the message that he was dead.

The second Vanguint recovered more quickly than Spike would have believed possible. The demon whipped his stake forward with his left hand, unable to bring the ax up. The stake's jagged point left a bloody furrow on Spike's right cheek.

Grabbing the demon's arm, Spike used his strength and leverage to snap his opponent's elbow. The Vanguint demon screamed in pain, then Spike reversed the broken limb, and sheathed the stake in his opponent's heart. Bloody froth covered his lips from the punctured lung that came with the abrupt penetration. The heart tried to beat around the stake, then quit.

The final Vanguint demon rose up in a fury, but he was more intent on getting out of Spike's immediate vicinity. As the demon turned to run, Spike stood and punched him in the back of his big head. The Vanguint went forward, tripping over his own feet.

Before his opponent could get up again, Spike

palmed the back of his head and slammed him face first into the floor. His teeth broke.

Holding on to the demon's head, Spike pulled him back and gazed into his eyes. "Who sent you here?"

"We came for the bounty on your head," the Vanguint demon answered.

"Dannek?" Spike asked, not believing the loan shark would so quickly decide to give up on him. After all, Dannek's usual plan included killing someone close to the person who owed him money.

"No. Somebody else. Got a posting here in Sunnydale. Somebody looking for side work. Wet work." One of the demon's eyes was swelling shut. "Offered five thousand dollars for your head."

Spike grinned. "Looks like it cost you four of your little pals."

"You killed them for free." The demon ran his tongue over his broken teeth and the empty spaces where his teeth had been. "Not very professional."

"Big mistake," Spike growled softly. "I kill four for free, the fifth one is free too." He drove his free hand into the demon's throat and broke his larynx.

As the Vanguint demon started to asphyxiate, his good eye rounding in horror, Spike grabbed hold of him with both hands and stood with his opponent over his head at arm's length. He surveyed the bar like a World Wrestling Federation champ. With a quick flick of movement, he threw the demon against the opposite wall.

The Vanguint demon's body slammed against the wall with bone-breaking force, then dropped to the floor. He jerked and grabbed his throat, but it was obvious he wasn't going to survive.

Spike reached under his jacket and took out his cigarettes. He shook one out, then lit up, holding the lighter in both cupped hands. Smoke eddied about his head when he breathed out the twin plumes. "Some of you probably know about the bounty somebody's placed on my head."

A few whispered conversations chased each other around the room.

"Just so you know," Spike went on, "this is the only warning you're going to get if you try to collect on it." His words were bravado. He knew it, and some of the demons and men seated around the stained table knew it too.

The Vanguint demon shuddered. His feet drummed against the floor for a long time. Then he relaxed, as if he'd gone to sleep.

Spike took another drag on his cigarette, then turned and finished the beer he'd been nursing. Inside, he was angry and scared all at the same time. He slammed the mug back onto the countertop, then swaggered through the tables and chairs.

Out on the street, Spike turned to the right and put his face into the blowing wind. Sunnydale was still active at this time of night, but a lot of the businesses had closed down and the late- and last-minute shoppers were heading home, where they could hope for relative safety from the monsters that prowled their city.

Footsteps grated against the pavement behind Spike. He kept moving, not hurrying, but keeping a deliberate stride. The wind was against him; he couldn't smell whoever trailed him, but from the sound of the footsteps he knew there were a number of them. As he passed a closed auto supply store featuring advertisements for NASCAR and Mr. Goodwrench, he glanced into the darkened glass.

Three lumbering shadows trailed him. From their immense size and general configuration, he guessed that they were the Qorqoth demons from the Alibi.

He ducked into the first alley on his right. A fire escape climbed the wall in zigzag fashion to his left. He leaped up onto the second-floor landing, crushed his cigarette out against the wall, and waited.

The Qorqoth demons approached the alley mouth with caution. Even though they were nearly twice his size and outnumbered him three to one, they respected his prowess.

Spike liked that.

"He's gone, Arrag," one of the demons said.

The center Qorqoth demon stepped forward and snuffled the air. He was tall and muscular, looking like he'd been roughly carved from anthracite. His features were large and angular, framed by a square jaw. A shelf of brow protected his deep-set eyes. His mouth opened, and a thick violet serpent's tongue darted out to taste the air. His hair stood up like a bird's, then lay back down in a smooth and shiny skullcap.

"I told you he knew we were coming," the third Qorqoth stated.

"Of course he knew we were coming, Doxxil," the first Qorqoth demon announced sourly. "How could he miss us?"

"Always with the sarcasm, Muullot," Doxxil snarled. "I swear, I'm getting tired of you griping so much."

"Me?" As much as they could, the Qorqoth demon's fierce features took on a look of disbelief. "I have a right to gripe. You got our inside man killed in a stupid bar fight in San Francisco chasing that Tolian demon that I told you was no woman."

Doxxil spat. "I hate San Francisco. I've always told you that. You can't count on the women being women. Newark's almost as bad. And the Tolian demon shouldn't have been wearing that dress."

The lead Qorqoth demon growled a warning. "Shut up. The vampire's still here."

Doxxil and Muullot glanced around the alley.

"Where?" Doxxil asked. "I don't see anything."

Arrag lifted his head and pointed his square chin at the fire escape. "There."

Spike felt the eyes of all three Qorqoth demons lock on him. "I've got to tell you," he said calmly, "if you picked tonight to come hunting that bounty on my head, you've picked a bad one."

A grin split the big Qorqoth demon's face. "I saw

what you did to the Vanguint back at the bar. I liked it. You've got some nice moves."

"Yeah, well, you've still got some of his brains on your boot there."

Arrag looked down and saw the brain matter. He stomped his hobnailed boot. Sparks spat from the thick nails as the metal rasped against the pavement. The bloody tissue dropped onto the ground.

"What do you want with me?" Spike asked.

"I could use a vampire."

The phrasing haunted Spike, reminding him of his final encounter with Buffy two days ago. "Never much cared for being used."

"Forgive me," the Qorqoth demon said. "I misspoke. We have an opening for . . . a partner."

"Not looking for partners."

"The job I've taken on pays a quarter million dollars," Arrag stated. "It splits five ways. I need another person to pull this off."

Intrigued, Spike asked, "What kind of job?"

"Theft."

"What's the merch?"

"An object."

Spike shook his head. "I don't like doing merch. Merch involves a buyer, adds one step—a very tiresome and unlucky step, I might point out—to an otherwise bearable way to get paid. I'm strictly a cash-and-carry kind of guy. Cash and bearer bonds. It's the only way to go."

"I'm betting fifty thousand dollars would go a long

way toward getting you out of whatever jam you're in," Arrag pointed out.

"Why me?"

"I liked the way you handled yourself back at the bar."

"Professional thieves, they don't go in for the knockabout stuff," Spike said. "Easy in, easy out. So quiet, you don't even disturb the house mouse. That's the way a pro wants it played."

Arrag smiled. "You've had experience at this?"

"Yeah." Immortal and unable to hold down a real job in the working human class but still having considerable cash needs—or wants—kept vampires and demons wrapped in the shadows and in crime. Spike had been a thief before. In fact, he'd been a thief several times.

"Even better," Arrag declared.

Spike had the feeling the big Qorqoth demon had been counting on a certain familiarity with thievery. "Not interested."

Arrag paused for a moment, then nodded. "If you say so." He turned and gestured to his companions. All three of them headed for the alley's mouth.

Fifty thousand dollars. And I'm letting it walk away when I could be earning it, paying Dannek off, and getting Buffy back. Beneath his breath, Spike cursed. Then he lifted his voice. "Hey."

Arrag turned around and gazed up at him.

Spike pointed with the cigarette, the glowing orange coal dancing against the night's shadows coiled in the alley. "I count four guys. Including me. Is that every man on this job?"

Arrag nodded. "Yes. It's a big job, but I like to keep things small and tidy."

"Four guys," Spike repeated. "So why five splits?"

"I take two shares," Arrag said. "It's my job. I put it together with the buyer and cased the site. I get paid handling expenses."

"My cut would be fifty thousand dollars."

Arrag stared at him. "Yes."

"Any upfront money?"

A big grin revealed Arrag's huge fangs. "To a man with a price on his head? No way."

"That could be a deal breaker."

"A minute ago, you weren't interested at all. An hour from now, you could be dead."

Spike cursed inwardly. *Don't come off as desperate. Whatever you do, don't come off as desperate.* He shrugged. "Okay, then. I'm willing to have a listen."

"Come on down and we'll talk over a drink. I'll buy."

"So where's the site?" Spike asked.

"Los Angeles," Arrag answered.

Unease twisted through Spike's guts. L.A. was Angel's territory these days. Spike had only been there once since Angel had left Sunnydale and set up operations there working on his personal redemption. Until that time, L.A. had been a fun place to occasionally go.

"You have a problem with L.A.?" Arrag asked.

"No," Spike replied, working to keep his voice neutral. "No problems. This trip, we're quick in and quick out, right?"

"No more than a night."

"Good enough."

Arrag studied Spike. "Somebody looking for you in L.A.?"

"Guy I'm thinking of, he's one of the do-gooders. He won't be involved in this."

"But you've got a history with him."

"I've been a vampire for over one hundred and twenty years," Spike said. "I've got history everywhere."

CHAPTER FOUR

Outside London, England
October 1887

The smell of blood pervading the carriage filled
Spike's nostrils as the vehicle rolled along the gently
winding road to the manor house on the hilltop.
White and waxen, the full moon sat on the hill
behind the house, and the forest beyond sank jagged
teeth into its belly.

Seated on the carriage's driver's seat, the blood
stink still fresh in his nostrils and the hunger of the
demon only partially satiated, Spike stared at the
moon and the manor house. The scene called out to
the poetic nature of his soul. If at all possible, he
thought he'd spend a little time with a quill and

paper tonight and see if he could find words for the poem that was falling together in his head. He thought Dru might enjoy the poetry. He knew she was definitely looking forward to the killing that Angelus and Darla had planned for the evening.

A low limestone wall, hand-quarried and hand-carried, ringed the manor house's grounds, but Spike knew from scuttlebutt overheard in the tavern the night before that Lord Hyde-Pierce owned a considerable amount of the surrounding forest. The three-story manor house, the three guest cottages, and the carriage house were likewise made of quarried rock rather than cut rock.

Gardens divided the manor grounds. Flower gardens lay in geometric order inside the limestone wall. Vegetable gardens and orchards occupied the grounds outside the walls. Rumor had it that Lord Hyde-Pierce also had a vineyard in France across the Channel.

Iron gates barred entrance to the manor house grounds. Uniformed guards stood at post in the gatehouse. Two of the men stepped from the gatehouse. One of them carried a lit lantern that swung in the darkness. Both men wore pistols in hip holsters and carried rifles at port arms.

Taking a fresh grip on the reins, Spike pulled back and slowed the horses. The animals didn't want to stop because they could smell the blood in the carriage as well. When he had first taken control of the carriage, it had taken several perilous minutes to get the horses under control. At the gate, they stopped and stamped and blew.

"Might I help you?" a portly guard asked. He lifted the lantern he carried to better inspect the carriage and the passengers. Light reflected from his graying whiskers.

"It's a little late for that," Spike replied. He wrapped the reins around the carriage brake.

"This here is private property, Guv." The guard took hold of the lead horse's bridle so he could control the animals if he had to. He kept his hand near the holstered pistol.

Spike dropped lithely from the carriage seat. "Don't address me like some commoner, you great lummox." He tugged his gloves on fiercely and threw back his coat a little to better reveal the good suit he wore. Possibly there was some blood on the clothing, but he trusted that it wouldn't show in the poor light of the lantern and the soft silver glow of the waxen moon.

The guard's face blanched at the sight of the suit, but he didn't immediately back off. "Well now here, fine sir, it's not often that I get the chance to see a gentleman a-drivin' a carriage."

"Earlier tonight, I had a carriage driver," Spike snarled. "A rather likable chap. Knew his place in life and wasn't so quick as to unsheathe his awkward tongue. But they killed him."

The guard placed his hand on the pistol butt and caught his comrade's eye. He gave a slight nod. The second man put his fingers in his mouth and gave a sharp whistle. Three other men stepped from the gatehouse.

"Who killed him, Guv?" the guard asked.

"The brigands we encountered tonight," Spike stated impatiently. "Your whole bloody forest is filled with brigands."

The carriage door opened abruptly. Angelus stepped down. He held his hands up at his sides to show they were empty.

The guard moved the lantern light to center on Angelus.

Angelus stood tall and broad-shouldered. He wore his dark hair tied back, full and natural instead of one of the powdered wigs that were still common among gentry. His clothing was dark and fit him well, and his white ruffled cuffs lent him an air of aristoc-racy.

"Perhaps I could explain our situation," Angelus said.

"You're Irish," the guard accused.

"I'm Irish on my mother's side," Angelus responded. His accent was faint but still noticeable to hardcore British ears. It was still a time in England when men hid their Irish origins. "My father was English. He loved my mother in a fit of passion. Till his dying day, he reveled in his love as much as he was shamed by it. And isn't that the way of the world, then? To have something that brings you both pleas-ure and pain?"

"When it comes to women," the guard agreed, "I'd warrant that's the truth of it."

"Gentlemen wouldn't talk about a lady so," a soft feminine voice announced. The carriage creaked a little as Darla stepped from inside. She wore a long dress that sheathed her trim figure at her corseted waist before flaring out. A small hat perched atop her head, and a modest veil masked her face.

The guard snatched his own hat from his head and bowed. "Excuse me, milady. I didn't know you were aboard the carriage."

Darla smiled. She wore her blond tresses pinned up. "It's quite all right. There was no way you could have known. I also have my sister with me."

Angelus held his hand out to the carriage.

Dru, dressed in similar fashion to Darla, took the offered hand, and stepped down from the carriage. The beautiful, slim-hipped similarity between the two women was enough to make onlookers believe they were sisters. Where Darla was fair-haired, though, Drusilla's mane was dark and rich.

If Spike's heart had still beat, he knew it would have beat faster every time he saw Dru. She was the love of his life.

"Ladies," the guard acknowledged with a sweeping bow. "You should hardly be out in the woods at this time of evening. Full dark came over two hours ago."

"I know that," Darla agreed. "But this was not by choice, I assure you."

The guard pointed to Angelus. "This man."

"My husband," Darla said.

"Your husband," the guard amended, "mentioned something of brigands."

"Yes," Darla said. "There were. Five of them. I believe they were poaching deer from your lord's lands when we came upon them. They were engaged in butchering a deer." She nodded toward Angelus. "My husband ordered the driver to stop the carriage so that he might intercede. I thought such an action, though noble in sentiment, carried a large amount of risk."

"Indeed, milady."

"But he has always been a brave man." Darla took Angelus by the arm.

"Very brave," Dru chimed in. "He's got the courage of a lion, he has. And the instincts of a wild hunting beast." She growled like a cat and clawed the air.

A pang of jealousy broke through Spike. After all, Angelus had sired Drusilla; he'd had her long before Spike had ever known her.

"As it turned out," Darla continued, "the men were brazen enough to put up a fight. They fired at us."

The guard raised his lantern and surveyed the bullet pocks on the carriage. Fresh white blisters showed starkly against the stained wood.

"It's a wonder that you weren't killed," the guard said gruffly.

"Our driver and the baggage handler were both killed," Darla explained. "We barely escaped. Even then, William had to climb aboard the coach when the horses panicked in order to keep us from smashing against a tree or overturning." She put a hand over her breasts. "I must tell you, I feared for my very life. I had thought we were all dead till William showed his mastery of the horses."

The guard ran a discerning eye over Spike. "Climbing out on a careening carriage was a brave thing to do, sir."

Of course it was, Spike felt like saying. But he didn't. He needed to stay in character. Otherwise, Angelus would get angry. Angelus had mapped out the evening's kills after hearing about Lord Hyde-Pierce in the tavern the night before. Tonight was supposed to be a night of bloodlust, but it was also supposed to be a profitable one. Lord Hyde-Pierce was reputed to be a wealthy man.

"My father owns a stable," Spike explained. Then he decided to make his fictitious father even richer. "In fact, he owns several stables. I'm used to handling horses."

"Does Lord Hyde-Pierce live in the manor house?" Darla asked, pointing to the house inside the wall. "We'd heard about him while we were traveling."

"Yes, milady."

"With everything that has happened," Angelus said, "I was hoping that we might prevail upon Lord Hyde-Pierce for a night's lodging."

"I know my lord," the guard said. "He would not turn a woman back into that dark night. Not when there are poachers—or brigands, as you say— about." He turned to Spike. "If you'll allow it, sir, I'll have one of my men drive the carriage to the main house for you. That's no job as befittin' a gentleman."

"Thank you," Spike said. He had to force himself to say that. Being polite and disguising his true nature didn't come as easily to him as it seemed to for Angelus. He walked back to Dru and helped her into the carriage, then helped Darla. He pulled himself through the doorway and took a seat beside Dru. Reaching between them, he took her hand, holding it in both of his.

Angelus heaved himself into the carriage also. The leader of the guard detail climbed up onto the carriage while another man went to the footman's stand on the back of the carriage. A moment later, another guard took the horses' reins and urged the animals into motion. The carriage bumped over the broken oyster shell.

Spike looked out the carriage window as the massive wrought-iron gates swung open. The lantern light from the guards remaining at post swung through the carriage's interior and briefly touched the congealing pools of blood.

Angelus's story hadn't been completely false. There had been brigands—of a sort—in the woods. Only it was the four of *them* who had been the brigands. They'd lain in wait and ambushed the carriage.

The carriage passengers had consisted of two men, two women, and three children. The driver and the footman had been the first to die. They had taken their time with the rest. Thankfully, the men had been close enough in size to outfit Angelus and Spike. They had hidden the bodies so that they wouldn't be found any earlier than morning. They planned to be gone by that time.

The driver halted the carriage in front of the manor house. The footman quickly dismounted and ran around to the carriage's side. Opening the door with a flourish, the guard helped Dru and Darla from the carriage, then stepped back as Angelus and Spike stepped out.

"Newton," a husky voice called out. "Bring them into the house."

"Yes, milord," the guard posing as footman replied. He gestured. "This way, ladies and gentlemen."

Angelus took the lead, stepping in beside the guard. Darla walked at his side, one step behind.

Spike took Dru by the hand and trailed after them. Lanterns lit the covered entrance to the manor house. Four figures stood in the light, including the guard from the gatehouse and the lord of the manor.

Lord Hyde-Pierce was a shriveled human being who looked more like a corpse brought back to life under a skilled mortician's hand. He was tall and rapier thin, frail enough that a strong wind might break him in two. The powdered wig left faint dust on the shoulders of his dark suit.

From the scant details that Spike remembered, the man had served in the Crimean War in the 1850s. Upon his return to England, he'd taken over his father's shipping business, used his foreign contacts to gain access to new ports and new markets throughout the world, and increased his family's already considerable wealth.

"I am Lord Hyde-Pierce," the old man stated.

Angelus gave the man the false names their group traveled under.

As he neared the house, Spike felt the resistance that would prevent him from entering the home of any living person without an invitation from a person who lived there. Hyde-Pierce stood to one side of the door, obviously waiting for the ladies to enter first.

Angelus and Darla hesitated by the door. Entry was impossible without an invitation.

"Please," the manor lord said, waving toward the door, "my house is your house."

And just like that, the power that had been preventing the vampires from entering the house fell away.

Angelus grinned at Hyde-Pierce. "Thank you, milord."

"I only wish I could do more," the old man said. "I feel partially responsible for the horror you have experienced this night."

"Oh no, milord," Darla insisted. "Your generosity has more than made up for that inconvenience."

❋ ❋ ❋

Spike sat awkwardly at Hyde-Pierce's long table in the manor house's banquet room. Candelabras decorated the table, and servants kept the food coming. Evidently, the lord had opened his larders for his guests in an unconcealed effort to impress them.

Sixteen people sat around the table. The fact that all of them sat comfortably offered testimony as to how large the table and the room were.

"Would you care for more wine, sir?" a servant standing at Spike's elbow asked.

Spike tapped his crystal glass in acquiescence. He scarcely paid attention to the ruby liquid splashing into the glass. Instead, his attention was riveted to the young woman seated to the manor lord's left.

Her name was Lyanka. Spike remembered her name from the introductions, although he remembered few others who were at the table.

Dark red hair, the color of coals burned to their dying embers, framed an angular face as clear and pure as porcelain. Lyanka was a beautiful woman. Her clothing did not hide the trim figure beneath.

She concentrated on Lord Hyde-Pierce. She laughed at his jokes, and she *oooed* and *aahed* at the man's war stories. Lord Hyde-Pierce had introduced her as an entertainer, and the women around the table had acted as if that were the most scandalous thing they had heard.

Whenever she had a chance to speak, she invariably turned the lord's attention to some facet of his collection. First as a lad working in his father's shipyards, then as a soldier, and finally as the owner of the shipyards, Lord Hyde-Pierce had acquired a considerable collection of arcane objects. Many of them were supposed to be mystical in nature, or were claimed to possess powers or an affinity for good or bad luck.

Even that discussion bored Spike. He was ready to kill someone, to show all the gentrified people at the table the true meaning of fear.

Instead, he sipped his wine and bided his time, listening to Lord Hyde-Pierce ramble on in his dried-out voice.

And he watched the red-haired woman with growing curiosity.

"Would you, naughty, wicked Spike?" Dru asked. "If I asked you to nicely?"

"Would I what?" Spike lay on his back and stared up at the ceiling of the borrowed room Lord Hyde-Pierce had given them for the night. He took a deep drag on the Spanish cigarillo he'd found among the belongings of the people they had murdered earlier in the evening.

"And there you sit, playing your little games with me," Dru said. "Like a spider with a fly, you are. Or a flame drawing in a moth."

"What do you want?"

"Why, to kill her. Kill her dead. Pour her blood and fill my cup till it runneth over."

"Kill who?" Spike tried to focus on her words

instead of the last drifting smoke ring he'd blown toward the spackled ceiling. They had just finished making love and lay twisted in the sheets and bedding.

"The lovely redheaded woman who sat beside the lord. The one who read palms and promises futures what she ain't got. The one who got my naughty, wicked Spike all in an uproar, she has." Dru hoisted herself up on her side. She placed one hand under her head to support it. The fingernails of the other hand trailed down his midsection, leaving a line of delightful tingles in their wake.

"Why would I kill her?"

"Because she has got your eyes, the windows to your soul, and turned your head from my direction. She did not give birth to you, Spike. I did. I am your sire."

Taking another drag off the cigarillo, Spike gave that consideration. There were a lot of people Dru didn't like. He didn't kill all of them, but he had killed most. Of course, he had killed more than she had asked him to kill, so that request was still somewhat novel.

Dru grinned at him with what would have been a child's innocence if madness hadn't been gleaming in her eyes. "There's another reason too. Another reason. Another reason for me and for you."

Uneasiness squirmed through his mind and stomach. "What other reason?"

"Because she can poison your dead heart, my

naughty Spike. Because she thinks she's the Queen of Hearts, like one of the cards in her deck of misfortune."

Give in a little, Spike told himself. *You're not bloody perfect, and she knows you aren't. That's part of why she loves you.* "I only looked at her for a little while."

"Her voice can rob the music of my voice, Spike. Soon you won't hear the coo in my words. I won't be your little lovebird anymore. I'll molt in a gilded cage of your empty love and be so . . . so . . . sad."

Spike rolled his head toward Dru, trying to ignore the fact that her fingernails were deeply embedded in his tender flesh. "No," he whispered. He pushed her dark hair back from her heart-shaped face. "No, my love. I only have eyes for you."

Dru searched his face with her gaze. Spike knew that if she sensed or believed he was lying, she would hurt him terribly. She had done so in the past. That was another thing he really loved about her: the unexpected love and hate that she would show him.

"You love me, don't you, my naughty Spike?" she asked.

"Yes," he whispered again. Then he cupped the back of her neck in his hand and leaned in to kiss her. His brain spun with the contact, and he felt his need for her escalate till it became a burning brand. Surging up, he covered her body with his.

"Stop," she sang. "Not yet. Not now. Naughty Spike must kill the redheaded sow." She squeezed him till he stilled, letting him know she would tear him open if she decided to.

He started to object, but she laid a crimson-nailed finger against his lips. "No," she said. "I want you to tell me that you only have eyes for me. And when you do . . ." She laughed. "When you do, I want you to be holding her poisonous eyes in your fists." She smiled. "A gift from you to me, and then your lover I'll be."

Frustrated, Spike peered down at her. He hungered for her touch and her kisses, and knew that he would have neither again till she decided to give in. "I'm supposed to wait on Angelus's signal, beloved."

An eyebrow arched. "Are you Angelus's man?" she asked. "Or are you a mouse? A quiet little mouse who creeps through the house afraid of the farmer's wife's carving knife?"

"I'm my own man," he told her, staring forcefully into her eyes.

She gazed back at him. She smiled. "A carving knife. A carving knife. Empty her head with a carving knife and bring me her lying eyes. Then you can be my man if you truly want with all your heart."

"Yes." Spike nuzzled her neck. "Always your man."

"Then go now. The sow awaits." Dru pushed him from the bed that they had shared.

Spike tumbled to the floor and got up slowly. He stood naked before her, bathed only in the light of the single candle that burned on the bedside table.

Dru sat up in bed. She made no move to cover her nudity other than to pull her knees up to her chest.

He picked his pants up from the floor and pulled them on. "Do you know which room she is in?"

Dru laughed at him. "Scent her out, my sweet William. Open your nose, open your nose. Even a mouse can scent the cheese."

"Angelus isn't going to like this." Spike left his boots off. He pulled his suspenders over his shoulders and left his shirt off as well.

"You shouldn't care," Dru replied. "You're not sleeping with Angelus. I am your bed warmer. I will share her eyes with you. She has one, she has two. One for me and one for you."

"All right," he conceded, because it was easier to give in to Dru's demands than to fight them. He started for the door.

Dru licked her lips. "Bring me her head. Bring her head to the bed. She can be the head of the bed."

Spike smiled at her. "With a rose between her teeth." Then he opened the door and stepped through.

Out in the hallway, he cleared his lungs of smoke, then took a deep draft of air. He didn't catch the woman's scent strongly, but it was there, and it was enough to get him moving. The bloodlust stirred inside him, no longer satiated by the lovemaking he'd shared with Dru. He was fully a predator once more.

He went to the staircase, taking advantage of the

pale moonlight that streamed through the window at the end of the hall. Now that he was a vampire, he could see better at night.

In the first-floor hallway, Spike moved slowly. He kept his nose in the air, sniffing for the scent of the woman's herbal perfume and the sweet sweat stink of her. She smelled of vanilla due to the perfume, but her flesh carried the hint of citrus.

He paused at each of the doors, quickly finding the one that he wanted. Trying the knob, he found—without surprise—that the door was locked. He stepped back and scented the air again.

Two scents. A woman's and a man's. She's not alone.

A pang of jealousy burst within him. He couldn't help wondering at the emotion. He didn't know the woman, had barely met her, and hadn't even exchanged pleasantries with her. But she had definitely had an effect on him.

Impatient and not possessing lock-picking skills, Spike drew his right hand back and straight-armed the door. His palm met the wood sharply.

Cra-ack!

Wood splintered, and the lock gave way. The nails came out of the wood with sharp, short screeches.

Startled by the amount of noise he'd made and the way that it tore through the quiet of the guesthouse, Spike stood frozen for just a moment. Then he gathered his senses and ran through the door.

A single figure sat up in bed. "Who's there?" a man's voice demanded.

Spike didn't answer. Only then did he realize that he was silhouetted in the doorway due to the courtesy lantern that burned in the hallway and the moonlight streaming through the window.

The man raised an arm quickly.

Spike barely had time to recognize the hard outlines of the pistol and move to one side. A foot-long yellow-and-white muzzleflash leaped from the barrel. The bullet missed by inches. Gunpowder stink filled the modest bedroom. Then Spike was on the man, bearing him down onto the bed.

The fight didn't last long. Spike killed the man almost effortlessly. However, his victim got off another shot in the meantime, and voices filled the hallway outside the guest room.

Spike cursed as he rose up from the dead man. No one else moved in the room. The woman hadn't been there after all. Only her scent had lingered. He threw the corpse to one side and raced to the doorway.

Chaos erupted in the hallway. Several men in nightshirts and caps stood halfway out into the hallway. Two nervous women looked out from behind their husbands.

"Look!" one man cried. "Its face! It's some Hell beast!"

Only then did Spike realize he wore the demon's face that revealed his true nature. He grinned when he saw the fear that he inspired. Fear was power— not as strong as love, but most people never knew true love, not like the love he shared with Dru.

He threw himself out into the hallway, going for the room immediately across from the one he had invaded. He fisted the man's nightshirt and yanked him from the room, throwing him into the opposite wall with bone-shattering force.

The man died on impact, his neck broken and rolling loosely on his shoulders by the time he dropped to the floor.

His wife screamed and backed away from the door. But she couldn't escape Spike. Obeying the bloodlust that filled him, he went after her. Three shots echoed in the hall behind him a second after he felt the burn of a bullet tearing through his right side. The other two bullets dug into the wall where he'd been standing.

Across the room, he grabbed the woman by the back of the neck. She was corpulent, but his vampire's strength enabled him to handle her like a child. Holding her off the ground, he drove his stiffened fingers into her abdomen, tearing flesh, then ripped her open and spilled her entrails like gutting a cantaloupe. He dropped her and left her to die on the floor, already starting to lose her senses from the pain and the shock.

Sensing movement behind him, Spike turned and saw a man standing in the doorway. The man carried a shotgun, a fouling piece that he'd perhaps brought with him to hunt while on Lord Hyde-Pierce's grounds.

"Die, you hellish beast!" the man yelled. He pulled the trigger.

Even with his quicker speed, Spike couldn't dodge the shotgun blast. The buckshot tore into his chest and midsection. One of the pellets caught him in the lower left jaw with crushing force. He staggered back, then regrouped and hurled himself at his opponent.

Mouth open in shocked disbelief, the man fumbled for another cartridge for the shotgun. Spike hit him with a doubled fist and hardly any finesse.

The man flew backward with half his skull caved in.

Irritated, knowing Dru wouldn't back off on her decision till he brought her the red-haired woman's head, Spike staggered out into the hallway. His guts burned from the pellets that had torn through his flesh, but he knew he would survive.

He looked at the other people in the hallway. Unable to hide his nature, he opened his mouth and screamed his defiance.

They ran, heading for the guest house's front door.

"What the hell are you doing?"

Jerked partially out of his bloodlust, Spike spun and stared at the stairwell he had descended. Angelus stood there, naked as the day he had been born.

Angelus glared at the people fleeing the guest house. "You idiot! Those shots have probably alerted everyone here in the manor. Catching them all now is going to be hard."

"We'll get them," Spike said confidently. "They can't escape us."

Without another word, Angelus's face morphed,

and he launched himself with outstretched arms at Spike. The impact drove them both backward. Trapped by Angelus's greater weight and greater strength, Spike struggled to slide out from under his grandsire.

Angelus leaned in, and Spike had no doubt that the other vampire was about to kill him once and for all.

CHAPTER FIVE

Sunnydale, present

Spike woke from the nightmare, still feeling Angelus's hands around his throat reaching out of the past over one hundred years ago and a continent away. He pushed the memory from his mind. Too many bad things were associated with those days. Of course, there were a lot of good things too.

Sitting up in the seat, Spike glanced around, surprised that the vehicle wasn't in motion. Neon and fluorescent lights splashed against the windows.

"Are you back with us?" Arrag asked from the driver's seat of the luxury van.

"Yeah," Spike mumbled. "I'm with you." He

peered past the Qorqoth demon and discovered that they were parked in front of a convenience store. "We still in Sunnydale?"

Arrag nodded toward the store. "Only long enough to pick up a few things."

Through the convenience shop's window, Spike saw that the other two Qorqoth demons were foraging from among the aisles. Both of them were quickly filling their arms with snacks and beer. Spike reached for his cigarette pack, took one out, and lit up.

Three other people stood at the convenience store counter. According to the big Coca-Cola clock on the wall behind the clerk, it was almost midnight.

Spike felt slightly heavy. He hadn't fully recovered from the wounds he'd suffered at the Alibi, hadn't drank anything but pig's blood and outdated blood from a local hospital supply in months, and had drank way too much liquor while in the company of the demons. He hadn't just been getting to know his new companions; he'd been trying to drink Buffy off his mind for a little while.

After the drink-laden, mutual-admiration fest, they'd retired to the fully loaded van Arrag had purchased for the job. Four captain's chairs took up the front and middle of the vehicle, leaving the back end for the equipment Spike guessed they might need to pull off the job.

Two other men, dressed in faux-gangsta clothes, stood only a few feet from the store entrance. They looked human. The longhaired blond guy danced and sang to the beat of the boom box playing at his feet. The other guy, bigger around but shorter, nodded his head in time to the beat.

Dealers, Spike realized. *Or front men for demons.*

The violence inside the shop erupted without warning. After laying their chosen goods on the counter, Muullot, or Doxxil—Spike wasn't certain which—reached for the clerk behind the counter. A blade flashed in the demon's hand, and a spray of blood from the clerk's slashed throat covered the cigarette products behind the counter.

One of the customers at the counter tried to run. Doxxil or Muullot scooped up a two-liter bottle of soda from the rack beside the counter and heaved it at the running man. The two-liter bottle caught the man in the back of the head and propelled him four feet to the door. Glass shattered as the man's face slammed into the door. He flew through the wreckage and collapsed on the pavement.

Inside the convenience store, the other Qorqoth demon flailed with his fists and some type of club weapon. Both the humans went down. Hefting one of the bodies, Doxxil or Muullot threw the body toward one of the front windows. The corpse—and Spike was sure that it was a corpse—exploded through the glass. Blood spattered the jagged edges of the opening left behind.

The two guys standing around the boom box at the front of the store scattered.

Doxxil and Muullot came through the convenience store's doorway. They laughed and joked and shoved each other as they walked over the body of the dead man.

"They don't look very professional," Spike said.

Arrag looked at the two demons approaching the van. "Not at the moment. But once they're on the job, they're solid. And I have to look after them. They're my sister's kids." He started the engine. "I let them blow off a little nervous energy now, kill a few people, they'll be calmed down by the time we reach L.A."

The two demons halted by the gas pump, destroyed it with a few punches and kicks, and stood back as gasoline poured out onto the ground. Doxxil or Muullot took out a book of matches, struck them, and tossed them into the growing pool. The gasoline caught fire at once, leaping up in a cheery but deadly blaze.

Doxxil and Muullot ran for the van as Arrag drove toward them. Flames wreathed the gas pump. Spike could already feel the heat through the window glass.

"You must really like your sister," Spike observed.

The two opened the van doors, one dropping into the front passenger seat and the other sliding into the seat beside Spike. Arrag kept the van in motion, rolling from the flaming gas pump with increasing speed.

"Man, Muullot," Doxxil said from the front seat as

he turned to face his brother, "did you see the look on that clerk's face when I cut his throat? He didn't even see it coming. Couldn't believe I'd done it."

"I know. And did you see that throw with the two-liter bottle? I'm telling you, dude, I could play NFL."

Doxxil pushed a bag toward Spike. "Want some cheese curls?"

Spike looked at the demon for a second, just short of being too long and turning the encounter insulting. "No thanks," Spike said. "I'm trying to cut back."

Looking hurt and uncertain, Doxxil pulled the proffered bag back.

"You know what we should have got?" Muullot asked as he gazed out the back window at the raging fire that was consuming the convenience store pump. "Graham crackers and marshmallows. We already got chocolate." He held up a bag of candy bars. "We coulda made s'mores."

Both brothers laughed and high-fived each other.

Morons, Spike thought. *I'm traveling with escapees from a loony bin.*

The gas reservoir buried beneath the convenience store's paved drive suddenly exploded. Broken cement, earth, and rock belched into the air, chased immediately by a gout of flames that created a huge rolling black-smoke cloud. Several small pieces of debris rattled against the van. The heat inside the vehicle grew intense, then went away.

Spike laid his head back on the seat and closed his

eyes as the brothers rated this fire compared with other fires they had set. Arrag searched for a station on the radio, quickly settling on a blues channel.

"Hey," Doxxil said. "Let's listen to something else. I get tired of that music."

"What do you have?" Arrag asked.

"Picked up an audio book in the store." Doxxil held the CD up proudly. "*Erotic Confessions of the Old Woman Who Lived in a Shoe.* Should make the trip interesting."

Terrific, Spike thought. He tried to focus on the goal. This was a fifty-thousand-dollar job. He just had to remember that.

But fifty thousand dollars only covered so much annoyance.

Los Angeles

Hard-driving rock and roll blasted from the club's sound system as Angel stepped through the doorway of McCarty's Flesh Fantasy. He raked his gaze around the club, searching for any sign of the gypsies Cordelia had seen in her vision.

A central stage area where a nearly nude dancer gyrated captured most of the attention of the club's patrons. The dancer wore a cowboy hat, leather chaps, and high-heeled red leather cowboy boots with silver rowels. Her blond hair flew as she moved, and her smile was too white, ersatz. Whatever real emotion had once been there had left a long time ago.

Two other smaller stages occupied the back corners of the room. One of the stages was made up to resemble a cloud. The other was a giant birdcage. Most of the patrons appeared to be bikers, longshoremen, demons, and blue-collar workers. It was a place where hustlers came to lay on the con, where dealers came to sell, and misery loved company as long as it came with longnecks, nachos, and nudity. Smoke billowed around the dim lights in gray patches of fog.

"Man," Gunn said, staring at the club, "this place is every bit as bad as the other one."

"Two Flesh Factories," Wesley said. "Who would have guessed?"

Angel pressed on through the crowd. The first Flesh Factory they had visited had been pretty much the same as the second. Only the first club had been listed in the phone book. They'd lost time hanging out there and waiting for the gypsies.

A hostess stepped up before him. She was too thin and hollow-eyed. Her dark hair was cropped close, and she wore white spandex that glowed almost fluorescent blue in the dim lighting.

"Can I get you guys a table?" the hostess asked.

"Not yet," Angel replied.

"The owners don't like gawkers," the hostess warned. "They want to see money trading hands."

"All right," Angel said. "A table."

She guided them back to a table littered with beer bottles and glasses near the birdcage in the back. "There's also a two-drink minimum."

"Bring us two drinks each." Angel sat at the table with his back to the wall and placed money on the table, the price of the drinks and a tip. "Then we'd like some privacy."

The hostess shrugged, finished partially cleaning the debris from the table, and walked away.

Gunn and Wesley sat to Angel's left and right.

"Not exactly a first-rate establishment, is it?" Gunn asked. He was young and slender. His dark skin and shaved head glowed with the dim lighting. He'd become a product of the streets, and had gotten a vampire-fighting force together with his sister before he crossed paths with Angel. Unfortunately, his sister had become a casualty of that war. But Gunn had signed on with Angel because Angel hit harder and deeper into the demon hordes that infested Los Angeles. "And yeah, that was a rhetorical question."

The cowgirl gathered her money at the end of the song and quit the stage. A leggy brunette dressed in a yellow slicker and wearing a fireman's hat stepped onto the stage. She carried a fire ax in one hand.

"They do have women," Wesley observed.

"Yeah," Gunn said. "And some of them even have heartbeats." He nodded toward the vampire woman in full demon's face gyrating wildly on the cloud stage across the room.

The waitress returned with the beers and placed the bottles on the table. She walked away without a word.

Angel continued studying the crowd. With the assortment of people and demons, it would have been possible to miss a few gypsies.

"They could already have come and gone," Wesley said. "Cordelia's visions tend to be current. We lost considerable time at the other one."

"I know," Angel said.

"If we missed this," Gunn said confidently, "we'll make up the difference. With Cordy and Fred both going through the books looking for the object Cordy saw in her vision, we'll get a break."

A rectangle of light suddenly opened in the wall between the cloud stage and center stage on the other side of three smoke-fogged pool tables. Gunn and Wesley noticed Angel's line of sight and intensity.

Angel stood and crossed the room toward the door. He moved quickly, avoiding the men scattered across the floor as well as the nearly nude dancers out among the audience trying to sell table dances.

A mixed batch of demons stood around the pool tables. Humans were in the minority. Chairs lined the wall to the left. Men filled the chairs, all of them getting lap dances from the women working the floor.

Angel narrowly avoided the pool cues, drawing angry stares from the players. He made his way to

the door, dodging past a drunken Bleyorick demon
hugging the pay phone for support as he promised
someone that he'd never go clubbing again if she
would only come get him this last time.

The crack in the wall that delineated the concealed door grew a little wider. Sharp voices pene-
trated the thick curtain of sound that cascaded
throughout the club's sound system as the DJ introduced a new dancer and started another rock and
roll song.

Trying to stay low-key for the moment, Angel
rapped his knuckles against the door.

Hesitantly, the door opened a little wider. A frog-
faced Wiatar demon dressed in biker's leathers
opened the door. Scars framed his oblong face and
ran over his scaly pale yellow-green skull. His ears
were ridged like a fish's fins and flared out as he
looked at Angel.

"Bathroom," Angel said.

"This ain't the bathroom, dude. Gotta go down the
hallway." The demon pointed down the hall.

Spying through the open crack, Angel saw a man
in black standing with his back to the door. A chill
touched Angel, then the gypsy turned to look at him.

The gypsy had a flat face with heavy, Slavic features. A scar crossed the right side of his face, narrowly missing his eye. A neatly trimmed mustache
framed his razor-blade slit of a mouth. A hint of
recognition dawned in his dark eyes.

The Wiatar demon sensed that something was

wrong. He shrugged a shoulder and popped a chopped-down shotgun at the end of a Whipit sling into view from under his long coat. The movement was obviously practiced, allowing him to grab the weapon immediately.

Angel kicked the door, driving it back into the Wiatar demon. "Down!" he yelled to Wesley and Gunn. He crouched as well.

The shotgun blast was slightly muffled inside the room, and barely fought back the loud rock music. A hole the size of a pie plate opened up in the door as the buckshot tore through.

Hooking his fingers at the door's edge, Angel stayed low, swung around the door, and launched a side kick as soon as the Wiatar demon was visible. His foot caught the demon in the stomach and drove the air from his lungs.

Angel's sweeping glance inside the room revealed a dozen gypsy warriors inside the room. The hidden area was set up for comfort, containing couches and chairs, a table and more chairs, and a big-screen TV with a PlayStation 2 gaming system hooked up. A group of Wiatar demons sat clustered around the TV and PS2.

For one frozen moment, time stood still in the room. Then one of the game characters on TV yelled, "Get out of the car!"

Angel swung his left arm up and knocked the shotgun away before the Wiatar demon could fire again. He stepped into the demon, brought his right fist up from his side, then twisted his hips to slam the blow into the demon's face. The demon dropped the shotgun and flew backward.

The gypsies acted in concert, suddenly rising up and lashing out at the Wiatar demons. Blades flickered in the room's light as they were bared.

Reaching under his duster, Angel ripped his battle-ax free and took two long strides to the right. Wiatar demons tried to intercept him. He used the ax, cutting through the flesh-and-blood demon barriers that jumped up in his way.

The Wiatar demons favored firearms—from shotguns to large-caliber pistols to submachine guns—and the string of staccato explosions filled the large room. As quickly as the demons unlimbered their weapons, though, the gypsies cut them down.

"Treachery!" one of the Wiatar demons yelled.

Gunn and Wesley followed Angel through the door. Both of them engaged Wiatar demons. Wesley stooped and picked up the shotgun from the first demon Angel had fought. Throwing himself down to avoid another demon's pistol blast, Wesley pulled the shotgun to his shoulder while lying on his back and fired at point-blank range.

Blood and gore splattered across the wall behind the demon.

Gunn stepped in to battle the nearest Wiatar demon while Wesley got to his feet.

Angel whirled, moving out of the field of fire as a massive handgun cracked off a round almost in his ear. He came around hard, getting a two-handed grip on the ax haft like a homerun hitter swinging for the fences. Coming up under the Wiatar demon's outstretched arm, the ax blade bit deeply and took all the wind from Angel's opponent.

Spotting the next Wiatar behind the one he'd killed, Angel left the ax in place, gripped the handle, and ran the falling corpse back. The dead demon collided with the living one, and they both went down. Freeing the ax, Angel turned his attention to the living demon as the Wiatar extricated his pistol from under his dead companion and took aim.

Angel swung the ax just as the demon fired. The ax split the demon's skull at the same time that the bullet struck Angel in the chest with the force of a sledgehammer. Pain ripped through Angel, followed almost immediately by cold shock.

He pushed through the pain, knowing from the look of the demon's smashed skull that he wasn't getting up again. Angel yanked the ax free and looked for Gunn and Wesley.

Gunn was locked in combat, battling a Wiatar demon with his sword and just getting the blade over the demon's rifle barrel. The point sank into the demon's throat, cutting off his thunderous cry of rage.

Wesley was on his knees. He wore a bandolier of shotgun shells draped across his chest from one shoulder. The demon that had carried the shotgun lay sprawled in death at his feet. Wesley thumbed two shells into the sawn-off weapon's double barrels and snapped the shotgun closed. He rose to his feet in one lithe move.

"Down!" Wesley roared to Gunn.

Gunn went to ground at once. A Wiatar demon fired a machine pistol, and the bullets passed over Gunn's head. Wesley fired the shotgun into the demon's face.

Flesh stripped from the demon's skull in a bloody froth. He staggered back and died, dropping clumsily to his knees, then falling forward.

Gunn freed his sword and rose to his feet.

Lights died in the room, smashed by flailing weapons and bullets that left pockmarks in the wall. The large-screen television exploded in a burst of sparks that resembled a miniature Fourth of July party.

Angel stepped from the path of a shotgun blast. One of the pellets ripped through his side, leaving a burning swath of pain in its wake, but he avoided the brunt of the attack. Holding the ax haft in both hands, he stepped to the Wiatar demon's right and drove the steel-capped end up into his opponent's face.

The meaty impact lifted the Wiatar from his feet and deposited him in an unconscious or dead heap on the floor ten feet away.

Angel surveyed the battle site. A curved, wrought-iron stairway led up to the second floor at the back of the room. An irregular line of Wiatar demons and gypsies spanned the distance. A Wiatar pulled himself up the stairway, following a gypsy only then disappearing up into the second floor.

The Wiatar fired his mini-Uzi. The stream of bullets struck sparks from the staircase's metal rails, then chopped into the gypsy. Paralyzed by the bullets, the gypsy tumbled back onto the demon, knocking them both to the floor. The Wiatar tried to get to his feet and bring his machine pistol up at the same time.

Angel hacked the demon's arm off and sprinted across him. He avoided conflict with the gypsies; they were human. He wanted questions answered, but he didn't want to hurt any of them. Pausing at the bottom of the curved stairway, Angel peered up into the darkness that filled the second floor. He scented the air, but only smelled the demon and gypsy blood.

The hidden door that opened into the club pulled open, and a bouncer armed with an extended stun baton stepped into the room. Wesley pointed the shotgun at him, and the bouncer made a swift exit.

"They're going to be in here soon," Wesley said.

"And if they're not, the police will," Gunn said.

Angel took the stairs two and three at a time. The steps rang and vibrated beneath his weight. The countervibration that started up almost immediately let him know that Gunn and Wesley were at his heels.

Leaving the dim light of the first-floor room

behind him, Angel stepped into the darkness of the second floor. He almost tripped over a dead gypsy. The current state of decapitation offered unimpeachable testimony as to his state.

Angel kept moving, listening to the adrenaline-laced pounding of demon's feet and gypsy boots against the wooden floor. Mixed in with those sounds was the furtive scurrying of rat's claws. The building was infested with the creatures.

Crates, old and new, occupied the second floor. The long, large room had been used as a combination storage space and dumping ground for decades. The fecund stench of death clung to the place, and if the remnants of a body or two weren't among the debris, Angel would have been surprised.

Bullets shattered a crate near Angel's head. Glass shards tumbled free of the crate, then the weight of the crates on top of it crushed it and sent all of them tumbling.

Angel broke from cover to avoid the falling crates. As he crossed the uneven space between the stacks, he caught a glimpse of a window near the back of the room where the gypsies clambered through onto a fire escape. Few Wiatar demons remained. However, the Wiatars' firearms made even their lesser numbers deadly. A burst of gunfire drove a gypsy over the side. The muzzle flashes reflected from the luminous eyes of the frightened rats lying low among the stacks of crates and piles of debris.

A gypsy woman, limned by moonlight, stood

framed in the window for an instant. She was beautiful, dark-skinned, and copper-haired. Almond eyes the color of gray ice flashed, reflecting the gunfire.

Her delicate lips framed a single word that Angel didn't understand. She held her hand up beside her. Pale green embers gathered in her palm. Then she hurled her hand forward.

Like miniature fireflies trained to be an air armada, the pale green embers flew into the room. Instead of targeting the Wiatars, though, the embers struck the rats and showered them in a brief luminosity.

The woman turned her head to survey the effects of whatever she had done. Moonlight shone over her neck, highlighting the multicolored tattoo that ran beneath her jaw to her shoulder. The tattoo was of a jeweled hawk in full flight. The indigo blue feathering stood out in sharp contrast to the red claws and yellow eye.

Memory tugged at Angel's attention. The tattoo looked familiar. He knew in an instant that he had seen it before. The past drew him back into its seductive embrace, but at the same time he saw several rats stand on their haunches and scent the air.

Noses wiggling, whiskers scraping the air, the rats turned their hollow gazes toward the surviving Wiatars. High-pitched shrills filled the large room. Then the rats attacked.

CHAPTER SIX

Outside London, England
October 1887

Anger fueled Angelus as he locked his hands around Spike's throat in Lord Hyde-Pierce's guesthouse. Surprise, as well as his greater size and strength, gave Angelus the upper hand temporarily. He bore Spike to the ground, covering the other vampire's body with his.

Frightened shouts from the lord's guests rang out all around them. Shots blasted into the stillness of the dregs of night that still kept dawn at bay.

Spike pulled his left foot back and shoved it into Angelus's stomach. Unable to hold on, Angelus felt his grip slip free. He tried to recover, but Spike drove him away with his leg. Shoving himself up, Angelus rose to his feet.

"Stop!" Spike shouted.

Angelus faced the younger vampire. He saw the fear in Spike's eyes and he fed on it. For seven years, Spike had been getting used to the idea that he was immortal, with the ability to live forever. Now, mortality came back at him in a rush, ripping away the privileged world he had been thrust into by Dru's crimson kisses.

"You don't want to kill me," Spike said. He crouched over. He wiped his mouth with a hand and looked surprised to see blood there.

"Sure, I do," Angelus said, taking a step forward.

"Not me," Spike insisted. "You want to kill the humans."

"Well," Angelus said, continuing forward, "that's going to be harder now, isn't it? I mean, what with them scattering like a covey of quail before an overeager hound." He attacked, feinting with a hand, then kicking Spike in the crotch.

"More! More!" a feminine voice screamed with childish delight. "Hit him harder! Break his bones!"

Spike stood back. A surprised look formed on his demon's visage. "Dru?"

Clasping her hands together, Dru beamed at him. "Oh, you should see yourselves! Like splendid champions you are! I could watch you forever! I swear on me mum's grave that I could!" She glanced from

Angelus to Spike and back again. "Oh please, don't let me interrupt! You were doing famously!"

"Dru!" Hurt showed in Spike's eyes.

Angelus couldn't believe the emotion that was there. Spike was softer than him, always somehow remaining in tune with the dead heart that lay still and silent within his chest.

"Oh don't worry so, William," Dru cooed. "Angelus won't harm you. Not truly. At least, if he does harm you, it won't be permanent, and he will never kill you. After all, he made you through me. He is your grandsire, you know."

Angelus calmed. Dru's madness, if anything, was enlightening. The four of them were there together. They could get more done working together than by battling one another.

"Perhaps Angelus doesn't love you," Dru went on, "but he does take pride in you." She smiled at Angelus, and he clearly saw the dark insanity that lingered there.

"And even if you don't take pride in him, you at least know that killing one of our own will not serve you in this instance," another voice said reasonably.

Angelus shifted his attention from Dru to Darla. She stood farther up the stairwell.

"If one of Lord Hyde-Pierce's guests reach town," Darla said, "things could go badly for us."

"No one will come from town tonight," Spike said. "They won't dare come here if they hear of what we're doing."

"Not tonight," Darla agreed. "But come morning, what townsman won't have heard of the four travelers that stopped at Lord Hyde-Pierce's manor for the night that turned out to be vampires?"

"We'll be famous," Dru crowed in delight. "The people in this area will tell stories about us." She touched her fangs with her tongue. "Even stories that they may use to scare children with." Her eyes grew wide and round. "Won't that be grand? To scare so many children?"

"We'll also be hunted," Angelus said. Dru's grasp of reality was still shattered, and she didn't see herself as vulnerable. "If so much as one of them gets away, we'll know no peace for a while."

"Lord Hyde-Pierce, should he survive this night, will post a reward for our capture or our deaths," Darla said. "Even if he does not survive, one of his cronies might even post a reward based on descriptions of us."

Angelus licked his lips. "Hyde-Pierce is going to die."

Darla passed Dru and came to Angelus's side. She took him by the arm. "Not immediately, beloved," she said. "First, we must discover where Lord Hyde-Pierce hides his valuables."

Turning his thoughts to the treasure they had come seeking, Angelus licked his lips again. The blood flow from his split flesh had diminished.

Angelus looked at Spike. "You'll live," Angelus announced.

Spike eyed him levelly, not backing up an inch now. "And so will you." He licked his teeth with his tongue, making certain he showed them off well.

His arrogance is growing, Angelus thought. The temptation to resume the battle, to teach Spike once and for all who was the master, thrummed strongly within him.

Darla's grip tightened on Angelus's arm. "No," she whispered. "Leave this matter for another time."

After a moment, Angelus nodded. The four of them didn't always travel together. Even Angelus and Darla didn't always travel together. But, sometimes, there was truth in the old saying "the more the merrier." Laying siege to Lord Hyde-Pierce's home tonight would not have been done—or would have been planned as a straight theft without the massacre involved—had Spike and Dru not been along.

"Take the woods," Angelus told Spike. "Track down any that might have been fearful enough or possess enough common sense to flee."

"I don't see why I have to—" Spike started to protest.

So quick that even Angelus's eye could not follow with his heightened senses, Darla flicked out a hand that bristled with fingernails. Two of her nails sliced Spike under his chin. Twin rivulets of blood wept down his neck.

"Don't argue," Darla ordered. "Otherwise I'll aid in your destruction."

Spike quieted.

"Kill them all," Angelus instructed Spike. "Stay out there to make certain of it."

Irritation showing on his features and in his body language, Spike nodded.

"Dru," Angelus said.

Dru clapped her hands excitedly. "Yes?"

"The stables," Angelus instructed. "Set all the horses free that are still locked up there. I don't want any of Hyde-Pierce's men to have a chance at escape who haven't already taken it."

"I will," Dru replied, smiling viciously. "I love horses. Do you want me to kill them? The horses, I mean?"

"Not unless it's necessary."

"Oh, but I think it will be necessary."

"Dru," Darla said in a steady voice, "save some of the horses. We'll want a few of them to carry away the treasure Lord Hyde-Pierce is supposed to have."

Dru nodded seriously. "All right, grandmother. I will. I'll save some of the horses."

Running feet suddenly sounded outside.

"Two by two, men," a male voice instructed. "Into the hallways first, then we'll secure each of the rooms on the ground floor."

"The guards," Angelus said.

Spike grinned a little and wiped at the blood under his chin. He licked the crimson from his fingertips. "Well, at least that means we won't have to go looking for as many."

Angelus leaned over to the lantern on the wall. He

raised the hurricane glass and blew the flame out. Embers clung to the wick, and a streamer of smoke curled toward the ceiling. Darkness descended over the hallway.

Some of the arriving guards carried lanterns, but the lights only made them easier targets as they stepped from the darkness.

Covered in blood, though little of it was his own, Angelus ran at the manor house window on the east side of the building. The guest houses surrounding the main building held only corpses now. More dead bodies littered the grounds between the structures where Angelus and Darla had run them to ground. The guards had tried to fight, but the night belonged to the vampires. The gardens that had been so carefully cultivated and worked now had bodies strewn among them.

Flames wreathed the stables and carriage house. Angelus didn't know what Dru had done, but the scent of burning horseflesh and smoke filled the night air. Every now and again, he heard her madness-inspired laughter.

Metal glinted at the window when Angelus was only six long strides away. He recognized the rifle barrel, then saw the shadowy outline of the man holding the weapon. The muzzle flashed, and Angelus heard the bullet split the wind beside his ear.

He already carried three bullet wounds that Darla

would have to clean out later. Although the weapons didn't threaten his existence, the probing necessary to pull the spent bullets out of his flesh was a painful experience.

Two strides from the window, Angelus leaped into the air and smashed through the glass panes and curtains with his feet. He landed awkwardly but rolled into a standing position with a fair amount of grace.

Three guards hunkered down behind the window rose from their positions. They leveled their weapons, aiming at his chest.

"Go ahead!" Angelus roared, throwing his arms wide and acting as if their bullets would cause him no concern at all. "You can't kill me! You can't hurt me!"

All three men fired. Only one of the bullets struck Angelus, catching him in the middle of the stomach. He resisted doubling over in agony only through a sheer effort of will and past experience with being shot.

The men started reloading their weapons.

Then Darla launched herself through the broken window. She caught two of the men around the neck and bore them to the floor. Her flashing fangs found the throat of one of the men while her right hand tore the throat from the other.

Angelus darted forward, brushed the rifle aside, and grabbed the guard's lapels. The man screamed in terror, and the sound was music to Angelus's ears. He whirled and tossed the man over his hip, throwing him down on top of the long banquet table where they had dined earlier.

The table broke, smashing to the floor. Angelus followed his prey, leaning in and tearing his throat out with his fangs. Hot blood splashed in his face. He drank it down, not worried about spilling it because there was so much more and it had been only moments since he had last fed.

When his opponent rolled lax in his grasp and the frenzied heart no longer beat, Angelus pushed up from the dead man.

Darla stood as well. She ran a forearm along her lower face to brush away the blood. A smile showed white and clean against her crimson-stained cheeks. The nightdress that she had taken from those they had killed in the forest earlier hung in tatters. She had ripped the garment away above the middle of her thighs to allow herself greater freedom of movement.

Angelus felt his lust for her grow within him. Whenever they killed together, especially when it was a mass slaying like at the manor house, his need for her intensified. They had been friends and lovers and rivals for over 130 years. Still, the spark between them persisted.

But now is not the time, he told himself. He nodded to her, and they ran through the house. After decades of slaying together, they knew each other's moves. No words needed to be spoken.

More of Lord Hyde-Pierce's servants, as well as a

handful of guards, hid in rooms on the first floor. Angelus and Darla slew them all, not taking any time to feed on them. He knew their hunger was satiated to a degree, enough so that they were willing to take their time with the last few kills.

Lord Hyde-Pierce, dressed for battle in hunting gear, carrying an elephant rifle and a .455 Webley pistol holstered at his hip, led the last-stand effort at the top of the stairs leading to the second floor.

"Leave my house, hellspawn!" Hyde-Pierce roared. "I've seen your kind before. I knew what you were from the moment I heard about what you were doing in my guest house."

"You haven't killed me before," Angelus taunted.

"We've never crossed paths," Lord Hyde-Pierce stated. For an old man, he held the rifle surprisingly steady.

Just before the rifle's left barrel exploded in sound and fury, Angelus whirled to his right.

Nimble and quick as a fox, Angelus ran for the balcony. He leaped, using the great strength he'd gained as a vampire, and pulled himself over the railing in one lithe move as Lord Hyde-Pierce and his guards turned to face him. Lantern light spilled across the wall, bringing Angelus into sharp relief. But he was already in motion, running toward the men.

From the corner of his eye, he spotted Darla hurling herself up the staircase. They had discounted her because she was a woman, and that was going to be the death of some of them.

Lord Hyde-Pierce fired his second shot before he was ready. The big rifle's recoil shoved him back against the wall. The bullet ripped through the guard standing between Angelus and the lord. Entrails, flesh, and blood splashed over Angelus as the bullet eviscerated the man. He caught the dead man in one hand and flung the body over the railing. Catching the next man's arm as he tried to point his pistol, Angelus broke the limb and reached for the man's head.

Darla snapped the neck of the first man she grabbed, then ran her stiffened fingers into the throat of the next. Already off-balance from firing the big rifle while not properly set, Hyde-Pierce tumbled down the stairs as Darla tried to clear the two dead guards away from her.

Roping an arm around the last surviving guard, using the broken arm for leverage, Angelus cupped his chin and twisted his head viciously. The neck popped loose from the spine. The man was dead before he hit the steps. He threw himself from the top of the steps, jumping to the floor just as Hyde-Pierce rolled to a stop at the bottom of the steps.

The old man had lost his rifle along the way. Weakly, eyes out of focus in the shadows, he reached for the pistol holstered at his side.

A pool of oil from a shattered lantern leaked across the floor of the great room. A moment later, the oil ignited with a gentle *whuff*. Black, malignant smoke curled toward the ceiling. Moonlight shone through the parted curtains and made glistening pearls of the scattered oil droplets.

Angelus hunkered down beside the old man. He plucked the pistol from Hyde-Pierce's grip before he could pull the trigger.

A shadow moved across the floor near Angelus. When he glanced up, he saw Spike standing there. "Is anyone left in the forest?" Angelus asked.

"No." Spike was covered in blood from head to boots. "They're all dead." He looked around. "I counted guests on the way through the house looking for you."

Angelus was impressed. Usually Spike wasn't so methodical. Killing was starting to agree with him, even though he had lost his first blush with it. Perhaps, aside from the railroad spike through the heads of those who had tormented him, he wasn't very creative, but he was thorough.

"I didn't see the woman," Spike said.

"What woman?" Angelus asked. He had slain women on his way through the guesthouses.

"The beautiful one at dinner," Spike answered. "Her name was Lyanka."

Angelus remembered the copper-haired woman from dinner then. He hadn't paid her much attention, but he had noticed that Spike had.

"Where was she?" Angelus asked, knowing that Spike would have the answer.

"In the guesthouse," Spike replied. "Where we were."

Angelus nodded, understanding what had happened earlier. Dru's jealousy and Spike's own predatory needs had sent him in search of the woman.

"Was she in the room when you got there?" Angelus asked.

"No."

"The strumpet was there," Dru said as she entered the room. Her nightdress hung in rags about her, revealing her pale flesh. She didn't even make a pretense at modesty. She put a thumb to her mouth and licked the blood from it. Straw littered her hair, and the stench of burned horseflesh clung to her. "She walked into her room like a fiery moth, drawing William's eyes to her like moth eyes." She glanced at Spike. "Sweet William couldn't keep his moth eyes off her. He kept staring after her. Like she was some little dish of ice cream that he couldn't quite get his hands on. But I knew she was an ice maiden. A chill vixen with wintry kisses that would freeze the heart of any man. I wanted her eyes. Such nice eyes. Eyes for you and eyes for me. Always dot the eyes and cross the tees."

The missing woman posed a problem. The initial plan had called for complete control over the lord and his servants. The unexpected guests had been one wrinkle that had only been added to by Spike's actions.

Angelus looked at Hyde-Pierce. "Where is she?"

The old man shook his head. "I don't know." His voice was hoarse and strained. His countenance seemed to pale before Angelus's eyes.

Beside them, the pool of oil continued to spread as the flames warmed the liquid. The fire had burned away all the oil in spots and was now feasting on the wooden floor.

"Who is she?" Angelus asked. He knew they had been introduced over dinner, but he'd scarcely paid her attention. She was a woman, and one not of much use to him.

Hyde-Pierce hacked and coughed. A bubble of blood burst across his wrinkled lips. He must have broken a rib during the long fall down the stairway.

"An actress," Hyde-Pierce replied. "She knew something of cards. She claimed to read fortunes. She knew so much, so very much."

"Knew what?" Angelus asked.

"History. Literature. Even folktales." Hyde-Pierce turned his head toward Angelus and touched his face with his fingers. "It is good to have you home, Peter."

Peter had been Hyde-Pierce's son, dead fourteen years now after an accident involving a railroad line his father had invested in. The scuttlebutt in the village outside the forest was that the old man had never quite gotten over the loss of his son.

Suspicion dawned inside Angelus. "What did the woman talk to you about?"

"Some of my collection, dear boy." Hyde-Pierce smiled gently. "Just some of those old bits and pieces of history I found here and there that you never quite warmed up to. She knew so much. Even knew marvelous tales that I . . . I . . ."

Abruptly, the old man's breath blew out of him. His eyes glazed, and Angelus knew he no longer saw anything in the mortal world.

Angelus dropped the body. His mind filled with suspicion. He locked eyes with Darla.

"That woman didn't just happen by," Darla said. "The men with her said that they picked her up in the village. She posed herself as a doxy."

"'Posed herself as a doxy'?" Dru repeated shrilly. "She revealed herself. Like a peacock. Spread her feathers and showed you everything and drew you in with your moth's eyes so that she could burn you blind." She glanced reproachfully at Spike. "And *you*. There you were sniffing around after her like some misbegotten hound, you were. A cute, naughty hound, but a hound who forgot that he belongs to me."

Angelus left Spike and Dru bickering.

"She's a thief," Darla said, joining Angelus at the bottom of the stairs.

Angelus vaulted the dead men, running with agile grace on the open steps. "Yes." There was no other reason for the woman to be there. Years of experience, especially with the seamier and more desperate side of life, led him to his assessment.

At the top of the stairs, Angelus glanced along the hallway leading to Hyde-Pierce's collection rooms. After dinner, the lord had brought his dinner guests up for a brief visit.

Light from the twisting fire spreading across the manor house floor darted along the hallway to the closed double doors. Smoke curled along the ceiling and grew steadily thicker, like fog rolling in from the sea. The crackle and pop of the dry wood echoed in Angelus's ears. The fire would swiftly claim the manor house and all the dead in it. That suited Angelus because the event would cover much of what had happened there.

Together, Angelus and Darla went forward. The door was unlocked, but something prevented it from being opened inward. Setting himself, Angelus threw a shoulder against the door. Hinges ripped free of the frame, and he plunged inside.

The collection room was dark now, and the shadows made the flickering candlelight at the far end even more noticeable. The woman, Lyanka, held the candle in one hand while she stood in front of one of the glass display cases scattered across the floor. She froze, looking at Angelus at the edge of the bubble of light the candle put off.

Angelus smiled. The woman *was* beautiful. Her face was grim and determined. He saw the fear in her eyes, but she wasn't giving in to it.

In one smooth motion, she threw out a hand and spoke harsh words the like of which Angelus had never heard before. Blue shimmering took shape in the air between them and rushed in on him.

Even though he'd been taken somewhat by surprise, Angelus was still in motion before the shimmering caught him. A wave of incredible force caught him and hurled him back into the wall, sending him crashing through built-in shelves that held books and objects. If he hadn't already been in motion and managed to avoid most of the impact, he was certain every bone in his body would have been broken.

Darla was in motion even as he fell, moving like a feral beast with all the speed she could muster. Angelus gathered his feet beneath him. The demon inside him refused to be left out of the kill.

Lyanka threw out a hand again. Another blue shimmer gathered form. This one, however, was weaker than the first. The shimmer caught Darla head-on, but only knocked her backward a few feet.

Angelus took heart in that. Apparently whatever powers the woman possessed had limitations. No magic was inexhaustible. He rushed toward her. She lifted her hand and spoke again. This time he managed to dodge the force, though it overturned three glass display cases behind him. Glass shards scattered and slid across the polished wood floor.

Panicked as she was, Lyanka still responded like a professional. She turned her attention to the glass display case in front of her as she reached under the traveling cloak she wore and brought out a pistol. She broke the glass display case with the pistol butt, then turned the weapon on Angelus. The sound of the shots exploded inside the room.

The woman's marksmanship was amazing under the circumstances. Two of the rounds tore into Angelus's body and knocked him from his feet. Pain ripped through him with blinding intensity. He struggled to get to his feet.

Darla came out of the smoke-laden darkness, coming up behind the woman when she inadvertently blocked the light of the candle she carried. Lyanka reached into the glass display case and took out a green-tinted metal rod nearly a foot long. Mouth open wide to expose her fangs, Darla grabbed the woman and attempted to bite her.

Lyanka whirled, showing obvious training as she slid free of Darla's powerful grip. Darla's fingers tore the other woman's blouse and exposed a multicolored hawk tattoo on her neck. Purple sigils marked the flesh around the tattoo. Scratches leaked blood down her heaving breasts.

Hunger stirred within Angelus as he reached his feet. He wanted the woman, wanted to taste her and feel her fear.

Still in motion, Lyanka pulled the flickering candle flame to her lips as Darla came at her again. For a moment Angelus thought the weak candle flame was going to go out. Then the woman's lips opened, and she breathed out.

Fire exploded from the woman's mouth and enveloped Darla.

Overcome by the fiery blast, Darla stepped back and howled in pain. Her flesh blistered, blackened, and cracked. Flames clung to her tattered dress. She panicked and tried to run, feeding the flames clinging to her garments.

Angelus stared at the woman. Her lips curled up in a smile, and she said, "Choose, vampire." Then she turned and ran.

Knowing there was a good chance that Darla wouldn't live through the flames, Angelus swept a tapestry from a nearby wall and ran for her. He wrapped the tapestry around her and bore her to the ground. Several frantic moments passed as he smothered the flames. Darla writhed and howled, kicking at him and struggling to bite him as the pain drove her temporarily insane.

Spike and Dru entered the room. Surprise and the flames clinging to the collection cases lit their faces.

"The woman," Angelus growled as he fought to control Darla. He believed he had most of the flames out, but he knew the pain from the burns were most likely intolerable. Due to her vampire nature, Darla would survive and would be inconvenienced only for a short time before her wounds healed completely, but the pain would be unpleasant for some time.

"Where?" Spike asked.

"Back there." Angelus nodded toward the rear of the room.

"No you don't, love," Dru said, pulling Spike back. "I'll find her. And I'll have her sow's eyes and peacock feathers when I do." She ran forward, but Spike followed at her heels.

Angelus sat and held Darla as spasms shook her. She was still out of her mind with the pain.

CHAPTER SEVEN

Los Angeles

"Angel!"

Responding to Wesley's voice, Angel dodged back from the approaching wave of shrieking rats streaming through the building. Wesley stood around the corner of a stack of crates and didn't see the rodents racing toward them on wicked claws.

"Rats," Angel said.

Wesley looked puzzled. "She got away?"

Angel swept by Wesley, retreating from the rats. He grabbed Wesley's jacket and yanked him into motion just as the first of the rodents put in an appearance. Their eyes glittered ruby red in the moonlight.

"Oh," Wesley said weakly. He ran, following Angel through the twisting maze of debris. *"Rats."*

A pool of rats dropped from crates with fat *plops* and joined others that oozed from the piles of debris to cut off one of the avenues of escape. Angel took the only other opening, almost running into Gunn, who raised his sword in defense.

"Rats," Wesley gasped.

Gunn shook his head. "Don't worry about it. She's got what—the alley or the rooftop? She won't get far."

"No," Wesley said, pointing at the massed creatures racing after them. "Rats."

Gunn cursed as he joined Angel and Wesley in running. "Oh man, and *really* big rats too."

A Wiatar demon stumbled from the shadows in front of Angel. Rats covered the demon. The rodents chattered and tore at the Wiatar with their claws and teeth. Overcome by the weight of the rats, the Wiatar fell to the floor. The rats continued ripping into him. His arms and legs quivered, and his attempts to fight grew weaker.

"Oh man," Gunn said in a low voice. "That is harsh."

Angel silently agreed. If they couldn't escape the rats, he knew they'd all be brought down.

Turning the next corner, trusting his sense of direction even though things had gotten confusing on the building's second floor, Angel stared at the wall that suddenly filled his vision. They stood trapped between two tall rows of leaning crates that stretched to the ceiling.

"Wrong turn?" Wesley asked.

"Yeah," Angel said. He couldn't help but think of Connor. *Once upon a time, your dad was a big, bad vampire. Until the day rats ate him.*

"Okay," Gunn said. "Escape route is out. Backup plan is—"

"Working on it." Angel turned and watched as a wave of rats swarmed into the area between the stacks of crates.

"Maybe we need to work a little faster," Gunn suggested anxiously. "We got four-footed Cuisinarts chomping away all our think time here."

Angel stepped in front of Wesley and Gunn. Gripping the nearest stack of crates, Angel set himself and pulled. With glacial slowness compared with the rampaging rats bearing down on them, the stack swung. Boards splintered as the weight shifted, and rotted wood gave way. The horde of rats disappeared beneath a deluge of broken crates, rotted foodstuffs, and out-of-date appliances and parts. A choking dust cloud rose up from the floor.

"Come on," Angel said, leaping to the top of the pile of debris and running for the exit door that could now be seen. With surefooted grace, he spanned the distance over the debris, then dropped to the floor and continued running. Rats had collected on the bodies of the fallen gypsies and Wiatar demons.

Gunn and Wesley ran at his heels, tumbling and nearly falling, but getting once more to their feet each time.

Only corpses remained in the first-floor room. Angel ran across them and paused at the doorway to the club. Peering around the corner, he saw that the club was in pandemonium. A bouncer stationed near the doorway turned and saw Angel. The big man started to raise the baton he carried, but Angel slapped the blow away with his ax haft and drove the bottom of the ax haft into the man's stomach. When the guy bent over, Angel slammed the ax handle into his temple and sent him to the floor in an unconscious heap.

The club patrons poured out the front door onto the street. The shrill *whoop-whoop-whoop* of arriving police sirens grew closer.

One of the dancers, this one halfway clad in a green, black, and white spandex superhero costume that hugged every curve, tried to run past Angel. He grabbed her, too fast for her, and held her for a moment. "Where's the back door out of here?" Angel demanded.

Hesitation froze the dancer for a moment, then she yanked her head toward the back of the club. "Back that way. Through the dressing rooms."

Angel went quickly, passing overturned chairs and tables. Some of the women were still in the dressing rooms getting their personal effects together. There were no screams of outrage at being invaded, but there were several curses.

The club's rear door was heavy security issue. The alarm was clearly marked. A few dancers and patrons stood in front of the door, obviously trying to get past the door.

"Somebody blocked the door from the other side," a man said. "Can't get the door open."

"Move," Angel ordered.

Noting his bloody and disheveled appearance, as well as Gunn and Wesley in the same state, the crowd stood frozen.

Wesley lifted the shotgun and fired into the ceiling. Trapped by the small enclosure, the deafening blast ricocheted between the walls. Shredded ceiling tiles tumbled to the floor like heavy confetti.

"Move," Wesley barked.

The crowd retreated at once from the door.

"Way to go, Wes," Gunn said.

Angel shoved against the panic bar across the door. Nothing moved. He scanned the door, hooked his fingers into the reinforced door frame, and tore it loose. Once the door frame was gone, getting to the door was easier. He pulled, using all of his strength, and pulled the door back in against the natural bend of the door hinges. Metal shrieked, but the door gave way, peeling back like the top on a sardine can.

Someone had parked an old pickup against the club's back door. Barely enough room remained, even with the door torn away, for Angel to crawl through. He dropped to the alley and looked up at the second floor.

Smoke billowed from the smashed and broken windows, followed by twisting tongues of flame. A fire escape clung to the wall like a broken-backed snake. Nothing moved on the fire escape or on top of the building.

Angel moved on out into the alley, followed by Gunn and Wesley as the crowd pushed them forward. Glancing toward both ends of the alley, Angel headed in one direction and pointed in the other.

"The streets," Angel said. "Go." He ran. At the corner, he peered around in time to see the gypsy woman climbing into a taxi. No name marked the taxi doors.

Gypsy cab, Angel thought.

In the next instant, the taxi pulled away. Red flashers of arriving police cruisers reflected from the windows and the back glass. Then the vehicle vanished into the shadows that guarded the dark heart of the city.

". . . bring you this breaking news from the streets," the female newsanchor announced. "So far, no one admits knowing what caused the violence that claimed the lives of over two dozen people at this night club."

Chavula Faa studied the image on the screen. Police cars, ambulances, and fire trucks occupied the street in front of the club. He recognized the neon name of the club at once: McCarty's Flesh Fantasy. There were only two such clubs in the metropolitan area. He had learned that fact tonight.

The newsanchor was a pert brunette Asian who wore her hair in a razor-cut along her jaw. She spoke confidently into a microphone headset. "There is some speculation among the police that tonight's events were gang-related. McCarty's Flesh Fantasy has long been a public eyesore, according to some local citizens I've talked to, a place with an enduring history of violence. Police investigators at the scene have confirmed that the club has been the site of past problems, including drug dealing and zone infractions on the part of the exotic dancers who work here."

Faa leaned back in the padded chair of his downtown L.A. office. He was a tall, broad man with swarthy skin that spoke of his heritage. Most people mistakenly thought he was Slavic or Middle Eastern. In truth, he was neither. He kept his head shaved and looked like he was in his mid-thirties, far younger than he really was. He wore round glasses that he knew made him look nerdish and somewhat vulnerable, and black khakis and a maroon-and-black pullover sweater.

The look was one he had deliberately cultivated, a look that had occasionally graced the covers of *Time, Newsweek, Business Week, Wired, PC Gamer,* and, three times—two of them issues with J.Lo and a popular *Star Trek* actress—*Maxim*. He had a public facade that everyone knew, but no one outside of his immediate corporate office knew much about him. No one even knew his true name. He had one public name that he did a lot of business under, but there were several other names that no one could attach him to.

He was a successful businessman who had made his riches in start-up dotcoms and backed those initial profits with solid design entries into the business software sector as well as the video-gaming industry. He had also developed software used by computer graphic effects crews in Hollywood and international marketing programs.

Chavula Faa was worth billions, but no one knew exactly how much because he hid most of his wealth under other identities. Occasionally, a business or an investigative reporter would come close to unveiling all those hidden identities. Seven times over the past sixty years, partly because he had been guilty of political indiscretions during the Second World War regarding deals he had made that had turned major profits, he had almost been found out. All of the people who had come close to making the discoveries that would unveil him had been dealt with. The bodies of four of them had never been found.

"How many people were killed and hurt at the club?" the off-screen newsanchor asked the reporter.

"I don't have an actual count," the pert brunette replied. "But as you can see from the activity behind me, those numbers are going to be considerable."

The images on the television screen showed emergency medical people and firemen interfacing with the police officers. The quick were separated from the dead, and those who still lived were carried off on gurneys. Red-and-white striped sawhorses and yellow POLICE—DO NOT CROSS tape sealed the area off.

Faa lifted a wireless-phone headset from the desk and pulled it on. The keypad attached to his belt. He tapped a speed dial number.

"Yes," a deep, gruff voice answered on the second ring.

"I am looking at a disaster," Faa said as he pushed himself up from his chair. The phone was heavily encrypted; he didn't have to worry about the signal being intercepted. "Tell me that you retrieved the piece." He spoke in the language that they shared, not their native tongue because he was still learning that, but the language that his people had come to know and been brought up in for the last millennium.

"I cannot, Master Faa."

"What happened, Tobar?" Faa asked.

"We were about to close in on the club, following up on the information you had given me about the robbery, when the vampire arrived."

"How did the vampire come to be there?"

"I don't know, master."

"Is he working with Gitana?"

"From all accounts I have heard, Gitana and her people tried to kill the vampire just as the Wiatar demons did."

"What happened?"

"The vampire was looking for Gitana. Or perhaps he was looking for her people."

"How did he know about them?"

"I don't know."

Faa hated that answer. The people he worked with, especially Tobar, who handled much of the clandestine work that needed to be done, were supposed to know things.

"Perhaps," Tobar said, realizing he had made a mistake, "he saw us last night and mistook Gitana's people for us."

Unease slithered through Faa. Ignoring the desktop computer on the massive kidney-shaped desk that allowed him access to the world, he reached into one of the lower drawers and took out a notebook computer. He opened the notebook and brought the OS to life.

"Does the vampire yet live?" Faa asked.

"Yes, master. He and his companions escaped the Wiatar demons, Gitana's people, and the police."

The notebook computer screen cleared. Faa located the file he was looking for and opened it as well. The computer was heavily encrypted and even protected with defensive spells. No one could get near the device without considerable risk, and even if a trained person did, the OS contained a number of defensive programs.

A graphic file of a drawing materialized on the screen. Two faces stared back at him, both of them carefully rendered in pencil. The parchment pages the images had been scanned from were over one hundred years old.

The faces were young and evil. They would never age, and their hearts would always remain dark.

Faa tapped keys. The images shrank and moved to one side, moving over slightly and becoming 3D renditions built by the computer software. Before Faa's eyes, the faces changed, taking on demonic features that he recognized as belonging to vampires.

The images flipped back and forth, becoming human, then vampire, then human again.

Angelus. Faa knew the face of his current enemy, though he didn't know where the man was or what name he wore these days. But he was definitely involved in the present situation.

"Are you certain that the vampire doesn't have a piece of the Bridge?" Tobar asked.

"Yes." The Bridge of Journeyhome consisted of seven pieces. During the last three weeks, Faa had accumulated five of those pieces. Two remained yet to be secured. One of those Gitana had managed to get her hands on, and the other remained missing.

"Then how is he involved in this?"

"I don't know." Faa looked at the two vampires on the screen. He tapped another key, bringing up a digitally enhanced picture of Angelus at the docks. Like the drawings, the picture had been rendered in 3D as well.

Angelus had changed his image over the years. He wore his hair short these days, and he had gone clean-shaven. His clothing bore no identifying marks, and gave no indication of what he was or what he did.

But he had not lost the skills of the warrior that had been written of in the journals that he had acquired all those years ago.

Faa remembered being impressed by the vampire in Prague when they had met. It had been 1891, four years after Lyanka had encountered the vampires at Lord Hyde-Pierce's manor house. Lyanka had found the first piece of the Bridge of Journeyhome in Hyde-Pierce's vast collections.

She had also been the first of their people to figure out what the device might be. Only she had given credence to the stories their people had handed down from the eleventh century, when the Aryans forcibly assembled great armies and decided to invade Muslim lands.

Their people had been gathered from all the other peoples the Aryans had swept up from India and what was now Eastern Europe to fight their wars for them. They had fought that war for a hundred years and more. And they had become gypsies, as had the rest of those people, no longer a part of their own culture but a settling of the multicultural backgrounds that had invented its own language, beliefs, and ways of doing things. After all that time, none of those in the army could return home. Their homes had become whatever they could carry in packs on their backs or stow aboard a *vardo*, the unique wagon home of the gypsies.

"You said the vampire has been involved with the Bridge before," Tobar said.

"Yes," Faa replied.

"And there were others."

Faa tapped the computer keys again. The faces of two women joined the faces of the two male vampires. Angelus and Spike were the two men. Darla and Dru were the women. He had the names from the stories told after 1887 and 1891.

"Yes," Faa said. "There were others."

"Lyanka was involved with them. Perhaps she told them the story of the Bridge."

"No," Faa said. He had read her journals. They had been covered in the blood of her family, whom he had slain to get those books. "They knew nothing of the Bridge." He paused, then pulled up another file.

Images of the illustrated manuscript that had been written back in the eleventh century, when their people had been first integrated in the Aryan army, appeared on the screen. Over the years he had hired the world's best linguists—human as well as demon—to decipher the language. When she had possessed the manuscript, Lyanka had done the same. She hadn't enjoyed much better success than he had.

During the long years of hard fighting, the language had been mostly lost. Getting identified by humans as well as demons had marked Faa's people as prey, and they had been hunted. They had been robbed, used, and killed by those who had come for them.

But now Faa knew the story.

He clicked the mouse, shifting through images of their people serving as cannon fodder for the Aryans, then examined the images of the world that lay at the other end of the Bridge of Journeyhome. The world lay idyllic, showing grand, sweeping cities and beautiful forests and waterfalls. It was a fairyland.

When his people had first arrived here, they had talked of their homeland, of the wondrous things that had been there. In turn, bedded down with people who had become little more than savages due to the incessant war against the Muslims and serving the overbearing Aryans, they had found themselves the victims of ridicule and violence.

In time, they had learned to be quiet and not talk of those things, revealing little of the personal magic they possessed that became weak and diluted over the passing centuries as they mixed their blood with that of the humans. None of the original arrivals had survived in the wars. Only their children had gone on. Many of those had turned away from the heritage others tried to keep alive, not wanting to embrace their new lives so much as to keep safe from their old ones.

"Do you know where Gitana is?" Faa asked.

"Not yet."

"But she has the piece?"

"I know only that the Wiatar demons do not. We captured one of them that escaped the police and talked with him. He said they had shown the piece to

Gitana, though he did not know her by that name, and were awaiting payment. When the vampire broke in, Gitana killed the Wiatar holding the piece and claimed it as her own. He did not know if she escaped the building."

"Where is the Wiatar demon now?"

"Dead, master. After I talked with him, I felt he knew too much about your business."

Faa nodded in satisfaction. Death was preferable to letting anyone live that knew more of his business than he wished. "Find Gitana, Tobar."

"I will, master. But this is a large city, and she moves around."

"She will not leave," Faa said. "She knows I have at least one of the pieces of the Bridge. She also knows I am here."

"I will not fail you, master."

"I know you will not, Tobar." Faa broke the connection and stripped the headset from his face. He returned to the window and peered out.

Los Angeles was still alive and restless. The city mirrored his own state. People would die in L.A. tonight, and some of those deaths would be by his hand.

But the vampire . . .

Never in the acquisitions of the other five Bridge pieces Faa had taken over the last few days had the vampire put in an appearance.

So why now? What has drawn him here? Is he drawn to the Bridge, or is he drawn somehow to

Gitana? There is the history there with Lyanka. But she would have killed him if she had been able.

Faa rubbed his chin in thought. He had risked much in coming this far with his pursuit of the pieces. But all that he might win drew him on. He turned his back to the hanging moon and stared at the notebook computer open on his desk.

The last image he had pulled up from the file showed a castlelike structure set high on a mountain over a forest filled with exotic animals. He didn't know if the forestland creatures actually existed, or if the castle-structure did. Perhaps they were only imaginings left over from stories told to Lyanka or gathered by her as she'd set out to find the true heritage of their people so that they might also find their destiny.

The phone rang, jarring his thoughts. Crossing to the desk, knowing that no one would call one of his private lines without good reason, he glanced at the Caller ID. The number belonged to Lilah Morgan, of Wolfram & Hart. She was the attorney currently representing his interests in Los Angeles.

Faa pulled the headset on and clicked the Connect button. "Ah, Lilah," he greeted in the East Coast accent he'd chosen for the Thomas Ivers identity he presently chose to wear. "This must be important for you to call me so late."

"It is," Lilah agreed. "I also figured, knowing that you're rarely a man of leisure when you're in town, that you would be up."

"It's the night," Faa said truthfully. "I love the night."

"So do I," Lilah agreed in her most charming voice. "I find that more things are . . . *possible* during those hours. I hope I didn't interrupt . . . anything."

Despite the tension that filled him, Faa grinned at his reflection in the window. He was a handsome man, and he liked that fact. Lilah was ambitious. He had seen her ambition the first time they had met. She was drawn to him because he radiated power, because he radiated menace. Even if she didn't get that feeling from his physical presence, she had access to all of his Thomas Ivers files.

"No," he told her. "No interruptions. While I'm currently here in L.A., I'm quite unattached."

"That wasn't what I was referring to," she said.

But they both knew that it was.

"How much have you seen of L.A.?" she asked.

"Not as much as I would like. You know how it is with business."

"Yes, I do. However, I'm also—if I might say so—an excellent guide of all things L.A. Museums and art exhibitions, if you like."

"And if I didn't want something quite so formal?"

Lilah hesitated for only a second. "I've seen some of those, too. And the ones I haven't seen, I've heard of. I'm not averse to doing a bit of exploring."

"Nor am I," Faa told her.

"Perhaps you should call me sometime," Lilah suggested.

Faa smiled like a wolf. "I'd like that." He enjoyed offering people hope, then snatching it away at a later date.

"So would I."

"Unfortunately," Faa said, "this was not a casual call."

"No. I've got good news."

"I could use good news."

"I think I've found the Czech statuary piece you were looking for."

Returning to the notebook computer, Faa called up the images of the Bridge of Journeyhome. The seventh piece had never been seen since it had been lost in the eleventh century. At least, it had never been seen by any of his clan or Lyanka's. Only half-remembered memories and legends had followed the piece. It had been lost several times.

"The owner is a collector much like yourself," Lilah said. "I've brokered buys for him in the past. Transactions where certificates of authenticity weren't possible but the pieces had to be guaranteed. He has his own experts."

"I'd like to talk to this man," Faa said.

"I'm working on it," Lilah said. "Like you, he prefers anonymity. The fewer people who know his business, the better."

Faa chafed against the time delay. When he had gotten the first piece of the Bridge of Journeyhome, he had performed auguries to discover what his chances were of discovering all seven pieces. The responses he had gotten indicated that, if all seven were to be found, they would be found quickly. Otherwise, ill luck would befall him and the pieces would be scattered again.

That luck was part of the enchantment that cursed the pieces. In 1891, he had possessed two of the pieces. Lyanka had been in possession of the one that had been missing for so long.

His demons had overtaken her in the Carpathian Mountains. She had chosen death over defeat. Faa had watched her fall from the bridge into the rushing river below. Later, he had found her body washed up on a bank. But Lyanka had not had the Bridge piece she had taken from Hyde-Pierce four years before.

Faa had lost the pieces in a fire only a few days later. For a time he had thought that they had been destroyed. But that was before he had learned they were virtually indestructible by physical means. Only magic—strong and black magic—could end their existence.

He had gotten three pieces again when World War II had ended and he had very nearly lost his life to Allied forces invading Normandy. Then, in South America, he had managed to find four pieces while living as a narco baron in Bagota in the 1980s.

"Who is this guy?" Faa asked.

"You know I can't tell you that."

"You're my attorney," Faa pointed out.

"Wolfram and Hart also represent him."

Irritation and frustration grated within Faa. "Perhaps I should seek a separate counsel," he suggested in an even tone.

"You could," Lilah responded. She sounded a little cooler, a little more guarded. She sounded a little uncomfortable as well, but she wasn't weakening. "I think, especially at this premature juncture in the negotiations, that choosing to do so would be inadvisable."

Faa restrained his immediate impulse to beat her down with words and threats. After all, he held the upper hand and she didn't know it. "What would you suggest, counselor?" he asked.

"That you wait till morning. Maybe a couple days. Let me see what I can set up. For his part, the seller is showing a definite weakness."

"What kind of weakness?"

"He likes a few things on your list," Lilah said.

"Which list?"

"Your personal list."

Faa stretched his neck and rolled his shoulders. Muscles and sinews popped and cracked. The personal list held items that were illegal for him to own.

"What does he want?" Faa asked.

"I don't know. He plays things cagily. In fact, he reminds me of you."

"I'll take that as a compliment."

"It was meant as one." Lilah paused, obviously waiting for him to say something that would offer further illumination on the situation. "At any rate, I'll give you a call in the morning to let you know how things stand."

"Do that."

"I think he'll do business. Maybe we can have a celebratory dinner after the dust settles."

"All right," Faa said.

Lilah said good-bye and broke the connection.

Faa punched the headset off, then walked to the desktop computer. He opened the DSL connection and pulled down a short menu. He and connected with Lilah Morgan's computer through a backdoor feature that was built into one of the software packages he had designed as an add-on to the OS.

The software package was a powerful tool and was offered cheaply enough that most businesses bought it, which had made Thomas Ivers a rich man. However, a pirate program available free on the Internet enhanced the original software bundle, making it faster and more invasive.

Most companies that did business off the books, like Wolfram & Hart, availed themselves of the additional program. What those businesses believed was that a software outlaw designer had written the code, intending to show up Thomas Ivers. No one knew that the two men were the same.

That software bundle, especially when connected to the illegal add-on and reinforced by a number of magical spells to get through Wolfram & Hart's mystical firewalls, provided Faa access through firewalls and counterintrusive measures. In seconds, he was on Lilah's machine, checking through images of her activities, including her phone calls.

Faa found the man's name almost immediately. Although Lilah had gotten a few calls, most of them had been of short duration. But there had been one to Willard Hargreave.

Two mysteries solved, Faa thought as he dropped into his chair at the desk. He clicked the phone, using the speed-dial function again to call Tobar. When the man answered, Faa said, "Forget Gitana for the moment. I have another target for you."

Tobar waited expectantly.

"Willard Hargreave," Faa said.

"The man who hired the Barkuk demons to pick up the Stone he had purchased through the Hong Kong dealer at the port," Tobar said.

"Yes." Faa had traced the piece for weeks, staying a step behind it till the Stone had left Hong Kong. He'd finally discovered the Stone was aboard *Swift Star* only hours before the ship had docked. There had been barely enough time to get Tobar and his people into place to intercept the Stone, and even then they had almost missed getting it because of the vampire.

"You want to strike against him now? I thought you wanted to wait."

Faa *had* wanted to wait. Tobar and his team had killed the Barkuk demons before they had made their getaway with the Bridge piece. Using his own magical abilities, Tobar had gotten the name of the go-between that had hired the Barkuk warriors. As it turned out, the go-between also used software—pirated, of course—that Faa had designed. He had broken into the man's computer files and discovered Hargreave's name.

Striking back against Hargreave when Wolfram & Hart hadn't known Thomas Ivers was interested in the shipment would have been an unnecessary risk. Even if Tobar had left no traces, Lilah Morgan could have possibly learned more than she should have.

Now it appeared that reasoning had been correct. In fact, Faa had to wonder if Wolfram & Hart was playing both ends against the middle and had somehow negotiated a favorable position by letting Hargreave know where and when the Bridge piece had come into the port from the East. How much did Hargreave know about the Bridge pieces?

"Not strike *against*," Faa corrected. "Hargreave is in possession of the final piece of the Bridge that Gitana does not have."

"Where can I find him?"

Faa tapped keys on the desktop computer keyboard. He entered the databases he had made himself privy to. "I don't know. Yet. But I will." And he lost himself in the cyber underworld of the city, hunting Willard Hargreave.

CHAPTER EIGHT

"So what is this thing?" Spike asked, gazing at the color snapshot he'd been given.

"Don't know," Arrag answered.

They sat in an L.A. bar that had seen better days but not better business, because the place was packed. The bar advertised itself as a sports pub, and even featured three ceiling-mounted big-screen television monitors that carried telecasts of ESPN's extreme sports.

But the sports weren't the club's big draw. Strippers from a dozen different demonic races worked the four stages—one center stage and three satellite stages—and drew catcalls and money from the crowd. If the bar had a name, Spike hadn't seen it. It was a surprisingly large warehouse-style structure tucked away in a rough neighborhood that didn't support much of anything. The bouncers meant business. They'd thrown five people out so far, all of them with broken limbs and one of them, Spike was certain, wouldn't live to see morning.

Arrag had negotiated a back booth directly under a neon beer sign that threw pink light over the photos he was showing Spike. The big Qorqoth demon sipped his beer.

Spike tapped the photograph he held. It was a close-up picture of a piece that looked ceramic or glass, a twisted brown-and-cream corkscrew shape that looked like a bull's horn with black ants crawling along it. Only, under closer inspection, he had seen that the ants were actually people. The image looked vaguely familiar, pulling his thoughts back to that night in Lord Hyde-Pierce's manor house outside London in 1887. "This thing, well, they gotta have told you something about it."

"My contact said don't drop it."

"So it's breakable then?" Spike eyed the object in the photo. *Breakable is at least something to know.*

"Maybe it's breakable," Arrag agreed. He took another sip of bear and shrugged. "Maybe dropping it will only wake up whatever's sleeping inside it."

Spike lifted his eyes to the Qorqoth demon's. He wasn't amused. They had arrived in L.A. less than an hour ago, and he wasn't looking forward to a long night hanging out with the Qorqoth demons in bars. But Arrag had insisted they stay together.

Arrag smiled, which wasn't a pleasant experience. "Just kidding."

"Kidding."

"You seemed nervous. I'm trying to get you to lighten up. I know when a guy's got the jitters."

"Now you're a clairvoyant," Spike said sarcastically. But he knew Arrag was right. He'd gotten more tense as soon as they'd entered L.A.

"Partial empath. On my mother's side. Not every Qorqoth demon wants to own up to something like that. Kinda dents the tough-guy image."

"Well, you're wrong this time."

After taking a measured sip of his beer, Arrag shook his head. "Nope. I can tell when you lie, too."

"I don't believe you."

"Gonna be interesting to find out, isn't it?" Arrag grinned.

"I'm in this gig for a cut," Spike stated bluntly. "A fifth of the profits."

Arrag was quiet for a moment. "Sometimes people talk to me about that whole 'honor among thieves' myth. That's a load of crap, you know."

"I know," Spike said.

Arrag's eyes narrowed. "Yeah, you do know."

Memories stirred within Spike. Past partners had betrayed him during other robberies. Very seldom had those partners gotten the upper hand.

"I do," Spike said. "Always somebody in the group who figures everything is better than just a piece of the action."

Doxxil and Muullot stood at the trio of pinball machines near the bathrooms in the back. They heckled each other as they operated the flippers and rocked the machine to get the most play out of the ball.

"When are we supposed to do this job?" Spike asked.

Arrag glanced at the clock over the bar. "I'm supposed to make a phone call in seventeen minutes. We'll get a time frame then."

"Seventeen minutes, eh?"

"Yes."

"It could go down that quick?"

"Guy I'm working for, he's in a hurry."

Spike finished his cigarette and stubbed it out in the glass ashtray between them. "Seventeen minutes doesn't give you much time to go on a recruiting drive if you suddenly get the feeling that I'm not going to work out."

A lopsided grin fitted itself to Arrag's face. "No. But there's still time to turn the job down."

Momentary panic shivered through Spike. Fifty thousand dollars seemed like it was almost lying in his hands. It was enough money to get everything back in Sunnydale straight again. It was enough money to get Buffy back into his arms—if she didn't decide to play the stubborn and stupid card.

"And, yeah," Arrag said, "if it came to it, that's exactly what I'd do. I don't owe anybody my skin. I make it a habit never to owe anybody who will use that debt against me."

Spike pushed his fears away, knowing that Arrag intended the comment as a dig. After all the years he'd put in, Spike knew he couldn't work scared. Pissed was okay, but not scared. He tapped the folder between them. "So what's the object in the pictures?"

"Art. Some kind of statuary."

"That's something you've got in your favor," Spike pointed out. "Something like this, I'd have no idea where to try to sell it. If I decided to betray you."

Arrag nodded. "That's what helps me trust you a little more. And why I'm telling you so much up front now."

"Whatever," Spike replied, leaning forward slightly. "I'll tell you this: You welsh on me, I'll track you down and kick your ass. What kind of reading you getting on that?"

Arrag chuckled. He flagged a waitress down and bought another beer. After he'd paid for the drink, he twisted off the top and took a drink. "Why don't you go watch the ladies for a while and let me get ready for my phone call?"

Nine minutes remained on the clock.

Curbing the angry rebellion that immediately resonated within him, Spike pushed up from the table. He walked away without a word, accidentally bumping into a large demon with snakes for hair.

The demon wheeled around on Spike, looking as though he was going to say something. His hair lifted and prepared to strike. Spike morphed into his vampire features. Recognizing who stood before him, the demon grimaced unpleasantly and walked away as his hair backed down grudgingly.

Spike crossed the room and stood at the front of the central stage. The dancers called the first row of seats around a dance stage "pervert row." Most of the guys scattered through the seats made catcalls, kept up a barrage of dollars that hit the stage floor, and reached for the pale vampire woman as she swung and shimmied past their outstretched arms.

As Spike watched, though, the woman stopped being the vampire dancer. She became Buffy instead, confident and seductive, two of the qualities that he loved most about her. Angel never could have thought of her that way. If he'd known the truth, that she had been sleeping with Spike, Angel would have been just as dumbfounded as Riley Finn had been when he'd broken into the crypt.

And he would have been hurt. Big-time.

Spike sipped his beer and savored the thought. Temptation coursed through him to call Angel while he was in town and tell him about Buffy, about how she'd been warming his crypt. Spike imagined how Angel would react to the knowledge that his pretty little girlfriend had taken up with big, bad Spike.

The image of Angelus reaching for him out of the darkness in Lord Hyde-Pierce's manor home over a hundred years ago formed in Spike's thoughts without warning. He flinched back slightly. *Okay, so maybe telling Angel doesn't come without some risk.*

The dancer finished her routine swirling around the brass pole in the center of the stage's runway. The crowd hooted and catcalled. Money hit the table like confetti in a ticker-tape parade.

Grudgingly, Spike gave up on the illusion of Buffy. Buffy was back in Sunnydale, probably still intent on giving him the cold shoulder. Or worse yet, trying to keep herself strong so she wouldn't *use* him again.

A waitress came by and took his empty bottle. She asked if he wanted another beer, but Spike declined. He glanced up at the clock over the bar. It was three minutes past Arrag's deadline. He glanced over at the Qorqoth demon's table.

Arrag was gone.

"You know, it's been over a hundred and ten years since he saw the tattoo on that woman or the object he says she took from Lord Hyde-Pierce's manor house," Fred said. "Maybe Angel just doesn't remember that event as well as he thinks he does."

Glancing up from the musty old book she was currently searching through, Cordelia checked Connor, who slept in a basinet near the hotel's counter. Connor held one tiny fist to his mouth and made small chewing noises. His breath pushed at the tiny fuzz on the light blanket she had placed over him.

She turned her attention to the drawing Angel had

made upon his return from McCarty's Flesh Fantasy. The drawing was intricately detailed, showing the small line of people along the horn's surface. At least, she assumed the object was a horn. Angel hadn't been specific about that. But what else could it be?

"It's been a long time," Cordelia agreed, "but Angel remembers a lot." That was part of the curse the gypsies had placed on Angel when they had reunited his soul with his body. He remembered every savage and evil thing he had ever done.

"He's got a lot to remember," Fred said. "I've never met anybody as old as him." She tapped computer keys in rapid syncopation without thinking. Her curly brown hair trailed down her back. She was slender and pretty, and always in motion from the nervous energy that filled her.

Cordelia envied Fred the skill she had at the computer. Fred was almost as good as Willow was. But where Willow tended to be absorbed by what she discovered on the Internet, Fred ended up being distracted and animated by it.

Fred looked up from the keyboard and monitor. Her glasses hung at the end of her nose. She pushed them up. "I don't mean to say Angel is old. I would never say that." She gave a frowning smile, as if uncertain of her own communication skills. "You don't think that's what I was saying, do you?"

"No," Cordelia answered. *'No' is safe, isn't it? 'No' pretty much sums up everything. 'No' doesn't lead to a lot of further conversation.*

"I mean, maybe Angel is two hundred years old," Fred went on, "but he doesn't seem any older than us."

"No," Cordelia said, "he doesn't."

Fred returned to pounding the keyboard. "But two hundred years . . . wow! I mean, that's like ten generations removed from us." She paused, her hands freezing for a moment. "Or maybe it's only eight. I guess that depends on how you wanted to declare a generation. You know, like an arbitrary number of years like twenty or twenty-five."

"Got it." Cordelia sighed. "Got the fact that it's been a long time and Angel has a lot to remember."

"A lot," Fred said emphatically. "Did you ever talk to your grandparents?"

"Yes." Positive answers kept Fred working, but they were so open-ended.

"Me too," Fred said. "But not—you know—when I wasn't here." She was referring to the five years she had spent in another dimension being thought of as a mad cow because she lived in a cave covered over with mathematical equations.

Cordelia kept flipping pages in the book on the counter in front of her. She was getting near the end of the thick book. She was also beginning to wish that she were out on the streets with Angel, Wesley, and Gunn tracking down information about the gyp-sies. After hours of searching through books and computer files, even with the added aid of the draw-ing Angel had done, she was beginning to feel like all her efforts were useless. Giles was supposed to be helping out in England as well, but so far the phone hadn't rung.

Fred froze. Her eyes remained trained on the monitor.

"Hey," Cordelia said. "Are you okay?"

"Yes," Fred answered. She pushed her glasses farther up the bridge of her nose. "I think I found it."

Reenergized, Cordelia pushed up from her chair and joined Fred at the computer. The image on the monitor looked a lot like the drawing Angel had done. "How did you find it?"

"Well, I just wrote a quick program that took into account the probable dimensions of the horn thing," Fred said. "And the description, of course."

Okay, Cordelia thought, *that's something I so would not have come up with.*

"I just figured that entering the probable spatial limitations might help us find the object," Fred went on. "Angel was pretty certain about how big this thing was." She adjusted her glasses again. "Of course, this was still pretty lucky. You were already searching through gypsy lore and history. If this thing was going to be found by looking there, I knew you'd probably have already found it. So I figured that it had to be recorded somewhere else and probably not attributed to gypsies in any way. This program was all I could think of."

"Right." Cordelia examined the object. Five pictures showed the object Fred had found. Two of the pictures were drawings, but the other three were digitized photographs. The object's lines were similar to the image Angel had drawn, and the color was brown and cream, just as Angel had said it would be. *Or had been at the time he'd seen it.* "So what is it?"

Fred scrolled down to the text beneath the picture. "According to this entry, which I haven't cross-referenced yet, this is a game piece."

"A game piece?" Cordelia thought about that, wondering how that description fit in with anything they knew connected to the past two days. "What kind of game?"

Fred adjusted her glasses and read quickly. "Doesn't say. Just mentions that it first surfaced in Germany in the twelfth century."

"So there are other game pieces?"

"Doesn't say," Fred said, continuing to read. "This article mentions that the person who found this believed it was part of a set, but none of the other pieces have ever turned up."

"So what happened to this piece?"

Fred scrolled down farther. "It passed in and out of the hands of collectors over the years. Until it finally disappeared. Ah! Wait!" She trailed a forefinger under a line of text. "It was rumored to have somehow found its way into Russian Crimea where it was thought to have been purchased by Lord Henry Hyde-Pierce. The game piece was also one of the objects listed missing during the massacre that took place at Hyde-Pierce's house in eighteen eighty-seven."

"Massacre?" Cordelia repeated. Angel hadn't mentioned anything a massacre. He'd only told them that he'd been in the lord's manor house the night the object was stolen by the woman with the tattoo that matched the tattoo of the woman at McCarty's Flesh Fantasy.

"Lord Hyde-Pierce, his servants, and his guests were all murdered during the night," Fred told her. She scanned the lines of text quickly.

"Who did it? Gypsies?"

"There's no mention of gypsies." Fred grimaced. "But this report does indicate that several of Hyde-Pierce's guests and servants had been drained of blood. 'And were mauled most savagely, as though by foul-tempered beasts.'"

"Read 'vampire,'" Cordelia suggested.

Fred adjusted her glasses and made a visible effort to regain control of herself. She failed. "That's pretty icky, isn't it? I mean, Angel was there, which means Darla was probably there. Along with Spike and Dru. They were all traveling together then, weren't they?"

A cold sensation skated down Cordelia's back on icy claws. "Yes," she answered mechanically. She looked at the sleeping baby in the basinet. "You have to remember, though, that was Angelus. Not Angel. Maybe they only had one body between them, but those two are very separate men."

"It gets kind of confusing," Fred admitted. "I mean, you look at Angel, see how he acts, and you don't see anything of Angelus in there."

"I know," Cordelia said in a quiet voice, thinking how she was going to have to probably explain that to Connor one day. *And Angelus is still in there,* Cordelia reminded herself again as she watched the sleeping baby. In fact, with the prophecy they had been investigating of late that might have something to do with Connor's supposedly impossible birth, Angelus's shadow seemed to be hovering nearer.

"So Angelus and company killed Lord Hyde-Pierce, his servants, and his guests," Fred said. "And they took the game piece?"

"Angel said the gypsy woman did." Cordelia remembered the woman's name after a moment. "Lyanka. Is there any mention of her in there?"

Fred read through the text again. She shook her head. "No."

"Of course not," Cordelia said. "That would be too easy." She sighed. "I'll get another book and start looking for game pieces."

"Oh," Fred said. "You might start with *Yigthereall and Other Demonic Games I Have Played,* by Brother Castor."

"The Mad Monk?"

Fred nodded, then shrugged. "One of them. Mad monks, I mean. The Roman Catholic Church made life difficult for a lot of priests and nuns. You know, having to study and make detailed reports of magic and demons and other stuff that officially didn't exist. You go through their early records, you find a lot of Brother Castor the Mad, Father Vincent the

Insane, Sister Justine the Unbalanced. Mother Theresa the You've-Got-To-Be-Kidding." She shrugged. "Maybe not the last one. That was a little creative license on my part."

Cordelia started for the offices where they kept the books Angel had assembled over the years. "Do you know where that book is?"

"East wall," Fred replied instantly. "Fourth shelf down. About a third of the way over."

"No exact book placement?" Cordelia asked with subdued sarcasm. Fred had a near-photographic memory.

"It will be the seventh or the tenth book," Fred answered. "Depending on whether Wesley replaced the two-volume set of *Menacing Divinations* and *Again, Menacing Divinations*. And Rochester's *Worlds That Die Screaming in Flames.*"

"Is Wesley having trouble sleeping at night?"

"No. Just trying to find out more about the prophecy."

Cordelia looked at the designated bookshelf in the office. She found the book exactly where Fred had said it would be.

"You might want to be prepared," Fred warned from the outside room. "That book has a lot of illustrations. Kinda stomach-churning. It's even more confusing when they're mixed with a very painful eroticism."

Curious, Cordelia flipped through the pages. Highly detailed and brilliantly colored illustrations depicted a number of different acts that were lewd and lethal.

"Ewww!" Cordelia said. "Ewww, ewww, ewww!"

"I know," Fred replied sympathetically. "Some of that stuff you're never going to forget."

Panic thrummed inside Spike as he searched the club for Arrag. If the Qorqoth demon called the robbery off, he wouldn't exactly hang out an official notice, would he? But he would be tempted to put a stake through the heart of any vampire that knew what the object the demon crew was going after was, Spike realized. He suddenly felt vulnerable seated at the front of the club.

A cool hand touched the side of Spike's face.

He whirled, face already changing into that of the demon, his fangs growing.

The dancer on the stage drew back. She was a voluptuous Kassarian demon, one of the few demonic races that seemed built solely for pleasure. Her spotted green skin held an iridescent shine under the stage's spotlight. A darker green mane of hair gleamed and trailed down her spine to her rump. She drew back into the fog created by the stage machines with a smile. Her catlike tail flicked from side to side.

"Easy," she said. "I just don't much care for guys seated up front not paying attention to me."

Spike grew aware of two of the club's bouncers headed in his direction. Both of the big demons carried truncheons—not exactly standard legal issue on the club scene, but the establishment didn't seem to care much for rules.

Backing away from the stage, Spike dropped a fistful of one-dollar bills at the dancer's feet. He gazed around the club, searching for the Qorqoth demons. Even Doxxil and Muullot had abandoned the pinball machine.

Spike began to get paranoid. Desperation had pushed him into the deal with the demon eggs, and even deeper desperation had put him in L.A., where Angel was. He pushed through the crowd of patrons, tables, and chairs. A lot of attendees stood, making it hard to see across the length of the club.

A hand fell heavily onto Spike's shoulder. He caught the hand almost effortlessly, turning with superhuman speed to face the hand's owner.

Doxxil looked back at him, blinking in pained surprise. "Hey dude, you're hurting my hand."

Spike didn't release the demon's hand. "Where's Arrag?"

Doxxil hooked a thumb over his shoulder. "Over there. Said for me to come keep you company while he talks."

Peering through the smoky haze that filled the club, Spike saw Arrag speaking on a pay phone. Reluctantly, Spike released Doxxil's hand.

After finishing his phone conversation and hanging up the handset, Arrag approached Spike. "You okay?" the demon asked.

"I'm fine."

"You look antsy."

"I'm a player," Spike said. "Not a patsy. You want to run a tight operation, fine. But I'm going to be part of that operation or I'm out of here."

"All right." Arrag started walking. "What do you want to know?"

"Who is the target?" Spike fell into step beside the demon.

"A man named Willard Hargreave," Arrag answered. "Hargreave's a multimillionaire. Lives in L.A. Out in Laurel Canyon. He keeps out of the news."

"Did you know the site was in Laurel Canyon?" Spike asked.

"Not until just now."

"Would it have mattered?"

Arrag shrugged. "Did it matter to you?"

Spike ignored the question. The whole bit had been about fifty thousand dollars cash, not geography. But they were dealing with geography now. "Laurel Canyon is filled with actors, actresses, and other movie people—not to mention old money. Power people with a lot of cash wrapped up in security. This isn't going to be a walk in the park."

"A walk in the park doesn't exactly pay fifty thousand dollars, does it?"

"A walk in the park generally won't get you killed, either."

If you're lucky, Spike couldn't help thinking. He followed the demon outside the club into the cool black wind that blew in off the Pacific Ocean and scoured the two-lane street sandwiched in between blocks of two- and three-story buildings.

Cars lined the street on both sides, lodged up in angle parking in front of the buildings. Two other places, both looking like clubs, and one place with a blue-and-green neon image of a pizza or a world globe hanging in the window—Spike chose to believe the place was a pizza shop and not a geography store—remained open. Passersby traveled in twos and threes, probably for safety in numbers. Few of them were human.

"There is one other thing," Arrag said. "Give me your hand."

Spike bought himself some time while he lit a cigarette, cupping his hands to shield the lighter flame from the blowing wind.

Arrag stood in the neon-tinted shadows outside the unnamed bar and patiently waited.

Not seeing anything amiss, Spike extended his left hand, setting his left foot forward also so he could kick or use his other hand with strength by whipping his body around if the need arose. He watched Arrag's eyes.

With blinding speed, Arrag slapped the back of Spike's hand. The bright steel of a blade concealed in Arrag's palm was briefly visible between the demon's fingers. When Arrag's hand passed, blood dripped from a two-inch-long cut across the back of Spike's hand.

Spike cursed and yanked his hand back, drawing

the brief, frightened attention of a small group of passersby, who hurried on and crossed the street. "What the hell did you just do?"

"Insurance," Arrag answered.

A burning sensation crept up Spike's arm. Then he saw the small inch-long bug tunneling into the incision in his arm. He reached for the segmented insect.

Arrag grabbed Spike's hand. Spike tried to shake off the demon's grip.

"Don't touch it," Arrag said. "If you do and you can't get it out—and I guarantee that you won't be able to get it out—the *vidovore* will tunnel to your brain and kill you."

Overcoming his immediate revulsion of the insect burrowing through his flesh, Spike watched as the insect climbed along his arm.

"What is it?" Spike demanded. He calmed himself. The creature was crawling through his flesh. If he had to, he could cut his arm open and get rid of the bug.

Arrag grinned. "It's a tracing beetle."

"What does it do?"

"It's not really alive," the Qorqoth demon said. "It's a mystical construct."

As Spike watched, the wound on his hand healed. The blood dried, and the flesh pulled together. The bug remained a small lump that tunneled up his arm till it reached a few inches above his elbow. Then the creature stopped.

161

"What does it do?" Spike asked again.

"Close your eyes," Arrag suggested.

"I don't think so," Spike replied, massaging the back of his hand. "Had about enough nasty little surprises tonight."

Arrag grinned. "You'll like this one."

"How about we skip to the *TV Guide* version?" Spike drew on his cigarette. As soon as he was out of sight of the others, he fully intended to get rid of the bug.

When Arrag nodded to them, Doxxil and Muullot walked away and disappeared into the nearby alley where they had left the van.

"Let's go," Arrag said.

"After you," Spike said.

Taking no offense, Arrag started toward the alley. Looking into the alley, Spike discovered the demon brothers had disappeared into the shadows.

"Where did they go?" Spike asked.

"You know where they are." Arrag kept walking.

Spike was certain that he was walking into a trap. He didn't like the feeling at all.

"Do you feel them?" Arrag asked a moment later.

"What's the trick?"

"No trick," Arrag said. "Stop and close your eyes. Think about Doxxil and Muullot."

Spike stared at the Qorqoth demon.

"I'm serious, Spike," Arrag said. "You've got to understand this."

Reluctantly, Spike closed his eyes.

"Do you feel them?" Arrag asked.

"No. I just feel stupid." *And vulnerable.* But Spike didn't mention that.

"Open your mind," Arrag suggested. "Be receptive. Try to feel them. And me. You know where I am."

"Yeah. You're right in front of—" Then Spike knew that was no longer true. Arrag was no longer directly in front of him. Fear snapped Spike's eyes open.

Arrag stood off to his left, exactly where the impression inside Spike had told him the demon would be.

The Qorqoth demon smiled. "You see now."

"No," Spike admitted.

"The *vidovore*," Arrag said, "has bound us. Until it's erased by magic, we'll stay bound. No one of us will be able to leave the others without the others knowing where he is." He shrugged. "Think of it as a GPS signal."

Closing his eyes again, Spike thought of Doxxil and Muullot. Almost instantly he felt the awareness of the presence ahead of him seep into his mind. Doxxil was ahead of him, and Muullot was behind him. The *vidovore*—the spell, Spike corrected himself—had turned his brain into a radar screen.

When he opened his eyes, Spike saw Doxxil stepping out of the shadows ahead of him. Glancing over his shoulder, Spike watched Muullot step around the corner of the club.

"Cool, isn't it?" Doxxil asked with a large grin. "My first time, it sort of freaked me out."

"Oh yeah," Spike said, but he was thinking that it

only meant that he couldn't cut and run from them if he wanted to. He switched his gaze to Arrag. "How long does the spell last?"

Arrag shrugged. "I don't know. I've heard stories of it lasting years. It's never been broken except by spell. I've heard three stories about bodies of partners bound by the spell that were later found by people who were looking for them."

"You've used this before?" Spike asked suspiciously.

Nodding solemnly, Arrag said, "Every job I've ever done."

"You might have told me about this."

"Would you have agreed to it?"

"I guess we won't know now, will we?"

Arrag was silent a moment. His voice was harsh when he spoke. "You're the one who brought up personal accountability on this job. With this spell in place, everyone *is* accountable. Try to leave before the job is done now, we'll back off the job, track you down, and kill you. Try to double-cross us, we'll track you down and kill you."

Spike grinned coldly as he flicked his cigarette butt away. "And if you try to stiff me or otherwise hang me out to dry?"

"You can track us down and kill us."

"What if you dissolve the spell?"

"I can't reverse the spell at this point unless you're willing," Arrag said. "We all have to be in agreement. That's one of the protective features."

Spike digested that. "What if somebody gets killed? Could be hard to get an agreement from a corpse."

"You're a corpse," Doxxil observed.

Muullot high-fived his brother, and they both cackled with glee.

"I'm a vampire," Spike stated. "Big difference."

"When you die," Arrag said, "your part of the spell ends."

"Except for your buddies being able to find your body."

Arrag nodded. "But no one needs your permission to end the spell. If you're dead and they know where you are—or don't care—they can break the spell without you."

"What if you die?" Spike asked. "Can Tweedledee and Tweedledum end the spell?"

"No. But you can find someone who can."

Spike considered that. For the moment he was bound to the others. But that wasn't forever either.

"Running's not an option from this point on," Arrag said.

Spike nodded. "I was thinking the same thing myself. When do we do this job?"

"Now," Arrag said, turning and starting through the alley toward the van. "We do it now."

Spike took a moment to himself, pausing to light a cigarette and consider his options. They were even worse than when he'd left Sunnydale.

But the money remained out there to be earned

as well. Fifty thousand dollars could change his world. Fifty thousand dollars could get Tarl Dannek off his neck and give Buffy that wake-up call she needed. He blew out a lungful of smoke and followed after the Qorqoth demons.

He didn't have a choice. He'd already rolled the dice on the play. He could only hope he didn't crap out, didn't come up snake-eyes. Pushing his fears aside, he clung to thoughts of Buffy. She would come back on her own. He felt that in his heart. When she did, he wanted to be able to welcome her with open arms and a clean slate. The money would make that happen, and he'd see to it that she never left him again.

CHAPTER NINE

Gypsies, Charles Gunn had come to the conclusion after a couple hours of searching, were hard to find. He roamed through the neighborhood around the bar where he, Angel, and Wesley had encountered the gypsy group. It was amazing how many people hadn't seen anything.

An LAPD cruiser rolled by on the street. Two policemen rode in the front seats. Both of them sent challenging stares his way.

Conditioned by life on the street, Gunn dropped his eyes and made an effort to look nonthreatening. *I'm just a guy out too late. Coming home from work.*

He held on to that thought as the LAPD cruiser kept going and disappeared around the corner.

Angel was hitting his usual street sources, and Gunn figured that was probably the literal truth of the matter. Snitches around the city, some of them human and some of them demon, feared Angel when he got on a tear for information. Gunn had seen Angel work.

Wesley was following up with the local magic shops and spell dealers. With the way the young woman leading the gypsies had thrown the rat spell, it was a lock that she might be connected with the local magic scene.

So far, Gunn hadn't had much to show for his effort. He was beginning to feel like he was wasting his time. He wanted to check in with Cordelia and Fred, mostly to hear Fred's voice because the way that she talked to him gave him hope. In all his years, he'd never met anyone who had turned his head the way that Winifred Burkle had. The experience was nice, totally unexpected, and he was taking his time enjoying it.

"Hey, man."

Gunn moved smoothly, stepping into the shadows in front of a consignment shop that had closed for the night. He peered up at a window a floor above him.

A small boy sat in the window. The soft blue glow of a television backlit him, flickering as images marched across the screen. He was no more than seven or eight, his unruly hair sticking up as he sat in the window. His skin was coal black, looking blue where the light from the television burnished it.

"What are you doing up, little brother?" Gunn asked.

"Can't sleep," the boy said.

"Window's not a safe place for you to sit."

A frown creased the boy's face. "You're not my mom, man."

Gunn smiled at the boy's natural rebelliousness. "No, I'm not. But you dropped the dime here. I was just throwing in my own two cents."

"Been sitting in this window for a long time. I know what I'm doing."

"I suppose," Gunn agreed.

"Anyway, I'm not the one being chased."

A chill thrilled through Gunn. "What do you mean, 'chased'?"

"Guys are following you," the boy said.

Gunn shifted his attention from the boy to back along the street. For a moment he thought the shadows hugging the walls, the street corners, and the alleys might be moving like window drapes in a light breeze. Then he felt certain that was just his imagination.

"What guys?" Gunn asked.

"Don't know. Didn't get a real good look at them. Seen you was a brother, thought maybe I'd clue you in."

"I appreciate that," Gunn said. "But maybe you were imagining things."

The boy cursed, and the harsh words tumbling from his lips surprised Gunn for just a second. "I don' imagine nothing. You wanna be a fool, you go on an' do it by yourself." He stepped back inside the apartment without another word and pulled the window down. City lights gleamed from the glass surface.

Gunn felt like he owed the boy an apology. Then a car shrilled rubber around the street corner to Gunn's left. The headlights flashed across the darkened window of shops across the street. Slewing wildly, the vehicle came to a halt in front of Gunn, facing him with the headlights on bright.

Putting a hand up in front of his face, Gunn peered through the harsh light. The car was a station wagon, at least twenty years old. Scarred, wood-grain panels ran down the sides. The engine leaked oil, and the smell of the burning fluid permeated the street.

The doors opened, and gypsies stepped out. They carried pistols and raised them immediately.

Gunn cursed, turned to his left, stayed low, and ran. Bullets chopped into the brick wall behind him. He kept his arms raised protectively, shielding his head like the bullets would somehow bounce off his hands and not core through his skull.

He ran around the building corner and ran down the first alley he came to. The way was narrow, hopefully too narrow for the big station wagon.

Tires shrilled again on the pavement. Lights

swung behind Gunn and played on the alley walls in front of him. His shadow suddenly appeared on the wall to his right, looking long and lean, then shifted and stretched out on the pavement in front of him as the car roared up behind him.

The alley turned out to be plenty wide enough to admit the station wagon. Pistol shots cracked the air.

Gunn kept his eye on the other end of the alley. That was the only thing that could matter. He stayed focused like a batter who'd just put a blooper into short outfield and was streaking for first base.

When he was almost upon them, two gypsy men shifted in the shadows on either side of the alley. Too late, Gunn saw the rope stretched taut between them. Gunn tried to gather himself and leap into the air to clear the rope. Instead, the rope caught him just below both knees. He fell as pain screamed through both legs.

As he tumbled across the coarse alley floor, Gunn watched the station wagon bear down on him. Lying on his back, thinking that surely at least one of his legs had to be broken and aware that neither of them were working correctly, he watched helplessly as the station wagon closed the distance.

One of the gypsy men stepped forward and unsheathed a long knife. The man put the bared blade against Gunn's throat. The other man pointed a pistol at Gunn's head.

"Okay," Gunn said, lying very still, "if you want me to raise my hands, just let me know."

The station wagon shifted as a door opened. Heels rang against the pavement.

Gunn peered up through the shifting smoke that eddied through the station wagon's headlights only inches above his face.

The gypsy woman, the one from the bar earlier with the hawk tattoo on her neck, stood and stared down at him. She was beautiful, but her features held a hint of cruelty. Her eyes were narrow and hard. Gunn had the immediate impression that she had seen too much.

With slow grace that denoted strength, confidence, and training, the woman lowered herself to her haunches within easy reaching distance of Gunn. Gunn lay there with the knife at his throat, afraid of taking a breath that was too deep because the blade would surely slice his flesh.

"You work with the vampire," she accused in a flat voice.

"Don't know what you're talking about," Gunn said. "You've got me mixed up with the wrong guy."

A half-smile tugged at her lips. "You're lying."

"No," Gunn said, "I—"

The woman gestured. The knife-wielder pushed his blade tighter against Gunn's neck, forcing his head back.

"Okay," Gunn said. "I'm lying. I work for the vampire."

* * *

Willard Hargreave had a fortress surrounded by a veritable kingdom in Laurel Canyon outside Los Angeles proper. Once off the main highway, Arrag piloted the van through the back roads that twisted and threaded across the hillside landscape.

Spike saw the house as Arrag drove by it. Armed security guards stayed on the premises, according to the file Arrag had. Sometimes the men went out with dogs to walk the perimeter.

Hargreave had purchased the place two years ago from a director of a successful television series who had gone on to launch a renewed attack on obscurity. During the first eighteen months, Hargreave had commissioned work on the house. The original structure had been razed to the ground, and a three-story, sprawling mansion had been raised. A swimming pool and Jacuzzi, tennis courts, and riding stables had been added. Two guesthouses sat apart from the main house.

"We're not stopping?" Spike asked.

"Not here," Arrag answered. "We'll park farther in at another house we have access to."

"What kind of access?"

"You'll see."

A few minutes later, Arrag pulled the van into an A-frame bungalow built back into the hillside. The edge of the front deck stood twelve feet off the ground while the back of the house was anchored in the hillside. A shell-covered driveway led into a separate garage below and to the left of the house.

Reaching into the bag between the van seats, Arrag took out a garage door opener, pointed it at the garage, and pressed the button. The garage door went up smoothly, and the lights came on. He pulled the van inside.

Doxxil started to get out.

"Wait," Arrag ordered.

Doxxil left the door closed.

Pressing the garage door opener again, Arrag closed the door. "No sense in alarming the neighbors," the Qorqoth demon said, putting the garage door opener into the glove compartment.

Doxxil got out, followed by Muullot.

"Aren't you worried that the owners might come home?" Spike asked.

"Mr. and Mrs. Appleby won't be home for nine more days," Arrag said. He walked to the rear of the van and opened the doors. "They're on-site in Australia trying to negotiate on-location shoots for a made-for-television movie. Fran Appleby is a location scout for a major studio. George Appleby is a reasonably successful daytrader. The trip is a working vacation."

"So we have run of the house," Spike said.

"If we need it." Arrag started taking out equipment bags. "Depends on how the heist goes. If we get in and out tonight, with no problems, then we leave before morning. However, if something gets blown at Hargreave's, we have a bolt-hole to come back to."

"Playing Mr. and Mrs. Appleby?"

"Playing Mr. and Mrs. Appleby's time-share partners. I've got legal paperwork that shows us as that. The house is registered with a time-share manager. If the police call to check up, there's even a blind in place at the company."

"But you guys are demons."

Arrag shrugged. "There are a lot of demons that work in the movies. Contracting. Special effects. Producing. You just don't see them. Only their front men."

Spike grudgingly admitted to himself that the Qorqoth demon was amazingly thorough.

"Impressed, aren't you?" Arrag asked.

"Smooth operation," Spike said.

Arrag shook his head. "It'll be a smooth operation if we make it back out of here tonight."

"When do we make the launch on Hargreave's?" Spike asked.

"Now," Arrag said. "We cut through the woods till we reach the back of Hargreave's estate." He turned to the demon brothers. "Let's go."

Angel made his way to the hotel's main foyer. He was tired and ached all over. Spots and smears of blood showed on his clothing, mute testimony to the backbreaking—literally—work he'd been doing. Thankfully, it hadn't been *his* back that had been broken.

He'd scoured his usual haunts for criminal demon activity, pumped all the usual suspects, and ended up with exactly zilch. The leads about gypsies he had gotten had put him onto the trail of two gypsy groups currently operating in L.A., but neither of those groups had a woman member with a hawk tattoo on her neck. Both encounters had turned bloody, but he had gotten away without killing anyone.

In the foyer, Angel crossed the room to the weapons chest, grabbed a cleaning towel, and started mopping the blood from the ax.

Cordelia, Fred, and Wesley sat at the counter. Piles of books surrounded the computer. Tape held computer printouts on the wall behind them.

"We found the object you drew," Fred told him.

A little of the tension filling Angel lessened. "That's good."

Cordelia looked up at him. "Maybe not."

Angel finished cleaning the ax and put the weapon away as the tension returned. Nothing had ever been easy since he'd come to L.A. "Is it bad?"

"Potentially," Wesley said. "It's just that there's so much conjecture about these seven pieces, no one knows for certain what they do."

"Seven pieces?"

"Yes. And we're not even certain about that."

"Why seven?"

"Seven is a mystical number," Wesley said. "The head has seven entrances for the senses. Two eyes to see. Two ears to hear. Two nostrils to smell. A mouth to taste."

Angel looked at Cordelia. "Where's Connor?"

"Sleeping. I just fed him. You missed it."

A twinge of guilt crawled through Angel. He crossed the foyer and ducked into his office for a moment. He watched Connor sleeping in the basinet, taking brief solace in the fact that his son was safe from harm.

Then he returned to the present war.

"Seven pieces," Angel prompted when he stepped behind the hotel's front desk. He glanced at the clock on the wall and saw that it was 10:18 P.M. The night was still young.

"Potentially seven pieces," Wesley said.

Angel scanned the wall behind the front desk. The center picture was the drawing he'd made of the object that Lyanka had taken from Lord Hyde-Pierce's manor house all those years ago. Three other pictures, one of them a sketch by someone else and two of them photographs, showed the piece from different angles.

Seeing the pictures gave more weight to the present situation.

"But we don't know if this piece is the one the Barkuk demons were at the port for," Angel said.

"No," Wesley agreed. "However, it is a strong possibility that the Barkuks were there for one of the other pieces."

Angel looked at Cordelia. "You saw one of the pieces in your vision."

Cordelia nodded and moved to the wall of pictures. "Not the one that you drew. I told you that earlier. But I did see this one." She touched one of the pictures.

Like the one that Angel had drawn, the piece Cordelia identified had sketches made of it as well as photographs. In the single color picture, the piece was brown and vaguely triangular in shape. Turquoise lines threaded through the piece.

"Looks like a rock," Angel said.

"Yes," Fred replied. "A sedimentary rock. Formed of layers and layers." She adjusted her glasses as she studied the picture. "That's why you have the blue striations. But, looking at the geological aspects of the rock, I don't think it was naturally formed." She glanced back at Angel. "Of course, I couldn't really make a judgment about that without seeing this piece."

"The rock wasn't naturally formed?" Angel echoed.

Fred looked uncertain for just a moment. "I'm only guessing." After the long, hard years in Pylea, her insecurities hadn't completely gone away.

"I'll take your best guess," Angel said gently.

"And I agree with her assessment," Wesley said.

Fred gave Wesley an appreciative smile. Turning her attention back to the photo, she traced the turquoise striations with a finger. "If you look at the gradations, you'll see that they're uniform. The thicknesses, at least in the picture, are the same."

Angel looked at the picture more closely. The detail was something that would have escaped him. "So what does that tell us?"

"That the rock was grown," Fred said.

"Grown?"

"Sure. The same way a pearl is grown." Fred pushed her glasses up. "Only maybe not by putting it into a clam and waiting so long."

"We found a legend attributed to this piece," Wesley said. "From the Han dynasty in China. Its loose translation is 'serpent's pellet.' According to the legend, the pellet brought its owner good luck."

"That's one of the things that all seven pieces have in common," Cordelia said. "They were all said to have brought their various owners good luck."

"At least, until those owners were killed," Fred pointed out. Then she looked incredibly embarrassed as she glanced at Angel. "I mean, by other people. Not you, Angel."

Angel couldn't think of a comment to make, so he let it pass. His past life wasn't an open book, but his friends knew what he'd been. The most important thing was that they recognized his efforts to be a better person.

"Was the luck real or imagined?" Angel asked.

"There are stories around the ownership about each piece," Wesley said. "Some of the tales are more easily accessible than others because some pieces disappeared before others, but they're all there. From everything we've been able to find out, the pieces did bring their owners good fortune."

"The downside was that other people were willing

to kill them for the pieces," Cordelia said. "We found plenty of stories about that, too."

"The Chinese legend holds that the serpent's pellet came from the belly of a huge snake," Wesley said. "A monstrous serpent, big enough to swallow a cow, crawled out of a flooded river, supposedly washed from some other world, ate a man and later threw up the stone because it couldn't digest it."

"Who was the man?" Angel asked.

"The legend indicates that the victim was a foreigner, one of a band of people who had gone into China while fleeing attackers."

"Who were the people?"

"According to the story, the people were travelers. Musicians. Handymen. Traders. And they were skilled in the art of fortune-telling."

A possibility came to Angel's mind at once. "Gypsies?"

"One does naturally leap to that conclusion," Wesley said.

"Might not be much of a leap," Angel said.

"The Chinese journal keeper believed that the serpent ate the man and turned him into the rock," Cordelia said. "To me, it's pretty obvious that the guy had the rock, got eaten, and the snake threw up the rock."

"Or maybe didn't throw it up," Fred pointed out.

"Right," Cordelia said. "But who would want to write, 'I found this rock in a pile of snake poop,' if it was going to be remembered for posterity?"

"Especially seeing as how the rock was later given to the emperor as a gift," Wesley said.

"When was this piece last seen?" Angel touched the drawing he'd made.

"The last record of it was with Lord Hyde-Pierce," Fred said.

"He brought it home from the Crimean War," Angel said.

"Right."

Angel surveyed the other pieces. "The other pieces were found there also?"

"No," Wesley replied. "They've shown up all around the world. This piece was last seen at the nineteen thirty-nine World's Fair in New York City." He tapped one of the black-and-white photographs. "It was part of an archaeological exhibit. Part of a small collection of Egyptian artifacts that had lately been brought up from the Valley of the Kings."

Angel looked at the piece. "The Egyptians had one of these pieces back then? I thought they were first written about in the twelfth century."

"They were," Wesley said. "I was rather surprised."

"We did further research," Fred put in. "Some of the pieces on display at the World's Fair were actually taken from a tomb raider. The rock was shown because it was found with the other items and was believed to be a crude bust of Anubis, the jackal-headed god."

Angel studied the round piece that had two

triangular projections. "Doesn't even look close."

"A matter of perspective, I would surmise," Wesley said.

"If the rock had been found in the nineteen sixties," Cordelia suggested, "someone might have said it was a crude bust of Batman."

"Where did the pieces originally come from?" Angel asked. "I'm on information overload here. I understand that they were scattered all around the globe, and that they're maybe a source of good luck for their owners."

"The furthest back we've been able to track them," Wesley said, "is to the twelfth century. We found mention of them in records kept by the Aryans during their war against the Muslims."

"The gypsies were supposedly created by those wars," Angel said.

"Quite right. The Aryans gathered people from several smaller nations and forced them to become warriors."

"They were cannon fodder," Angel said. "Chewed up between two massive armies."

"Yes." Wesley moved down the wall and pointed out illustrations. "Different accounts mention the pieces. Some say there were five pieces. Some say six. A few mention that there were seven. Two accounts suggest that there was an inexhaustible supply of them."

"But there are seven?"

"We've found only seven," Wesley confirmed.

"There were a few scattered reports of the pieces in Watchers' journals. None of them put the seven pieces together."

"But another book did," Cordelia said. She hauled out a massive, dusty tome. Stylized golden script along the book's spine read *Windows to Other Worlds*. Smaller script added *A Translation*. "According to this book, the seven pieces were used as a scrying device."

Scrying, Angel knew, was one of the oldest magics performed. Healing and life extension came first, but the power to see into far and distant places, to spy on an enemy, or to search for a lost item in a bowl of water, oil, or blood was just as ancient a tradition.

"The gypsies gathered the seven pieces and used them to peer into other worlds," Cordelia said.

"That's what all of this is about?" Angel asked. "A window?"

"Not a window," a cold voice said. "When placed together and used properly, the Seven Foundation Stones form the Bridge of Journeyhome."

Surprised, knowing that his lack of attention to the hotel's front door was proof that he was tired, Angel looked up and saw the gypsy woman with the hawk tattoo on her neck standing just inside the door. Dressed in black, she carried a long sword at her side.

"Hello again, vampire," she said.

"Lyanka," Angel said before he knew it, even though he knew it couldn't be.

CHAPTER TEN

Stare Mesto, Prague
February 1891

"A circus is such a tiresome thing," Darla said. "All noise and movement. So much attention and so little meaning."

Angelus walked the long expanse of the Charles Bridge over the Vltava River. The cold wind blew in from the north. "A circus is a good hunting ground. Anonymity. Good cover. Lots of humans drinking and carousing." He smiled at the gaily colored tents at the other end of the bridge in Stare Mesto, the old city of Prague. "And then there are the gypsies to blame for it all. What more could you want?"

Darla sighed. "Perhaps. But you also have all the great unwashed masses in attendance."

Boats slid by on the dark surface of the river below. Oars slipped into the water and created miniature waves as the oarlocks creaked. Lanterns hung from the prows and turned the dark water into patches of green and brown around the reflections of the light.

"I love the circus," Dru said. She walked arm-in-arm with Spike. "I love the candy and the fruits and the animals. Fuzzy and big and loud and fast. I want to tickle the lion's nose when the lion-tamer sticks his head into the lion's mouth. Maybe a pigeon feather." She scoured the ground.

Peddlers lined the bridge. Sweet cakes, fruit, puppets, musical horns, small drums, and wine were offered for sale. Scantily clad women offered even more delights. Angelus's grasp of the Romanian language was rudimentary, but there was no mistaking what they had in mind or how much they wanted as payment.

"I do like the clowns," Dru said with childlike wistfulness. "I hope they have clowns. Funny clowns and sad clowns. Clowns with faces that aren't their own. Maybe I could show them my face. Do you think they would like it?"

Angelus focused on the circus. They'd first heard of it in a tavern earlier that evening. According to the man they'd talked with—then later robbed and killed in the alley behind the tavern—the circus had come to the city two days ago. The gypsies were already outlasting their welcome, though. Theft and robbery had increased throughout Prague. Angelus doubted that the increase in crime was solely the work of the gypsies. Like himself, the presence of such a handy scapegoat emboldened others.

"If they don't have clowns," Spike said, "I'll make them sorry for lifting your hopes."

"I'm quite capable all by myself of making clowns sorry," Dru said. "Their makeup runs. Their eyes run. They break so easily. Snap, snap, snap, and usually they're all done."

Spike frowned.

Angelus ignored them. They were in one of their relationship swings again, and this time they were bickering. Their fighting, Dru's belittling of Spike and Spike's own increasing violent tendencies and need to prove himself, had gotten them temporarily too well known for them to safely travel in England and France. They'd come to Prague to seek anonymity.

Being around the pair when they were fighting was hard for Angelus. Spike and Dru hadn't yet learned that the secret to a long-lasting relationship—especially between two potentially immortal people—lie in being apart sometimes and maintaining interests outside the relationship. Or maybe, they preferred to fight and make up. To Angelus, that was a waste of time.

Over the years, Angelus had taken different

lovers. Darla had as well. In the early years, he had been jealous of her affairs. Then he'd learned how boring the sameness of a person could be if too much time was spent together. Especially considering that neither of them changed much.

The only thing that he never tired of was violence. He loved the kill, loved the terror he could bring to other people. The savage joy he had at being able to break a person's heart and his or her hopes was intoxicating, a drug whose power would never wane. Many times, Darla had brought him a new lover, and they had killed the girl or woman together.

Spike was jealous because he had been apart from Dru for eleven days. He had joined Angelus in a robbery that had gone wrong nearly a month ago and had them running from a pack of lord's men for nine of those eleven days. They had finally managed their escape, killing a number of their pursuers in the process, and returned to Prague.

During that time, Dru had taken a demon lover for a short while. Darla had told Angelus about the affair while they'd made love, then told him about the men who had chased her in Angelus's absence. She'd even gone into detail about some of them she had bedded, and the tales had only forged fires in their own rediscovery of each other.

As a result, Dru's barbs and Spike's angry despair made them ill-met companions. Angelus hoped the promise of the circus—all gaiety and derring-do, spiced with the promise of easy prey and the Vltava

River as an easy means of disposing of the bodies—
would at least provide a night's amusement.

The circus had set up in a few streets of the old
city. Torches hung at the front of the patched tents
where special shows were performed. Gaslight
lamps lined the street, adding to the light that filled
the heart of the city. Drummers around the area beat
a frantic rhythm that echoed and rolled through the
narrow streets of the old city.

The *vardos,* the colorful wagons that were both
transportation and homes for the gypsies, sat nearby.
Horses were tied to ground tethers.

The gypsies looked foreign in their homespun
clothing, broadcloth shirts tucked into breeches and
big boots, accented by cloaks. Their dark skin, mustaches and beards on the men, and colorful scarves
and dangling earrings set them apart even from the
mixed populace of Prague.

The gypsy women performers went scandalously
attired, wearing little clothing despite the chill wind.
They rubbed their bodies with bear fat to provide a
small layer of insulation against the chill and make
their flesh gleam as if covered by heavy dew. They
rolled their hips as they walked among the crowd
and extolled the virtues of the shows the audience
stood ready to watch.

"Come watch the acrobats as they challenge death
on the high wire," one of the young women said.
"See the lion tamer as he bravely enters a cage filled
with man-eating lions and tigers brought here from

the savage coasts of darkest Africa. Watch the beautiful women as they display horse-riding skills that won the favor of sultans and sheiks and kings."

Angelus stood with Darla at the outer edge of the crowd. Pickpockets, primarily gypsy children, drifted through the crowd in the wake of the barely dressed young women. One small boy, no more than eight or nine, approached Angelus.

Turning, Angelus grinned mirthlessly at the boy, freezing the youngster in his tracks. "Try to touch me, boy, and I'll slit your throat."

The boy's eyes widened. He turned and fled.

Angelus laughed. It was the circus; anything could happen.

"You shouldn't have warned him," Darla chastised.

"Oh?"

"No," she said. "You should have let the little thief get closer, then snapped his arm when he tried for your purse. His bleating cries of pain would have been music to my ears."

Angelus roped an arm around Darla's shoulders and pulled her close. There were times, like this, when he loved her like no other. Of course, there were other times that he didn't want to be around her at all. But he enjoyed the good times. "I should have snapped his arm, should I?" he asked, nuzzling her neck with his lips.

"Yes."

"So are you starting to look forward to the circus?"

She smiled a little and captured his head in her arms, stilling his lips upon her neck. "Perhaps. But only a little."

"We'll find someone interesting to kill," Angelus promised.

"Soon?" Darla sighed as he nibbled at her neck again.

"Soon," Angelus said. A gypsy man who strode out into the midst of the audience captured his attention.

The gypsy stood naked to the waist. His upper body gleamed from bear fat. Scars marked his flesh, telling of past harsh experience with knife and pistol ball wounds. He carried a long-necked bottle in one hand and a flaming torch in the other.

"I am Bavol!" the man shouted. "Come watch me swallow fire!" He took a deep swig from the bottle. The nearby drummers paused in their drumming, drawing the crowd's interest even more with their absence.

Pulling the flaming torch up to his lips, Bavol breathed out. A large fireball spewed into the air. The flames roiled and curled inward, creating a storm of fire for a few brief seconds. The crowd dodged back as if expecting the fiery mass to fall among them. Instead, the alcohol the gypsy fire-eater had breathed out was consumed, and the flames disappeared. Only a few wisps of smoke drifted into the air, torn to bits by the northern breeze.

Applause filled the area. The drummers resumed their cadence at a more fevered pitch.

Bavol bowed deeply, then blew another fireball into the air.

"That's a cheap trick," Spike announced as he moved up only a few feet away. He cupped his hands and lit one of the cigarillos he constantly carried whenever they were available. "Give me a bottle of whisky, I could do the same thing."

"Without burning your face off?" Darla asked.

Spike snorted derisively. "Of course. That little stunt is nothing. A child could do it."

"Perhaps," Dru acknowledged. "Still, Bavol is a fine-looking man. He has eyes like a crow's, all hungry and jealous. The kind of eyes that would make a good soup." She trailed the backs of her crimson fingernails down the side of Spike's face.

Angelus saw the pain in Spike's face as Dru's comment scored a direct hit. *Stupid,* Angelus thought. *You love too hard, Spike. That makes you easy prey for Dru's fangs.*

For all of Spike's growing tough-guy swagger, Angelus knew that the younger vampire gave himself too quickly to softer emotions.

Bavol turned and headed back into the main tent. A barker stood out front, offering admission for paying customers. The line formed quickly.

"Do you want to go in?" Angelus asked Darla.

"I'd rather get someone to eat and go back to the hotel." Darla looked at him and sighed. "But you would rather do this, wouldn't you?"

"The night is ours," Angelus entreated. "Come

morning, we'll be once more trapped in the hotel room." They avoided company at the hotel during the day for the most part, and never went out. Thankfully, they had enough money for the moment to stay in one of the most expensive hotels in Prague. When they were up and about during the day, entertainment—whether in the form of music or conversation with other travelers—was possible without leaving the hotel and risking the sun's unforgiving rays.

"If we must," Darla said.

Angelus took her hand in his and kissed her fingers.

"Oooooh, how romantic. Like lovebirds sitting on a limb in a taxidermist's shop. Together forever until the moths eat their feathers off." Dru moved toward them, deliberately swishing her long skirts. She was dressed as a noblewoman. She took Angelus by the arm. "I remember when you were my little lovebird."

Angelus stared at her pointedly, knowing she was seeking only to further enrage Spike and drive him mad with jealousy. "That was a long time ago."

Spike knew that, though he never talked of it. The subject was one of the things he never seemed able to get around. But he chose not to address it because Angelus had laughed in his face at his jealousy. If he could have broken Dru away from them for all time, Angelus had the distinct feeling that Spike would have.

"That was a long time ago, Dru," Angelus said quietly. He didn't want Spike or the people around them to overhear. "And it's over."

Dru pushed up against him suggestively. "One day soon, Angelus, perhaps you'll see me in a more favorable light. A light like the molten heavens, like a comet streaking from the sky."

"Not when it will cause problems."

Anger showed on Dru's face, but it quickly winked out of existence. She put on a smile as if his words meant nothing. "One day, Angelus," she repeated. She walked away, emphasizing her hip sway.

"She's going to be trouble," Darla said.

"Maybe," Angelus admitted. "But I can handle her."

"*We*," Darla said. "We can handle her."

"You're the one who seems to prefer her company."

Darla smiled. "I like her. Under the proper circumstances, she amuses me."

"Your amusement carries a stiff price."

"Amusement always does. But I know that she amuses you as well."

Grudgingly, Angelus nodded. "At times. Not this evening." He gazed around the crowd.

A woman stood outside a small red-and-white-striped tent farther down the street. She was turned in profile, but there was something familiar about her. Memory stirred within Angelus.

"Are you coming?" Darla asked.

Angelus squeezed her arm reassuringly. "In a moment. You go ahead and I'll join you."

Suspicion showed on Darla's face. "Where will you be?"

Angelus leaned down and kissed her on the lips. "Finding something else to amuse us. Go. I'll be along." He gave her a gentle push.

With obvious reluctance, Darla went.

Knowing he would pay for his insistence at some point later on, Angelus watched her lead Spike and Dru into the big tent. Then he turned and walked through the crowd toward the small tent where the woman was.

The sign over the tent read: FORTUNE-TELLER.

A man beat Angelus to the woman. She took him by the arm and guided him into the tent. He was only inside for a few moments before he returned. Without waiting, Angelus ducked into the tent, filling the small doorway with his size.

The woman sat at a small square table covered with a red cloth. She wore a scarf, bangle earrings, large bracelets, a peasant blouse, and a long skirt that made her look very different from how she'd looked fourteen years ago in Lord Hyde-Pierce's manor house. Her makeup made her sultry and challenging instead of demure. Despite the passage of time, she didn't look like she'd aged. Her hands gathered the cards spread before her on the red cloth, expertly sliding them together.

"Sit," she invited without looking up. She nodded to the straight-backed chair on the other side of the table.

Angelus sat. With amused patience, he awaited her recognition.

"What question is it you want answered?" Lyanka asked, squaring the cards as she gathered them. "Would you want to know about your current lover? Whether she is true to you? Or would you know of your next love? Perhaps it's money that interests you. Is there a possible inheritance you want to know about? Or a business undertaking you're considering?"

"I only want to know one thing," Angelus said.

"Tell me then." Lyanka stacked the cards in her supple fingers. "We can discuss a price for my services."

"What was it," Angelus asked, "that you took from Lord Hyde-Pierce's home that night?"

Lyanka looked up, her eyes and nostrils widening slightly. She placed the deck on the table before her. "Hello, vampire," she said.

Angelus showed her a mocking grin. "Hello, thief."

"I sometimes am reminded that this truly is a small world," Lyanka said.

"And this is one of those times?"

"Yes."

"I was thinking the same thing myself."

"What are you doing here?" she asked.

"I came for the circus," Angelus told her. Then he shrugged. "Maybe to claim a victim or two. I did not expect you."

Lyanka waited. "And now that you have found me?"

"I don't know," Angelus admitted. "You make me curious." He gazed around at the small tent. "Even more so now that I find you in these circumstances."

A smile curled her beautiful lips. Light from the small lantern hanging from the center of the tent two feet below the fabric played over her auburn tresses where they peeked out from beneath the scarf. "You're risking your existence by coming here."

"I could have killed you before you knew I was here."

Confidently, she leaned forward. "I only wish you had tried. The spells that I have in place to protect me would have burned you to a crisp before you touched me."

"You could be lying."

Lyanka held out her hand. "Touch me, vampire. Given your nature, you won't be able to touch me without building up some kind of strong emotion. That's all that's needed to set off an avalanche of spells. Take measure of what I'm telling you for yourself."

Angelus leaned forward. She didn't flinch, didn't draw her hand back. Her eyes held steady, returning the harsh glare of his gaze. He smiled and leaned back without touching her.

"Afraid?" she taunted.

"Cautious," Angelus admitted. "I remember what you were capable of back at Hyde-Pierce's manor house."

"So do I. I've never seen so many people in one place so savagely killed."

"I would have killed you, too. If I'd had the chance."

"I'm only sorry that I didn't kill you when I did have the chance."

Angelus gazed at the cards in her hands. "So now you're a fortune-teller."

She smiled. "I've always been a fortune-teller."

"And a thief?"

"Not a thief," Lyanka responded. "I didn't take anything that truly belonged to Hyde-Pierce."

"You took something."

"Something that wasn't Hyde-Pierce's to have."

"Were you hired to take it?" Angelus asked.

"No."

Angelus was intrigued. Mysteries sometimes alleviated the boredom that came between stalking and killing. Mysteries also created vast amounts of frustration within him. Darla didn't much care for them.

"So Hyde-Pierce had something personal of yours?" he asked.

"Something," she replied, "that was not his to have." She shuffled the cards. Her fingers moved delicately. A heavy garnet ring on her right hand caught the lantern light and reflected bloodred.

"What are you doing here?" Angelus asked.

"Traveling."

"These are your people?"

Lyanka leaned back in the chair. "Some of these people are mine, yes."

"Your family?"

Her brow wrinkled. A wary gleam dawned in her eyes. "If they were, do you think I would tell you?"

Angelus laughed. "No. But if I have to guess, I may have to kill a lot of other innocents before I find anyone else close to you."

"Kill them if you want, vampire," she told him. "None of these people are my family. But they are friends. And I will tell them of you. They know about vampires and other demons. Cross a gypsy, vampire, and it will be the undoing of you."

"You wouldn't believe how many people have told me that over the last hundred and forty years." Angelus smirked. "Yet, here I am."

"Yes. You are here. And we have yet to see what that means, haven't we?" With quiet dexterity, Lyanka began dealing the cards.

Angelus recognized the Celtic cross pattern she used.

"Do you know this form?" she asked.

Angelus looked at her, knowing something in his eyes had given him away.

"You don't need to answer," she said. "I know that you do. Many fortune-tellers believe that the Celtic cross is the most powerful spread of the cards that can be done."

An icy anxiety thrilled up Angelus's spine. He was aware of magic, had seen arcane power in several places, but didn't like it because he couldn't control it. He silently wished that he had not entered the tent, or had tried to kill the woman outright when he saw her. Of course, then he would have found out if she had mystical defenses in place the hard way.

"This is the Knight of Wands," Lyanka said, turning over the middle card under the second one she had dealt. The card showed a knight holding a long staff seated on a rearing horse. "He represents you. At his best, he is confident, charming, a risk-taker, and passionate."

"So far," Angelus said, "so good."

She looked at him. "That isn't you. You have all the negative tendencies." She tapped the card. "You are superficial and cocky. At times, reckless and foolhardy. You never know rest or true content, and you're always ready for a fight."

"That's just your opinion."

"Believe what you want," she told him. "But you know the truth." She turned over the second card on its side atop the first. The illustration showed a young man gathering swords from a battlefield while other men walked away. "The Five of Swords crosses you. The card speaks of your own self-interest and your loss of morality."

"I'm a vampire," Angelus said. "Those things are my nature."

"Those were in your nature before you became a vampire," Lyanka said. "You are stuck in this position, and it will take much to change you. Live life as you currently do, and you will never know true peace." Relentlessly, she flipped over the third card set a few inches below the first two. The card depicted the devil with a man and a woman standing at his feet. "The Devil symbolizes the ignorance and self-indulgence you have always had in your life. Instead of fighting against those things, you have embraced them."

The woman's words bored into Angelus's mind, making him remember his years in Galway with his father. He and his father had never agreed on anything. But his father had been greatly surprised when young Liam had come home a vampire and slain the entire family. Angelus still relished those memories, but they were bittersweet. Although he had taken back control of his life from his father, there remained a lot of unfinished business he hadn't expected. His father had never approved of him as a person, and that was something he now knew would be missing forever.

The fourth card, placed to the left of the first two cards, was the Moon.

"This is your past," Lyanka said. "You've always known fear of the unknown. You have always been lost, not knowing your place in life."

"This is a waste of time," Angelus snorted.

"Is it?" Lyanka looked at him with a raised eyebrow. "I feel the magic in the cards tonight, vampire, stronger than I have felt them in years." She revealed the fifth card and placed it a few inches above the first two. "This is the Nine of Wands. It signifies your belief. You believe yourself to be a warrior, strong enough to be able to take whatever you want."

"What does it say about the power to close the mouths of gypsy fortune-tellers who won't shut up when I tell them to?"

Lyanka placed the sixth card to the right of the first two. "This lies in your future." The card was the Hanged Man, with an illustration of a young man with a glowing head hanging upside down from a cross. "At some point your world will turn around. You will have to surrender to a greater power to undergo an emotional release. You will have to give up control over your own life and accept the direction of a higher power."

Angelus laughed and cursed. "Do you know how foolish this sounds?"

As if drawn by the cards, interested in spite of herself, Lyanka turned up the seventh. "The Two of Wands signifies that you see yourself as being powerful and strong. You enjoy your feelings of superiority and relish authority."

Unable to sit still any longer, Angelus stood.

Lyanka flipped over the eighth card. "The Chariot symbolizes how others around you see you. To them, you are a force of will, a man used to getting what he wants. You are strong and dominant."

"That goes against what you say lies in my future," Angelus said. "If the people around me believe I am a force to be reckoned with, why would I bother to give up control over my own fortunes? No one can make me."

The ninth card was the Tower, depicting a castle

tower wrapped in flames. "Because you will experience a downfall. You will be given back what you have lost, but you will have to learn things about yourself and the world that you have not already acknowledged."

"No!" Angelus leaned forward, placing both his hands on the table. For the first time, he felt the power of the spells that protected her from him. Blue sparks hissed in the air between them. He also felt a vague certainty that she spoke the truth. *But it's her truth,* he told himself. *She's just playing with me, trying to summon up an ignorant and superstitious fear to chase me away.*

Lyanka looked up at him. Only a little fear showed in her dark eyes. "Careful, vampire. Get too close to me and you'll burn."

Angelus resisted the impulse to wipe the cards from the table. He wasn't sure what reaching in so close to her would trigger.

Lyanka looked at him for a moment. "We are interlinked, you and I. I don't recognize the bond between us, but I know it is there."

"Liar!" Angelus's voice was hoarse. More than anything, he wanted to kill her, to exert his control over her and make her shut up.

Without breaking eye contact, Lyanka turned over the tenth and final card.

Unwilling but unable to stop himself, Angelus looked down.

"The Knight of Swords," Lyanka said. "This is a

friend of yours. He is known to you now. He is tactless and rude, a man who can be graceless in his statement of the truth as he sees it. He is harsh and controlling, prone to criticism and sarcasm. Believing he is always right in everything that concerns him, he does not care much for other people."

Angelus stared at the figure of the knight wielding the sword while mounted on a rearing horse. There could be only one person her reading alluded to.

"You know him," Lyanka accused.

"Lies," Angelus said. "You feed me lies to set us at each other's throat."

"You've already been at each other's throat," she told him. "You will be again. There will always be animosity between the two of you. You have had what he treasures. And one day he will have what you treasure, when you are weaker and not as uncaring as you are tonight, and you will hate him for that as well. Your lives will be mixed for a long time to come."

Angelus seized on her words, recognizing the opportunity before him. "If we're going to have our lives mixed for a long time, then he and I aren't going to be killed anytime soon, will we, thief?"

She grimaced, as if only then realizing what she had said.

"How about you?" Angelus asked. "How long are you going to live?" He changed his features, sliding into the mask of the demon.

Lyanka moved back only a little. "I won't die tonight, vampire."

"We'll see, thief." Angelus reached for her slowly. The blue sparks returned as his hand neared her. He felt the strength of her spell and knew that he could break through. But that would only trigger worse things.

Without warning, she ducked toward him.

Flames erupted along Angelus's arm. Cursing, he drew his arm back and used his own cloak to smother the fire. His seared flesh burned and ached immediately. He drew back as she stood and approached him. He felt the pressure increase and backed away from it.

"Go away, vampire," she ordered. "Go away before I decide to kill you tonight."

Maybe she was bluffing. Maybe her power wasn't that strong. Angelus didn't know. But his arm hurt, and he didn't want to risk it. "Another time," he threatened.

"Another time," she agreed, "and I'll be just as ready."

Growling curses, Angelus turned toward the doorway, changed his face back into human features, and stepped into the night that draped Prague. He kept walking and he knew from listening that she didn't follow.

As he walked through the noise and movement of the circus, Angelus kept his burned arm wrapped and held protectively against his stomach. People veered away from him. He knew Darla would be waiting on him inside the circus tent where the performers went through their paces, but he didn't care. His anger and the pain he felt made him want to lash out at someone.

He turned his steps toward the Charles Bridge but automatically avoided the light of the lanterns hung at the entrance. He cursed the woman, cursed the night he met her and the fact that she had been able to escape him at Hyde-Pierce's manor house. That had been Spike's doing. If Spike had simply listened and gone along with the plan instead of giving in to Dru and his own lusts, every person in those houses would have died that night.

Footsteps—several of them—closed in on Angelus.

Angelus turned. His hand automatically dropped to the pistol he wore beneath his cloak.

A tall gypsy man led the seven other men that approached him. The leader was tall and broad-shouldered but slim-hipped. His black hair was a flowing mane scarcely controlled by the light blue scarf over his head. A fierce mustache split his handsome face, and a goatee curled up defiantly from his chin. His clothes spoke of a casual acquaintance of wealth. His cloak was colorful, patterned in purple, red and yellow, making him stand out from the surrounding crowd. "Stay your hand," the man said. "We mean you no harm."

Angelus kept his hand on the butt of the pistol he kept at his belt. It was an American Colt, a short-barreled .36 caliber he had traded for when he'd arrived in Prague. If bullets didn't dissuade the men in front of him, he still wore a rapier.

"Stop right there," Angelus ordered in English, then spoke in Romanian to the best of his ability.

The man stopped and held up a hand. The men around him stopped as well.

"Impressive," Angelus said sarcastically. "You've got them trained. I guess I'll have to watch your act."

"Who are you?" the man asked in English.

"Someone who doesn't like answering questions."

Irritation showed on the man's face. "My name is Chavula Faa. I own this circus."

"Great," Angelus said. "I'm sure you and your circus will be very happy." He wondered what he had done that had caught the man's interest. Then he thought of Spike, Dru, and Darla, thinking perhaps they had drawn the man's attention first. He hadn't checked on them to make certain they were well.

Faa glanced over his shoulder. A slim woman only as tall as his shoulder stepped forward. She was young and beautiful, but her face was filled with despair.

"Do you know him?" Faa asked in Romanian. "Do you know what he is?"

The young woman traced a symbol in the air. The effort glowed faintly, then faded. She waited a moment, then nodded. "Vampire," she said.

The men stepped back a little, and their hands sought their swords. In spite of the situation, Angelus couldn't help smiling. Darla wouldn't like it, if she wasn't already involved, but he welcomed a fight. Action would salve his pride at having to back down from Lyanka. Of course, he didn't intend to let the woman get away forever.

Faa waved the slim woman back and studied Angelus with renewed interest. "Blood drinker," Faa said. "What business did you have with the woman?"

Angelus looked pointedly over Faa's shoulder at the woman standing there. "I've never seen her before."

Faa grimaced in displeasure. "Not this woman. Don't play games with me. My men saw you talking to the fortune-teller."

"I had my fortune told," Angelus said.

"You're not here for amusement, vampire."

Angelus grinned at him coldly. "It might be fun to kill you."

One of the gypsy men stepped forward. He was big and broad, dwarfing the first man and Angelus as well. He bared a blade in one fist that was too short to be called a sword and too long to simply be called a knife. A white scar split his left eyebrow and ran the length of the left side of his face to his jaw. The scar stood out starkly against the dark flesh.

Faa put a hand in the middle of the big man's chest, stopping him in his tracks. Rings decorated the circus owner's hand.

"No, Tobar," Faa commanded.

The young giant stepped back.

Faa regarded Angelus. "You have no love for the

fortune-teller," the circus owner said. "I was told that."

"Your spy must be very good," Angelus said. "I didn't see him."

"The woman is a thief," Faa said.

Angelus didn't comment. Maybe Faa already knew that, or maybe his spy had relayed that he had called the woman that.

"Has she stolen anything from you?" Faa asked.

"Is it any business of yours?" Angelus demanded.

"It could be."

Knowing that he wasn't going to be permitted to leave without answering, Angelus considered his choices. He could fight and risk possible death or injury—as well as Darla's ire. Or he could answer. Also, during his long years of experience dealing with others, he knew that Faa's own curiosity about the woman was exploitable.

"No," Angelus answered. "She's never stolen anything from me."

Faa glanced over his shoulder at the woman there. She nodded almost imperceptibly. When Faa turned back to Angelus, a smile was on his face. "Then why are you interested in the woman?"

"The reasons are my own."

"Maybe we could discover we have similar interests," Faa suggested. "Over a bottle of wine."

"I'm not that—" Before Angelus could finish, Faa produced a small bag and tossed it into the air. Angelus drew the pistol with one hand and pointed it at the center of the man's chest as he caught the small bag with his other hand. Avoiding the bag while standing with the bridge to his back was impossible, and he preferred to have some kind of control over it in case it turned out to be bad.

Tobar started forward again, but Faa threw a hand out to stop him.

Angelus felt the heft of the bag as well as the shapes of the coins within.

"Gold," Faa said. "For the time you spend listening to me."

Weighing the bag in his hand, Angelus said, "I'm listening."

CHAPTER ELEVEN

Los Angeles

"Not Lyanka," the young woman standing in the hotel foyer said in a sharp voice. "My name is Gitana. I am Lyanka's granddaughter."

Angel looked at the woman, seeing the differences now. Gitana's face was a little more full, and she looked younger than Lyanka did the last time Angel had seen the woman.

"Look," Cordelia said, coming around the counter, "I don't know who you are, and I don't know who your grandmother was, but you can't just come barging in unannounced."

Gitana swung her sword toward Cordelia, not

intending to strike her but to back her off. The blade swung to a stop only inches from her throat. Cordelia didn't back up, and started to slide into one of the martial arts forms Angel had trained her in.

Angel caught Cordelia's arm and pulled her back. "Don't," he whispered. He had no doubt that the gypsy woman would kill Cordelia. The trespasses he'd made against her grandmother were unforgivable. The life of anyone who stood with him would be forfeit in the young woman's eyes after the things she thought he had done.

"Angel," Cordelia protested, trying to break free of his grip.

As gently as he could, Angel maintained control of Cordelia and put her behind him. He felt Cordelia resisting him. Glancing over his shoulder at her, he said, "Please, Cordelia."

Reluctantly, Cordelia halted her struggles.

A small smile tweaked the corners of Gitana's mouth. "Very good, vampire."

"His name is Angel," Cordelia snapped defensively.

"Angel," Gitana said. Her dark eyes never left Angel's. "A corruption of the name we know him by. We knew him as Angelus. He was the murderer of my grandmother."

Angel felt Cordelia's eyes on him but refused to meet her gaze. He kept his attention on the young woman and the gypsy warriors who had followed her into the hotel. They were death.

"I don't know who you are," Cordelia said, "but

Angel hasn't been Angelus in about a hundred years."

"There was that short time back in Sunnydale," Wesley volunteered.

Glaring over her shoulder, Cordelia said, "Thanks for all the support."

"But he never left Sunnydale," Wesley went on, trying desperately to cover his mistake. "At least, not that we know of."

"Remind me never to let you testify at the character hearing," Cordelia said.

"Her mother wasn't murdered in Sunnydale," Angel said. "Lyanka died in eighteen ninety-three. In Romania. In the Carpathian Mountains." He glanced from Gitana to Cordelia. "But I didn't kill her grandmother." He looked back at Gitana. "Your grandmother was a brave woman. She was trapped on a bridge over a river in the Carpathian Mountains. Chavula Faa had demons at both ends of the bridge. There was no escape. She chose to cut through the bridge and take her chances with a fall into the flooded river."

"She died there," Gitana accused.

"She didn't plan to," Angel said. The memory of the woman's long plunge into the river haunted him. But not as much as what had happened afterward. "She planned to escape. She didn't survive the river."

"If it hadn't been for you and the other vampire," Gitana stated, "my grandmother never would have been trapped that night."

Angel couldn't argue that.

"What other vampire?" Cordelia asked.

"Spike," Angel answered without looking at her.

"You were with Spike?"

"We weren't always enemies," Angel reminded.

"Oh yeah," Cordelia said. "Pre-soul days."

"Of course," Angel went on, "I've pretty much always thought he was a jerk. Self-involved and narcissistic."

"And malevolent."

"Always that."

Gitana watched them talk, and her interest grew more curious. "'Pre-soul'?"

"Angel got his soul back," Cordelia said. "The Cliff's Notes version: He's no longer a soulless vampire. He's now a vampire with a soul and he's fighting on the side of good. Earning redemption points because of all the evil he did while he was just a bloodsucking death machine."

Angel and Gitana both looked at her.

"Did I miss anything?" Cordelia asked.

Angel couldn't answer.

"And don't look at me like that," Cordelia told Angel. "There's no way to pretty up what you were before you got your soul back. Besides, she already evidently knows all about that side of you. I'm not telling any family secrets here." She glanced back at the young gypsy woman. "So if you're a good guy, you need to back off. And if you're not a good guy, you're going to get your ass kicked."

Before Angel could move, Gitana reached for him. He could have broken away before she touched him, but he chose not to, though he did shift his weight so he could get away quickly in case she wielded the power that her grandmother had. A whisper of electricity rocketed through his skull.

Gitana took her hand back. "You do have your soul back."

"*Hello*," Cordelia said in exasperation. "Didn't I just tell you that?"

"I have never heard of such a thing," Gitana said.

"Believe it," Cordelia said. "That's why Angel set up this help-the-helpless investigations agency. That's what we do: Help the helpless. So maybe if you're looking for some help—"

"I'm not looking for help." Gitana waved to the men behind her. One of them retreated outside.

A moment later, the front door opened, and two men entered carrying Gunn. He was trussed up with rope and gagged with a sock, his arms trapped behind his back. His captors tossed him on the floor between Gitana and Angel.

"Charles!" Fred gasped. She started forward around the counter. Wesley caught her and restrained her. She fought against him while he whispered in her ear. Gradually, Fred quieted, but tears tracked her cheeks.

Gunn looked worse for the wear. His eyes were bloodshot. His flesh held dark welts that promised to be bruises by morning. Slowly, carefully, he rose to his feet and stood swaying. He spat out the sock.

Speaking through bloody and swelled lips, Gunn said, "'S'okay. I'm okay. I just got waylaid in the alley looking for gypsies. Told you there was safety in numbers."

Gitana strode forward confidently, staying just out of Angel's quick reach. She kept the sword naked in her fist.

Most of the warriors who flanked her carried automatic weapons, shotguns, and machine pistols. Angel knew if the situation turned ballistic that Cordelia, Gunn, Fred, and Wesley might be instant casualties.

And Connor still slept in the room beyond. The thin walls wouldn't stop the bullets. Angel marshaled the fear that vibrated within him. It was amazing how much fear he knew these days with the addition of his son.

"If you're not looking for help," Cordelia said, "what are you doing here?"

"I came hunting the vampire," Gitana replied. "Just as he was hunting me."

"He wasn't hunting you," Cordelia said.

"Then why was he at the club where I was conducting business with the Wiatar demons?"

"I sent him there," Cordelia said.

Gitana switched her gaze to Cordelia. The gypsy woman traced a symbol in the air with her left forefinger that glowed faintly for a moment. "There is something . . . different about you. You aren't as human as you look."

Cordelia crossed her arms over her chest. "Not a compliment."

Before Cordelia could say something else, Wesley interrupted: "Cordelia has undergone some changes lately. She has visions. That's how we knew about the club. But we knew nothing of you."

Gitana pointed her chin at Angel. "He did."

"Only when I saw you there," Angel said. "And only then because you look so much like your grandmother."

"She should have killed you at Hyde-Pierce's home when she had the chance."

"She tried," Angel replied.

"We were at the club," Wesley said, "because of these." He pointed at the wall of pictures. "What did you call them? The Seven Foundation Stones?"

"What do you know about them?" Gitana asked.

"They seem to be part of a mystical device," Wesley said.

Angel let Wesley handle the conversation. He knew that his own involvement exacerbated the situation.

"From everything we've learned and been able to guess," Wesley said, "these Seven Foundation Stones form a scrying device to look into other worlds." He tapped the pictures. "According to the files we found, the language on the Stones has never been deciphered." He took his glasses off and cleaned them. "From what I see, based on my involvement with the translation of several documents and objects while I was with the Watchers Council, I suspect that the language isn't human."

Gitana stopped in front of the pictures. "You weren't looking for the Stones?" She stared in disbelief at Angel.

"The Stones have been out there for centuries," Wesley pointed out. "I don't know how long you've been searching for the Stones, but—"

"For all of my life," Gitana said.

Wesley nodded. "Yes. Well, we haven't been looking for them at all. At least, we didn't know that the Stones were what we were looking for."

"How did you learn about the Stones?"

Angel relaxed a little, still thinking about Connor in the next room. His son was so small and vulnerable that his heart ached. He didn't know what kind of woman Gitana was, but he didn't want to find out if she would stop short of killing children.

"We were contacted by a friend," Wesley answered. "That friend asked Angel to look into a shipment from Hong Kong that arrived last night at the Los Angeles docks. Our friend didn't know what the object was, only that it was important. Unfortunately, Angel lost the object that our friend asked us to look for when the Barkuk warriors made good their escape."

Angel remained quiet, knowing that whatever part he took in the conversation might make the situation worse. Wesley's calm, neutral manner remained factual and open.

"The Barkuk warriors didn't escape for long," Gitana said. "They were hunted down and killed. The object that they had given their lives for was taken from them."

"There were gypsies there that night too," Wesley said.

"We did not go there," Gitana said.

"Then there is another group of gypsies running around L.A. hunting the Stones," Gunn said.

"Yes," Gitana said. "They follow a man named Chavula Faa."

"The man Angel said trapped your grandmother and caused her death?" Wesley asked.

"Yes." Gitana surveyed the pictures hanging on the wall.

"This Faa guy is still alive?" Cordelia asked.

"He lives."

"Then he's got to be really old."

"Chavula Faa *is* old," Gitana said. "He is the oldest of us all. My people are not human, and they are very long-lived. Chavula Faa has lived for centuries."

"Not human?" Wesley repeated.

"We are not gypsies," Gitana said. "We are Kalochner. In my native language, what I know of it because we have lost much since we first came to this world, we were called the Light-Bringers. In our world, we were very special."

Fred went to one of the books piled on the hotel

desk. She opened the thick volume with a thud that rang through the hotel foyer. Looking embarrassed, she said, "Sorry." She turned pages. "Just remembered that I read something about the Kalochner."

"There was little mentioned of my people," Gitana said. "My forebears made certain of that."

"Oh, there's very little," Fred agreed. She found the page she was looking for. "The Kalochner weren't even thought to be real. Kind of a myth. Twelfth-century Muslim records indicate that there was a group of people in the armies the Aryans amassed to battle them that had Kalochner people among them."

"My ancestors," Gitana said.

"They were the ones that were supposed to have taught the gypsies magic and fortune-telling," Fred said. "That's really all there is to the legend. And the fact that they were interested in the Stones because they used them to peer into other worlds to find secrets and spy on the Muslims."

"My ancestors didn't peer into other worlds ferreting out secrets," Gitana said. "Or spy on the Muslims. The magic that my ancestors brought to all the peoples that became the gypsies was their own. In those days, there were no gypsies. There were only peoples who had been ripped from their homelands by the savage armies of the Aryans, who wanted the lands and wealth of the Muslims. Over the years, they melted into one people. At least, that was how they appeared in the eyes of outsiders. But inside the gypsy families, we recognize the differences that make us unique."

"How did your people come into this world?" Wesley asked.

Gitana looked at the pictures on the wall. "Through the Seven Foundation Stones. When placed together in the proper pattern and activated by a spell, they become the Bridge of Journeyhome."

"Not an entirely original name," Cordelia observed.

Gitana swiveled to face her. Fire danced in the gypsy woman's eyes. Angel took an instinctive step forward to protect Cordelia.

"It was," Gitana said in an icy tone, "the only name we had for it. My ancestors forbade its true name to ever be spoken. So they called it the Bridge of Journeyhome."

"Why did the Kalochner people come to this world?" Wesley asked.

Gitana waited a moment, then reached a decision. "Because the gifts that they had were unique even on their world. There were others in that world who wanted to exploit their gifts. They wanted to use the powers of my people in their constant warring. In the beginning, before their arrival here in this world, we were pacifists. They had chosen to lay down the weapons of war to live in peace with one another and even the outer empires."

"Judging from all the guns and swords you guys are carrying around," Cordelia stated, "you didn't have any problems reverting back to nonpacifist ways."

Gitana bridled slightly, gripping her sword more tightly, then let her breath out. "We had no choice. After we arrived here, the Aryans found them and forced them into servitude in their armies."

"How many of your people made the trip to this world?" Wesley asked.

"Over three thousand." Sadness flickered in Gitana's eyes. "More than half that number didn't survive the trip. My ancestors had no way of knowing about the diseases they would be exposed to here. Especially in the filthy camps the Aryan army maintained. But they were so desperate to leave their world because they were all fugitives. Those Kalochner who were not controlled by one kingdom or another for their own purposes were hunted down and killed. Ignorant villagers and even city-dwellers believed the Kalochner capable of killing with a single glance."

"The Evil Eye," Gunn said.

"Many have called it that. Here as well as there. And some of our people could place a curse on others that caused death, but only after considerable effort."

"A curse," Gunn said as if in disbelief.

"A few still have that power today. My grandmother, Lyanka, was very powerful." Gitana shrugged. "Perhaps I have the power. I have never tried. A curse is a very powerful thing, and even the person who summons it has no real power over it once those forces are unleashed."

The words fell like leaden hammers in Angel's ears. He pushed the memory away before it could surface, and concentrated on what Gitana said.

"Those superstitious people didn't stop to think that if my ancestors had possessed so much power, they wouldn't have been at the mercy of the kings and princes." Gitana paused. "My ancestors were enslaved, hunted, and slain in their own world. They spent years hiding out from the different kingdoms and forming the Seven Foundation Stones in the bellies of dragons. When the Stones were finished, they had to track down those dragons and kill them."

"Doesn't sound very peace-loving," Cordelia said.

"In my ancestors' world, dragons are things of great evil. They are cruel and plotting beasts. And my ancestors were very desperate. They could no longer hide. They were too well known in their world. So they earned the enmity of dragons as well."

"And they found little comfort in this world when they arrived," Wesley said.

Gitana nodded. "Still, they survived. It was all they knew to do. But they hid their ways and the fact that they were from another world. They had children who stepped further away from the old ways and fought with their parents over the knowledge that was denied to them. Many of them felt they had the power of my people, but they weren't trained in their use except in small ways that provided modest incomes for them. Most were taught the arts of healing and fortune-telling. There were a few that were handed down the knowledge , all of them chosen by the elders and trained to keep our ways and remember the world we had fled from. But every now and again, one of those who were untrained had the power of my people manifest strongly in them."

"Chavula Faa was one of those," Angel said.

At first, Gitana looked as though her anger was going to get the better of her. Then she released it. Slowly, she sheathed the sword she held, but she did not tell her men to stand down.

"Yes," she answered. "He is. Though he is of mixed heritage, as all of my people are these days, the power within him is strong. There is no way to cancel that out. Even some of the true gypsy children that were born to human women and never knew our ways carry traces of the abilities of my people."

"Was your grandmother one of those that were chosen?" Wesley asked.

"No." Gitana straightened her spine and stood a little taller. "My grandmother did not agree with the Kalochner Elders. She believed that our people should embrace their heritage. So she set about trying to find the Seven Foundation Stones in defiance of the Elders." She paused. "My grandmother believed that we don't belong on this world. So much time had elapsed in our world that she hoped things had changed back on our homeworld. She believed that we should at least investigate the possibility."

"Lyanka took one of the Stones from Hyde-Pierce's house that night," Angel said.

"Yes. She searched for the Stones all the time during those days as well as later. She found a second Stone only days before you helped get her killed."

The accusation hung heavily in the hotel foyer for a time. Angel felt the weight of the truth in Gitana's words.

"At that time, Chavula Faa had at least two of the Stones," Gitana continued.

"And he wants the Stones to activate the Bridge of Journeyhome?" Wesley asked.

Gitana nodded.

"Why?" Gunn asked.

"Because he intends to go back into that world and conquer it," Gitana said. "With the weapons that have been made in this world, the people there will have no chance."

"How do you know that?" Cordelia asked.

"Because of the visions that are capable once any three of the Stones are together," Gitana answered. "When three of the Stones are gathered and the proper spells are used, brief, uncontrolled glimpses into the world where we came from is possible. From what I have been told, the people have not progressed there as this world has."

"Have you seen into this other world?" Wesley asked.

"No. But I have the journals my grandmother left before her death."

"Why did you come here?" Cordelia asked.

Gitana looked pointedly at Angel. "To kill the vampire. To warn you others to stay out of our business. This man"—she indicated Gunn—"told me that you were not vampires, and that you had no idea what was going on."

"Killing the vampire is so not a good idea," Cordelia said. "We could help you get the Stones. That's what we're good at."

"We're not exactly 'the helpless,'" Gitana said.

"So we'll go beyond the scope of what we normally do," Cordelia said. "We'll help those who can help themselves get what they need done a little faster. You know, pitching in to make a big job a little smaller. I'm thinking saving a whole world from a would-be despot's invasion would probably pony up some serious redemption brownie points." She glanced at Angel with a hopeful expression. "If you're up for that. You're the one with all the history issues."

Angel maintained his silence.

"No," Gitana said. "I won't trust the vampire."

"And he's not going to stay out of it," Cordelia said. "Not now that he knows what's at stake. Trust me on this. I know him."

"Cordy," Gunn said with a note of desperation that slurred a little because of his puffy lips. "Could I maybe talk to you? I mean, lately I've been thinking that maybe some things just aren't any of our business. If we're gonna get killed by the bad guys *and the good guys,* maybe we should just sit this one out."

"Gitana does seem to have a handle on things," Wesley agreed.

"She does," Fred added. "And the phone has rung a few times this evening. There are other cases we can look into. Cases with demons and other monsters that truly helpless people need help with."

"Can't," Cordelia said with a little exasperation. "Vision, remember? The Powers-That-Be obviously have decided that we're supposed to be involved with this one."

"What do you know about Wolfram and Hart?" Angel asked.

Gitana shook her head. "I'm not familiar with either of them."

"Not an 'either,'" Cordelia said. "Wolfram and Hart are a law firm that specializes in demony things. They've got people everywhere."

"People, demons, monsters, and pretty much anything else that is creepy," Fred added. "They're not good people."

"Why should their names mean anything to me?" Gitana asked.

"Because Wolfram and Hart were involved with the attempted theft in Hong Kong and on the L.A. docks," Angel said.

"How do you know?" Suspicion gleamed in Gitana's eyes.

"Because my friend told me," Angel said. "And if Wolfram and Hart is involved, you're going to need help."

"We don't need your help."

"You have one of the Stones," Angel said. "How many does Chavula Faa have?"

Gitana hesitated. "Four. Possibly five. We have no way of knowing."

Angel nodded. "Maybe Wolfram and Hart know."

CHAPTER TWELVE

The security guard standing in front of Spike's hiding place within a weeping Japanese willow was one of the Urike demon tribes from Alloch. Spike didn't know which tribe because he wasn't that familiar with the tribal tattoos mapped across the demon's broad, flat face. But identification didn't matter because Spike knew all Urike demons shared one trait in common: Every one of them had a keen sense of smell.

Standing almost eight feet tall and covered in violet scales, the Urike demon was built lean and muscular like a racing greyhound. His pointed ears lay pinned back against his hairless skull as if they'd been pulled back. His double set of arms and hunched back made him resemble a praying mantis to a degree. But the face was anchored around a broad, wet nose that snuffled constantly as he scented the air. His forked tongue flicked out, staying and vibrating for a short time while he tasted the wind.

Got my scent, Spike realized. *Doesn't know where I am yet, but he will.*

"What are you waiting on?" Arrag asked over the headset Spike wore.

Knowing there was nothing to be done for it, Spike morphed his face, bringing all his demonic strength and speed to the forefront. He was less than fifty feet from Willard Hargreave's mansion. Backing out of the operation wasn't an option.

The Qorqoth demons waited on the other side of the security wall. All of them wore radio headsets. Arrag had assigned him as point man for the break-in because the security system depended a lot on heat sensors.

As a vampire, Spike's body signature read at the same temperature of the land, as long as he'd been in the area to get acclimated and didn't carry residual heat from somewhere else. Arrag had shut Spike in the van and turned the air conditioner on for a time just to be certain.

Spike lunged for the Urike demon just as he started to turn around. The Urike demon carried an assault rifle, but he'd been trained well in the weapon's use. Spike knew that from the way the demon kept his finger outside the trigger guard until he was ready to fire.

Grabbing the assault rifle, Spike tore the weapon away before the Urike demon could slide his finger inside the guard. Even without his lead weapon, though, the Urike demon wasn't defenseless. His massive jaws opened, saliva dripped from the sharp teeth, and fetid breath came out in a rush that clouded Spike's face. At least the demon wasn't human.

Spike made a Y of his hand and jammed it into the Urike demon's throat. The blow was strong enough to crush a normal man's windpipe, but Spike didn't know if he'd succeeded with the guard. Urike demons could also take a tremendous amount of bodily damage before they went down.

The demon said, *"Hurrrkkkk!"* and staggered back. But he lowered his hunched shoulders and brought all four hands up to defend himself.

Spike feinted, as if he were going to launch himself at the demon, then dropped to the ground and swept the Urike's legs from under him with a vicious kick. One of the demon's legs snapped like kindling.

"Huurrrkk! Huuuurrrrrrkkkk!" the demon cried hoarsely as he went down. If the windpipe wasn't crushed, it was at least paralyzed. He couldn't yell for help. He rolled over onto his stomach and tried to push himself to his feet.

Throwing himself on top of the demon's back,

Spike locked his legs around his opponent's mid-section, cupped both hands under the Urike's chin, and twisted. For a moment he didn't think he was going to be able to turn the demon's head, then it went in a rush and the vertebrae ratcheted and shattered with a series of cracks.

Spike rode his dying opponent to the ground. He waited till the final spasms and quivers had raced through the Urike demon's body. When he was certain the security guard was dead, Spike stood and pulled the corpse into the shadowy shelter of the weeping Japanese willow.

"What are you doing?" Arrag called over the headset.

"Urike demon," Spike said, tucking the final arm of the demon's four out of sight beneath the drooping tree branches. "Familiar with those?"

"Four arms?"

"And a keen sense of smell," Spike agreed. "He was onto me. I had to take care of him."

Arrag cursed quietly and competently. When he was done, he said, "A dead guard means an empty slot in a security detail. You've just set a time clock on our operation, and we don't know when it goes *bang!*"

"Probably when the on-site security guards start beating the bushes," Spike said. "I didn't have a choice. You get that?"

Arrag remained quiet, but Spike heard him breathing over the headset.

Remaining hunkered in the shadows, watching

Willard Hargreave's house with cold dispassion, Spike tried not to think of the fifty thousand dollars that might be slipping through his hands with the turn of bad luck. He took the dead demon's assault rifle, figuring it might come in handy. He wanted a cigarette but he knew he didn't dare.

"Make up your mind," Spike growled into the headset's mouthpiece. "We came here to rob this place. You can either help me or go home."

"Help you?"

"I'm going in. With or without you." Spike rose from the shadows and started for the house.

"This isn't how we planned it."

"These things never go completely according to plan," Spike replied. "Get over it. Get with the program or get out." He moved with all the speed he could muster. This far into the security net, the motion detectors were absent. They were used primarily for the outer perimeter.

"All right," Arrag agreed reluctantly. "We're staying."

Greed has a way of building courage, Spike thought wryly, knowing it was what propelled him now. He dropped into position beside the first-floor back door they had chosen as an exit point into the house. He reached into the chest pouch he wore over the dark clothing Arrag had given him to wear and took out the electronic lockpick.

The device was no larger than a cigarette pack, and only half as thick. The dulled gray finish assured that the thin moonlight wouldn't reflect from the surface. He freed the wires attached to the device from the Velcro restraining strap.

Using a cordless battery-powered screwdriver, Spike carefully removed the cover of the electronic lock on the door. He examined the wires with a mini Maglite flash he held between his teeth, found the three that he wanted, then attached the alligator clips from the electronic lockpick. The teeth of the clips were razor-sharp and sheared through the protective plastic coating over the wires instantly. He switched off the mini Maglite and put the flash back in his chest pouch.

He pressed the activate button and watched as the LCD panel started cycling through the electronic tumblers. The operation took only seconds. Arrag had access to cutting-edge equipment.

The final tumbler clicked into position in the eighth slot.

Tentatively, knowing they really didn't have another way into the house if the electronic lockpick didn't work, Spike reached for the doorknob. It was locked. The door bolt didn't depend on the electronic mechanism.

Cursing, dying for a cigarette, Spike reached into the chest pouch again. He took out a small crowbar no bigger than a pencil.

"What's wrong?" Arrag demanded.

"Your information about the bloody door wasn't entirely correct," Spike said. "It didn't have just the electronic lock on it. There's still an old-fashioned bolt."

"Then break it. Since you killed the guard, we're in a hurry. You compromised finesse."

Spike placed the mini-crowbar against the lock, then drew back his hand. He slammed his hand forward. The crowbar ripped through the old-fashioned locking mechanism. Bits and pieces dropped inside the room on the other side of the door. From the spongy noise they made, Spike guessed that they'd hit carpet.

Still, he was nervous when he tried the doorknob again. For all he knew, an execution squad armed with flamethrowers was waiting on the other side of the door. He already had the impression Willard Hargreave wasn't the kind of guy to screw around. When the knob twisted easily in Spike's hand, feeling mushy and loose, he stood to one side of the doorway and pushed the door inward.

Nobody stood in the foyer. Also, there was no resistance to his entrance as there would be if the residence was owned by a human. A demon's home didn't have the same rules as human habitation.

Well, we're due a bit of luck, Spike reassured himself.

The foyer was black with shadows, which was exactly how he had expected it to be. Spike went forward, able to see partially in the darkness, but trailing his fingers lightly along the left wall to keep his bearings all the same. He had memorized the big house's layout from the blueprints that Arrag had been given by his contact, but he knew that sometimes blueprints provided on a job didn't always stay up-to-date.

These did, though. Willard Hargreave had ordered his house built and had kept it to the specifications.

Spike passed through the foyer and into a kitchen and an ornate dining room beyond. The rooms were wired for thermal sensors, which made them off-limits for the flesh-and-blood guards on the premises. That was the weakness Arrag had decided to exploit when he'd gone over all the information, which was why Spike's complicity in the robbery was so important.

Video cameras backed the thermal sensors, but with the rooms as dark as they were, Spike felt certain that anyone watching the screens would only have seen the darkness as he passed through. Thermal imaging, using software that could read body heat of a normal living being, would also be blind to his passage.

A guard passed through the great room outside the dining area. He was also a demon, but thankfully wasn't a Urike demon that might scent Spike. When the creature's soft footfalls receded down the hallway beneath the switchback stairs that led to the massive second story, Spike eased out and continued.

He bore to the left, aiming himself at the huge study located near the center of the house. Another electronic lock barred the double doors there. He took out the electronic lockpick and screwdriver again. In seconds, the LCD screen was pulling up the tumblers.

"Are you in?" Arrag asked.

"Have I called?" Spike countered. He took the alligator clips off the lock's wires.

"Clock's ticking. Tick, tick, tick."

"And I'm getting there. I'm inside the study now." Spike pulled the door open, made certain there was only dark and inviting gloom inside, then stepped into the room.

"The control panel—"

"I know where the control panel is," Spike snapped. He made his way to the other end of the room.

The study was an exercise in history. Ancient Chinese statues, vases, and paintings shared space with European nautical charts and ship's plunder that included Spanish gold doubloons and Egyptian jars. Floor-to-ceiling bookshelves lined walls that were sixteen feet tall. Thick beams decorated the ceiling.

Thermal sensors lined the top of the high walls, trained down on the center of the floor. Spike knew that if he'd been a living breathing entity with a heartbeat, he would have set off alarms immediately. The study was one of the "safe" rooms inside the house. No one living was allowed in those rooms.

Still, for all the pomp and splendor in the room, it held an air of being a workplace. Whoever Willard Hargreave was, he spent a lot of time in the room.

"Have you—," Arrag asked.

"Quiet," Spike interrupted. "I need to hear if anyone is coming in after me."

Arrag cursed.

Spike shouldered the assault rifle, letting the weapon hang by its strap straight down, and crossed to the massive desk that looked as though it could have been used as an antiaircraft carrier. Plush leather and teak furniture finished out the room, comfortably building an intimate work area as well as a more relaxed area for business dealings consisting of three sofas and a big-screen HDTV.

Moving quickly, Spike reached under the desk and felt for the concealed button Arrag's information said would be there. When he found the button, he pressed it. A section of the desktop popped free, rose a few inches, then flipped over to reveal a sophisticated monitor.

"All right, then," Spike whispered to himself, "come to Papa." He dug in the chest pouch for the computer key card Arrag had given him. *Moment of truth. Is this really a robbery, or has Arrag set you up to take the fall?*

The key card slot was just below the blank monitor. Spike slid the car into the slot.

The monitor came to sudden brilliant life.

Spike felt an immediate rush of fear and anxiety. He was deep inside treacherous territory if things were going to go bad. Fighting his way out of Hargreave's house would have been hard if not impossible. Situated in the center of the house as the study was, there were no windows, no immediate means of escape. He was boxed.

He took the assault rifle's pistol grip into his hand and triggered the key card. *The card is a facsimile,* Arrag had said, *that is so close to the original, the reader will never know.*

Spike watched the data streams across the computer monitor. He forced himself to think of Buffy in his arms. That was the focus, everything that he was prepared to die for at the moment. He remembered Angelus taunting him, telling him that love would one day be the death of him.

But I've got her now, Angel, Spike thought fiercely. *You walked away from her and she took up with me. I'm everything she could possibly need. She knows love when she sees it. You hold back because you have a fear of what's right and wrong. But I've never held back. Never didn't go for something I really wanted. That's the difference between you and me.*

The green numbers changed shapes with dizzying frequency. With stomach-churning suddenness, the numbers froze and exploded across the screen.

Surprised, Spike took an involuntary step backward. He expected alarms to shrill, but the noise never came. Then the screen changed again, bringing up a schematic of the house alarm systems.

He pulled the pencil-thin mike to his mouth. "I'm in."

"Then shut down the alarms," Arrag replied. "We

don't want to be here when the sun comes up in the morning."

Spike silently agreed. He could almost feel the fifty thousand dollars in his hands. It had been so long since he'd actually needed that kind of money that he'd forgotten how much space that kind of cash took up. Would the cash fit in a briefcase or a suitcase? Of course, that depended on whether the bills were hundreds or twenties.

Too bad you can't give it all to Buffy, he told himself as he entered the disarming codes. He had an image of Buffy lying naked on a plush bed covered in silk as he cascaded fifty thousand dollars over her.

Reluctantly, Spike turned his thoughts from the fantasy as he continued entering the codes. He watched as the alarms went benign across the back landscape behind the house. When he was finished, a narrow corridor was left open between the overlapping fields of heat sensors and motion detectors.

"Okay," Spike said over the mike. "It's all good here."

"You're sure?" Arrag asked.

Irritably, Spike said, "Pop on over and have a look for yourself then. And make sure you remember that the alarms might be down, but you've still got flesh-and-blood security on the premises."

"We're on our way," Arrag said.

The radio went dead in Spike's ear. He hated that. He wanted to be kept up with what they were doing. But Arrag had planned for the blackout in communication while they negotiated the distance between the wall and the house. Electronic devices could still be detected, and there was a chance of communications bleed-over that might be picked up by the on-site security staff.

Satisfied that he'd done all he could with the alarm systems, Spike pushed the buttons that returned the unit back inside the desk. He turned his attention to the floor-to-ceiling bookshelf behind the desk. He kept the assault rifle in one hand, finger curled outside the guard.

Scanning the titles on the bookshelves, he pulled out a copy of *Slaughterhouse 5* by Kurt Vonnegut on the first shelf and felt it lock into place. He slid free a copy of *1984* by George Orwell on the third shelf. He followed the selections by choosing *Behold, the Man* by Michael Moorcock on the sixth shelf.

When the third book was locked into place, the bookshelves neatly divided and folded back accordion-style to reveal a massive walk-in safe. The solid wall of steel that made up the door and the large hinges testified to the door's proof against even uncommon thieves.

Arrag had promised that his nephews were excellent safecrackers. That remained to be seen, and Spike hadn't been overly impressed with the brothers so far.

The safe door looked imposing and impenetrable. Muullot and Doxxil might take one look at the vault in the flesh, so to speak, and throw up their hands.

No, Spike decided. *They brought explosives. If they can't take out the electronic locks, they'll still want to try the explosives.*

Still, Spike couldn't help speculating about what lay behind the massive vault door. Fifty thousand dollars was only the opening bid on tonight's action. As long as they managed to get away with the item they'd been hired to steal, Spike felt free to take whatever else he could put into his pockets.

Hopefully, Willard Hargreave had packed a lot of cash or jewels inside the vault. Surely there were at least a few bearer bonds tucked inside. The guy was an international dealer.

Spike stood in the shadows of the room beside the open bookshelves. He kept the assault rifle angled down, ready to bring the weapon up if one of the guards happened to stumble onto the little break-in that he had going on.

Or, in case this is still all a setup, he told himself as he listened to the long silence stretching from the headset.

His mind worked constantly. He'd always been creative. Angelus had been the straight thinker among them when they'd been a group: he, Angelus, Darla, and Dru. Angelus could plot and plan with the best of them, terribly lucid and practical. But Spike's gift and curse lay in the fact that he was creative. He always saw more than one side to an issue, more than one path to a destination.

Creativity bred paranoia. Spike had carried

around a headful of paranoia for over a hundred years and, during the last couple, his life had taken really strange twists and turns. Loving a slayer was a death wish of sorts. But he'd followed his heart, cold and dead as it was. Maybe it didn't beat, but the passion remained.

He waited in the darkness, certain that someone in the group had betrayed them. There was no honor among thieves. He felt certain his companions would sacrifice him in a minute to get what they wanted. He'd be a fool not to acknowledge that fact.

Time passed, only ticks of the clock, but years of paranoia.

Either Arrag had betrayed him, Spike thought, or Arrag had betrayed them all. Then again, Muullot and Doxxil could have conspired against their uncle and the new guy, figured on blowing both of them away and taking everything they could. *No love lost for a vampire*, Spike admitted reluctantly. And maybe, because he'd seen times before when large amounts of money were about to change hands, one of the brothers had set up all of them.

Somewhere in the house, a clock struck midnight.

The witching hour, Spike told himself. That thought led him to Willow, and from there he immediately remembered the rest of Buffy's entourage. Xander and Anya, bickering as usual as the wedding neared. Dawn, still trying to come to grips with her mother's death. Tara and Willow working at figuring out their own places in the world and with each other after Willow's magic addiction. None of them was perfect. Each in their own way was as flawed as Spike was. It was those flaws that bound them.

Standing there unannounced in the study of Willard Hargreave's mansion, Spike realized how far from home he really was.

Not for long, he promised himself. Still and not breathing, he heard the night sounds of the whispered movement. He lifted the assault rifle and aimed at the door.

Quietly, Arrag and his nephews filed into the study.

"Put that away," Arrag commanded.

Spike raised the assault rifle but he didn't put the weapon away. They were armed as well.

"Took your time," Spike groused.

Arrag surveyed the massive vault, then glanced over his shoulder at Spike. "Watch the door."

"Sure." Spike flipped the Qorqoth demon a rebellious salute. He walked to the door and put his back to the wall so he wouldn't be seen by anyone who entered the room.

Muullot and Doxxil placed their equipment bags on the floor behind the desk. The demon brothers hauled gear from the bags, moving with an economic precision Spike never would have guessed either of them possessed.

Arrag brought the monitor up from the desk again. The soft glow bathed his harsh features. The light changed as he flicked from frame to frame to check the other security stations.

"We're good," Arrag said softly as he looked up at Spike. "As long as they don't find the body of the Urike demon."

Spike didn't say anything. Maybe he'd take some crap over killing the Urike demon, but—if they were successful—he'd be taking fifty thousand dollars too. That was all that mattered.

As long as they don't turn on you, Spike told himself. He held the assault rifle across his chest. And he waited.

CHAPTER THIRTEEN

"Evil never sleeps."

Recognizing the voice, Lilah Morgan automatically closed down the files she was working on at the computer. She tapped another key, sending them to her PDA in her jacket through wireless Ethernet that connected the machines, and erased the files on the desktop computer's hard drive.

She glanced up at her visitor and smiled. "Angel." It wasn't a greeting; the acknowledgment stood more as a challenge.

The vampire stood in front of her desk. As usual, he wore black. But there was something different about his dark eyes. He looked a little more haunted than usual.

Weakness? Lilah wondered, and her pulse sped up a little at the possibility. A conscience was a burden someone in her business couldn't afford. She took a pencil between her fingers and peered over it at him. The pencil had a wooden barrel and was something of a weapon in case the unannounced visit turned ugly.

Security was only seconds away, but Lilah knew if she called for them, things would turn violent in an instant. Despite the best vampire-detection equipment Wolfram & Hart had access to—and they had access to the best, including some they didn't invent themselves—Angel seemed able to come and go at will through their offices.

"I trust that I interrupted something nefarious," Angel said.

Lilah glanced at the clock on the wall. She smiled. "It's just after midnight. Prime time for nefarious doings." She leaned back from the desk but kept the pencil in her fingers. With satisfaction, she realized her hands weren't shaking.

Only a short time ago, Angel had threatened to kill her if she ever tried to harm Cordelia Chase again. Lilah sometimes had nightmares about that encounter. As an attorney for Wolfram & Hart, she had access to files that showed what Angel had been capable of as Angelus. Properly motivated, the experts assured her that he was quite capable of returning to that savagery.

Last year, when Darla had been returned to life as a human to be used as a hostage against Angel, and subsequently turned back into a vampire by Drusilla, Angel had declared war on the law firm's offices. A proper blood tide had ensued. Several of the firm's senior partners had ended up as casualties.

"In this case," Lilah went on casually, "a bit of political blackmail. Senatorial indiscretions." She wrinkled her nose as if she disapproved but couldn't keep the smile from her lips. "Mundane stuff, actually. Almost boring. But I can use it."

Angel nodded and stepped farther into the room. He peered out the window at the night-darkened city beyond.

"This isn't a social visit," Lilah observed.

He faced her, his handsome features cold and dispassionate. "No." And that simple word resonated with all the dislike he had for her. "The only thing social about you is the diseases you and this law firm manipulate on a daily basis."

"Oooh, venom."

"A little maybe."

Lilah studied him. Knowing why he was there was no stretch of the imagination. "You want something."

Angel remained silent.

"I don't read minds," Lilah said, "and there's no other reason you'd be here." She felt a little smug. "For you to come here means you've rounded up the usual suspects and come up empty. Your street sources are dry, or this was something that was never in the streets. No matter how much you try to put it off or put a different spin on your reasons for being here, you're going to have to put it on the table so we can kick it around."

"Last night," Angel said, "there was an attempted robbery at the docks. A ship called *Swift Star.*"

"It was in the news," Lilah said, remembering the story. "Not much mention. I barely noticed it."

"But you noticed it."

"I'm in the crime business." Also, she knew that one of the other partners in the firm had some business on that ship that had been kept on stealth mode.

"You're on the wrong side of the crime business," Angel said.

"You say wrong; I say lucrative. Depends on your frame of reference."

"What I want to know is what interest Wolfram and Hart had in *Swift Star.*"

"I wouldn't know."

"You would."

Lilah paused, wondering if she could use the obvious need and immediacy that she felt radiating from the vampire. "I need some incentive."

Angel gave her a cold eye, and Lilah felt fear rush through her. When he was terrifying, he was even more attractive. She couldn't help feeling the pull, and acknowledging it—even if only to herself—was worse because she knew he didn't feel that pull and wouldn't care that she did. There was something about power that drew out the worst, the darkest, and the most passionate sides of her. And Angel was a player, a true champion of the Powers-That-Be.

"I've paid ahead," Angel said. "You're still alive

after everything you've tried to do to my family."

"Killing me wouldn't help you." Although she tried to state that in a calm manner, Lilah felt the tension of the moment.

"The enemy I know is better than the enemy I don't know," Angel agreed. "That's why I'm here, and that's why you're still alive."

"Then you know you can't threaten me. If you kill me, you lose that known entity."

"I can threaten you. I did. Now you're up to bat."

"Whatever was on *Swift Star*," Lilah said, "isn't in my caseload."

"Someone here at Wolfram and Hart represented a buyer or a potential buyer for whatever was taken from that ship."

Lilah waited.

"Check into it," Angel suggested. "I know you can."

"I also know that you wouldn't be here just to return somebody's property."

"No."

"Then what's this about?"

He was quiet for a moment, then spoke softly, "Lilah, don't try my patience. Not on this."

She heard the quiet desperation in his voice and lost herself for a moment in thought as she tried to figure out what might cause that.

"What are you going to do with the information?" she asked.

"Put some pressure on. Shake up the situation and see what falls loose."

Lilah put the pencil away, feeling entirely safe now. She was in a position to deal. That was her best position. "Give me a little more. Let me know what I'm looking for."

"Why?"

"Because the guy you're looking for has some pull in this office," she replied. "If he's screwed up somewhere, maybe I can use that to my advantage."

"And you get to step on others along the way."

Lilah made a moue of her lips and shrugged. "Just a perk. You don't have to make a big deal out of it."

Angel's face hardened. "Get me a name."

"Tell me what I'm looking for." Lilah set her elbows on the desktop and laced her fingers.

After a momentary hesitation, Angel reached into a pocket of his duster and pulled out a sheaf of folded pages. "There are three objects there. Art. I think one of them was on *Swift Star.*"

Lilah took the papers and spread them out on the desk. She recognized two of them at once. One of them she had negotiated for Thomas Ivers four years ago. Amazingly, the other was one that Willard Hargreave had offered to trade to Ivers for something of Ivers's private collection. "All three of these pieces were supposed to be coming in on the ship?" she asked.

Angel hesitated. "I don't know."

Don't know, Lilah mused, *or not going to tell?* She studied his face but couldn't make up her mind either way.

"But you know," Angel accused.

Taken aback by his declaration, Lilah struggled to save ground. "What are these pieces?"

"That's not the issue."

"I could help more if I knew more."

"You could also hurt more if you knew more." Angel stepped toward her, and the movement was filled with threat. "Tell me who finessed the transport from Hong Kong on *Swift Star*. That had to be an attorney. Someone with international scope. A lot of legal tape has to be cut on transportation of art or artifacts."

Lilah considered her options. Every time he showed up in her office, things got tense. And there was never enough time to assess the situation properly. Usually they got a feel for each other immediately, each knowing in seconds who had the superior position. She hadn't won often, but she had won.

The question now was in how she was going to parlay Angel's interest into something she could use.

"The name," Angel prompted.

"Wynowski," Lilah said. "Bill Wynowski. He's an attorney specializing in investments and tax cases. Off-shore accounting. That kind of thing."

"What did Bill Wynowski do?"

"He brokered the deal for the piece."

Angel tapped the three papers on her desk. "Which piece?"

Lilah leaned forward and tapped the one on the left. "This one."

A flicker of recognition passed through Angel's eyes, but he quickly hid it. "You're sure?"

"Yes."

Angel picked up the papers and put them back inside his duster. "Who is the client?"

"I don't know." Lilah was already planning and plotting. If Angel went after Wynowski and ended up with Willard Hargreave's name, she could be held blameless. Wynowski would have been the one to give up the client, not her.

Angel wouldn't tell; he needed her in place just as she needed him on occasion. After all, the subject of his son still occupied a large amount of the time expended by the research-and-development arm of the law firm. This way, she kept the vampire close and she could get rid of Wynowski, who had more seniority than she did.

Even more, if Angel should get away with the art piece that Hargreave had, Ivers would undoubtedly still want it. Sooner or later the billionaire would learn about Angel and about her relationship with the vampire. Ivers would have to come to her and ask her to help. That would put him closer to her, and it would give Wolfram & Hart outside sources to put further pressure on Angel.

It was a desperate gamble, but Lilah didn't see how she could not come out a winner.

"If you're lying—," Angel said.

"I'm not," Lilah interrupted. "Whatever *Swift Star* carried as cargo, the deal was Wynowski's."

Angel hesitated, then nodded. "Where do I find Wynowski?"

* * *

Standing guard, even though Spike was in a house that was more or less a fortress and had armed security guards on the premises, turned out to be somewhat boring. He kept the assault rifle close to hand, though.

Arrag kept himself busy, dividing his time between watching the security cameras and prodding Muullot and Doxxil. The brothers were making surprising headway with the massive vault behind the study's bookshelves.

All the idiocy that was so much a part of their behavior when they were with each other disappeared. Muullot and Doxxil moved in tandem, hooking up drills and acid delivery systems, almost silently boring into the guts of the vault door and unleashing cancers that ate through metal, circuitry, and polycarbonate.

Spike's thoughts centered on Buffy, imagining how things had been between them before Riley had walked into the crypt and caught them together. Even with his eyes open so he could watch the Qorqoth demons, he could see Buffy, could feel her warm skin—so unlike Dru's—pressed against him. He felt her breath on his shoulder, heard her cries of need and passion, saw her eyes looking back into his.

—isten to me. Hear me. You've got to—

I hear you, Spike thought as he remembered those moments stolen from her friends and from her patrol.

—me! You can't let them ta—

Spike frowned. That didn't sound like any of the conversations he had ever had with Buffy.

—need you! Please!

There, Spike told himself. *That sounds much better.*

—killed me!

The voice turned frenzied, and even though he'd pushed Buffy past any point of control, Spike knew that he'd never elicited that tone of voice in her. Something was wrong.

A haze formed in front of him, a misty shifting that blurred the Qorqoth demons and the vault at the other end of the room out of focus. The cold of the grave, something he barely remembered but could never truly forget, shivered down Spike's spine.

—killed me! You were there! You were to blame! I hated you!

Spike blinked rapidly in an effort to clear his vision.

You had a hand in my death, William! You did not act—

Guilt washed over Spike as he remembered how Buffy had sacrificed herself to save Dawn. There had been no other way then. Long, bitter months had passed before Willow figured out the resurrection spell that had brought Buffy back.

—could have saved me! You chose not to! You and—

Spike knew that wasn't true. He'd tried to save

Buffy. He hadn't been strong enough. Then he realized what the voice had called him. *William.* Buffy had never called him William until that time three days ago in the crypt the day after the demon eggs had hatched.

He stood straighter and glanced around.

With a quick movement, the whirling fog that was there and not-there in front of his eyes coalesced into a wavering, translucent form that had about as much physical consistency as a flashlight beam playing on dust motes.

Features pushed forward from the whirling morass. They were feminine, beautiful and angry and scared all at once. Her hair fluttered in disarray over her shoulders. She wore a gown, something that shimmered and looked soft, something that was meant for the intimacy of a boudoir.

In one frozen instant, Spike recognized her. She was Lyanka, the gypsy woman he'd seen Chavula Faa's demons pursue up the treacherous trail that had wound through the Carpathian Mountains back in 1891.

No, he corrected himself. *I first saw her at Lord Hyde-Pierce's in 1887. Then I met her again in 1891.*

And I died in 1893, William, Lyanka told him. *I died when I cut the bridge free and plunged into the river while you and Angelus and the baying demons Chavula Faa loosed upon my trail watched.*

"I remember you," Spike whispered, and he felt shamed by his part in the woman's death.

More than that, though, he remembered her kisses.

CHAPTER FOURTEEN

Stare Mesto, Prague
February 1891

"Who are you?"

Looking at the woman he'd first met at Lord Hyde-Pierce's manor house in 1887, Spike felt dismayed she didn't recognize him. Of course, he'd been introduced under an alias that he himself didn't remember.

Still, it stung that she didn't remember that she had met him before—especially since he had been prepared to kill her to please Dru. After all, he sometimes still dreamed about her, and—after Angelus had told him he'd discovered her at the circus—he'd been excited about the prospect of meeting her.

Then Angelus had told him he couldn't kill her. In fact, the plan was for neither of them to kill her. Spike hated that. Killing someone was much easier than skulking about. Skulking was really not his forte.

"My name is William, lady." Spike chose to address her in a courteous tone. He took her hand in his and delicately kissed the back of it as he bowed. "At your service."

Lyanka smiled at him, but it was as if at some hidden joke. She gazed around the small outdoor café in the old city.

Lanterns hung on the low wall surrounding the courtyard were kept dim. The café was a place where lovers met for brief trysts, where foreigners gathered to meet others who spoke their native tongue, and where travelers met to discuss the hardships of the roads into and out of the city.

"You're here alone?" Lyanka asked.

"Regrettably," Spike acknowledged. He glanced around as well. Minutes after he had followed the woman through the city and to the café, he had entered the courtyard and taken a corner table. He had not expected her to approach him.

Lyanka looked at the money he'd left to cover the price of the hot chocolate he'd ordered. The coins lay naked on the tabletop.

"Were you leaving then?" she asked.

Spike wished a facile answer would fall into his mouth. He used to think he'd been so good with those. But his confidence in himself waxed and waned with Dru's attentiveness to him. "I was," he admitted.

Lyanka gazed into his cup. "With your hot chocolate hardly touched?"

Spike lowered his voice. "Truth to tell, lady, I am trying to develop a taste for chocolate. It's all the rage in London these days, but I can't quite bring myself to it. Not as long as there is tea."

She smiled at him. "You try to be a fashionable man."

Spike nodded. "It's manners, lady, that separate us from the beasts. Don't you think?"

"I'm no lady," she replied.

"Well then," he said gallantly, "you should be."

Her grin positively dazzled. "Well, Sir William of the Silver Tongue, you certainly have the words to turn a woman's head."

Despite his chagrin at getting caught watching her and the blistering argument he'd undoubtedly have with Angelus once he admitted that she had caught him, Spike felt flattered. He also felt appreciated, something he hadn't felt in weeks around Dru. He hated it when they fought, but that seemed to be part of the whole mix that made them the couple that they were.

Of course, that relationship was made even harder by the periods of madness that seemed to come onto her every so often from the cruelties she'd suffered at Angelus's hands. Spike felt certain Dru would be more attentive to him if only it were she and him. But there was still a lot he was learning from Angelus and Darla about being a vampire that Dru might forget to teach him.

He still remembered the morning after she had turned him, how he had mistakenly stepped out into the sunlight and caught fire. Dru had laughed while he had run back to the horse trough near the carriage house where they had spent the night making love. She'd never mentioned that he wasn't supposed to go out into the sunlight. He'd never forgotten.

And now there was the Slayer. The idea of a young girl selected to be the champion of the world fascinated him. No matter what her powers, Spike didn't see how a young girl could hope to stand against the demons that inhabited the world. But Angelus had spoke of her as if she were some sort of divine instrument.

Perhaps Angelus and Darla were determined to be overly cautious about encountering a slayer, but Spike was starting to look forward to it. There was something erotically alluring about facing an opponent whose sole purpose for existence seemed to be to kill him. One day soon, he hoped to face a slayer. Then he would see the true measure of himself.

"Well then," he responded to her compliment, "if my words have sufficiently turned your head, perhaps you'd care to share my table."

Lyanka glanced around at the other tables. "I've already been rather forward in asking your name. I also find myself bereft of my companions, and I know a young woman should be properly chaperoned in the city. Don't you think it would be scandalous if I now joined you at your table?"

"Lady," Spike declared, looking into her beautiful eyes, "I live for scandal."

With only a little more invitation, Lyanka joined him at his table. Conversation was a little stilted at first because neither of them wished to talk truthfully about why they were there, but they found a commonality in places they had seen, poets they enjoyed, and childhood stories because both of them had been ostracized as children.

When Angelus had first mentioned he had seen Lyanka at the circus and that he wanted to keep an eye on her, Spike had been in the mood to simply kill the woman out of hand. After all, she had caused all kinds of problems for him four years earlier.

He had not counted on falling in love with her, but that was exactly what he'd done in a matter of hours. When the café finally closed, he'd taken her for a long walk through Stare Mesto. She knew more about the city than he did, and he'd delighted in her stories, some of which she admitted she'd made up on the spot.

They parted before the dawn. He'd insisted on escorting her back to her hotel, and she had only put up mild resistance. He hadn't kissed her at the door because that would have been too forward, but he had wanted to.

That impulse surprised him. Spike was consumed with his love and lust for Dru. He had needed her ever since she had turned him, ever since he'd tried to turn his dying mother into a vampire to save her, and had pierced his mother's heart with a stake when she had turned on him.

There had been no one else who had even come close to caring about him.

But in the space of an evening, knowing that poets recognized that love could set a heart aflame with only a glance, Lyanka had made Spike feel that she cared what happened to him.

Glancing up at the graying eastern sky, Spike hurried across the street, dodging around the carriages that carried early risers or were ferrying home those who had been out all night carousing. He stepped into the safe shadows of the alley, trusting that he would find a way to the hotel to the west where they were presently staying while the shadows remained long and certain.

Before he knew it, a hand reached for him, seized his shirtfront, and slammed him back against the alley wall. Spike morphed immediately, feeling his face change as his fangs extended.

Angelus stood before him. Anger twisted his features. "What the hell were you doing?" he demanded in a hoarse voice.

Spike swept his arm across Angelus's wrist and broke the hold as he stepped to the side and back to create distance between them. "What's wrong with you?"

"I asked you to watch the woman, William," Angelus snarled.

Spike got the impression Angelus was barely holding himself back. He kept his hands loose and ready before him. "I did watch her," Spike argued.

"You weren't supposed to let her see you."

"That couldn't be helped."

Angelus cursed, then turned on his heel and paced the alleyway. "I knew I shouldn't have asked you into this. There are too many people to watch. That damned woman and Chavula Faa."

"Who is Chavula Faa?" Spike asked.

Angelus waved the question away. "Don't worry about it."

Spike took a cigarillo from his pocket and ignited it with a Lucifer. When he had the tobacco going properly and his temper under control, and even wore human features again, he said, "Did it ever occur to you that I might be more help if I knew what was going on?"

"No, William," Angelus answered angrily as he spun and faced him. "If I'd wanted you to know all of my business, I'd tell it to you. That's why I only tell you what I want you to know."

"Then you're right. You shouldn't have asked me into this," Spike said.

Angelus cursed again. "I had no one else to ask. It isn't like we're back in the countries we're most familiar with. Your bloodlust has seen to our present state of affairs."

Spike ignored the comment. Perhaps Angelus wanted to pout about it now, but during the killing spree he'd been impressed and intrigued by the lengths Spike had been willing to go to learn his craft. "Maybe you should tell me what's going on."

"No."

"You needed help. Otherwise you wouldn't have talked to me. When you didn't ask Darla first, I guessed there was some robbery in the offing."

"There is robbery in the offing," Angelus snapped.

Spike considered his next course of action carefully. "Who is the gypsy man I've seen you talking to?"

"Again, that's none of your business."

Spike drew smoke into his lungs then let it out. "I've done some checking, too. They tell me he owns the circus."

Angelus doubled his fists and started forward. "Damn your eyes, William! Do stay out of this!"

Spike took a step back, but he wasn't afraid; he only wanted to give himself room to avoid an attack and return a blow or kick of his own. "I can't stay out of this," he replied evenly. "You brought me into it."

"That was my mistake."

"Does Darla know about the woman?" Spike asked.

"No. And if you tell her, I'll rip that dead heart of yours from your chest."

A pang of worry and pain stabbed through Spike. "Have you fallen in love with this woman?" *Please don't let that be the case!* Angelus already had

Darla's love, when she chose to give it, and these days Dru was more interested in spending time with Angelus than with him.

"No!" Angelus denied. "She tried to burn me at Hyde-Pierce's home, and she would kill me now if she had half a chance."

"When did you find out she worked as the fortune-teller for the circus?"

Angelus hesitated. "That first night. The first night we went to the circus."

"You didn't tell me then."

"No."

Spike considered that. With Angelus telling him anything at all, he knew that Angelus was running out of options and the stakes were high.

"Why haven't you already killed her?" Spike asked. "For what she did at Hyde-Pierce's?"

"I've been paid not to."

"Paid?" The concept staggered Spike.

Angelus nodded. "I was paid by Chavula Faa."

"The circus owner?"

"Yes."

"Not to kill her?"

"Exactly," Angelus said. "She's a thief. You saw that for yourself at the manor house."

"So?"

"Chavula Faa believes she is here in Prague to steal something as well. He wants to know what it is."

"Why doesn't he ask her? Or have one of his men follow her?"

"Because he is trying to act as a confidant for her. He doesn't want her to lose trust in him." Angelus shook his head. "I don't know everything he has going on, but his gold is good. And there may be more gold at the end of it. If not, I can always kill her then."

"Do you have any idea of what it is Lyanka"— Spike hesitated—"what the woman is going to try to steal?"

"No. I've been looking into that while you've been watching her. I haven't discovered anything."

"Do you remember what she stole at Hyde-Pierce's?"

"Yes."

"There was money in the manor house," Spike said, "and she passed that up in lieu of the statue she bundled out of there."

"I know."

"For a true thief, cash is easier to handle and easier to use. You and I know that."

Angelus growled in agreement. "There's something more to this, William. I'm puzzled, and I want to know what it is."

Spike smoked the cigarillo quietly.

Angelus glared at him. "She knows who you are now, William. You're going to be worthless when it comes to following her."

"Not necessarily," Spike said. "As a gentleman caller, I might be able to take up even more of her time. She works nights out at the circus. After that, I might be able to squire her around the city. I can see to it that she has no free time."

Angelus smiled. "Until the night she decides to steal whatever it is she's after."

"In which case, when she avoids me, we'll know to watch her more closely." Spike watched Angelus through the curling smoke. "Either way, this could be a good thing."

"Perhaps, William," Angelus said sarcastically. "Unless she loses interest in you before tomorrow night."

Exhausted, Spike fell back into the sweat-soaked sheets. Lyanka fell beside him, naked and rosy with perspiration. Her breath felt soft on his cheek.

"I've never before met any man like you, William," she said.

He rolled on his side and stared at her. "Is that a good thing or a bad thing?"

She touched the corners of his mouth with her forefinger. "Oh, it's a good thing. Over the years, I've been courted by a number of men."

"You make yourself sound positively ancient."

"I'm older than you think."

Spike laughed at her. "Then I had best be prepared. Should I come calling tomorrow night, I'll expect the most horrid hag ever."

Lyanka covered his mouth with her palm. The scent of her blood mixed with her sweat nearly drove him crazy with desire. But he restrained the bloodlust within himself. He could always feed on someone later. Perhaps one of the prostitutes that trafficked in the narrow alleyways. For the moment, though, he wanted to enjoy the fire in the fireplace of her hotel room.

Dru still remained cold to him despite his advances and gifts and poetry. Only last night he'd shown up to walk Lyanka back from the circus and out to a late dinner wearing a black eye Dru had visited upon him. Dru continued to carouse and take lovers, becoming so excessive that Darla was getting cross with her and insisting that Angelus do something about it. Of course, Angelus was thoroughly enmeshed in figuring out what Lyanka was doing.

Out of them all, though, Spike figured that he was having the best time. He was in love, and he felt certain that Lyanka was in love with him too. He couldn't help wondering if she would have felt so relaxed with him if she had known he had crept down the stairs of Lord Hyde-Pierce's guesthouse to murder her.

But that wasn't an issue. She hadn't known that then, and she didn't recognize him now.

"Don't you dare say such terrible things, Sweet William," Lyanka said.

Her careless address of him, the first time in such a manner so like Dru's, momentarily cut him to the quick. Guilt assailed him and stilled the happiness he felt inside at Lyanka's attentions.

She caught the change in the mood at once. Spike

had never met a woman who seemed to know his every thought so well.

"I said something wrong, didn't I?" she asked. She rolled on top of him, worry creasing the laughter from her features.

Spike hugged her, relishing the warmth of her body. "Not you," he said. "Just a voice from the past. A ghost."

Lyanka smoothed his brow. "Someone who hurt you?"

"Yes."

"If I knew who it was, I'd be tempted to tear her eyes from her skull."

"Now that's a bit harsh, don't you think?" Spike disentangled himself and reached for his pants at the side of the bed. He took a cigarillo and Lucifer from his pocket. He lit up, and the brief flame revealed her face a little more.

Lyanka drew away. "Do you still have feelings for her, William?" She brushed hair from her dark eyes.

Spike breathed out smoke. "No," he said, and the instant he lied he knew that Lyanka knew he was lying.

Hurt showing in her own eyes, Lyanka turned away from him.

"I'm sorry," he apologized. "That was a lie. There are still feelings."

"Do you love her?"

Spike hesitated. "Yes."

"As deeply as you say you love me?"

"I don't know. I've never compared the love I feel for you both. Nor do I wish to now."

Lyanka remained turned from him. "Is that where you are? With her? When you're not with me?"

"No. For the last four nights that we've been together, I haven't seen her." That was the truth. Spike wasn't even sure if Dru was coming home these days. He'd been so caught up in all the new and unexpected experiences he was having with Lyanka that the pain Dru had caused within him had dimmed.

"But you haven't forgotten about her?"

"No."

"Why do you think that is?"

Spike paused to gather his thoughts. "She was my first love. No one will ever replace that."

Lyanka said nothing.

Spike wished she would tell one of her stories about a piece of art or history or a poem she had read so the uncomfortable silence stretching between them would be broken. He had never meant to hurt her like this—even if he later killed her.

And he'd never known that he could feel her pain.

"When I say *flower* to you," Spike said softly, "what do you think of?"

Lyanka waited for a short time before answering. "Purple lilac, I suppose."

"Why?"

"I don't know. It was my mother's favorite. We always seemed to have it around the *vardo*."

"And most likely lilac was what your mother used to teach you the word *flower.*" Spike paused. "That's how it is with first loves, Lyanka. At least, that's the way it is for me. But life doesn't stop with first flowers or first loves. It continues on because there are more loves and flowers. Now you know several flowers. And how many lovers have you had?"

"A gentleman wouldn't ask." Lyanka turned to him then, and the smile he knew so well was back in place. "But I do know what you mean. I remember my first love too."

Spike really didn't want to hear about it, but he knew he had no choice.

"I taught him some of the magic that I know," she said. "He had talent for it. Not many of my people these days do. Not for the more involved things outside healing and fortune-telling."

"What happened?"

"I had a secret. Something I had ferreted out from our legends. A thing that had almost been forgotten. I made the mistake of telling him."

"Mistake?"

"He betrayed me." Lyanka lay next to Spike, curling in close and laying her hand over his heart. He quickly picked up her hand from his chest before she noticed that his heart wasn't beating.

"That must have been hard to live with," Spike said as he held her.

"It was," Lyanka admitted. "But it got a little easier after I killed him."

Maybe that wasn't proper bedroom conversation, but Spike found himself falling for the woman just a little more. Then her lips found his again, and he didn't think anything for a long time.

Two nights later, Lyanka drugged him, stole the object she had come for, and escaped before Angelus or Chavula Faa knew. Spike had felt betrayed and angry. He had hated the fact that she had somehow seen through him, knew what he was there for, or had simply decided to jettison him when she chose to move on.

Most of all, he hated the fact that he had developed feelings for her. The emptiness within him created a morose nature that broke out in increased savagery, especially after Angelus wouldn't forgive him the mistake of trusting the woman or pointing out that her escape was his fault. But the morose nature and violence pushed Dru out of whatever funk she had been in, and she'd sought him out again. Her love once more became the balm he needed, his reason for living for a time.

Spike didn't see Lyanka again until the night Chavula Faa's demons caught the woman high in the Carpathian Mountains and trapped her on the bridge. That night, Lyanka had died and he'd never expected to see her again.

CHAPTER FIFTEEN

Los Angeles

Spike stared at the dead woman standing before him.

Lyanka wore the gypsy riding leathers she had worn that night in the Carpathian Mountains. She didn't look any worse for the wear, not like she had when he and Angelus had found her body later.

Except for the fact that I can see through her now, Spike reminded himself.

"What are you doing here?" Spike asked. He glanced through her at the Qorqoth demons, but none of them seemed to notice the ghost. He spoke quietly enough that his voice didn't carry. Arrag's attention remained on the security systems and the brothers were focusing on breaking into the vault. He was just the guy standing at the door, a redundant alarm system.

I need your help, Lyanka told him.

"You're dead."

That's why I'm a ghost, she told him impatiently. *And you're also partly to blame for me being in this state.*

Spike shifted, starting to move away. He'd dealt with ghosts before, and those experiences had never gone well. He didn't know what had brought Lyanka's ghost here now, but he knew things were going to go badly if he didn't get away from her.

Lyanka reached for him. Her fingers passed through his duster, but he felt the coldness of her grasp and the shock was enough to stop him in his tracks.

I can touch you harder, Lyanka threatened.

Across the room, Arrag glanced up at Spike from the monitor. "Anything wrong?"

Spike didn't know what to say for a moment, then realized that the Qorqoth demon couldn't see the ghost. She was there to haunt him alone.

"No," Spike replied. "Everything's jake."

Jake, Lyanka taunted. *You've been watching too many tough-guy movies, William.*

Spike put an edge in his voice. "The name is Spike."

All right, Spike.

"And if you knew what I was talking about," he

added, "then maybe you've been watching too many movies. Thought you'd be busy being dead."

I'm walking the Ghost Roads these days, Lyanka said. *I see all kinds of things. In this world and others. That's how I knew you were here tonight.*

"Beat it," Spike advised. "That little love spell you put me under back in eighteen ninety-one had an expiration date that didn't even make it into the twentieth century."

Like me?

The guilt over her death returned full force to Spike.

I was one of the throwbacks to my people, Spike. I was three hundred seventy-two years old when I died in that river. I could have lived for hundreds more, could have gotten to know my daughter and my granddaughter better. But you helped cut that time short.

"What?" Shock coursed through Spike. She'd always seemed human, *smelled* human, to him.

Lyanka studied him. *You don't know what this is about, do you? The robbery you've agreed to?*

"Look," Spike said, "I came here to do a job, make some money. Go rattle your chains somewhere else. I got over you a long time ago." He spoke softly, hoping Arrag couldn't hear him over the slight noise the brothers were making.

Lyanka smiled. *You never get over your loves. Haven't you noticed that? Your heart isn't as dead as you'd like to think it is.*

"I'm involved right now."

And how is that working out for you?

"Fine," Spike said hoarsely. "Just fine. Couldn't be happier."

Somehow, I doubt that. You never have seemed to have had much luck with women. And now the Slayer? Pining after a woman who is as much a hand-me-down as Dru? Angelus had her first.

Anger surged through Spike. "It's not like that."

Isn't it? I've kept up with you. I can see a lot from the Ghost Roads. Lyanka touched the side of his face. The feel of cool, clean spring water flowed over Spike's cheek.

"Thought maybe you'd have better things to do than check up on me."

I do. I've been standing as a guardian for a long time, but have been able to do so little because my connections to this world have been tenacious.

"Having a problem getting the family to whip up a séance to see Granny?" Spike taunted.

No. My ability to manifest myself and influence actions has always been centered around the Stones.

"What Stones?"

Lyanka looked at him with a trace of sadness in her pale eyes. *Do you know what you're here after, Spike?*

"Art," Spike replied. "Some kind of statue."

It's one of the Founding Stones. The Stone that I died with that night in the mountains when I cut the bridge to escape Chavula Faa's demons. And to escape you and Angelus. The river tore the Stone away from me, as you know, but it turned up again later. The Stone has to surface eventually because of its magical nature. The Seven Founding Stones find one another just as they surely push one another away. They have a magical affinity for one another and their place in this world.

"I don't know what you're talking about," Spike told her.

Lyanka reached for him. Instead of being threatening, the gesture was tender. *You're still upset with me for sneaking out on you all those years ago.*

"I caught hell for that for the next two years," Spike said. "Until we caught up with you again." He didn't want her to know how her leaving had surprised him and hurt him—even without the influence of the spell.

And you betrayed me to Chavula Faa, Lyanka said.

"I didn't—"

Lyanka didn't hear him out. She raised her voice and spoke over him. *We don't have much time.*

"We?" Spike repeated. "And time for what?"

They've come for the Stone. You can't let them have it.

"Me?" Spike couldn't believe it. "You've chosen the wrong vampire to haunt, Lyanka. I've signed on to help that crew get whatever they're supposed to get out of that vault. If it's some kind of Founding Stone, then they're going to get a bloody Founding

Stone. I'm getting fifty thousand dollars for my time and my trouble."

And you believe that money will help you with your star-crossed lover?

"Damn right it will," Spike growled.

You can't let them have the Founding Stone that Willard Hargreave has here. We can't allow that. After you betrayed me—

"I didn't betray you," Spike said. "I only—"

Lyanka stepped closer to him, invading his personal space so that her body meshed with his. The chill of her presence filled him, in direct opposition to the memory of those fireplace-warmed nights in Prague.

I gave my life trying to keep that Stone out of Chavula Faa's hands, she said.

"When you cut that rope and broke the bridge, you thought you were going to escape."

Did I? Would you have taken that chance? Even though you were a vampire?

Spike didn't answer, but they both knew he hadn't dove into the river after her.

Lyanka's "voice" exploded in his mind as she grew more frustrated. *There are Seven Founding Stones. When used in conjunction with one another, they open a doorway to another world. My world. The world my people came from.*

Spike looked at her, watching shining silver tears cascade down her face. They dripped from her chin and disappeared before they struck the study floor.

I learned about that world, she entreated. *I dug for knowledge about it from the old books and parchments the Elders wouldn't let most people into. Only a handful of people knew about the Bridge of Journeyhome. I made the mistake of falling in love with Chavula Faa's brother. He wasn't ever the conniver and power monger that Chavula was. He was just a foolish man that trusted his brother too much.*

Spike felt the pain echoing in her words.

Chavula Faa killed the Elders, Lyanka continued. *He killed them and took their knowledge for himself. Only my family and I knew the truth about the Founding Stones and the Bridge of Journeyhome.*

Spike cursed himself, cursed his weakness for listening to the ghost, knowing he didn't want to be any part of this. He was there to earn fifty thousand dollars. That was all. He needed to stay focused. Instead, reluctantly, he asked, "How long has Willard Hargreave had this Stone?"

It has been in his possession for years. Until now, it has been safe. Hargreave, like Hyde-Pierce, has no idea what the Stone is. Or the power that it brings.

Spike stared through Lyanka at the vault. Doxxil and Muullot continued working at a feverish pace while Arrag manned the security monitor. "Do you think it will be safe here?" He couldn't believe he was actually thinking of tripping an alarm and blowing the robbery. If he did that, he could kiss the fifty thousand dollars—plus whatever he could steal from the vault once the door was open—good-bye.

No. Chavula Faa knows the Stone is here. He has five of the Founding Stones already. My grand-daughter has another. And this one is here. I have been able to keep watch over him at times because of the Stones, but not always because his magic has gotten more powerful. The only thing that makes him vulnerable is his wanderlust. He is like a true gypsy in that respect. Moving requires time to set up his safeguards, and there is no place that can't be reached through the Ghost Roads.

"These people aren't working for Chavula Faa?" Spike asked.

No. They're working for a man at Wolfram & Hart.

"Then Chavula Faa still won't have the Founding Stone. It'll work out for you. Maybe somebody else will have it, but you'll still have your haunting privileges."

Lyanka slapped him. Although her hand passed through his head, the numbing cold that followed created enough of an impact facsimile that his head turned.

"Are you all right?" Arrag asked, peering at Spike from across the room.

"I'm fine," Spike replied. He tried to avoid the reproachful look the dead woman gave him.

"You're acting strange," the Qorqoth demon persisted.

"Getting antsy," Spike replied. "We've been here a long time. I thought you said they were good."

"They are good. I'm more worried about the body of the Urike demon you left out there."

"It's not like I could have eaten the thing," Spike muttered. "I'm a vampire, not some flesh-eating zombie." His irritation at the whole situation grew. He'd been lured into a bad deal by an old and—somewhat—trusted friend, lost out in love, was in debt to a loan shark who had forced him to leave Sunnydale, was presently in town with Angelus, who might be tempted to rip his head off if he discovered him, had thrown in with a trio of Qorqoth demons who probably didn't have his best interests at heart, and was in the middle of stealing an object that was haunted.

None of this was his fault. He hadn't asked to be betrayed, abandoned, destitute, in unsafe territory, or desperate. He wanted a cigarette badly but knew that the mansion was festooned with smoke alarms.

William, Lyanka said, *please.*

"No," he said.

There's a world at stake.

"Not my world. Not my problem. And mentioning stakes? Not a good PR move with a vampire in the picture, love."

William . . .

"Go away," Spike ordered. He started forward and stepped through her in an effort to remind her how insubstantial and inconsequential she was. But even as he moved through her, suffering through the coldness that had been left by her presence, he felt her hot gaze on the back of his neck.

"Bill," Angel called, throwing up a hand and putting on a fake salesman's smile.

Startled, perhaps a little tipsy from the party he'd been attending for a client, Bill Wynowski turned and blinked at Angel. The Wolfram & Hart attorney was a small, round-shouldered man. He was bald, his hair carefully slicked down on the sides, and might have been in his early thirties. He wore a dark suit and carried a leather Gucci briefcase in one hand.

The underground parking garage offered only private parking, so Angel had been forced to walk in from the street. The guy managing the kiosk had been talking on a cell phone and had barely noticed him.

Lilah Morgan's information about her fellow employee had included a listing and license plate number for Wynowski's personal vehicle as well as the party. Once she had the information about the Mercedes, Fred had hacked into the Department of Motor Vehicles, gotten the car's GPS code from the insurance company files, and located the vehicle before Angel could drive to the building where Wynowski was supposed to be.

Angel had stood in the shadows by the car and waited. There was no way he would have gotten past the client's apartment security. Less than five minutes had elapsed, but even that brief time had left Angel alone with dark thoughts that thundered out of the events of 1893 in the Carpathian Mountains. He heard Lyanka's dying voice again and again.

Then, thankfully, Bill Wynowski, attorney-at-law for Wolfram & Hart, had stepped from the nearby elevator with four other people. A couple split off immediately, leaving the lawyer in the company of two young women who were definite hardbodies dressed up in evening wear. Wynowski stood out dramatically.

"You know, ladies," Wynowski said suggestively, "the evening doesn't have to end here." The guy didn't have a confidence problem.

"Oh yes it does," the platinum blonde said with a look of disgust. "You want to use us to make an impression with your buddies, you pay for the privilege. But your pockets aren't deep enough to buy that kind of service."

The brunette shoved her finger into Wynowski's soft chest, driving him back. "And renting arm candy doesn't mean you get to paw me every chance you get."

"I told you that was an accident," Wynowski protested.

"The first time," the brunette said, "I bought that. But the second and third?" She shook her head vehemently. "Nuh-huh. No way. No how."

"You almost broke my finger."

The brunette grinned at him, but there was no

humor. "On second thought, maybe we need to go to your car for a few minutes. If I'd known I *hadn't* broken your finger, I wouldn't have let go."

Wynowski stepped back.

The women turned and left.

Cursing beneath his breath, Wynowski headed for his Mercedes. He manipulated the ignition, then the door lock with his keypad. The car chirped twice in response.

Angel came out of the shadows rapidly. Anxiety thrummed within him, and he allowed the feeling free rein to a degree. He shoved an arm forward, catching the Mercedes's door and slamming it into Wynowski, trapping the lawyer halfway inside the car.

Wynowski opened his mouth to scream.

Covering the lawyer's mouth with a hand, Angel said, "Scream and I'll snap your neck." He stared into Wynowski's eyes. "Do you understand?"

Shaking, the little lawyer nodded.

"I'm going to talk," Angel said, "and you're going to listen. When I'm finished, you're going to give me a name and an address. That's it. A name and an address."

Wynowski's eyes were round with apprehension behind his glasses. Slowly, as if uncertain if he was supposed to respond at all, he nodded.

"*Swift Star*," Angel said. "I want to know about the art shipment from Hong Kong. The one the Barkuk demons almost got away with. Only they were later found dead. Who was the shipment for? Understand?"

Wynowski nodded.

"No screaming." Angel leaned on the door a little harder to emphasize his point and Wynowski's inability to defend himself. Then he removed his hand.

"Willard Hargreave," Wynowski whispered. He quickly added a Laurel Canyon address. "He hired the Barkuk demons to arrange the transport once the piece reached L.A."

"Good." Angel took some of his weight from the car door.

"But Hargreave didn't get the piece," Bill said. "It was stolen later from the . . . men he'd hired to transport it once it reached the docks."

"Who got the piece?"

"I don't know."

Angel stared at him.

"I swear to God, I don't know. I heard it was some gypsies who killed them and took the piece, but I don't know. I wasn't there."

"Who is Hargreave?"

"Just a collector. A demon. He plays the stocks. I help him move his money around. That's all I know."

"Okay, then," Angel said, relaxing. "I don't have to mention that if I find out that you called ahead and warned Hargreave that I'd talked to you that I will come back, do I?"

"No," Wynowski whispered, shaking his head. "But there's something else you might need to know."

Angel looked at the man.

"There are thieves at Hargreave's house tonight."

"How do you know that?"

Wynowski shook with fear.

"Talk." Angel leaned harder on the door. "How do you know thieves are there?"

Air hissed out of Wynowski as the door pressed against him. Angel eased back on the door.

"Because I hired them," Wynowski said.

"Why?"

"To steal something."

"From your own client?"

Wynowski shrugged and looked apologetic. "There's another man who wants something that Hargreave has. I'm trying to broker a deal for the other client to get it."

"What is it?" Angel demanded.

"A statue. A weird rock thing. It's nothing really, but it reminds me of the thing that was stolen last night. Don't know how anyone can even call that thing art. Hargreave has it insured, so it's no big deal. He has a lot of things. He's just an obsessive collector. Probably never even looked at the thing again after he bought it."

"The other client has been putting pressure on you to get this piece?"

"No. It's just that he's a big client at the firm. Lilah Morgan handles him. He's one of the reasons she's gotten the promotions she has the last few years. I thought maybe if I got the piece and gave it to him, maybe he'd think about, you know, seeking another counsel."

Desperation vibrated inside Angel. "How long have the thieves been at Hargreave's?"

"Twenty, thirty minutes. They're supposed to call me when they're done."

"How are they supposed to contact you?"

"My cell phone."

Angel held out his hand. "Let me have it."

Wynowski pulled his cell phone out with difficulty.

"Who are the thieves?" Angel asked.

"Qorqoth demons. The leader's name is Arrag."

"Who's the other client that's interested in the rock that Hargreave has? Lilah's client?"

Wynowski hesitated.

Angel leaned on the door again, harder, then let up.

Wheezing, Wynowski croaked out, "Ivers. Thomas Ivers."

"The name doesn't ring a bell."

"He's a dotcom guy. Heavy into software. Great guy to meet. Friendly. Impressive."

"And he's an art collector?"

"I heard through the grapevine that he was looking for this piece." Wynowski paused, then looked whipped. "Actually, Hargreave told me Ivers was looking for this piece while I was helping him with the other piece. Hargreave considered getting the second piece quite a coup. There's like a set of these things or something."

"Calling either one of those men," Angel grated in a harsh, cold voice, "would be a big mistake." He held up the cell phone. "Calling in and canceling your phone service would be a mistake."

"Got that," Wynowski said, nodding his head. "I know who you are, Angel." He looked stricken, thoroughly cowed. "*Mr.* Angel. You can count on me."

Without another word, Angel turned and walked away. He felt badly about the way he had dealt with the man, but there was a lot at stake. Even his friends didn't know what was truly on the line when the dice rolled.

A cold chill settled over his shoulders as he walked out onto the street. His past constantly reached out for him, but for just a moment he would have sworn he could hear Lyanka whispering in his ear.

He remembered how he had last seen her, how her body had been broken and bloodied by the river. She'd lived for a time, but only a brief time. But in that time she had marked him forever.

Cordelia sipped latte from the Starbucks container as she stood behind the hotel counter and watched their uninvited guests. *If they'd been vampires,* she thought sourly, *we'd never have had this problem.*

In the foyer, Gitana gazed out at the street. Her warriors lounged on the round seat in the center of the lobby and on the floor. Pizza boxes lay scattered everywhere. Despite the tension of the situation, a few of them talked and joked.

"Very professional, aren't they?" Wesley asked at Cordelia's side. He looked worn and haggard.

Cordelia knew she didn't look much better. The mystery surrounding Connor's birth had been hard on all of them. At first, the changes around the hotel involving bringing Connor home, then Angel's sudden zealousness in protecting his son and being everything he could for him had tested all of their friendships. But now with the uncertainty of the Prophecy hanging over their heads and their inability to figure out what it was while trying to deal with the continuing chaos that broke out daily around them, they were getting stretched past their limits.

Cordelia gazed at the gypsy warriors. "They are."

"It's reassuring in a way," Wesley said. "I mean, with Chavula Faa and his henchmen out there somewhere."

"Or scary," Cordelia pointed out. "They're on our side for now, but the instant Gitana changes her mind and declares us the enemy, they'll kill us."

"There is that," Wesley agreed reluctantly.

"Maybe they'll just torture us and maim us," Gunn said, joining them.

"Cheery thought," Cordelia said.

Gunn shrugged. He carried a spiked morning star over one shoulder. "At least we'll get to live." He stared hard at the warriors and raised his voice—a little. "And ain't no way I'm gonna let that happen without cracking a few heads and kicking some butt."

Wesley and Cordelia stared at him.

"Nice speech," Wesley offered.

"Coulda been better," Gunn replied. "Think they heard me?"

"If they didn't," Cordelia said, "you could work on the speech, punch it up a little, and try again."

"I just wish Angel would get back or call." Gunn frowned. "I don't like the idea of us being held hostage while he's out fronting Lilah."

"Angel didn't want company, anyway," Cordelia said.

"They didn't exactly give him a choice," Gunn said.

"Even so," Wesley said. "Angel wanted to handle this by himself."

"I got that vibe too. This kinda feels like personal business for him. Only we're going to get caught in the fallout. Kinda like these whole last few months have been. What with Holtz and his crew showing up wanting to kill Angel."

"Angelus did kill Holtz's family," Wesley said.

"I know." Gunn sighed. "Didn't say the man didn't have his reasons. Just pointing out we were already up to our eyeballs in death and destruction before the gypsies got here."

"There's more that Angel's not telling us," Cordelia said.

"I agree," Wesley said.

"And that's another thing I don't like about the situation," Gunn stated. "If I'm going to put my head on the chopping block, I'd like to know why I'm putting it there."

"Angel has a hard time talking about Angelus," Cordelia said.

"You talk about them like they're two separate people," Gunn said.

"They are. Or were. Or however that works out."

Wesley stared at Gitana. "Whatever Angel is keeping from us," he said, "that woman may know. Possibly it would behoove us to know more." He looked at Cordelia.

Gunn looked at Cordelia as well. "Yeah."

"Me?" Cordelia asked. "You want me to ask her?"

"Don't just come out and ask her," Gunn suggested. "Girl talk. Get her to chat. She's got such a mad-on about Angel killing her granny, maybe she'll just mention it."

"In casual conversation?"

"I doubt," Wesley said, looking at the gypsy woman again, "that woman is very used to anything casual." He looked back at Cordelia. "Still, I would wager it would be a good investment of time. I couldn't imagine that she's taking the waiting any better than we are."

Cordelia knew that was true. Angel had his cell phone with him, but he was either out of range, choosing not to answer, or . . .

Or he's dust, Cordelia forced herself to think even though she didn't want to. *In which case we're all waiting around here for nothing and Chavula Faa could be closing in on the Founding Stones.*

"I'm not the only woman here," Cordelia pointed

out. She glanced meaningfully at Fred, who was still busily searching through archives on the Internet. So far, they hadn't turned up any more history on the Founding Stones. Chavula Faa had been a ghost in a few documents on gypsies, a rogue and an outlaw even by freewheeling gypsy standards, who had vanished in the 1920s.

"Look," Gunn said, "Fred is great. I like Fred a lot. But Fred is not the one I'd send in to get covert information with casual chatter as her primary weapon."

"I agree," Wesley said.

"But you'd send me?" Cordelia asked, not knowing whether to take that as a compliment or be upset because they would send her into the lion's den.

"You're all we got," Gunn said, nodding.

Cordelia gave him a withering look. "So not what I wanted to hear."

"What?" Gunn said. "What did I say?"

"Perhaps you could have been a bit more delicate," Wesley suggested.

"*Delicate?*" Gunn gave a derisive laugh. "We got an army of gypsies armed to the teeth sitting in our lobby. Angel is out searching for magic rocks that will open the doorway to another world. We're risking going up against a major bad guy with some serious mojo on his side. And I'm not being delicate enough?"

Cordelia held up a hand. "Okay. Okay. I'm going to go talk to the witchy woman. If I don't come back,

Connor needs another bottle in fifteen or twenty minutes."

"Cool," Gunn said. "I can do that."

"And a diaper change. I don't want him lying there in a wet diaper."

Gunn frowned. "No prob." He turned his hands palms up and shooed Cordelia toward the gypsy woman.

Cordelia turned and crossed the lobby, conscious of the gazes from the gypsy warriors. Some of them watched her because she was a potential threat to their mistress, but she knew some of them watched her because she was a woman.

Standing at the glass door facing her own reflection, Gitana moved her eyes slightly. Cordelia knew that the other woman had spotted her reflection approaching. Two of the warriors standing near her got up and took defensive positions.

"Let her pass," Gitana ordered.

The guards moved away but remained nearby.

"What do you want?" Gitana demanded. She did not turn around but stared at Cordelia's reflection in the glass.

Oh, this is going to be easy, Cordelia thought. "I thought maybe we could talk. You know, woman to woman."

"Talk," Gitana said.

Cordelia thought about how to approach the subject, then gave up. There was no way to be subtle about it. She faced the woman squarely. "You make

Angel nervous. Now I know he's got this thing about gypsies ever since they returned his soul to his body and let him remember every atrocious thing he ever did as a vampire, and then there was that whole go-to-Hell scene he did after Buffy kind of killed him, but you make him more nervous than I would expect him to be even after all that. I don't think you've told us everything you know."

"You think I should," Gitana said flatly.

There is something! Cordelia's heart sped up, but even though she felt she was on the verge of success, she also felt scared. If there was something, Angel really was nervous about the situation and she wasn't just imagining it.

"Yes," Cordelia said. "You should."

"Why?" Gitana sounded only mildly curious.

"Because we're trying to help you find the Founding Stones."

"Angelus killed my grandmother. I hardly knew her. I was only a child when she was murdered."

"He's not Angelus. At least, he's not Angelus anymore."

"And you trust him?"

"With my life."

Gitana looked at Cordelia's reflection in the window. "Yes," the gypsy woman said. "You are."

Cordelia didn't know what to say to that.

"We pay for our sins in this life," Gitana mused. "Do you believe that? In spite of all this forgiveness you're espousing?"

"Yes." Cordelia had seen more than her share of suffering, her own as well as that of others. "But I also believe in forgiveness and redemption. That's one of the things Angel has taught me. Not taught me, I mean, but one of the things I have seen in him. He can fail, but he's not afraid to acknowledge failure, then pick himself back up and keep going. It's one of his best traits."

At that moment, Connor awoke and howled. The baby's cry was unmistakable in the quiet that lay over the lobby.

Gitana turned to face Cordelia. "That was a baby," the gypsy woman said.

"That was the TV." The woman's instant interest made Cordelia feel defensive. "Probably on a timer and just came on."

Connor continued yelling for his bottle. Gunn left the counter and went to the back office where the baby was resting in his basinet.

Gitana was in motion before Cordelia knew it. The woman swept past her. Cordelia reached for Gitana, then had her hand snatched away by one of the guards.

"Let her follow," Gitana called without looking over her shoulder.

Sandwiched between a pair of guards, Cordelia followed Gitana into the back office. Gunn was just picking the baby up from the basinet.

"Whose baby is this?" Gitana demanded.

"Mine," Gunn answered.

"Mine," Cordelia said at the same time.

They looked at each other, then stepped toward each other and locked in an embrace like they were a loving couple.

Gitana regarded them with a wry smile. "Strange. He doesn't appear to favor either of you." She lifted her hand toward Connor.

The baby stared back at her. Soft light glowed from Gitana's hand and bathed his face. He blinked at her. Then he shoved his fist into his mouth and started gnawing. Drool ran down his round chin.

"This is the vampire's child," Gitana said incredulously as the light went away and she lowered her hand. "I didn't think such a thing was possible."

"It's not," Cordelia said, stepping forward to take Connor from Gunn. "You're wrong."

"I'm not wrong," Gitana said. "And you weren't either. But Angelus isn't nervous. He's afraid."

"Afraid of what?"

Surprisingly, a look of sympathy showed in Gitana's eyes. "Angelus never planned on having a child. How could he?" She shook her head. "They say the sins of the father are visited upon the child. Can you imagine the hard life this child will have?"

Fear rattled Cordelia's chest, and she didn't know how to stop it. She wrapped her arms protectively around Connor. She looked into the baby's eyes. *Where is your father?*

CHAPTER SIXTEEN

Angel crossed Willard Hargreave's landscaped grounds under the cover of a cloudy moon less than twenty minutes after he'd quit the apartment building where he had encountered Bill Wynowski. The drive had been frantic, and he'd kept the information about Hargreave to himself rather than sharing it with Cordelia, Fred, Wesley, and Gunn. Sharing it with his friends meant potentially sharing it with Gitana and the gypsies she'd encamped at the hotel. He didn't know that he was ready to do that.

Almost to the big house, Angel caught the scent of something dead. Following the stench, he located the body of the Urike demon hidden under the weeping willow.

The angle of the demon's neck offered mute testimony that the creature was dead. The fact that the body was hidden told Angel that he hadn't been the only one to invade Hargreave's premises that night. Wynowski had been right: The robbery crew was already on-site.

Amazingly, though, some of the scent that clung to the demon's corpse reminded Angel of Spike. Angel pushed the thought from his mind because he knew that couldn't be true. Spike was in Sunnydale, not in L.A. Memories of Lyanka and all those bloody days over a hundred years ago was summoning up ghosts.

Leaving the corpse where it was, Angel waited till a security guard passed only a few feet away, evidently taking a smoke break while he made his rounds. The man never stopped moving, though, and continued on his way without ever knowing Angel or the dead Urike demon were there.

A few seconds after the guard disappeared from sight, Angel broke cover and ran for the main house. From the coolness of the Urike demon's body, the creature had been dead nearly an hour. Despite the outward appearances of the wall, the powered gate, and the tech that watched over Hargreave estate, the security was somewhat lax if the security teams hadn't noticed a man missing for nearly an hour.

The question was whether the thieves were still on the premises or if they had already gone.

When he reached the house, Angel flattened beside the door at the back. The back door had seemed the easiest point of entry. He climbed the steps and glanced at the door, spotting the electronic lock. Frustrated, knowing that he didn't have the equipment he needed to get past the door, he considered his options.

Breaking into the house would alert everyone, including the thieves, possibly before they were able to finish the robbery. Waiting for the thieves to leave when they were finished with the robbery might make them vulnerable. Of course, he was alone and might not be able to take a group of Qorqoth demons on his own. If they got past him, they might vanish with the Founding Stone. Then they'd call Wynowski's cell phone, which he had, so he might still have a chance at them.

The downside was that if the thieves escaped, the Founding Stone might be floating free for a few days before he was able to track it down. And Thomas Ivers was still an unknown quantity in the mix.

Before he could make up his mind, his eyes still focused on the electronic lock, Angel heard a gentle rustle of noise behind him. By the time he swiveled his head around, he found himself staring at a dark-clad gypsy man who shoved a submachine pistol into his face.

The submachine pistol's front sight cut Angel under the chin. From his mode of dress and the night-vision goggles hanging around his neck, Angel felt certain the guy was not one of the thieves or one of the security teams.

"Busy night, isn't it?" Angel commented.

The gypsy didn't answer. Over the man's shoulder, Angel saw other movement through the trees. *So much for the security systems.*

"You're not a Qorqoth demon, are you?" Angel asked.

The gypsy maintained his stolid appearance.

"That's bad news," Angel said, "because that means you guys just got here too." He set free the demon inside him, borrowing the enhanced strength and speed as his face changed. He slipped a hand behind the gypsy's head and slammed him face first into the glass window of the back door.

A brief stutter of automatic gunfire from the submachine pistol lit up the night before the gypsy warrior dropped lifelessly to the steps.

Then the alarms around the mansion began howling.

I gave my life to protect this Founding Stone, Lyanka told Spike. *All I'm asking is a few minutes of your time. A few minutes of an immortal life. That's not much to ask after everything we shared, William.*

"What we shared?" Spike put as much irritation into his words as he could. Either his voice carried more than he thought or else his body language attracted Arrag's attention.

The Qorqoth demon shot him another suspicious glance.

Spike turned his back to his comrades in crime. "Look," he said. "What we shared was a love spell you bewitched me with. And if I hadn't been out of sorts with Dru, you probably never would have been able to work that particular piece of magic. You got me when I was weak."

I got you because Angelus left spying on me up to you while he dallied around spending Chavula Faa's gold.

"You want to tell me those days meant anything more to you than a frantic roll in the hay?" Spike challenged.

Lyanka folded her arms across her breasts and even looked embarrassed. *You're insufferable.*

"And you're a nag." Spike took out his cigarette pack. "God, outside of *A Christmas Carol*, I didn't know ghosts could be such nags."

The Founding Stone needs to be protected.

"Haunt somebody else," Spike suggested. "Have them protect it. Me, I just want to nail down my fifty large and get back to what I call a comfortable existence."

With the Slayer. Lyanka arched her brows.

"That makes a difference to you?"

She's going to break your heart. You're unlucky in love. I knew that the first time that I laid eyes on you. That was another reason why I chose to enspell you. You believe in love, William. You want it above all things.

"You know what?" Spike fitted a cigarette between his lips. "You're bloody wrong."

No, I'm not. Lyanka looked sad and she shook her head. *I'm not wrong, and you know I'm not wrong.*

"Get away from me."

I can't. You're my last hope.

"Why me?"

Because you helped kill me. You owe *me.*

"I was there when you died," Spike objected. "That's not the same thing. I didn't put you up in those mountains."

You betrayed me to Chavula Faa.

"I did *not*."

Doxxil's voice, filled with excitement, drew Spike's attention. "Arrag," Doxxil called. "We're through the door."

Spike turned around, holding his lighter in his hands, cigarette dangling from between his lips. He watched the brothers grab hold of the huge vault door. Together, the demons hauled the vault open.

Lights were on inside, illuminating built-in drawers and shelves that held statues, paintings, vases, and other items. Spike hoped that a lot of the drawers had money, gems, or bearer bonds. He wanted a bonus for tonight's operation.

Lyanka stepped in front of Spike. *Please. You can't let them have the Founding Stone.*

Arrag grabbed a flashlight and headed inside the vault.

Without thinking, Spike lit his cigarette, took a deep drag, and exhaled smoke. The smoke cloud rose up in the still air inside the study. Only an instant later, the smoke set off the alarm inside the room.

Arrag jerked around at the sound, then saw instantly what had happened. The Qorqoth demon unleashed blistering curses.

Before the strident scream of the fire alarm could go off again, another alarm system shrieked to life.

Moving quickly back to the security monitor, Arrag checked the screen. "Intruder alert," he snapped. "Not the smoke alarm. Someone has breeched the grounds." He glanced up. "Let's get what we came for. Now!"

Doxxil and Muullot heaved the vault door open more.

"Spike," Arrag commanded, "guard the door. Anyone comes in, you know they're not with us. Kill them."

As Arrag led the way back into the vault, Spike spat out his cigarette and crushed it underfoot. He got a better grip on the assault rifle and made sure the safety was off.

Lyanka moved in front of him. *William! Please! I know you once cared for me! Spell or no spell, those feelings you had were real! A woman always knows when she is truly loved!*

"Yeah, well, there are a lot of you ladies out there who don't seem to care," Spike replied. He thought of Dru, and in almost the same instant thought of Buffy as well. None of them ever truly understood him.

I care.

"Too little and way too late," Spike said.

She touched him with a hand and the chill spread down his cheek to his neck. *I had to try to save my people. I still do.*

Before Spike could reply, rapid gunfire ripped through the noisy alarms.

Wait, Lyanka said, then she faded from view as fast as breath on a cold windowpane on a chill spring morning.

Spike trained the rifle on the doorway. He glanced at the vault, thinking how many opportunities he was probably missing by not being inside. He imagined Doxxil and Muullot filling their pockets with gems and bundles of cash while Arrag found the prize they'd come for. *And I'm gonna go home empty-handed. Except for the fifty thousand I signed on for, and which I'll be handing most of to Tarl Dannek because I ended up getting sodded over with those damned demon eggs.* He cursed loan sharks in general and friends in particular.

When Lyanka rematerialized in front of him, Spike was so startled, he slid his finger over the assault rifle's trigger and almost blasted her. "That was stupid!" he told her. "I could have killed you!"

Lyanka stared at him. *Again?*

"Go away."

I can't. Lyanka moved closer to him. Her face took on a pleading look. *Chavula Faa's men have just arrived. They're out on the grounds now, fighting with Hargreave's people. They'll be in here any minute. You've got to get away. You've got to get the Founding Stone away before Chavula's men find it and take it.*

"Brilliant idea, pet," Spike said sarcastically. "We're working on that very thing."

A Urike demon shoved his ugly face through the study doors. Spike squeezed the assault rifle's trigger and shot through Lyanka. The bullets hammered the demon's face into a thousand bloody pieces. The decapitated body slumped between the doors just ahead of a hail of bullets that splintered holes through the doors.

"Spike!"

Turning, Spike glanced back at the vault and saw Arrag emerging. The Qorqoth demon shoved the rock that Spike recognized from the pictures into the backpack.

"We've got it," Arrag said. "Let's go."

"Gonna be hard to go back out the way we came in," Spike said. He emptied the clip into the door, blowing holes through the woodenpanes himself. He replaced the spent clip with one of the full ones he'd taken from the Urike demon he'd killed out on the grounds. "Got security guards out in the hallway."

"Over here." Arrag ran to the right side of the room. He ran a penlight over the shelves of books, and moved selected volumes.

A section of the floor opened up.

Swapping the empty magazine for the remaining full one he had, Spike raced across the room, trying to ignore the fact that Lyanka floated across the wooden floor without apparent effort to remain at his side. "What's this?" Spike asked, peering down into the dark hole.

"Hargreave is a man with many enemies." Arrag shone the flashlight down into the hole, lighting up the narrow confines of the tunnel below. "He has an obsession about leaving himself escape routes. The mansion is riddled with them, but we weren't supposed to use them if we didn't have to. This is the one for the study."

"So this is why you said if we got caught in the study we wouldn't have to worry."

Arrag flashed a tight grin. "This escape route only opens up if the alarm system has been triggered and the vault is open." He played the flash beam around the edges of the hole. "Otherwise, the hatch would open and all you'd see is three-inch-thick steel plating. That's why we couldn't use this route to get into the house."

William! Lyanka called.

A spherical object bounced into the room. A second later, a loud *bamf!* echoed through the study, and vile yellow smoke spewed from the sphere as it continued to roll into the center of the room.

"Smoke grenade," Doxxil said, pulling his black turtleneck up to cover his nose and mouth. "Maybe tear gas. We gotta go."

Arrag dropped into the escape tunnel and led the way. Doxxil and Muullot quickly followed.

Spike turned and looked at the vault with con-
flicted emotions. *All I need is time to make one run
through there. Just one run. If this guy's as wealthy as
Arrag makes him out to be, I can go back to Sunnydale in style.*

In the next instant, three black-clad gypsies wearing gas masks spilled into the room. They carried
automatic weapons and came up firing.

Bullets cut the distance across the room. Most of
them chopped into the hardwood floor or into the
walls, but two of them caught Spike high up in the
chest. Raw pain split his concentration. Snarling and
howling with agony, he raised the assault rifle and
fired into the center of the trio, raking the barrel
back and forth.

The bullets caught two of the gypsies and spun
them away like dervishes.

Those are Chavula Faa's men, Lyanka said.

Spike didn't care. Anyone who hurt him like that
was going to die or be dusted. The molten pain of
the bullets stayed sharp in his chest as he dropped
into the escape tunnel.

Arrag stood below, quickly affixing what looked like
small boxes with wires sticking out of them to the walls.

Spike scanned the boxes, knowing them from past
experiences. "Explosives?"

Arrag nodded. "C-4. Get moving. I can't wait on
you all day."

Spike ran, feeling the cold front that was Lyanka's
ghost nipping at his heels. Memories of those nights

spent in her arms in Prague filled his brain. He also remembered how he'd felt when he'd watched her die. Those had been horrible, long moments.

Of course, he amended, *that was when I thought she was going to stay dead and I'd never see her again.* It had been sad, but had at least seemed permanent and offered closure.

Arrag's heavy footsteps pounded after Spike.

In the darkness, with only the Qorqoth demons' bouncing flashlights illuminating the tunnel, Spike didn't know how far they traveled. He knew the explosives Arrag had planted around the opening had detonated before they'd scarcely gone fifty yards. The blowback had knocked them all from their feet, but they had scrambled back up, all of them bleeding from their noses and ears from the tremendous concussions.

The tunnel ended abruptly.

Doxxil looked panicked for a moment as he played his flash beam around the suddenly tight enclosure. Then he spotted the ladder rungs built into the wall. He climbed to the top and released the hatch, opening to a view of trees immediately above the exit. The starry sky stood out between the branches.

Glancing back the way they had come, Spike saw no signs of pursuit. He took only small comfort in that, then climbed up after Muullot. By the time Spike reached the ground level out in the woods north of Willard Hargreave's property, Lyanka was already waiting.

William. The ghost sounded desperate. Her face held fear and pain. *You can't do this. You don't know all the people you're putting at risk. Chavula Faa has no mercy in his heart. Look at what Faa is doing to Hargreave's security people and all the staff.*

Despite himself, Spike glanced back through the trees and farther down the hill. Hargreave's mansion sat surrounded by flames. The temporary hearing loss he suffered from the C-4 explosions dulled the hammering *whop-whop-whop* of the rotor blades of the sleek executive helicopter that floated above the landscaped grounds. The machine hovered like a vulture waiting for the sun to warm broken-backed prey left on a highway.

Think of what he will do to my people. Some of them are children.

"Leave me alone," Spike muttered. He worked hard to convince himself that none of this was his problem. But he had been part of the reason Lyanka had ended up on the bridge in the Carpathian Mountains with no place to run.

"Did you say something?" Arrag had to shout to be heard.

Spike looked at the Qorqoth demon and shook his head. "No."

"Then let's go." Arrag took the lead, and they ran through the woods. They avoided properties they knew to be as equipped with heavy security as Hargreave's mansion had been. They made good time, and the demons' heaving lungs sounded like bellows around Spike.

Behind them, explosions and gunfire continued to rock the countryside.

Minutes later, Spike and the Qorqoth demons reached the relative safety of the house they'd been given keys to. They gathered at the garage door while the savage din coming from Hargreave's house thundered.

William. Lyanka's voice was harsh and demanding as the five of them gathered and looked toward the sounds of battle.

"What?" Spike snarled before he thought about it.

The three Qorqoth demons stared at him, bristling at his tone of voice.

Take the Founding Stone from them.

Remembering that the demons didn't see the ghost, Spike held his retort and only shook his head. Arrag and the others would think he was just trying to clear his head, but Lyanka would know that he was answering her.

You have to, the ghost said. *I'm not giving you a choice.*

Spike turned his back to her, looking at the Qorqoth demons looking at him. "Well? Are we just going to stand here, or are we going to go?"

Arrag held a shotgun at his side, his hand around the pistol grip. He held the rucksack with the Founding Stone in his other hand. "What's going on, Spike?"

"Nothing," Spike answered.

Slowly, Arrag shook his head. "You haven't been the same since we got inside the study."

Doxxil and Muullot flanked their uncle. Both of them had swords. All their faces were masks of blood from the ear-and-nose leakage.

Spike wiped at the blood on his own face. "Tonight was not exactly what you had planned. Things got a little ragged in there."

"Not my fault," Arrag replied.

"No," Spike agreed, not wanting the demon to think that he thought it was. "Just ill luck. That's all."

"Remember when I told you I could tell if you were lying?"

Spike waited.

"Well," Arrag said, "you're pinging my radar pretty seriously now."

Sighing, knowing he didn't have a choice, Spike said, "That damned hunk of rock you picked up back there is haunted." He waved to Lyanka. "Ever since I stepped inside that study, I've had this ghost yapping at me."

Arrag glanced in the direction Spike indicated, but from his expression, Spike knew that the demon didn't believe it.

"Why haunt you?" Arrag asked.

"Because she thinks I betrayed her and got her killed."

Arrag's eyes narrowed. "Did you?"

"No."

Arrag was silent for a moment. "That's not quite the truth."

Spike silently cursed the Qorqoth demon's empathic abilities.

See? Lyanka said triumphantly. *They know you killed me too.*

Spike turned to her, at the end of his patience and totally frustrated. He couldn't believe the holier-than-thou expression that was on her face. Even if she was right, didn't she realize she was still dead?

"I did *not* kill you," Spike said.

"He's lost his freakin' mind," Muullot said to Doxxil. Unfortunately, with the temporary hearing loss that all of them had suffered from the explosives, he had to talk loud enough for Spike to hear him as well.

"I have not lost my freaking mind," Spike argued, turning to face the brothers.

Muullot and Doxxil took a step back and raised their swords defensively.

"Just take it easy, Spike," Arrag advised. "We're all friends here."

But Spike could tell that they weren't. The Qorqoth demons stared at him with animal wariness in their eyes.

"If that rock is haunted," Doxxil suggested, "maybe none of us should be around it."

"I've heard about stuff like this," Muullot added. "You add a ghost with anything, that's a recipe for disaster."

"So now you guys are gourmet ghostbusters?" Arrag demanded.

Neither brother said anything in reply.

Gunfire and explosions continued to sound back in the direction of Hargreave's mansion.

"This rock," Arrag said, hefting the rucksack, "is worth a quarter million dollars the instant we deliver it to our buyer. We're not going to be around it long. And the ghost can go with the rock if she wants to."

If you let them take the Founding Stone, Lyanka said to Spike, *if you go with them, I will go to the Slayer. I will tell her what you have done. I will tell her about the night that you got me killed, and I will tell her about the night you did not help me save my people when you could have.*

"You can't do that," Spike said, turning toward Lyanka.

I can.

"Buffy won't see you."

She's the Slayer. I know she's seen ghosts before.

Spike knew that too. During the intimate talks he'd had with Buffy, she had mentioned Lucy, the ghost of a slayer she had met in a crypt. And there were others her friends had seen.

She'll see me, Lyanka threatened. *And I'll tell her. You won't go back to your little lover as a champion, William. You'll go back looking like the spoiled, selfish child you can sometimes be. She's already found fault with you.*

Spike wanted to scream. He didn't know how

much information traveled over the Ghost Roads, but he knew it was a lot. He felt completely boxed in. How could everything he was doing get so bollixed up? He'd done it all for Buffy—well, at least most of it.

"Spike?" Arrag called tentatively.

Take the Founding Stone, Lyanka ordered.

"Spike?"

Take it now, William!

Feeling trapped, Spike stood and didn't know what to do. Everything seemed to be coming down on him at once. More than anything, he knew he couldn't live with losing Buffy. And if Lyanka told Buffy how he'd screwed this up, how he'd made the mistake with the demon eggs even bigger, he knew she wouldn't forgive him.

No one in the history of the world can possibly have screwed up so much in so little time, Spike promised himself bitterly. *You've got to have set a new world record.*

"Spike?" Arrag called. "Don't listen to the ghost. Just stay away from the ghost. Stop listening to the ghost and back away now."

Doxxil and Muullot put their hands over their ears and started saying, "Na-na-na-na-na-na-na," like they were going to be infected by a ghostly presence any moment.

In that instant, Spike knew he was going to be the one to break the covenant they had between them as fellow thieves. He was going to betray them.

Betrayal is easy for you, Lyanka accused him.

Spike didn't know if she was referring to what he was about to do, or if she thought he was going to betray her. He looked at Arrag, knowing that he didn't have a choice. "I'm sorry, but I've got to—"

"Kill him!" Arrag ordered, bringing the shotgun up.

CHAPTER SEVENTEEN

Lifting the assault rifle, Spike aimed toward the center of Arrag's chest and squeezed the trigger. The bullets slapped into the Qorqoth demon's flesh and knocked him backward in stumbling steps. Panicked, knowing the Qorqoth demons would kill him if he gave them the chance, Spike didn't stop firing till the weapon cycled dry. Arrag would be the worst of his one-time partners to face in a fight.

Roaring in shock, fear, and rage, Doxxil and Muullot threw themselves at Spike with their swords uplifted.

Spike reacted automatically, stepping to one side

and blocking Doxxil's sword with the barrel of the assault rifle so hard that the Qorqoth demon stumbled in front of his brother. Both demons went down in a heap. Reversing the assault rifle, Spike slammed the metal-plated butt into the demons' heads repeatedly, feeling like he was playing a weird riff on Whack-A-Mole.

Bloodied and battered, Doxxil and Muullot went down. Neither brother seemed to have the strength to get back to his feet.

Spike! Lyanka yelled.

Turning to face the ghost, Spike roared, "Back off! Haven't you done enough yet to jinx me?" He didn't feel bad about killing Arrag or beating the brothers bloody; they would have killed him if they could have. They all deserved to die after turning on him like that.

What hurt Spike most was that he might have screwed up the deal for the rock or the Founding Stone or whatever the hell it was. He needed that money. He needed Buffy. More than anything, he wanted to be back in Sunnydale in his crypt—properly fumigated, of course, and with candles and maybe a few rose petals strewn about—and have Buffy in his arms.

Get the Founding Stone, Spike, Lyanka said.

Spike paused only long enough to feed a fresh magazine into the assault rifle. Then he strode toward Arrag.

The Qorqoth demon was shaking through his

death throes. His eyes moved wildly in their orbits. Blood misted his breath and flecked his chin.

"You shouldn't have panicked," Spike told the dying demon. "Your own fault. You were a pro. You should have known to hold it together. You should have trusted me to do the same. You made a stupid mistake, and you died stupid for it." He shook his head. "That shouldn't happen to anybody."

Arrag reached for him, but the demon's hand dropped lifelessly back to the pavement. Blood pooled all around the Qorqoth's corpse.

Spike rifled through the demon's pockets and found the keys to the van parked in the garage. He grabbed the straps of the rucksack and hoisted it over his shoulder. Keeping the bloodstained assault rifle in one hand, he ran to the garage door, knelt to hook his free hand under it, and yanked the door up.

The garage door locks shattered with harsh metallic screams. Shrilling on its runners, the door slid up into the housing slightly off-track. The security lights exploded with white-hot incandescence. Braying burglar alarms added to the din already coming from Hargreave's mansion.

So much for lying low, Spike thought as he used the electronic keypad to open the van's door and slid behind the wheel. He dropped the rucksack between the captain's chairs, then keyed the ignition and smiled a little when the engine caught the first time. Arrag took good care of his tools.

Everything was going well until Lyanka materialized in the passenger seat. "What the hell are you
doing here?" Spike demanded.

You're not leaving me! she yelled back at him.

Spike didn't waste time arguing, and it wasn't like
he could actually stop her from coming. He dropped
the transmission into reverse, then turned and
peered back over his shoulder at the garage door.

Why did you set off all the alarms?

"Because you pissed me off and because I bloody
well felt like it. And I didn't want to give Tweedledee
and Tweedledum time to recover. If they're going
to." Spike stomped the accelerator. The tires burned
the pavement as they fought for traction. When they
grabbed hold, the van shot out of the garage like a
gazelle bolting in front of a lioness.

Doxxil—or Muullot, Spike wasn't sure—stood up
and stumbled into the van's path. The Qorqoth
demon was obviously still dazed from the beating
Spike had given him. The impact broke the doors
loose at the rear of the vehicle, then the van jumped
and jerked as the tires rolled over the demon's body,
followed by Arrag's corpse.

You hit him! Lyanka cried, twisting around in the
seat to stare at the two demons Spike had driven
over.

"Speed bumps," Spike growled. "I hate speed
bumps." He cut the wheel sharply as the van slewed
out into the street. Lights were already on in
several of the surrounding houses. He pulled the

transmission into drive and floored the accelerator again, reaching down to snap the lights on. The beams cut tunnels in the darkness that filled the quiet neighborhood.

What are you doing?

"Getting out of here." Spike took the next corner on two wheels and never backed off the accelerator. He aimed the van rather than drove it, scraping the vehicle against cars parked at the sides of the street and hammering through yard ornaments and signs.

Where are you going?

Spike glanced at her. "I hadn't thought that far ahead yet. You see, I hadn't figured on having to kill the guys I pulled this job with. That kind of caught me unawares. So now I'm just making it up as I go along. I'll work out a plan when I have time to sit down and think again."

Without warning, Lyanka screamed and pointed ahead of them.

Jerking around, alerted by movement in his peripheral vision, Spike saw the dark bulk of the huge service van almost too late. He yanked on the wheel and barely got out of the larger vehicle's way as the driver honked frantically. The service van caught the van's side, anyway, and scraped the entire length, shredding the side mirror and throwing up a fireworks display of sparks in all directions.

Cursing, Spike kept control of the steering wheel. He caught sight of Lyanka getting thrown through the windshield, but—since she was a ghost—she slid through without breaking anything or needing an exit. He glanced up at the rearview mirror and watched her get to her feet in the middle of the street behind him.

Good riddance to bad ectoplasm, Spike thought as he took the next turn in the street. He hoped he remembered his way out of the neighborhood. He'd paid attention coming into the area, but he was amped up now and couldn't trust what he was remembering without a doubt.

He reached under his duster, felt his own blood smear across his hand from the two chest wounds, and took out his cigarette pack. He shook out a smoke, then got his lighter, cupped both hands on the steering wheel, and lit up. The first deep drag felt great. Life suddenly seemed good again. It was also possible that he could get out of the entire situation smelling like—

"Crap!" Spike bellowed as Lyanka materialized in the rearview mirror seated in one of the chairs. "I thought you were gone for good."

I died for that Founding Stone, William. You won't get rid of me with a slight traffic accident.

Spike blew out smoke, then rolled down the window to let it out. "That's fine," he said. "I'll be rid of you soon enough."

What are you going to do?

"Me?" Spike smiled like a cat. "I'm gonna call up Arrag's buyer and finish this little transaction." He pointed the cigarette at her reflection in the rearview mirror. "If you want to keep haunting that hunk of rock, you're welcome to it. I hope you and the new owner are happy together."

Lyanka folded her arms and looked smug. *You don't know who Arrag's buyer was. I can see that in your thoughts.*

"Well then," Spike said, "you should also know that I've got the buyer's phone number memorized. Arrag wasn't as careful as he'd thought he was being when he was flashing paperwork around."

More anxious, obviously reading the truth in his words, Lyanka leaned toward him and said, *The Founding Stone needs to be taken to my grand-daughter.*

On a stretch of clear highway now, Spike fumbled through the caddy at the bottom of the dashboard where Arrag had kept all of his personal stuff, including maps, a GPS, and a cell phone. He grabbed the cell phone and punched in the numbers he'd seen in Arrag's paper.

The exchange was located in Los Angeles. Below the number, in Arrag's neat handwriting, a short message said, *Wolfram & Hart. Bill.*

"Get Bill to do it," Spike suggested. *If Bill's a guy instead of just a note of where to send the bill.*

Lyanka reached for him, but her hand passed through him, leaving a trail of cold goose bumps. The cell phone crackled with interference but didn't quit ringing.

Spike kept his foot heavily on the accelerator. It

wouldn't take long before the sheriff's department responded to the attack at Hargreave's mansion.

The phone rang four times.

Spike was almost ready to give up when a man's voice answered. "Hello." The voice was incredibly and unbelievably familiar at the same time.

Disbelief filled Spike as he recognized the voice. He was paralyzed with shock for a moment. Then he punched the End button and broke the connection.

Lyanka sat up straighter in the passenger seat. *That was Angelus!*

"Can't be," Spike argued. Angel couldn't have been the buyer for the piece. *Unless he's got himself onto a bad deal, too.*

I knew his voice. So did you.

Spike dropped the cell phone in his duster pocket. Renewed agony flashed through him from the two wounds in his chest.

Angelus is here in Los Angeles, Lyanka said. *I have heard of him. I was told he was different, that he had been rejoined with his soul.*

"Oh, he was different all right," Spike said. "That was a real bothersome experience. You wouldn't believe the whiner he turned into. 'Oh, all the evil I have done. I have been such a bad, bad vampire. Yadda, yadda, yadda.' I tell you, it was enough to make you hurl." He shook his head wearily. "By the time Angel left with his tail tucked squarely between his legs, everybody was ready to dust him."

What about Darla? Surely she stood by him.

"Nope. Darla was pretty much sick of the whole 'poor me' scene too. And, lately, she's had her own problems." Spike smoked and tried to think but it only made his head hurt. "Darla's dead three times now. I heard she was human for a time too. Till Dru came along and turned her into a vampire again. Where she went from there, I have no clue. I don't bother to keep up." He glanced at her. "I thought you knew all this stuff."

Lyanka shook her head. *No. I knew about you, William, because I was closer to you than any of the others. I don't know how I'm tied to this world, other than through the Founding Stones, but I know that you're part of that. You became part of it when I met you. Or maybe I had the feelings I had for you because you were destined to be part of the recovery of the Stones.*

"No way." Spike pointed at her with his cigarette. "You know what that bit of business back then was? Bad bloody luck. That's all. I know about bad luck because I've had me a ton of it lately. You're just the latest in a long line." He pressed the Redial button on the cell phone, thinking maybe Bill—whoever he was—only sounded like Angel.

"Hello?"

Damn, but he sounds like Angel. Gunfire sounded in the background, just like what was no doubt happening back at the Hargreave mansion. Spike made himself remain calm. "Bill?"

There was a pause. "Spike?"

Cursing, Spike punched the End button again. There was no doubt about it: That was Angel, all right. But what the hell was Angel doing answering Bill's phone?

Crouched down inside a smoke-filled hallway inside Willard Hargreave's mansion, Angel looked at the viewscreen on the cell phone he'd gotten from Bill Wynowski less than an hour ago. The phone had Caller ID as part of the service package.

UNKNOWN NUMBER.

Whoever had called had made two attempts. Both times the Caller ID had flashed UNKNOWN NUMBER. The second time, though, Angel had thought he'd recognized Spike's voice at the other end of the connection, even in spite of the noise all around him.

Gunfire echoed through the hallway, but the bursts were growing more sporadic. Hargreave's on-site security team wasn't a match for the gypsies, but they had no choice about fighting. The gypsies hadn't invaded the mansion and the estate grounds to take prisoners. They'd come to kill and to conquer, and they had done that virtually within minutes.

Angel pocketed the phone and stayed flat against the wall. The rumble of voices reached his ears from both ends of the hallways. After he had put the first gypsy's head through the window to set off the alarms, the others hadn't been shy about showing themselves. The only plus had been that the mansion's security team had boiled out to intercept them and had provided at least a small diversion for Angel to make his way inside. The fact was, he was able to prove that whoever Hargreave might be, he was also not human. Either that, or the arriving gypsies had already killed him.

Knowing that the lower floor would be sealed off first and escape from there would be almost impossible, Angel turned and made his way to the far end of the hallway. Entering the great room, he spotted a guard posted at the double-wide front door. Angel waited till the guard had his head turned, sweeping his gaze over the outside grounds, then bolted for the long staircase that led up to the mansion's second floor. He leaped to the top stair in three great bounds, throwing himself to the floor behind the railing as a large man he recognized from a long time ago entered from a hallway on the other side of the room.

The big man had changed somewhat over the intervening years, but his size set him apart. Angel hadn't seen many human men as big as the man. He tried to remember the man's name but couldn't. The thing Angel did know was that the man had been one of Chavula Faa's warriors back in 1891 at the circus in Prague, and in 1893 in the Carpathian Mountains.

"Yes," the big man said. He had lifted his left arm and was talking into a microphone affixed to his wrist. "No, master, the Founding Stone has not been found yet. We are looking now, but I believe that whoever reached this place before us has already taken it. We will continue the search as long as we are able, but I have been told that the law enforcement agencies have been notified and are on their way."

Moonlight skated through one of the second-story windows overlooking the great room. The silvery illumination touched the scar splitting the man's eyebrow.

"No, master, we'll stay here as long as you see fit," the man continued. "There has been no sign of the vampire."

A gypsy came running up, holding a walkie-talkie in one hand. "Tobar," the man called.

Tobar looked at the gypsy coming toward him. "What?"

"The helicopter pilot has spotted something you should know about." The man stopped and hooked a thumb over his shoulder. "There was a gun battle about a mile away. The phone lines we've tapped into to monitor the neighbors have indicated that three demons have been left for dead there. A vehicle fled the house where they were."

"Get the helicopter down there," Tobar ordered. "I want to know who those demons are and where that vehicle is."

The gypsy sprinted away, cradling a submachine pistol and talking into the microphone at his wrist.

Tobar turned back to the first guard he was talking to. "Get this house shut down. If Hargreave is still alive, I want him brought in that way."

The man spoke into his own microphone.

"Master," Tobar said, "I will keep you apprised of the situation."

A red laser dot suddenly tracked across the floor in front of Angel and got his immediate attention. He was in motion, rolling sideways, even as he looked forward and saw the gypsy warrior who had stepped from the hallway in front of him. Bullets tore into the hardwood floor where Angel had been, ripping long splinters from the elegant finish.

Angel flipped to his feet and grabbed a heavy Chinese vase in a nearby niche in the wall. He threw the vase toward the gypsy with all his strength. A burst of gunfire shattered the vase in midflight, but most of the jagged shards still slammed into the gypsy warrior, staggering him for a moment.

By then, Angel was in motion, driving his feet hard against the floor as he streaked for the window at the other end of the hallway at the top of the second-floor landing. More bullets fired by Tobar and the other guard in the great room smashed the railing to pieces, staying within just inches of him.

Steel security bars covered the window. Angel stopped in front of the window as bullets thudded into the wall, ceiling, and floor around him. He kicked the steel bars twice before the frame gave way and ripped free of the wall. Once the bars dropped away, he threw himself through the window. A round caught him in the shoulder, knocking him off-balance. He landed face first on the ground, his shoulder screaming in agony.

Dazed, spitting dirt from the flowerbed, Angel climbed to his feet. Solar-powered ground-effects lights threw off his night vision, blurring the figures in the distance that were already closing in on his position. Bullets tore holes in the ground, destroying hibiscus, bougainvillea, and roses in a panorama of colors.

Angel ran, ignoring the pain in his shoulder. His stride was off at first, not quite in sync. Then his arms and legs got together, and he ran at full speed. He left the gypsies behind. Maybe they were faster than a normal human, but they were no match for his speed.

When he reached the high security wall around the estate grounds, Angel leaped up, caught the edge, and hauled himself over easily. He turned to the right and ran the mile and a half back to his car. He leaped into the Belvedere and shoved the key into the ignition, getting underway immediately. So far, the highway was empty.

He took Wynowski's cell phone from his duster pocket and checked the Caller ID again.

UNKNOWN NUMBER.

Angel pressed *69 and Talk, hoping that the redial function would allow him to get through to the phone number the caller had dialed from. The phone rang and rang. No one answered.

Irritated, Angel put away the captured cell phone

and took out his phone. He didn't want to leave a trail in case Wynowski decided to have the records of his cell phone activity pulled.

Lorne answered on the first ring. "Angel Investigations. We help the helpless."

"Lorne," Angel said, surprised to find the demon on the other end of the line.

Before his club had been blown up shortly before Connor had been born and Darla had died in the alley, Lorne had been the host of Caritas, a karaoke club that catered to humans as well as demons. Lorne was an Anagogic demon and a native of Pylea, the dimension Fred had accidentally fallen into. After finding a portal of his own, Lorne had crossed over and made his way to L.A., following his interest in singing. He had, for a time, been very successful.

After the club had blown up during a battle over Darla, Lorne had moved into the hotel. The last few days he had been scouting for a new location for a new Caritas, or a job—whichever came first. Although he'd proven invaluable during the events in Pylea and other cases, Lorne insisted his first calling was as an entertainer, not an adventurer.

"Angel," Lorne effused, "baby. You have been such a bad little detective. Not calling in like that." He made *tsk*ing noises. "You know everyone has been worried to death about you."

"I had something to do," Angel said.

Lorne lowered his voice, dispensing with the lighthearted banter and becoming intensely serious.

"You know, if I had known that I would be stepping into a hostage situation here at the office, I wouldn't have come back. I could have spent another couple of days with a friend. Someone could have called and warned me."

"Didn't think to call," Angel said truthfully. "We've been kind of busy the last couple of days."

"Doesn't help me not be a hostage." Lorne sighed as though he were carrying the weight of the world. "By the way, I want you to know this is a very *tough* crowd. I came in, saw the entire gypsy wardrobe thing going on, and thought this was a shoe-in for Cher's 'Gypsies, Tramps, and Thieves.' You know, the whole, 'I was born in the wagon of a travelin' show.' Thought I'd get a good response, if not rave reviews."

"Probably not a good choice," Angel said.

"I kind of got that when they shoved a gun in my face and told me to sit down and shut up."

"Hard to miss."

"I didn't have to buy a vowel after that," Lorne agreed. "Though I could have moved a bowel."

"Where's Cordelia?"

"This is the brush-off?"

"Got things to do," Angel said.

"What are you doing?" Lorne lowered his voice. "A lot of people around here—we'll call them gypsies who aren't into classic rock—are getting antsy. There's talk of killing people because you haven't been answering your phone. I wouldn't have been fond of the idea, anyway, because I like the people they're planning on killing, but now that I'm one of those people, I like the whole idea a lot less."

"Is that Angelus?" Gitana demanded in the background.

"Whoops," Lorne said. "Busted. Hold on." His voice retreated from the phone. "It's nothing. Just checking on my dog. Wanted to make sure that Fluffy was doing all right after the big snip. When I took him in to the vet, both of us were cringing, I tell you."

"Let me have that phone," Gitana ordered, coming closer with each word.

"You want to talk to my vet?" Lorne asked.

"It's after one o'clock in the morning," Gitana said. "You really expect me to believe a veterinarian is up tending to your dog at this time?"

"Fluffy is a very special dog," Lorne insisted.

"Give me the phone or I'm going to shoot you through the head."

Lorne returned to the phone. "Angel? Gotta go. Take care. I'll be seeing you soon. I hope. *Chow*."

"Angelus?" Gitana said a moment later.

"Yes," Angel replied.

"Where are you?"

"On my way in. I found one of the missing Founding Stones."

"Good. Bring it back here and your friends will live."

"I can't. I didn't get to it in time."

A tense silence followed. Then, when she spoke,

Gitana sounded angrier. "You're playing with the lives of your friends. And with the life of your son."

A pang of despair rocketed through Angel. He'd known keeping Connor a secret from the gypsies was going to be impossible. "If you know about my son, then you know that I'm as involved in this as you are, Gitana. Think about it. My son is already at risk because of Lyanka. Getting those Stones back to you may be the only hope my son has."

Gitana was quiet for a moment, then spoke in softer tones. "What happened?"

"There's another collector involved. His name is Willard Hargreave. His house was broken into tonight, and a lot of people were killed. The story will probably be on the news in minutes."

"I'm listening."

"I saw Tobar here," Angel said. He shrugged his shoulder, trying to ease the throbbing pain that filled his arm. "Do you know Tobar?"

"If Tobar was there," Gitana said, "he was sent by Chavula Faa."

"Agreed."

"Did they get the Stone?"

"No. Someone else did."

"Who?"

"I don't know. Yet. I'm working on it. Does the name Thomas Ivers mean anything to you?"

"No. Should it?"

"I don't know. His name came up in a conversation that I followed up on. I wanted Cordelia to check up on him, find out what she could."

"You're on your way here?"

"Yes. I'll be there in twenty minutes or so."

"I'll get Cordelia."

Angel listened to the indistinguishable voices in the background for a while. Then Cordelia picked up the handset.

"Hello? Angel?"

"Here, Cordy."

"Waiting around to see if my head ends up on a pike?" she said with a note of exasperation. "So not good."

"I'm on my way there."

"I know. I knew you wouldn't run out on us." Cordelia hesitated. "There's something you need to know. Gitana knows about Connor. She knows he's your son."

"I know."

"After that, she also said that she knew you would do what you could to help her. I thought she was threatening Connor, but she said she didn't have to."

"She doesn't have to," Angel replied.

"Because Connor is already threatened," Cordelia said.

Angel didn't want to answer, but he knew he had to. Cordelia was his friend, and for now she was a mother figure for his child. He was coming to realize there was a lot of power in that. It was easier than it had ever been to talk to Cordelia.

"Yes," Angel admitted.

"I need to know what's at stake," Cordelia said in a gentle but firm voice. "We need to talk."

"We will," Angel answered, but he didn't offer to tell her everything. He was afraid that once he did, Cordelia would respect him less. No matter what he did, he would never truly be free of the shadow that Angelus's past left.

Glancing to his left, Angel watched as a helicopter leaped up from the ground in the neighborhood near Willard Hargreave's estate. The aircraft heeled over and shot toward the city, letting Angel know his enemy could move and strike faster than he could.

CHAPTER EIGHTEEN

Chavula Faa stood on the helipad of the office building he owned and watched the Bell helicopter executive model touch down. The rotorwash slammed into him, pulling at his clothes and bringing in some of the night chill that seeded the wind coming in from the Pacific Ocean.

The lights of the city combated the hovering darkness of the night, giving it the appearance of a bottled city, cut off dramatically by the San Gabriel Mountains to the north.

Tobar opened the wide cargo door. Seats filled the cargo area. With his weapons strapped around him, the big warrior climbed from the helicopter, looking like a hero stepping from the belly of some incredible mechanical beast. Tobar stood outside the helicopter for a moment and swept the helipad with his fierce gaze.

Faa shook his head, letting the other man know it was only them on the building's rooftop.

Reaching back into the helicopter, Tobar hauled out a Qorqoth demon that was covered in blood. He carried the limp demon easily in one hand and dropped him at Faa's feet.

The helicopter pilot guided the aircraft back into the air, falling away from the building for a moment before gaining altitude.

Faa looked down at the unconscious demon. His legs were shackled together, and his hands were handcuffed behind his back. "This is the only one that survived?"

"There were two that still lived," Tobar said. "I didn't think the other one would survive the trip here. And I only had room for one."

"What about the other demon?"

"I killed him."

Faa surveyed the Qorqoth demon's dark clothing, seeing the blood that stained all his garments. "Are you certain these men were involved in the theft from Hargreave's mansion?"

"Yes. I questioned him. He told me he helped steal the Founding Stone from Willard Hargreave's home."

"Did he give the information freely?"

"He thought he was trading that information for the life of his brother."

"Now that you've killed the brother," Faa said, "he might be harder to talk to."

Tobar acknowledged that with a nod. "As always, I place my faith in you, master."

Faa let go of the argument. Tobar was the most loyal member of the men that followed him. His shortcomings over the years were few. "You said there were three Qorqoth demons. If you can account for them all, where is the Founding Stone?"

"There was a fourth thief, master," Tobar explained. "A vampire."

Wariness twisted inside Faa. "Angelus?"

Tobar shook his head. "Angelus was there, as I told you. But this was someone else. The Qorqoth demons used the vampire they had recruited to get past the heat sensors at the mansion." He nudged the unconscious demon with the toe of his boot. "This one, he described the vampire to me. He has a slight built, with peroxided hair and an English accent."

Faa looked at Tobar. "An English accent?"

"That's what he said."

"Did you ask the vampire's name?"

"I did, but that was after I executed the demon's brother and this one was reluctant to answer. I broke his fingers to get his attention, but he passed out from the pain." Tobar shrugged. "Or maybe his wounds are more serious than I had believed."

337

William. It can't be. Faa knelt beside the fallen demon. *Surely not both Angelus and William can be in L.A. at this time.*

After Lyanka's death, Faa had kept track of the two vampires—four, actually, counting the two women—but hadn't discovered much. Angelus had dropped out of sight around the turn of the twentieth century. Only occasional references came to Faa about William. None of the vampires had been involved with his clan or Lyanka's since.

Whispering the words of the spell, Faa placed his hand on the demon's bloodied head. Instantly, images flooded Faa's head. He saw the peroxide-haired vampire in the demon's thoughts, watched as they pulled the robbery off. Then the blond vampire shot the Qorqoth demon leader with an assault rifle.

But more than that, Faa felt the lingering effects of other magic.

Faa drew his hand back, ending the spell. "This one has magic on him. There is a binding spell on him that we can use to track the vampire. See to it that he's kept alive."

"I will, master." Kneeling, Tobar gently picked the unconscious demon up as if he were a child.

"The vampire was William," Faa said, still struggling with what he had seen.

"The one who has become known as Spike?"

"Yes." Faa remembered what he had seen. "William attacked them. He shot their leader and beat down the brothers."

"This one told me that. He said that Spike informed him the Founding Stone was haunted."

"Haunted?"

"By a woman."

Faa stared at Tobar and felt unsettled. The gypsy leader knew that ghosts existed, had even trafficked with some of them himself, but he'd never before heard of a ghost manifesting around the Stones.

It was, Faa knew, something to consider.

"What is the ghost's name?"

"This one was not told. Things happened very quickly when they went wrong."

"Where is the Stone?" Faa asked.

"I don't know. The vampire fled."

"Get this man into my office. A doctor is waiting. Once he is stable, we will use him to find the vampires. Then we will find the Stone." Faa gazed out over L.A., realizing he would have to leave soon, probably never to return for decades. He would miss the city too. But he thought of the beautiful world that lay across the Bridge of Journeyhome. It would be all his for the taking, and he had an army standing ready.

"Once we get this Stone," Tobar said, "there still remains the Stone that Gitana and her clan have."

"We'll get it," Faa stated calmly. "Gitana is in this city as well. She won't have traveled without the Stone. Once we find the vampire, then we'll find her."

"That is Chavula Faa," Gitana said, staring at the face on the computer monitor in the hotel lobby. "He has changed, but I would know him anywhere." She stood with Angel, Cordelia, Gunn, Wesley, and Fred at the counter. After Angel's return, she had lightened up and was no longer as defensive as she had been. But there was still no doubt that they were more prisoners than compatriots.

Angel stared at the hawk-faced visage. The picture was on the cover of *Newsweek*. It was the best picture Fred had been able to find of Thomas Ivers during her search. The man had been in other pictures, but he had always managed to get caught only partially, never a clear-cut shot. The *Newsweek* picture caught the man in three-quarter profile, but there was no mistaking his identity.

"I know him, too," Angel said, remembering how Faa had looked when they had first met back in Prague in 1891.

"Definitely a photogenic guy," Gunn commented. "With looks like that and all the money he's raking in, you'd think he'd have his face plastered all over."

"Doing that would make it somewhat difficult to conceal the fact that you're a man who has lived a few hundred years, don't you think?" Wesley asked.

"Okay," Gunn acknowledged, nodding. "There is that. But you can just look at this guy and know he's all about himself."

"Ow!" Pain blazed through Angel's shoulder as Cordelia continued to treat the gunshot wound he'd acquired at Willard Hargreave's mansion. He yelped again and pulled out of her grasp.

"Baby," Cordelia said, holding the bullet between the bloody jaws of the forceps.

"That was deep," Angel said, "and the flesh may be dead, but that doesn't mean it's unfeeling."

"Not you 'baby.'" Cordelia handed him the forceps. "*The* baby. Connor's awake and wanting a bottle."

"Oh." Angel took the forceps. He listened more intently and made out his son's plaintive cries. "I didn't hear him." He felt guilty about that. *I'm his father. I should have heard him.*

Wesley looked at Angel. "You probably would have if he'd cried again."

"She got him on his first cry?" Angel put the forceps on the surgery tray they'd been using. "And you heard it too?"

"Cordy is getting really good at hearing Connor when he wakes," Gunn said. "You'd think it was her mutant ability or something."

"You're probably just tired," Wesley said.

Angel felt the guilt eating at him. "You know what it is, don't you? With everything going on, the Prophecy and all that, I'm not spending enough quality time with Connor. I can't even hear him when he cries."

"That's not your fault," Wesley said.

"Of course it's my fault." Angel slapped antibiotic salve on his shoulder and tried to adhere a gauze pad to the wound. "Who else's fault could it be?"

"Let me get that for you," Gunn suggested, indicating the bandage.

"I can do it," Angel said, brushing Gunn's hands away. "Maybe I can't hear my kid when he cries, but I can still take care of myself." The bandage continued to refuse to fit. The gauze pad slipped repeatedly across the salve. He threw it on the surgical tray in disgust. "That bandage is defective."

"That bandage," Cordelia said, returning with Connor in her arms, "is fine. *You're* defective." She held Connor upright. "Hey, Connor, see who's here? See Daddy? Wanna watch me put a bandage on Daddy and see him cringe? C'mon. It'll be fun."

Despite the pain and doubt that he felt, the insecurity and guilt that nagged at him constantly, Angel couldn't help but smile at his son. Connor was magic. Exactly how magic he was remained to be seen, but for now he had that baby magic that made everything in the world seem to make sense and be somehow inconsequential by comparison.

"Hi, Connor," Angel said, smiling. That expression was getting easier and easier to do these days with Connor starting to take more notice of his surroundings and the people in them.

"Hi, Daddy," Cordelia said in a high-pitched voice. She waved Connor's arm. The baby grinned and cooed. "Take me, Daddy."

Gently, still in awe of how small his son was, Angel took Connor into his arms. He held the boy close, enjoying the powder-fresh baby smell of him. "Hey, little guy."

Connor cooed again, made big eyes, and grabbed

Angel's nose. Angel laughed at his baby and kissed him tenderly.

On the other side of the counter, Gitana stared at him coldly. Angel felt vulnerable, once more aware of the gypsy army that filled the hotel lobby. And Connor was now directly in the line of fire if anything bad broke out.

"Let me see your arm." Cordelia took the bandage from the surgical tray and applied it to the wound. With expert care, she wrapped the wound with an Ace bandage.

"And here's the little tyke's bottle," Lorne said, bringing a bottle from the kitchen in the back.

Angel looked at Lorne.

"What?" Lorne asked.

"You heard him too?" Angel asked.

"Well, of course." Lorne plopped the bottle into Connor's mouth. "How could I miss his little voice? Kid's got a great set of pipes. When I finish with him, he'll be quite the performer." He tickled Connor under the chin and made the baby smile. "Yes you will, won't you?"

Angel held the bottle and let Connor drink. He walked away to get a sense of privacy from the others. Time spent alone with Connor, without some earth-shaking emergency going on, was hard to come by.

Gitana stepped into his space, standing across from Connor. "We're wasting time," she said.

"We're gathering intelligence," Angel said. "We only now found out Chavula Faa is this Thomas Ivers guy. It would probably help if we found out a little more about him."

"We know he has a building downtown. We could go there."

Angel lowered his voice and put an edge into it. "If you want to head up a massacre, you're welcome to it."

"You're afraid," Gitana accused.

"You think we can just drive up to the building, tear through the doors, and beat Chavula Faa into the ground?"

"Works for me." Gitana put her hands on her hips.

Angry, Angel locked eyes with her. "I'm not getting my friends killed just because you're in a hurry."

"Time works against us. We have reason to believe that Chavula Faa has five of the Stones. I have been given visions by the Stone we have."

"The thieves have the last Stone," Angel said. "You have yours. For the moment, Faa can't do anything drastic. Whatever spell opens the Bridge of Journeyhome into your home world, he can't do it with only five Stones. Or even six."

Gitana crossed her arms and stared meaningfully at Connor. "You have a son, vampire. You stand to lose a lot if the Founding Stones are not removed from Chavula Faa's possession."

"I know," Angel said, making his voice as neutral as he could. The fear fluttered inside him, nearly making him nauseous. "Having Connor, knowing everything you know about how your grandmother died, you should know I'm taking this situation seriously. I don't want anything to happen to my son."

"Then put him down and let's get to work." Gitana took a step forward.

Instinctively, Angel fell back into a defensive posture, putting his right shoulder and leg toward Gitana so he could strike quickly while keeping Connor protected. He didn't know what the gypsy leader intended, but he knew she wasn't coming any closer to Connor without a fight. "Stay back from my son."

Anger blanched Gitana's features. She reached for the sword at her hip.

"*Okay*, now," Cordelia said, stepping in between them with her hands spread to keep them apart. "And that'll be enough of that." She stared at Gitana. "Don't you even think about cutting me with that unless you intend to kill me. Because if you do cut me and don't kill me, I'll tear your eyes out."

The gypsy warriors stood, most of them with submachine pistols and rifles at the ready in their hands.

Cordelia looked at the warriors. "I meant that whole eye-tearing thing in the kindest way possible. I really think if we work this out together we might stand a chance against Chavula Faa. Otherwise, we're just going to kill each other—or maybe you'll kill us—and you won't stand a chance against Faa. If you thought you could take him on your own, you'd already be there." She looked at Gitana. "Am I right?"

Reluctantly, Gitana sheathed her sword and waved to her men to stand down. "We'll wait. But only for a little longer." Without another word, the gypsy leader turned and strode away.

"That went well, don't you think?" Cordelia asked in a hoarse whisper. "I mean, nothing important got lopped off."

"Thanks," Angel said.

"Thanks?" Cordelia acted like she couldn't believe the word. "*Thanks!* What kind of response is that?"

Angel felt perplexed. "It was a thank-you, Cordelia."

"'Thanks' doesn't cover everything that's been going on the last couple days," Cordelia told him.

Angel looked at Cordelia, aware of the baby in his arms and that he was with the only family Connor would probably ever know. More than anything, Angel wanted to keep that family together. "You're right," he said. "It doesn't."

Cordelia looked a little surprised. "It's time to come clean, Angel. There's something you've been keeping back from all of us."

Angel remained silent.

"At first, I thought it was just this whole gypsy thing. You know, reminding you of how you got your soul returned to you after you—after *Angelus*—killed that young girl."

"Different clan," Angel said.

"I know," Cordelia replied. "And these people aren't even real gypsies. Not completely, anyway."

"No," Angel agreed. "Not completely."

"So what haven't you been telling us?"

Angel looked at the baby in his arms. The formula

sloshed in the bottle as he drank. Connor had always been a healthy eater.

"That night when Lyanka cut the bridge supports and dropped into the river," Angel said quietly, "she didn't die immediately. Spike and I went looking for her."

"Why?"

"Spike wanted to."

"To make sure she was dead? To take the Stone and turn some kind of profit on it?"

Angel shook his head, the memory coming clearer in his head. "Back in eighteen ninety-one, we met Lyanka at a circus that Chavula Faa owned."

"You haven't mentioned this part."

Angel shrugged. "Not much to tell. Faa hired me to watch her."

"You worked for the bad guy?"

"*I* was a bad guy."

"Oh yeah."

"What fascinated me was the fact that I didn't tear both their throats out. Would have probably saved a lot of trouble later. I figured Lyanka had it coming for the incident at Hyde-Pierce's—" Angel stopped. "I guess I left some things out when we talked about that."

"The massacre?" Cordelia nodded. "We covered it. Found Cliff's Notes on it."

"Oh." Angel tried to read her expression and couldn't. Even as much as they knew about him and his past, he knew there were occasional bits they discovered that still shocked them. What was even worse, when they weren't shocked or disbelieving, those incidents seemed to hurt worse. Accepting that they could expect the worst of him was hard. "Faa, I would have killed on general principals. He just had this cocky attitude that I couldn't stand. But he also had gold. And Lyanka had made me curious about what she was looking for at Hyde-Pierce's home."

"What did Faa ask you to look for while you were spying on Lyanka?"

"Rocks. I didn't know it at the time, but they were looking for the Founding Stones for the Bridge of Journeyhome. She was there in Prague to steal one of the Stones. Faa wanted the Stone too, but he didn't know where it was. He wanted me to find out and tell him, or get the Stone before Lyanka did. Or after."

"Why did Faa hire you?"

"Because Lyanka knew all of his people. She had powers. Faa's people were afraid of her."

"She knew you."

"Yeah. I just didn't know how well she knew us till it was too late. And Spike and I weren't afraid of her. We were also too cocky, too sure of ourselves." Angel kissed Connor's forehead. The baby wrinkled his face, then returned to drinking the bottle. For some reason, Angel hated confessing his past sins in front of his son.

"You spied on her and—"

"Actually, Spike spied on her. He and Dru weren't getting along. And I really didn't want to skulk around in the shadows."

"So you stuck Spike with it."

"Yeah. Following Lyanka around kept Spike and Dru apart, which is usually a good thing when they're following their homicidal instincts. I just didn't count on Lyanka spotting Spike and putting a love spell whammy on him."

"A love spell?"

Angel nodded.

"Lyanka was beautiful?"

"Spitting image of Gitana."

"She was beautiful." Cordelia sighed. "So Spike got seriously whammied by the love spell."

"He and Dru weren't together, and Spike's always been a sucker for love."

"He was weak *and* she was beautiful."

"Seriously whammied," Angel said.

"He betrayed you and helped her get off with the Stone?"

"No. She put another spell on him and knocked him out while she slipped away to steal the Stone. By the time I figured out something was wrong with Spike and discovered him in the hotel room, Lyanka was gone."

"She was smart."

Angel shrugged. "She ended up dead."

"So why did Spike go looking for Lyanka the night she took the header off the bridge? To get revenge? To kill what was left of her?"

Angel hesitated. "He was still in love with her. I saw it in him that night."

349

CHAPTER NINETEEN

Carpathian Mountains
April 1893

"The woman's dead, William. You're wasting our time and putting us at risk." Angelus sat his horse awkwardly as the animal stumbled down the steep mountainside. Pebbles clattered and shifted constantly beneath the horseshoes. He'd had to yell to be heard over the roar of the river to their left.

"She might have lived," Spike argued stubbornly. He stood in his stirrups and gazed anxiously into the rushing, whitecapped water that overflowed the banks.

"No human could have survived that fall into the river. And if the fall didn't do it for her, she would have drowned. She couldn't have fought that current." Angelus stood in his own stirrups and peered back up the mountain. The two limp sections of the rope bridge that Lyanka had destroyed in her desperation still dangled on either side of the high gorge, swaying and jerking in the wind.

The woman had disappeared into the white-capped water four or five minutes ago. Spike had set out in pursuit at once, savaging his foam-flecked steed to charge down the mountainside in pursuit. Angelus had not once seen her or the horse or the demons that had fallen in when she'd cut the bridge supports.

Chavula Faa's demons—the ones that had not been lost to the roaring river when Lyanka had sabotaged the rope supports—had stood on the side of the mountain pass Lyanka had ridden up to the pass. Their master had been trapped on the other side of the severed bridge. A few of the six-limbed demons had even thrown themselves into the river after the woman. The demons weren't bright. Eventually, though, their master had made his intentions known that they were to go downriver. Their dark shapes tumbled and galloped down the mountainside, quickly closing the distance between them and the vampires. For the moment, though, they were a quarter mile farther up the mountain.

The gypsy chieftain remained on the other side of the gorge, trapped for a longer time by the more craggy features of the mountains there. Where

Angelus and Spike were able to ride their horses down the mountainside, such an effort was all but impossible on the other side.

Angelus knew Chavula Faa still hoped to recover the Founding Stone that Lyanka had stolen only that day and carried to the bridge. Nearly two years had passed since the woman had bewitched Spike and left him unconscious and sprawled on the bed they had been sharing in Prague. When Dru had discovered what—and who—Spike had been doing in his spare time, she had blamed Angelus for her lover's infidelity. In a response that could only make sense to them, Dru had begun showering Spike with her affections again. Incredibly, no mention—by Spike or by herself—had been made of the affairs Dru herself had indulged in while in Prague.

After Prague, Angelus had never expected to see the gypsy woman again. Running into Lyanka again after six years had passed since the meeting at Hyde-Pierce had been unbelievable enough. But there Lyanka had been four days ago, in the same small traveler's inn on the eastern side of the mountains where Angelus had chosen to spend the night with Spike, Dru, and Darla.

The fortuitous circumstances were almost enough to convince Angelus of the luck-altering properties he'd since heard were gotten from the rocks Lyanka and Chavula Faa had sought. He had learned nothing more about the objects than that. And the fact that the rocks were ugly.

Even more convincing of that friendly magic was the arrival of Chavula Faa only two days ago. But that wasn't such a leap of faith because Chavula Faa had admitted that he had been on Lyanka's trail for almost two months, never quite able to totally catch up to the woman.

Angelus's horse stumbled over the rocky terrain and almost fell. Silvery sweat flecked the animal's hide. Angelus knew that if the horse did not get to rest soon, the creature would die and leave him afoot. The prospect didn't bother him. He didn't truly care for the animal, and the frigid winds raking the mountainside with icy claws might offer discomfort while he walked back to the small village nestled on the other side of the mountain, but the wind could not kill him. He wouldn't allow that.

Chavula Faa's demons were another matter. Even though they were supposed to be working together, Angelus knew the gypsy chieftain might well decide to destroy them in his anger over losing both the rock and the woman.

"William," Angelus called.

Spike ignored him, guiding his mount close to the riverbank's edge. The soft ground gave way beneath the horse's hooves, and occasionally the rushing river breached the bank and rose to the animal's fetlocks.

"William," Angelus called again. "Faa's demons are coming after us."

"They're coming after her," Spike replied in a tight voice.

"Perhaps," Angelus admitted, "but I don't think they'd mind killing us in the bargain if we saw our way clear to getting in the way."

"If they do," Spike said, "it would be by your bargain."

"The woman is dead."

"I don't know that."

"What?" Angelus let some of his irritation be heard. "Because you haven't seen her broken body?"

"I want to know for certain."

"William, damn it! As swollen as this river is, the current could carry her miles away before we ever find her. Dead or alive. And I'd wager that she's dead."

"I'm not keeping you here. Go if you want."

Angelus glanced back at the approaching demons and saw that they'd gotten closer. Only minutes remained before the first of the staggered line reached them.

"I'm not going to leave you," Angelus said.

Spike twisted in his saddle and locked eyes with Angelus. The younger vampire gave him a scathing look. "Why won't you leave me?"

Angelus didn't try to answer. It would do no good for them to fight there. The demons would overtake them, and they wouldn't be able to stand against them.

"You're just thinking that if I find her body, perhaps she'll still have that damned rock on her. Then you can sell it to Chavula Faa," Spike accused.

The thought had crossed Angelus's mind. Profit

was profit. But that wasn't the main reason to not leave Spike behind. Spike knew too many of Angelus's hiding places, places where he kept gold and jewels, and places where he sometimes dropped out of sight when people who hunted him came too close. Having Spike in enemy hands and talking could be a death sentence. At the very least, having Spike tell someone the things he knew could offer several problems Angelus didn't care to entertain.

Darla would be incensed as well. After Prague, Darla hadn't wanted any further dealings with the gypsies. She didn't know that Lyanka and Chavula Faa were in the small town.

"William, I followed you out here because you wanted to warn the woman."

"You didn't want to warn her."

"No," Angelus replied angrily. "I didn't. That woman would kill either one of us if it suited her. You're playing yourself as a fool if you think otherwise."

Spike turned back in the saddle and continued riding.

"You don't want to be down here, either," Angelus said. "You're still feeling some of the dregs of the love spell she bewitched you with. These feelings you're having, they're not yours. You need to work your way past them."

The growls of the panting demons behind them grew louder as they neared.

"Damn it, William!" Angelus said, kicking his

horse's sides and moving up to ride abreast of the younger vampire. He reached for the reins of Spike's horse, intending to seize control of the animal. "You'll listen to me or I'll—"

Spike hauled back on his reins. He pointed. "There! Do you see it?"

Drawn in in spite of himself, knowing that the demons were coming closer by the second, Angelus followed Spike's direction. At first, he didn't see what had drawn Spike's attention. Then he saw the woman's body riding the rough surface of the river. She clung to a rocky outcrop by one hand.

Before Angelus could say or do anything, Spike spurred his mount and dashed forward. The horse's hooves slapped through the river's overflow. Cursing, Angelus turned his own horse in the same direction and galloped after Spike.

A few feet shy of the woman, Spike hauled on the reins so hard, the horse reared high and fell over on its side. Spike was gone from the saddle by that time, already racing to the woman's aid. In two short steps he was splashing through the river up to his chest, barely able to remain standing against the force of the hurtling current.

"You're a damned fool, William!" Angelus called from the bank as he brought his own mount to a halt. "You're going to get busted up! Maybe even get killed if you get that thick block you call a head torn from your shoulders should the river catch you and tear you in half along the bottom!"

Spike slipped and fell and forced his way across the river, losing several feet of distance as he crossed. But in the end he slid along the water and managed to catch hold of the same rock that Lyanka clung to. He grabbed her around the waist and hung on.

"Angelus," Spike cried. "Help me. I can't bring us both back to shore." He spat and spluttered in the spray that hammered against the rock that only partially shielded them.

"Let her go. Save yourself." Angelus didn't bother stepping down from his horse. He glanced to the left as the horse stutter-stepped beneath him, and he saw the demons closing ranks, becoming a solid mass that thundered toward them.

"Help me!" Spike yelled.

Angelus remained resolute. "You're a fool, William. I don't have to die a fool's death with you."

"Help me!"

"Does she still have the rock?" Angelus asked. "The rock that Chavula Faa wants?"

"I don't know. Help me get her out of the water and we'll see."

"Find out if she has it."

"I can't. If I try, I'll lose my hold on the rock or on her."

Greed drew Angelus on. He cared nothing for the woman. But the thought of that rock and the gold that Chavula Faa—or even someone else—might be willing to pay for it rose in his mind. There was no guarantee that he and Spike would be able to get away from the demons, and having the rock might be a good bargaining point to buy their escape.

"*Angelus!*" Spike bawled.

Cursing himself for being as big a fool as Spike was even though motivated by greed and not some damned spell, Angelus threw his leg over the horse and dropped to the ground. He tied the horse's reins to a nearby brush, then walked into the river.

The current filled Angelus's boots and pulled his feet out from under him at once. He fell, slipped, tried to get up, and fell again. He maintained his efforts to get to the rock and finally managed to secure a hold on the rough surface.

Worn from his exertions and from the earlier long chase up and through the mountain, Angelus floated in the water on the other side of Lyanka. Angelus had difficulty putting his feet on the ground.

Lyanka's left eye was closed. The left side of her face was badly damaged. White bone showed through the wound, and even though the flesh still bled, the river washed the crimson away immediately. She stared at him with her right eye and her mouth moved, but the sound of the rushing water drowned her words.

"Together then!" Angelus called, spitting his words out against the river spray smashing across the rock. "And damn you if you slip or this woman drags us away, William!"

Shoving themselves from the rock, Angelus and Spike forced their way through the river. Spike slipped and fell once, causing all three of them to get washed twenty feet downriver. The woman came up gasping weakly for air. Her lungs sounded wet and diseased when she breathed.

Finally, in seconds—though the time seemed like hours, Angelus guided them all to the riverbank. Spike dropped to his knees, even his vampire constitution all but exhausted. With difficulty, Angelus remained on his feet and glanced up the mountainside. "They're coming," Angelus said.

Chavula Faa's demons were little more than a hundred yards away.

"William," Angelus said, "we've got to go."

Still on his knees, Spike looked at Lyanka. Pain wracked his features. "We need to save her."

"That's stupid," Angel said. Lyanka had fallen into the river a beautiful woman, but they had salvaged a monster. "Look at her. She can't be saved. Her skull is bashed in. She's lost an eye. One arm is broken, and the other probably is as well. Her legs are shattered. If her back isn't broken, I'll be surprised. She's spitting up blood, and that definitely tells me that her ribs have punctured her lungs." He laughed, unable to keep from taunting Spike. "Do you know what you did, William?"

Spike glared up at him.

"You saved a dead woman from drowning, is all," Angelus crowed sarcastically. "And now haven't you done well for yourself?"

"I can save her," Spike said. His features changed,

and his fangs elongated as he put on the face of the demon.

Lyanka's good eye widened in fear and loathing.

Angelus caught Spike's head as he leaned forward to bite the woman's exposed throat. "No," Angelus commanded. The woman already knew magic, and he was beginning to suspect she was something more than human because no one human could have survived the river.

If Spike did succeed in turning her, there was no telling what they would be dealing with when she regained her health and the strength that vampirism would bring. She had fought them, used them, and would have killed them if she'd been able. Being turned, becoming a vampire, might only sharpen those desires, or focus them on her.

"Leave me be!" Spike roared. He pushed and fought to be free of Angelus.

"It's the damned spell!" Angelus yelled, holding tight to the grip he had on the younger vampire. "If you were yourself, you wouldn't care one whit about this woman!" But he knew there was a possibility that Spike's feelings were genuine. The younger vampire was too quick to love, too weak in his need for it, too willing to overlook a loved one's failings once his heart had been given. That weakness was something that Angelus was certain would be used against Spike time and time again.

Lyanka held a hand up. She spoke a single word. A purple glow formed in the air between her and the vampires, then the glow exploded and blew Angelus and Spike backward a dozen feet.

Dazed and hurting further now, Angelus pushed himself up from the mud. From the ripped condition of his clothing, he was surprised that he wasn't in a million pieces. He felt like he had been worked over with sledgehammers.

Only a few feet away, Spike tried to get to his feet but slipped and fell. He looked dazed, barely conscious. Blood leaked from the corner of his ears.

Behind them, only a few yards shy of the horses, the six-limbed demons stopped and threw their heads up. They snuffled the air and hung back, obviously afraid of the woman's power. Perhaps if their master had been present, they might have rushed forward to do battle at his stern command. But he wasn't there, and they didn't rush in.

Angelus was thankful for small favors. The demons had stopped, and he was certain Lyanka had meant to kill Spike and him with her enchantment.

Lyanka rolled over on her side to face them. Her jaw was out of place and possibly broken. Missing teeth marred her mouth, and her once-beautiful lips were bruised and split. She pointed at them. "I put the evil eye upon you, vampires," she croaked in a harsh voice. Her words slurred and were indistinct to a degree because of the broken jaw, the missing teeth, and the smashed mouth. "And I name you. Angelus. William. I curse you, and I curse your get with all the power that I muster. May tragedy and hopelessness follow you to the end of your days. As long as the Seven Founding Stones lie in the hands of my enemies, you will forever more be cursed."

Angelus thought he felt a tingle, then in the next instant dismissed the feeling as being a product of his overstimulated imagination. Lyanka had no more power. If she had, she would have slain them where they stood when she'd had the chance.

Lyanka took one more ragged breath, then slumped back onto the ground. She lay, stretched and broken, like a child's rag doll. Overrunning its banks again, the river came up after her, washing over her body and pulling it a few inches closer to the rushing water again.

"William!" Angelus called out as he ran to the body of the dead woman. "Get up! Those damned demons are going to be upon us in a moment!"

Stiffly, Spike stood. "Is she dead?"

"As they get," Angelus replied. He ran his hands over her body, seeking secret pockets in her clothing, cloak, and boots, where she might have hidden the rock. "Get the horses."

Spike remained motionless.

Looking back over his shoulder, Angelus said, "Get the horses. *Now!* Unless you want to end up excreted into a pile of demon dung before morning."

The cautious demons growled.

Galvanized into action, Spike sprinted for the horses farther upriver. By the time he returned, Angelus was cursing furiously.

"No rock?" Spike asked.

"No." Angelus strode for the horse that Spike held. The demons broke their line as the next rush of water that flooded over the riverbanks caught Lyanka's body and moved it forward.

Angelus barely avoided the leaders of the pack as he used his spurs to force the creature into motion. Spike stayed behind him. Together, they continued riding, following the course of the river on the flagging horses. Behind them, the demons feasted on Lyanka's corpse and howled at the moon.

CHAPTER TWENTY

Los Angeles

"She cursed you?" Cordelia asked when Angel finished speaking.

Angel nodded. He still heard the dying woman's voice screeching in his ears.

"You never thought to mention this curse to anyone before?" Cordelia asked.

"It was a hundred years ago. She just seemed like a dying woman. Not someone who could work a curse. She was on her way out and she was trying to scare me. That's what I thought. I blew it off. At that time, I hadn't been cursed and had my soul returned to me. And I had no way of tracking down the Founding Stones."

"The soul return?" Cordelia said. "That was a good thing. Maybe painful, and definitely more guilt-ridden than a piece of Death By Chocolate cake the week before prom after you ordered the dress, but a good thing."

Angel looked down at the baby in his arms. Connor had finished his bottle and gone back to sleep. "Curses like that from a gypsy tend to spread to family, Cordelia. It could affect Connor."

"Maybe it didn't take," Cordelia suggested hopefully. "Lyanka was dying, and you said she would have killed you and Spike if she could have. Only she couldn't. She just kind of fizzled out. She could have just been putting up a front."

Tenderly, Angel stroked Connor's cheek as the baby breathed quietly. Connor's fingers twitched, and he balled his hands into fists at the contact.

Lifting his eyes to Cordelia, Angel asked, "Do you want to take that chance?"

Cordelia sighed and crossed her arms, hugging herself. "No. No, I don't."

"There's another wrinkle too," Angel said.

"That's us," Cordelia said brightly. "We never get the permanent-press type of trouble."

"I think Spike might be one of the thieves who took the Stone from Hargreave's mansion tonight."

Cordelia's expression sobered immediately. "Spike? As in, *our* Spike? The homicidal monster from Sunnydale Spike? Spike as in journeyed-to-L.A.-to-torture-Angel-to-get-the-Ring-of-Amarra Spike?"

"Yeah. Know any other peroxide-haired vampires?"

"You saw him?"

"Well, no. Talked to him over the phone."

"And you heard peroxide in his voice?"

"No," Angel said, regretting that he'd mentioned the hair. "I heard him."

"At the mansion?"

"Over the cell phone."

"He called you? How did he get your number?"

Knowing the story was getting tangled, Angel cradled Connor in one arm and took out the cell phone he'd taken from Bill Wynowski. "On this."

"And this is?"

"A cell phone belonging to a Wolfram and Hart attorney named Bill Wynowski. When I went to see Lilah tonight about the Barkuk demons angle, she gave up Wynowski." Angel considered the phone a moment. "Actually, I think she only gave me what she wanted me to know. I think she knew more than she told me."

"That would be the Lilah we've come to know and despise. So why did Spike call Wynowski's phone?"

"Wynowski was working for Hargreave," Angel explained. "Wynowski brokered the deal to bring one of the Founding Stones from Hong Kong."

"The one that Giles asked you to look for? The one that the Barkuk demons got away with?"

"Right."

"Still not getting the Spike connection."

"Wynowski was going to double-cross Hargreave," Angel said. "Wynowski knew that Thomas Ivers wanted the Stone as well."

"And we all know that Ivers is Chavula Faa now."

Angel nodded. "Judging from the stuff Fred and Wesley have been able to turn up on the Internet about Ivers, the guy is rich."

"Very rich," Cordelia agreed. "According to the reports I've looked at, Ivers is represented in California by Wolfram and Hart. Want to guess who his legal counsel is?"

"Lilah," Angel said. Irritation vibrated inside him as the pieces fit together. "She didn't give us the information for free. She was using us to squeeze Wynowski into a bad place. She protected her client's interests and possibly set Hargreave into the market for finding a new attorney."

"Loyalty's not a big factor at Wolfram and Hart. Once you sign your soul away on the dotted line, you're pretty much corporate material. Maybe you can't walk away from the firm, but you can screw over your fellow employees."

Connor shifted in Angel's arms.

"So Wynowski hires thieves to steal the Stone that Hargreave got from Hong Kong," Cordelia said.

"It makes sense," Angel said. "If we could check back, we'd probably find that Wynowski hired the Barkuk demons as well. This crew that invaded Hargreave's home, they were probably the second offensive."

"How did Spike get to be one of them?"

"I don't know."

Cordelia frowned. "Are you sure it was Spike? I mean, you've haven't exactly been getting plenty of sleep lately. Maybe you made a mistake."

Angel shook his head. "It was Spike."

Cordelia thought for a moment. "You said Tobar was told about three demons that were killed in Hargreave's neighborhood. If they were the thieves who took the Founding Stone, and if Spike was one of them and he called you after those demons were killed, that means he was still alive. Well, as alive as a dead vampire can be. It also stands to reason that Spike betrayed them and killed them. He called you, thinking that you were Wynowski, and intended to collect all the pay for the job. He got greedy."

"Sounds right."

"Do you think that he knew he was talking to you, not Wynowski?"

Angel hesitated. "I knew his voice."

"So it's a safe bet that he knew yours."

"Probably."

"That means he's not going to call back."

"I'm not the money guy," Angel said.

Cordelia massaged her temples. "What do you think he's going to do?"

"I don't know."

Glancing at the cell phone, Cordelia said, "I don't suppose you've thought about calling him."

"Didn't get the number," Angel said. "No way to call back."

"We might be able to get it from Wynowski."

"Wynowski's probably rabbited. He won't be back until the dust settles on this. If then."

"Maybe Lilah could—"

"I don't want to tell Lilah any more about what's going on than we have to. If she'd known more tonight, I don't think she'd have given up Wynowski."

"Pardon me, Angel."

Turning, Angel saw Wesley standing behind him. Gitana was at his side. Both wore grim faces.

"What?" Angel asked.

"There appears to be a new problem," Wesley said. "Or rather, an old one. But Gitana—and possibly, Lyanka—was not aware of it." He opened an old book. "In 1258, the grandsons of Genghis Khan—Mongke, Kubilay, and Hulegu—ruled the steppes. However, Hulegu lived in Persia and asked the caliph, al-Mutasim, to recognize Mongol sovereignty. The caliph chose not to. In return, Hulegu led a Mongol army into Baghdad and sacked the city, burning buildings and houses to the ground, raiding universities, and eventually massacring over eighty thousand people."

"Not exactly the History Channel here," Cordelia commented.

"I know that." Wesley looked more gaunt and hollow-eyed than usual. He turned pages in the book. "But you have to understand what was at stake here. There was an assassin's sanctuary at Alamut. The caliphs believed in maintaining a standing army of men who would give their lives to further Islam, men who would give their lives to take those of enemies to the Muslim empire. The sanctuary had a large library, books on a number of things that were never located in one of the legitimate libraries of science, law, trade, agriculture, and other such topics. Few of those books survived the Mongol raids. This is a copy of one of those books."

"Wes," Angel said, "could we hurry it up here?"

Wesley turned pages till he found an illustrated picture. He turned the book so that Angel and Cordelia could look at the page.

The five rock shapes on the page were unmistakable. One of them was the Stone Angel had first seen at Hyde-Pierce's mansion in 1887.

"Those are five of the Founding Stones," Cordelia said.

"Exactly," Wesley said.

"But there are seven."

"The Muslims never found all seven. The most they had at any one time were five, and then only for a brief period. This book deals with scrying and visions. Evidently those of diehard Islam faith held it in contempt because the miracles that are written about in its pages aren't the work of the hand of Allah. Most of the objects and events written about in these pages have to do with demons."

"The Stones," Angel reminded gently, knowing that Wesley believed the information was important.

"You'll remember that the Aryans built the gypsy armies to contest the Muslims by shepherding small villages and towns into their militia," Wesley said. "And that the Kalochner race got swept up into the same shortly after their arrival in this world."

"Yes."

"Well, after the Muslims got their hands on the Stones, the Kalochner put up a fierce struggle against the Muslims using the power of the Stones," Wesley said.

"That means the Stones were used for more than just a way home," Angel said.

"Yes. As borne out in this book. Together, the Stones provided a focus that intensified Kalochner powers. Not enough to change the outcome of the battles, evidently, but enough that the Stones garnered the interest of the Muslims. No doubt, they believed that the Stones manifested those Kalochner abilities rather than just enhancing them. Still, they discovered that proximity to the Stones brought out hidden talents that some of them possessed."

"What hidden talents?" Cordelia asked.

"Dreams, primarily. Most of those few who had latent extrasensory perception—at least, that's what I'm inferring from reading the text—developed visions that allowed them to glimpse places far from them. What international governments funded as 'remote viewing' geared toward intelligence gathering and target identification. In some cases, a few of the Muslims gained other abilities, including but not limited to, precognition, telekinesis, and healing."

"All of these," Gitana said, "are natural abilities for Kalochner people who carry the true blood of my people."

"Did those effects last?" Angel asked.

"No," Wesley said. "Only when the subjects who manifested those abilities remained within close contact of the Stones."

"The Stones were kept by the assassins?" Cordelia asked.

Wesley nodded. "Presumably to be used as weapons. During that time, Islam was the leading force in science and discovering the natural world. They studied many things."

"Including the Founding Stones," Gitana said impatiently. "The Muslims hunted the Stones within the gypsy army. They sought them out and found five of them before the Mongol invasion. During the battles, the Stones were lost from my people, scattered across those harsh lands, and many of my people were killed. According to this book, the Muslims discovered that once any five of the Stones are together, they work to draw the missing Stones to them."

"Unfortunately," Wesley said, "in this case they also drew the Mongols."

Angel considered that. "Someone can make the Stones seek out the other Stones?"

"Alone or in groups of two or three, the Stones act as compasses for the others. You can't know where they are precisely, but they will guide you in the general direction of the next. But any five of them working in concert seem able to juggle events and control destiny to a degree. They . . . enhance the probability that all seven Stones will be pulled together in the same spot at the same time."

"A spell triggers that?"

"The Stones do it naturally," Wesley said, closing the book. "It's not just by luck—good or bad—that all seven Founding Stones are here in L.A. The Stones are here because they've been drawn here."

"They possess a power unto themselves—," Gitana said.

"An *affinity* for one another," Wesley clarified. "A resonance or a harmony. Perhaps one of those terms would be a better way to describe the effect."

"And this power allows the Stones to influence events in the world to bring themselves together under the hand of one of my people," Gitana finished.

"Five Stones," Wesley said. "Let's be clear about that."

"Chavula Faa," Angel said.

"Exactly," Wesley said. "According to the book, three and four of the Stones had been gathered together before. Usually they enhanced their possessor's luck to a large degree, and there are cases cited in the book, for fortune or misfortune. But never five Stones all at one time."

373

"How did these assassins learn what five Stones together would do?" Cordelia asked.

"One of their number was of sufficient Kalochner blood and possessed power and knowledge of the Stones," Gitana said. "I recognized his name in the text. He was Djordji, also known as the Shunned One." She looked undecided for a moment, then raised her chin proudly. "There are only a few shunned ones in the history of the Kalochner, and most of those lived only short lives after they were declared to be shunned. Most of the descendants of the original arrivers remained true to my people."

"You believe that the events that brought the Stones together here were magically influenced?" Angel asked.

"Absolutely," Wesley answered.

"We tracked one of the Stones here," Gitana said. "That was the one you saw us getting from the Wiatar demons earlier tonight. That is the first Stone our group has had in almost thirty years."

"Why are the Stones here now?" Angel asked.

"Because Thomas Ivers—or Chavula Faa—must have only recently gotten a fifth Stone while here in L.A.," Wesley answered. "If there was a way we could know that, we'd have more information to better support the theory. But the Stone that Hargreave purchased was pulled here during the time frame that Chavula has been here in his Ivers identity."

"As was the Stone that we got from the Wiatars,"

Gitana said. "That Stone, I was told, came by way of Hawaii."

"Isn't this something Lyanka should have known about?" Cordelia asked, looking at Gitana. "You're acting like the whole five-Stone attraction is a big surprise to you."

"My grandmother," Gitana said in an icy tone, "was a wise and brave woman who learned of our heritage in spite of the fact that she was not one of those chosen to learn of the Bridge of Journeyhome. She learned the secrets she was denied, and she became a champion of our people."

"She also taught Chavula Faa's brother about the Stones," Wesley said. "He, in turn, taught his brother, which brings us to our current impasse."

Gitana gave Wesley a scathing look.

"That information about the Faa brothers was included in another reference I discovered about the Stones," Wesley said. "As was the fact that Lyanka killed the brother."

"My grandmother loved him," Gitana said defensively. "He betrayed her. His death was a small price to pay for all that he did. The knowledge that he gave his brother set Chavula Faa on her trail and doomed the Elders."

"Evidently early in the twentieth century," Wesley said, "Faa took it upon himself to track down and eradicate all the Kalochner Elders who knew about the Stones. Faa took possession of the Stones that the Elders had at that time, and the story was spread that the Stones' good luck had been used up and only bad luck remained." He paused and adjusted his glasses. "To dissuade others from wanting them, I assume. The Stones rarely showed up, at least in the texts we've been pouring through, since that time."

"Now they're all here," Cordelia said. "In L.A."

"So it would seem." Wesley grimaced. "There is one thing more."

Angel waited.

"According to the legends, the proximity of all seven Founding Stones manifests a huge amount of power. That power is supposed to open the Bridge of Journeyhome. But if the energy is not used in that manner, the energy will be released."

"Released how?" Angel asked.

"If it's not harnessed, possibly as an explosion."

"How big of an explosion?"

Wesley tapped his chin with his forefinger. "How much energy do you think it would take to open a doorway to another world? I'm sure I could get Fred to crunch some numbers for you."

"Ballpark figure," Angel said.

Wesley nodded and sighed. "With the location of the Stones as ground zero, I'd say we're safely talking about several city blocks." He paused. "It's a ticking bomb, Angel."

"Sitting here isn't going to help us," Gitana argued. "You can information-gather away all the time that we have to act." She gazed at Connor sleeping in Angel's arms. "I know you have as much at risk as we do, and I don't believe you mean us any harm, but we have to do something."

"Agreed," Angel said, his mind spinning out the angles. "The best defense is a good offense. Maybe it's time we put the pressure back on Thomas Ivers. Get your men ready."

Gitana wheeled away instantly and issued orders with crisp authority. Although the gypsy warriors had not slept in hours, they responded like components in a well-oiled machine.

"So what is the plan?" Wesley asked.

Angel walked toward the back of the hotel and put Connor back in his basinet. "Wesley, you're with me." He walked out into the main lobby toward the weapons locker. "Gunn, you're with me."

"I'm coming," Cordelia announced. "Fred and Lorne can watch Connor. He'll be safe, and they can continue to research."

Angel hesitated.

Cordelia pointed to her head. "The vision thing, remember? The Powers-That-Be have already taken a hand in this thing. Might be a good idea to have me on hand if they decide to offer us another tip. You know, make sure their chosen champion is aimed in the right direction."

Angel looked at her.

"And I'm no slouch in the fighting department," Cordelia pointed out.

"All right," Angel said. He reached into the weapons locker and started pulling gear on. He turned to Gitana. "How good are your people with security systems?"

"We left the *vardos* a long time ago," Gitana said. "And pursuing the Stones has never been without risk. My warriors are good at disabling security systems."

"Good," Angel said. "I can get in through systems without getting myself caught, but moving a small army through them is another matter."

"We can do it."

"Then let's start by cutting down the places Chavula Faa has to run and adding some pressure to his operations," Angel said. "We can afford to wait. He's pushing for the win."

CHAPTER TWENTY-ONE

Sitting here drinking is not going to make your problems go away.

Seated in a back booth at a sleazy bar in East L.A., Spike topped off his shot glass with whiskey from a bottle he'd purchased. "Drinking helps me think." He knocked the drink back, feeling it burn his throat all the way down. The whiskey wasn't smooth, just a step above rotgut. But it was cheap, and there appeared to be plenty of it. "Kind of streamlines the problems I've got facing me till I see a solution." He peered at the glass. "At the moment, I see the bottom of this glass, which is never a good thing."

Lyanka sat in the booth seat across from Spike.

She had her arms crossed and an irritated look on her face. *You're going to get caught before you get out of town.*

"And what would you have me do to prevent that?" *I'd have you kill Chavula Faa.*

"Excellent suggestion," Spike replied caustically. "I'll just call him up and see if he can pencil that in." He drank the whiskey and poured another shot.

If you can kill Faa, you'll be free.

"If I'd never come to L.A. looking for a quick fifty thousand dollars, I'd be free."

You'd still owe the loan shark. Dannek—wasn't that his name? Lyanka smiled at him sweetly. *Yes, I believe it was.*

Spike pointedly ignored her. He glanced around. The bar was a seedy joint that left dreams and responsibility checked at the door along with depression and frustration. It was a place where working men and demons came to drink, to dull their senses enough to get enough sleep to take on another day filled with wrecked hopes, savaged hearts, and backbreaking labor. At the moment, it was the perfect place for Spike to get quietly drunk.

Of course, getting drunk with a ghost yapping in my ear is going to be next to impossible. But Spike was determined.

Closing time was two A.M., forty-seven minutes, according to the clock hanging above the bar where the bartender chain-smoked and flipped through horse-racing forms. Spike knew he had time to get drunk.

Three men and one woman formed a band in one corner of the bar. A blue haze of cigarette smoke surrounded them. A lead guitarist, bass guitarist, drummer, and harmonica player riffed through a series of blues pieces. Occasionally, the woman—the lead guitarist for the group—worked her way through the lyrics of a song. Her voice was husky from years of drinks and cigarettes. A few of the obvious regulars sat at nearby tables and commented favorably from time to time.

How are you going to solve the problem with Dannek? Lyanka taunted. *If you could have killed him, you already would have.*

Spike eyed the ghost and wondered how much she did know about him. She knew about Dannek and about Buffy. Did she know about the chip in his head as well?

"I could sell the van," Spike said. "Arrag had enough toys and illegal goods on board that he could get me close to the money I need for Dannek."

Lyanka waved that away with a hand that seemed no more substantial than the smoke the sluggish air-conditioning cycled through the bar. *Even so, I will still tell Buffy of your part in my death and in losing the Founding Stone.*

"You know, Buffy doesn't look at me and see perfection," Spike said. "She knows what I am, how I am, and she still chooses to be with me."

Not lately.

"She'll change her mind again. Women are good at that. She's drawn to me in spite of herself, and she knows it." Spike knew he was telling himself that as much as he was telling the ghost. "This time apart is just . . . uncomfortable. It's not forever."

Shadows darkened Lyanka's face as she frowned. Smoke drifted through her eyes. *You are smug and conceited, William.*

"You count those as bad qualities?" Spike gave her a mock surprised look.

Lyanka ignored him. *What are you going to do with the Founding Stone?*

"Toss it into an alley," Spike replied. "Forget about it."

Lyanka sat bolt upright on the other side of the table. *You can't do that!*

"If I can't sell the damned thing, it's not worth anything to me."

You're a fool!

"Ah, and now you're trying to butter me up by playing to my good side." Spike poured himself another whiskey neat. "That deserves another drink." He toasted her. "In memory of your dearly departed health, and passionate nights spent in sweat-soaked sheets."

Leaning forward, Lyanka faced Spike. Her calm demeanor fired an instant warning shot through him. The fiery taste of the whiskey hung in his throat a moment too long. He almost choked. "What?" he asked suspiciously.

There's something you haven't considered. Something even I haven't considered.

Spike took his cigarette pack from the tabletop and shook one out. He lit it in his cupped palms and blew smoke out. "Gonna enlighten me? Or are you gonna keep me in suspense?"

I'm bound to that Founding Stone, William, she said sadly. *For whatever reason, my fate is tied to that of the Stone. If you allow it to fall into Chavula Faa's hands, what do you think will become of me?*

Cold apprehension filled Spike. The ghost was right. The possibility was something that he hadn't considered. He'd just assumed Lyanka could leave the Stone any time she wanted to. "You're lying," he said. "You can leave that rock if you want."

Really? Lyanka treated him to a half-smile. *Then maybe you'll tell me why I haven't already gone to my granddaughter and told her Hargreave had the Stone you stole tonight.*

Spike pondered that. Conflict rose within him, and he hated himself for the weakness that he had. He was a vampire, and he was selfish, and he should have been way beyond worrying about what happened to anyone else. Especially with a ghost, someone who was even more dead than he was.

Despite his harsh taunts and her anger, he remembered how it had been with Lyanka. She'd been a warm and generous lover during the few nights they'd spent together while he'd spied on her. She had kept him sane during that time in Prague when Dru's inattention and cruelty would have driven him insane.

Are you prepared to let Chavula Faa have whatever is left of me when he gets the Stone? Lyanka asked.

"Yes," he said, but his voice came out in a strained whisper, and he knew that she couldn't miss his lie.

Lyanka smiled at him and stroked his cheek. *Sweet William. You are harsh and you are fierce, but when it comes to matters of the heart, even a blind person would know how you felt.*

"Chavula Faa isn't interested in you." Spike made himself cling to that thought. She knew that he was soft, and she was using that against him. All he had to do was realize her threat as the lie that it was.

Do you think he would be interested in vengeance for all the years of frustration that I gave him?

Spike remembered the harsh-faced man he'd met in Prague and seen again in the inn deep in the Carpathian Mountains. The Chavula Faa that Spike had known would have paid for the opportunity to torture the ghost. And men like that, Spike knew, rarely changed. Some men were just born cruel. And heartless.

I remember that night in the river, William, Lyanka said in a soft voice above the blues tune the musicians played while the singer crooned softly. Aching pain haunted the music and the barely heard lyrics. *I remember when I fell, when the cold river drank me down and pulled me under. I remember how I'd thought I was dead, then somehow found the rock that I clung to that allowed me to live a few moments more even though I was sure I was dying.*

Spike remembered as well. He could still feel the cold river surging around his legs as he'd run out to her, could still hear Angelus's harsh voice ringing in his ears, commanding him to come back.

You came for me then, Sweet William, Lyanka went on. *Even though Chavula Faa's demons raced down the mountainside for you. Even though Angelus told you that you would only be pulling a dead woman from the river.*

"You weren't dead," Spike said quietly. The whiskey glass lay empty cupped inside his hand. He remembered how cold her body had been when he'd grabbed on to her, how weak and frail she'd seemed hanging there in the foaming jaws of the river. "You should have been dead, but you weren't."

I shouldn't even have been able to hang on to that rock, Lyanka agreed. *But I did. And you came for me when you shouldn't have.* She smiled. *I think that was the bravest thing I've ever seen anyone do.*

"It was stupid was what it was," Spike replied harshly.

It was noble. A truly heroic act.

"You ever take count of how many heroes are around after they've done something heroic?" Spike shook his head. "I'm not one for heroic acts."

Maybe you believe that you aren't, she told him, *but I can see inside your secret heart, William. Probably the Slayer can too. That's why she's been drawn to you.*

Spike shook his head. "That's animal magnetism. Nothing more."

Not for you.

Spike took a hit off his cigarette and held it. He knew that if he tried to answer any differently she'd only bust him for lying. "The Slayer is complicated."

Perhaps she is. But you're not. You've always known yourself. You've just sometimes lived in denial of it and tried to follow your darker nature.

Spike opened his right hand palm up on the tabletop. "You can read fortunes in palms. Is Buffy coming back to me?"

Lyanka regarded the open palm. A cold finger traced the lines carved into his flesh. "I could choose not to answer you until after you save me."

Spike closed his hand. "I won't save you for the price of an answer."

And I won't hold that answer from you. Lyanka regarded him with melancholy in her eyes. *She will come back to you, William. And she will put a challenge before you that will change both of your lives forever. Both of you will know the truth of your secret self, but that event will tear you apart. The cost you pay will be high.*

Hope rose within Spike. He wanted to be on his way back to Sunnydale. Whatever was coming that would bring Buffy back into his arms, no matter how daunting, he was ready.

You love her.

"Yes."

Lyanka's eyes searched him. *You've never known love like the one you feel for her.*

"Never."

As a woman, I should be jealous.

Spike grinned. "You are."

Lyanka smiled back gently. *Perhaps. But more than anything, I'm afraid of Chavula Faa. I don't know how a ghost can die, William, but I'm sure it won't be pleasant, just as I am certain that Faa will find a way to make that happen.*

Spike shook his head. "I'm one vampire, Lyanka. I can't save you."

You're more than you realize, William. One day you will come to know that. But for now, you are one. If you're going to save me, if you're going to save the Founding Stone from falling into Chavula Faa's hands, you're going to need help.

"I don't have anyone I can call on," Spike replied. He grinned thinly. "The only guys I thought I could count on in this city I had to kill because of you. I'm without resources."

Angelus is close to my granddaughter. I can feel their energies together. You have the phone. You can call Angelus.

"Angel," Spike said. "He's changed, remember?"

He will come. The words I hear of him along the Ghost Roads are that he is a Champion now. A weapon of the Powers-That-Be. He will know the truth of the Founding Stones. There's a reason that all of us have been brought back here. The Stone that binds me binds the three of us.

"Because of your curse?"

Lyanka smiled. *Perhaps. Or maybe in spite of it. I had thought both of you would be dust before now. Instead, you both yet live and you are here when Chavula Faa has nearly completed the set of the Seven Founding Stones. There must be a reason for that.*

Spike smoked, watching the coal of his cigarette glow bright orange in the dim bar. "Maybe this is the curse coming to fruition, Lyanka. Maybe Angel and I are supposed to get dusted helping you against Chavula Faa."

No. That is not meant to happen. How else would the Slayer come back to you?

A wolfish grin fitted itself to Spike's lips. "Maybe you lied about that."

I didn't.

"I only have your word on that. And you've got a heap of self-interest on your side."

The sadness never left her eyes. *I didn't lie about that, but I didn't lie about the test before you either.*

The sincerity in her words was sobering. Despite that, Spike hoped she was right. He wanted to believe her, but it was hard. He had been lied to so many times in the past, and many of those times he had lied to himself.

The answer lies within you, William. Do you believe the Slayer loves you? If you believe that, then you already have the answer to your question.

Spike stubbed his cigarette out in the overflowing ashtray before him. "Calling Angel is not a good choice."

It is, Lyanka said, *the only choice you have. The only choice either of us has.*

True to her word, Gitana's gypsy warriors did know their way around security systems.

Less than twenty minutes after the initial push into the building where Thomas Ivers's offices were located in downtown L.A. near the Staples Center, Angel stood inside the software designer billionaire's plush private office. Since it was not a home, and the fact that Chavula Faa wasn't quite human, Angel had no problem entering the rooms.

"Faa is not here," Gitana said. She stood at Angel's side with a bared sword in her fist. Wesley and Gunn flanked Angel on the other side. Cordelia stood just behind him.

"No," Angel agreed. "Doesn't look like he left much either."

"Doesn't look like he's coming back either," Gunn said.

Although the office looked like it was ordinarily probably neat, it now lay in disarray. One of the gypsy warriors brought up the desktop computer. The monitor came on, filling the room with bright light, but no OS appeared. The warrior opened the tower case, then shook his head in disgust. "Nothing," the warrior said. "The hard drives are missing."

"He was expecting us to come here," Angel said, walking around the room. "Faa is prepared to lose the Ivers identity. He's planning on it being a casualty of the war with us."

"He has a whole world to conquer once he has all seven Founding Stones, after all," Wesley stated quietly.

Angrily, Gitana hurled the blotter from the desk. "Then where is he?"

"I don't know," Angel admitted. "He's had hundreds of years to learn how to hide. Probably has another three or four identities here in L.A. alone."

"Maybe he left the city," Cordelia suggested as she started rifling the desk drawers.

"Faa wouldn't leave," Angel said, walking slowly around the room. He smelled Chavula Faa in the room. Despite the passage of time and the cologne the man wore, Angel could still smell the Kalochner man. "Not the city. There's too much at stake. The Founding Stones are right here for the taking. That's what he has to be thinking. We haven't done anything to dissuade him of that."

The phone in Angel's duster rang. He reached into the pocket without thinking, consumed by the need to find some way to get close to Chavula Faa. He punched the send key, opening the line, thinking that Fred or Lorne was calling. "Yes," he answered.

"It's me," Spike said.

"Spike." Angel's voice came out in a harsh grate.

Then he realized he'd answered Wynowski's cell phone, not his own.

Cordelia and Wesley looked up at Angel at once. Cordelia had encountered Spike in the past, and Wesley was familiar with the vampire from his duties as a watcher. Even Gunn seemed somewhat apprehensive, and he'd only heard some of the stories.

"What do you want?" Angel demanded.

"To meet," Spike replied. "Me and you, we got some unfinished business between us."

"There's a lot of unfinished business," Angel said. "Going to be a lot until one of us is dust."

Cordelia joined Angel. Her expression was sober, maybe a little worried.

Spike laughed, but there was a trace of bitterness in the sound. "You're looking for the Founding Stones and hunting for a man named Chavula Faa. Or maybe he's hunting you."

"He's hunting you, too, from what I hear. After the robbery at Willard Hargreave's mansion."

"Then we have something in common."

Irritation filled Angel. "You have a reason for calling?"

There was a pause. Angel heard Spike take a hit on a cigarette and release it. Faint blues music sounded in the background. Spike was in a bar, but that was hardly a surprise. It also wasn't much help. L.A. held any number of bars, and many of them—according to the digital clock on the wall—would be closing down in the next five minutes with the two o'clock A.M. last-call.

"I can't use the Stone," Spike said.

"So you're offering to sell it to me?"

"I'm giving it to you. As long as I know you're going to keep it out of Chavula Faa's hands."

"Why?"

"Because we got Lyanka killed all those years ago. We owe that to her."

The answer surprised Angel. "You haven't ever bought into guilt. Lyanka was a long time ago. You've killed a lot of people since then." He remembered the ferocity Spike had exhibited when torturing him only two years ago in a dockside warehouse.

"This is about Lyanka," Spike said. "You remember her, don't you? The woman you sold out to Chavula Faa in the Carpathian Mountains after you saw her?"

"I remember," Angel said, and guilt spread heavily across his shoulders and burned into his flesh. The burden rushed at him, almost too much to bear.

"We don't have a lot of time," Spike said. "From what I understand, Faa can track down these Stones because he has some of the others."

"He has five of them."

"Then maybe we have less time than either of us is thinking."

Angel looked at the empty offices. He was all out of choices. "Where do you want to meet?"

Spike paused as if hesitant. He named a bar and gave an address in East L.A.

"I can be there in fifteen minutes," Angel said. "If you're not there—"

"I'll be here." Spike's voice hardened. "But you come alone, Angel."

The phone connection clicked dead in Angel's ear. He punched the end button and dropped the handset into his duster pocket.

"That was Spike," Cordelia said.

"Yeah," Angel said.

"You're not seriously going to see him."

"He's got Hargreave's Stone," Angel said. "And he's by himself."

"Because he killed the other people who stole the Stone with him. Spike isn't someone you can trust."

"Cordelia's right, Angel," Wesley said. "For all you know, Spike has thrown in with Chavula Faa and this is a trap."

"All the more reason to go alone," Angel said. "If something happens to me, all of you can still act."

"At least take me with you," Gunn said. "One more guy isn't gonna—"

"No." Angel's voice was grim and final. He faced Gunn. "Look, I appreciate the offer, but Spike will leave if I don't show up alone. With Chavula Faa after him, Spike probably wouldn't get far, but Faa has more manpower than we have. Faa would get to Spike first, and then we'd lose that Stone." He looked at Cordelia and Wesley. "And I appreciate the concern."

"The concern's not misplaced," Cordelia replied defiantly.

"Definitely not," Wesley said. "Throughout all the Watcher records I have seen concerning Spike, he's proven himself time after time to be conniving, traitorous, and deadly."

"I know," Angel said. "He learned from the best."

It bothered Angel that they knew whom he was talking about, and it bothered him even more that he knew he was right.

CHAPTER TWENTY-TWO

Angel scanned the streets as he drove the Belvedere down the block that contained the address Spike had given him for the bar. Only a handful of men moved along the sidewalks, their shoulders hunched against the wind that blew in from the north. The area was desolate even by East L.A. standards.

At the alley near the tattoo parlor on the corner, Angel stopped and peered along the shadowed length. Overflowing Dumpsters lined the walls behind the small businesses. The stench of decay and urine tickled Angel's nose.

At the other end of the alley, a cigarette coal

glowed orange briefly. Wynowski's phone rang in Angel's duster pocket. He took the handset out and punched send. He waited without speaking. Only one person would call him on that phone.

"I'm looking at you," Spike said over the connection. "You coming out to play or not?"

The phone clicked dead in Angel's ear. The orange coal of the cigarette moved slightly, and a small cloud of gray smoke drifted up above the silhouette of the man framed by the van he stood beside.

Reversing the convertible for a moment, Angel backed up, then pulled into the alley. He sat in the car and studied the younger vampire.

Almost disdainfully, Spike leaned his back against the van. He tilted his head back and blew a smoke ring. "Playing hard to get, Angel?"

Without a word, Angel opened the Belvedere's door and stepped out.

Spike straightened and stepped away from the van. He moved into a martial arts stance, giving himself plenty of room to move. He stared at Angel over the hot, glowing tip of his cigarette. "You came alone."

"You thought maybe I wouldn't?"

Spike shrugged. "You've changed a lot."

"Not about the things that matter."

Spike smiled. "You used to be quite the killer."

"Still am. Just changed my prey. Where's the Stone?"

"I've got it. Don't get in a lather about it."

"Like you said, there's not much time. Chavula Faa's men could be closing in on this place even now."

"They've been chasing themselves then," Spike replied. "'Cause I've been hitting different bars every few minutes. The connection between the Stones isn't instantaneous, and it only points in the general direction without giving a distance reading."

"Took me almost twenty minutes to get here," Angel said. "That's a lot of time."

"This isn't the bar I called you from." Spike smiled. "I'm homicidal, not half-witted."

"That remains to be seen. You showed up here in L.A., ended up becoming part of this thing. Not exactly a statement for good judgment. Or even an instinct for self-preservation."

"If I'd known what this was about before I bought into it, I would have stayed home and cleaned my crypt." Spike took a drag off his cigarette and let the smoke out through his nose. "But I didn't have a choice about this any more than you did. Us being here like this? Lyanka says it was fated to be."

Angel narrowed his eyes. "Lyanka?"

Spike pointed to the shadows to his left. A puzzled look framed his features. "You don't see her?"

"No," Angel answered, wondering if Spike was trying to run a fast one by him. Spike was good at hiding secrets he didn't want known.

Spike turned and spoke apparently to empty air. "Why can't he see you?"

Angel stood his ground and listened to the car noises out on the street. Farther back in the alley, a man sleeping in a cardboard box whimpered pitifully.

Turning back to Angel, Spike said, "She says you can't see her because you don't want to believe she's here."

"I don't want to believe you're here either," Angel countered. "But here you are."

Spike showed a wry grin. "Not my fault. Like I said, we didn't have choice in this. The Founding Stones brought us here."

It wasn't just the Founding Stones, though, Angel realized. It was the vision that the Powers-That-Be had given Cordelia. And it was Angelus's bloody past, the one that he had shared with Spike. Angel knew it was that, at least in part, that was as much to blame for his involvement in the present situation as his standing as the champion the Powers-That-Be had declared him to be.

But Spike?

Having Spike present made no sense.

Except that he can see the ghost of Lyanka and you can't. Angel considered that. *Why can't you see the ghost?*

"I've seen ghosts before," Angel said, as much to himself as to Spike.

"I know. I'm seen some of 'em with you." Spike blew smoke into the air. "Evidently, though, you ain't seeing this one."

"What kind of scam are you trying to pull, Spike?"

"No scam. You're the one with the vision problem. I'd rather be on my way back to Sunnydale. Got somebody there waiting on me."

Angel knew from Spike's tone that there was more to the vampire's declaration than what was plainly stated.

Spike grinned smugly. "I hated to leave this one, Angel. Truly I did. And she was sorry to see me go."

"You expect me to believe that you're here because of Lyanka's death?"

"We had a part in it," Spike agreed. "And she ain't forgot that. She decided to call in the marker at Hargreave's house."

"That's why you killed your buddies? For her?" Angel knew Spike would find some way to excuse his acts.

Exasperation showed on Spike's face. "My *buddies* weren't my buddies at all. They were about to kill me. But I killed them first."

"Why were they about to kill you?"

Spike pointed at empty air. "Because of her."

Angel glanced at the space beside Spike. "Lyanka." He tried to make his reply neutral, neither supportive nor combative.

Spike sighed and shook his head. "Yes. Her. She won't leave me alone. They caught me talking to her and got suspicious of my behavior."

"They should have started out that way. Might have kept them alive."

Anger darkened Spike's pale features. "I'm not the only one who done something wrong here, *Angelus.*" He used the name as a taunt and as an accusation. "Part of this mess I'm having to help clean up is yours. You were the one who hooked us up with Chavula Faa in Prague, and you were the one who went to Chavula Faa and told him Lyanka was at the inn during that night in the Carpathian Mountains. I didn't even know either of them were there until you rousted me out of bed to go on that little midnight ride."

Angel agonized over Spike's words. All of them were true. He had been the one to see Lyanka that night, and he had gone to Chavula Faa as soon as he'd seen the gypsy chieftain ride into the village a few hours later. Chavula Faa had paid Angel for the information, but that hadn't been the main reason he had told Faa about Lyanka.

The main reason Angel had sold the information had been that he'd wanted to see blood shed. Somehow, though, Lyanka had gotten out of the village ahead of Faa's warriors, and then his demons. For a time, she had lost her pursuers in the mountains. Only Angel's knowledge of the mountain pass had put Spike and him within striking distance of the woman before she'd made her final stand on the bridge.

He still remembered how it had been, how she had managed to get away from them. For a brief moment, it had looked like she would get away entirely. But she hadn't. Chavula Faa had split his forces. The gypsy chieftain had led the group across the bridge that had intercepted her. He'd gone on far enough without finding her tracks or seeing her that he knew she had remained on the other side of the river. He'd caught her when he returned.

Then she had sawed through the bridge supports with a knife and sheer determination and desperation, and dropped into the river. The image of Spike holding on to her later in the river, calling out for help, trying to save her even after Angelus had betrayed her, remained sharp.

Angel couldn't accept that the ghost was there. He looked at Spike. "Why would she manifest to you?"

Spike hesitated, taking a drag on the cigarette to cover. "I don't know."

But Angel knew that Spike was lying. He did know why he could see her. Or he suspected. Sometimes ghosts come back because they are tied to events or places or things that had meant something to them.

Or to people, Angel realized.

Then he thought about what he knew of Lyanka. Her lover had betrayed her, and she'd been an outcast from the Elders of her people, trafficking in knowledge forbidden to her. There couldn't have been many people who wanted to be close to her. Gitana had said that even Lyanka's immediate family hadn't supported the quests the woman had gone on.

Over the years, Lyanka had probably had a number

401

of lovers. She'd been, as Angel recalled, a beautiful woman. But even with all those loves—stolen whenever she wasn't chasing a myth or a legend, or in turn being chased—how many had truly touched her heart?

Spike had. If the ghost was truly there, Angel told himself, it was because Spike had touched her heart. Or come closer to doing that than anyone else she had ever known. And knowing Spike as he did, knowing the capacity the younger vampire had for giving all of himself to a relationship, Angel also knew that such a thing was possible.

Despite being a bloodthirsty vampire with tendencies toward violence, Spike was also an incurable romantic. He gave himself without holding anything back. He had been weak in Prague when Dru had turned away from him, and he had been hungry. He had always believed he needed someone to complete himself. Over the years, Angel had seen women respond to that need. Angel had never been able to give himself so completely as that. Not even with Buffy. In the end, he'd walked away from her to find himself in L.A., to redeem himself. Even when rejected by someone he loved, Spike never left, never went away. He'd always stayed until even the bitter dregs were burnt off.

"Lyanka's bound to this Stone, Angel," Spike said, interrupting Angel's thoughts.

"What do you mean?" Suspicion rose inside Angel again.

"This Stone, the one that Hargreave had, it was the one she gave her life for that night on the bridge," Spike said. "When she cursed us with her dying breath, the spell bound us all to this Stone. She's told me that."

"And you believe her?"

"She's dead. Why would she lie?"

"You're a known liar," Angel countered. "Why would you tell the truth?"

"Because I don't have a damned choice," Spike roared. "I'm stuck here, same as you."

"Not the same as me," Angel said. "You've never been the same as me." The old anger swelled within him then. "Give me the Stone."

"You've got to understand the risks involved," Spike said.

"I do understand them. If Chavula Faa gets all the Stones, he can open a doorway to the world the Kalochner came from. With the military technology he's gotten his hands on in this world, he can hurt a lot of people over there. Over here, too."

"He's got to be stopped."

"I'll stop him," Angel said. "Give me the Stone."

Spike hesitated. "I'll bring the Stone."

"What do you mean?"

Spike shook his head. "I mean that you're not getting the Stone without me."

"That's stupid."

Spike shrugged. "That's how it's gonna be. You don't see Lyanka. Maybe you don't even believe she exists. But if Faa gets his hands on this Stone while she's bound to it, he can hurt her. I'm not going to have that happen. Somebody's gotta stand up for her in this."

"I'm working with her granddaughter."

"And you're working with me."

Slowly, Angel shook his head. "That's not happening."

"You can use another man," Spike said. "You can't tell me that's not true."

"Not you. No way."

"You're not listening to me." Anger turned Spike's face hard. He looked at a space to his right and spoke as if addressing another person. "He's not listening to me. I told you he wouldn't listen to me. We'd have been better off trying to do this ourselves the way I told you."

"I'm listening," Angel said. "I'm just not buying into the fact that you feel a need to help. Give me the Stone."

Without warning, Spike launched himself at Angel and drove a kick to Angel's midsection. Unprepared for the blow, Angel caught the kick squarely. Pain shot through him, paralyzing him for a moment. He flew backward against the opposite alley wall. He barely got his hands up to meet Spike's next attack.

Fred Burkle walked from the hotel galley to the lobby with two cups of freshly brewed hot tea. She moved carefully because she was too tired from spending hours hunched over the keyboard to trust her footing. Her eyes burned from staring at the monitor too long.

Worry gnawed at her reserves incessantly, but that was also what kept her going. Angel, Wesley, Cordelia, and Gunn were somewhere out there, perhaps even now battling against Chavula Faa and his minions.

Surely they would have called first, she told herself. Her brain, creative and practical as it was—and always leaning toward factoring in known facts to come up with resolutions to questions—some of which hadn't even been asked yet, insisted on summoning up horrible ends for her four friends.

For a moment, when Fred saw the gypsy warriors Gitana had left behind after the others had gone to confront Chavula Faa, she thought the men were just sleeping. She didn't blame them. The last two days had been hectic at the hotel, and she'd had no idea what the Kalochner warriors had been facing before they had arrived earlier that evening. *That was yesterday, wasn't it?* Time sometimes got confusing when Angel Investigations worked around the clock.

Then Fred saw the blood. Crimson pools of it lay everywhere, like a blood glacier had drifted through and left lakes and ponds and rivers and streams in its wake. Knives and arrows stuck out of the bodies of the dozen men that had been left to watch over Lorne, Connor, and her. Fred knew they hadn't been prisoners. At least, not exactly.

But they hadn't been free to go, either.

Unable to hold the cups of tea in her suddenly shaking hands, Fred dropped them. The cups shattered against the floor. Hot liquid splattered over her feet.

"Don't look, sugarplum," Lorne advised softly. He was off to her right, out of sight. "They're all dead. Killed while you were in there pouring tea."

Fred's breath caught in the back of her throat as she surveyed the dead. She couldn't turn away. It wasn't that they were dead, or that there were a dozen of them that were dead. Even before joining Angel's efforts at helping the helpless, Fred had seen a number of deaths in Pylea. She wasn't used to blood and gore, or even accepting of it, but she was no stranger to sudden and violent death.

"Fred," Lorne called softly. "Just relax. I don't think they want to hurt us. At least, they don't want to hurt us yet."

They?

Before she could turn to figure out what Lorne was talking about, Fred felt cold, naked steel slide along her throat. Her first instinct was to back away the instant she recognized that she had a knife at her throat. She'd been there before too.

A strong hand clamped the back of her neck, freezing her in place.

"Don't move, girl," a harsh voice said softly into her ear. "We want you alive, but we have the demon. And we have the child. Maybe we don't need you. Act smart, and you'll live."

"O—Okay," Fred said. She glanced out of the corner of her eye and saw the gypsy warrior standing there. Slowly, the man turned her around till she faced Lorne.

The Anagogic demon sat uncomfortably behind the high desk. His head tilted to one side while a gypsy warrior held a sword blade along his jawline. Connor was asleep in Lorne's arms. The baby had woken briefly after Angel had left, but Connor went to sleep again while Lorne sang lullabies to him.

A man with a shaved head stepped forward with a confident stride. Like his men, he wore athletic gear instead of the more traditional gypsy garb of Gitana's warrior.

Like the dead men, Fred couldn't help remembering.

"Do you know who I am?" the man asked.

"Chavula Faa," Fred answered, knowing it was the truth. "But you're also known as Thomas Ivers." Then she realized that maybe she shouldn't have said so much.

The corner of Faa's lips quirked up in a quick smile of amused surprise. "Correct. You work with the vampire?"

Fred hesitated.

"Tell him the truth, princess," Loren said. He looked uncomfortable with the sword at his throat. "This guy doesn't ask questions unless he already knows the answers. He and his little army crept in here undetected. Don't know how that happened. But they're good at what they do."

Faa smiled again, and the effort was completely mirthless and merciless. "Your demon friend is right. I know enough to know when you are lying."

"They went looking for you," Fred said. "To your offices." She paused, feeling more scared than ever. "I guess they're not going to find you there."

"No." Faa turned his attention to the dead guards. "Those are Gitana's men. I recognize them by their clothing and by the tattoos they wear."

Fred nodded.

"I also know that she left the Founding Stone with them. Where is it?"

Resolutely, Fred remained silent. She was a prisoner. If Faa wanted her dead, then she'd have been as dead as the guards.

Swift as a striking snake, Faa whipped his arm forward. His fingers wrapped around Fred's face.

Despite the situation, Fred started to struggle to get away. Then she felt like her body had been flooded with Novocain and her mind pried open like an orange. A moment later, Faa released her.

The gypsy chieftain turned and pointed to the desk. "There is a safe behind there. The Stone is inside."

"No," Fred said, feeling totally responsible. "You can't do that."

"I can," Faa told her in a low voice. "And I will."

Fred took an involuntary step forward, but Faa

slid a dagger free and tucked the point up under her chin, freezing her in her tracks. "No," he commanded softly. "There is one other task you will accomplish for me tonight."

This is stupid!

Bloodied and battered, Spike sat back on his haunches and glared at Angel. Angel sat equally battered and bloodied against the wall on the other side of the alley.

"It's not stupid," Spike told Lyanka. The ghost stood between them, her hands on her hips. "It's just how things are between him and me. They've been that way for a long time. He thinks he's Little Lord Fauntleroy or something. Look at his hair. Even after the fight, not a hair out of place."

Lyanka cursed in colorful language, getting particular about men in general and their ability to think for themselves.

"Talking to your imaginary friend, Captain Peroxide?" Angel knuckled blood from his mouth. "Pleading insanity isn't going to help you. When I get my second wind, I'm going to get up again and kick your butt."

"You just go ahead and try," Spike invited. He spat blood and smiled like his ribs weren't killing him. Over the years, he had trained with Angel. Even after the hundred years since Angel had gotten his soul back, they'd had occasion to fight. They were still evenly matched, and going head-to-head as they were, it was hard to find an advantage. "But while you're planning on delivering me a proper comeuppance, you've got to remember that you're wasting time. And allowing Faa's forces to perhaps close in on us."

"Is that what you were hoping to do by attacking me?" Angel demanded. "Delay me till Faa could get here?"

"Faa's not on his way here," Spike said. "Not yet, anyway. You just pissed me off."

"You could be lying."

"And I could be telling the truth." Spike shoved himself to his feet, swaying slightly for an instant as his senses reeled. He closed his eyes, reaching out for Doxxil, the surviving Qorqoth demon brother. A brief image flickered into his mind. "Faa's somewhere else. At a hotel. Getting into a safe. There's a woman there, a skinny brunette. An Anagogic demon. And a child." He opened his eyes and saw Angel standing across from him.

Suspicion darkened Angel's eyes. "How do you know that?"

"The Qorqoth demon that put together the Hargreave robbery," Spike explained. "He put a binding spell on all of us. Didn't know one of the Qorqoths was still alive until I felt him in my head a little while ago."

"This demon is with Faa?"

Spike nodded. "I saw him there."

"In the hotel?"

"Yeah." Feeling that maybe they weren't going to fight at least for a little while, Spike reached under his jacket and took out his cigarettes. He lit up and puffed contentedly. "That's what I've been trying to tell you. I'm stuck in this situation just as badly as you are. Even if I give you the Stone I have, there's a good chance Faa will come looking for me."

"Why?"

"You don't think he wants every Kalochner out there in this world to know what he's done, do you?"

Angel didn't reply.

"You always hated loose ends," Spike said.

Lyanka walked over to Angel. She reached out and ran her hands over him. "I don't understand," she said.

"Do you feel anything?" Spike asked.

"No. Should I?"

"Lyanka's trying to touch you."

Angel took a step away as if the experience was unsettling. "Those people you saw. Were they all right?"

"Yeah, but there were dead gypsies everywhere. Didn't look like Chavula Faa's people. These guys had some kind of traditional clothing on."

"They're Gitana's people."

"I didn't see Cordy there. You're still hanging with her, aren't you?"

"Yeah."

"Then who are these people?"

"Associates."

Spike smiled. "Then you're a growing concern. Next thing you know, you'll be opening up a branch office." He raised a hand and mimed reading a sign. "'Angel and Son.' Has a ring to it."

"Son?"

Spike knew that Angel was suddenly more antsy than before, but he had no reason for it. "Son. Daughter." He shrugged. "'Angel and Partners' just doesn't sound quite as colonial."

Relaxing a little, Angel came toward him. "I need that Stone, Spike."

Spike readied himself for battle again. "And you'll get it. It's just that I'm part of the package."

Stopping a few feet away, Angel held his distance. "I'd heard you were with Buffy."

Panic assailed Spike. If Angel knew—or even only suspected—that Spike had been involved with Buffy, Spike knew that they'd be battling to the death.

He doesn't know, Lyanka said, moving toward them and placing a reassuring cold hand on his shoulder. *Just stay steady.*

"Working with Xander, Anya, Willow, and Dawn," Angel went on.

"Buffy trusts me," Spike said. His throat thickened. He wanted to say more, to crow about the relationship he'd been having with the Slayer. But he knew that only one of them would walk away from the ensuing confrontation. If Spike had known that he would be the one to walk away, he would have bragged about it. At the same time, though, he felt certain that Angel would have known that the relationship with Buffy was over.

Temporarily, Spike told himself.

"I'm not Buffy," Angel said in a low, dangerous voice. "I know what you've done, and I know what you're capable of."

Convince him that you're just here to help, Lyanka said. Her voice held frustration.

Spike never took his eyes from Angel's eyes. "I can't," he told the ghost. "He knows me. He knows me as he remembers he was himself. He's the reason you ended up dead."

"Spike," Angel said. He was going to say more, maybe even threaten. But his phone rang then. He reached into one pocket of his duster and took out a phone. He answered the phone, but the ringing persisted. He took another phone from another pocket and tried again.

Spike waited. The conversation was brief. When it was over, Angel pocketed the phone and looked at Spike.

"Problem?" Spike asked.

"Those associates you saw in the hotel?" Angel asked. "Chavula Faa has them. He wants to trade them for the Stone you have or he's going to kill them."

"How did he know you were with me?"

"The associates Chavula Faa is holding called Cordelia first. She told Faa I was going to meet you.

I'd told him I did find you, and that I had the Stone."

Spike grinned. "Then you need me."

"I need the Stone."

Anger got the better of Spike. "Damn it, Angel! Why can't you get it through that thick head of yours that I can help you?"

William! Lyanka shouted.

"Because helping people is not what you're about, Spike," Angel said in a low, level voice. "You do things only when it suits you."

"It suits me to save Lyanka."

"Your invisible friend?"

Spike had to resist the temptation to strike Angel. "She's real. And you're wasting time you could be using to save your associates."

Angel appeared hesitant.

"C'mon," Spike entreated. "If Chavula Faa is calling the shots, he's gonna deal himself the best hand. From the bottom of the deck. And you can bet that if he offers to let you walk away from all of this, he's lying. The only way you're going to turn the tables on him and maybe get yourself and your *associates* out of the line of fire is by putting a joker into play."

"With you as the joker?"

Spike smiled. "If the card fits."

"You've got the Stone?"

Turning, Spike walked back to the van that had belonged to the Qorqoth demons. He tripped the electronic locks and reached into the compartment hidden between the two captain's chairs. He brought out a black leather bag.

"The Stone?" Angel asked.

"Yeah," Spike replied. "Plus a little surprise." He hesitantly offered the bag. "I figured that whoever I ended up dealing with—you or Chavula Faa—I might need an edge." He nodded to the bag. "One of the Qorqoth demon's tricks, that bag. The bottom's lined with plastic explosives." He shrugged. "Don't know how explosive it is, but it should at least guarantee a few seconds of confusion. Maybe even take out Chavula Faa if he's sitting on top of it when it goes off."

Angel took the bag and looked inside, recognizing the distinctive shape of the Founding Stone.

Spike smoked, and a small grin tracked his face. "Told you it was there."

"We're going to need more than a trick bag to give us the edge we need."

"All right." For a moment, Spike was caught up in the excitement that used to flow through them when they were planning and plotting. "What edge?"

Angel was quiet for a moment. "We need to get up close and personal. Chavula Faa is meeting us at an address near the ocean. Probably one of the properties he owns here. He has control of the battlefield, though. He'll have men ringing the place. Tobar is there."

Spike nodded. "Big guy. Scar through his eyebrow."

"That's him. He'll probably be set up on the hostages. They'll be somewhere close to Faa. If they aren't, I'll negotiate it that way."

"So what is the edge you want?"

Angel was quiet for a moment. "Remember Marseilles? De Beck and his family?"

Spike shook his head. He had *hated* Marseilles. "Not Marseilles."

"It's the only way," Angel said. "Are you in or out?"

CHAPTER TWENTY-THREE

L.A. shadows closed in around Angel as he drove to the address Chavula Faa had given him. He worked to keep himself calm, focusing on the plan and trying not to remember how much of it depended on Spike. Marseilles had been a risky thing for both of them, and Spike had to sell the current feint.

Connor was in danger, as were Fred and Lorne. Angel knew that Chavula Faa wouldn't hesitate to put any of them to death. They all knew more than Faa would want anyone to know about the Founding Stones. The cell phone rang. Angel fished the handset from his pocket and answered.

"Angel," Wesley said in a calm voice. "We're here."

Here, Angel knew, was a position two blocks away. He'd deliberately given Wesley, Cordelia, and Gitana the wrong address.

"We don't see Faa," Wesley went on. "Gitana is getting quite agitated."

"Faa's not there," Angel said.

Wesley waited.

Angel gave the address of the real meeting place. "Give me time to sell this thing before you bring in the troops."

"How will I know when is the proper time?"

"I'll call you. When I do, come running."

"All right." Wesley hesitated. "Good luck." He knew that Faa had taken Lorne, Fred, and Connor from the hotel.

As he handled the Belvedere, making the last turn to the night-darkened lot where major construction was taking place, Angel dwindled down inside himself. No emotion would touch him again unless he allowed it, and that wouldn't be until he was on the other side of the situation he currently found himself facing. It was a warrior's mindset. The technique was almost as demanding as letting loose the demon inside him while at the same time keeping control.

He raked his gaze over the yellow earth-moving equipment that filled the lot. Faa had chosen a good site for the exchange. The other buildings around the area were all small businesses that closed with the setting sun. There were no restaurants or bars, nothing that would encourage a late-night crowd. The hurricane fence surrounding the lot stood twelve feet tall.

Signs posted on the mesh advertised the presence of security. That meant that law enforcement presence in the area would be minimal.

Men rolled the double gates back smoothly as Angel neared them. He halted outside the gates, staring through the shadows that covered the uneven terrain inside the development area. Tall hills of gravel and sand and dirt framed the short road that ran into the development area.

One of the men flicked on a flashlight and waved Angel inside.

Angel drove through the gates, watching in the rearview mirror as the men locked the gates after him. He braked to a stop just inside the area and stared at the limousine parked fifty yards away facing him as a cloud of dust rolled over him. Several men stood among the tall hills and amid the earthmovers. All of them were armed.

Reaching into his duster pocket, Angel took out his cell phone and dialed the number Faa had used earlier to call him. The phone rang twice while Angel sat in the convertible and watched patches of dust drift in front of the headlights. If he had to, he could drive through the gates or the hurricane fence to get away. But Faa's trap was more than just the barricade.

"Yes?" Faa answered.

"I'm here."

"I see you."

"Yeah," Angel said. "I don't see you."

"I'm here."

"Show me. Or I'll throw this car in reverse and back out through your shiny new gates back there."

"Your friends' lives are at stake."

"My friends," Angel forced himself to say, "may already be dead."

"You don't trust me?" Chavula Faa's tone was mocking.

"Give me a reason to."

"After all these years we have known each other, Angelus."

"I want to know that my friends are alive before I come any closer."

"Very well."

One of the limousine's doors opened. Fred and Lorne got out, obviously handcuffed. Fred held Connor.

In a distant part of himself that Angel would have denied having access to, Angel felt a twinge of relief. He blocked the feeling away immediately. No one was safe till Chavula Faa was dead and the Stones were recovered.

"All right," Angel said. "I'm coming in." He put his foot on the accelerator and drove forward over the uneven ground. The convertible rocked back and forth like a ship caught out on choppy water.

Before he could get close to Fred, Lorne, and Connor, men with assault rifles stepped up in front of the limousine and blocked the way. Getting the message, Angel put the car in park, but left the keys in the ignition and the engine running. He opened the door and stepped out.

"Man, Angel," Lorne said, "you are a sight for sore eyes!"

Fred smiled at Angel hopefully. She glanced down at the sleeping baby. "Connor's all right. I swear he could sleep through anything."

Chavula Faa stepped out of the limo's rear seat. "You were supposed to bring the Stone," he said. "Please don't tell me you're playing games with it or I will be forced to kill one of these people to show you how serious I am."

"I've got it," Angel said, jerking a thumb over his shoulder. "It's in the back of the car. Brought you a surprise, too."

Faa scowled. "A surprise wasn't part of the deal."

"I think you'll like this one. Consider it more of a gift." Angel walked to the rear of the car. "You knew one of the thieves that took the Founding Stone from Hargreave's home."

"Spike."

"Right. He was the one with the Stone at the end. He killed his partners."

"How did you find him?"

Angel reached into his duster pocket, attracting the immediate attention of the guards around Faa.

He moved slowly, revealing the cell phone that he held. "I also found out who hired the Barkuk demons that tried to steal the Stone that arrived in the dockyards yesterday."

"Who?"

"Bill Wynowski." Angel opened the Belvedere's trunk. Moonlight fell across Spike's body lying inside. A short sword protruded from his chest. Blood matted his shirt and jacket.

"Hargreave's attorney at Wolfram and Hart?" Faa seemed genuinely amused. "I can't say I'm surprised that one of them would do such a thing, but Wynowski really didn't seem the type."

Almost effortlessly, Angel lifted Spike's body from the trunk of the car. "Here's your surprise." He threw Spike's body forward, but acted like he stumbled and ended up tossing Spike close to Lorne's and Fred's positions. They, as well as the guards, scooted backward.

Spike landed on his back. The sword jutted straight up from his chest. By all accounts, he looked dead as a doornail.

"He didn't like the idea of giving the Stone up and not getting paid for it," Angel explained. "We had a small disagreement." He smiled. "I won."

"So I see." Faa stepped away from the body. "He's not dead. He's a vampire."

Back in Marseilles, when Angelus and Spike had set up the De Beck family and stolen a fortune, the De Becks hadn't known that. They had believed that

Spike had been dead after Angelus had shoved a sword through him—till he had risen up and attacked them.

Faa wasn't going to be as easy to fool, but Angel knew that the man was aware he and Spike were not friends.

"He's not dust," Angel agreed. "But he's hurt. He's also yours. To do with whatever you choose. A bonus."

Faa nodded at one of his men.

The man stepped forward and yanked the sword, dragging it through Spike's flesh. Spike didn't move.

"Torturing him now isn't going to do much good," Angel said. "You're going to have to wait for him to wake up."

The man released the sword and stepped back.

Faa looked at Angel. "What about the Stone? Where is it?"

Reaching into the Belvedere's trunk again, Angel brought out the black bag that Spike had given him that contained the Stone. He started toward Faa with the bag.

"No," Faa ordered. "Hand it to one of my men. You stay there. I don't trust you."

Angel tossed the bag to the nearest guard. The guard opened the bag and Angel started counting down from twenty. He pressed the speed dial for Wesley's cell phone.

"It's here," the guard said.

"Give me the Stone." Excitement stained Faa's voice.

The guard took the Stone from the bag but hung on to the bag. He handed the Stone over to Faa.

—*nine, eight, seven,* Angel thought, keeping count. He glanced at Spike.

"Did you know that this is the first time seven Founding Stones have been together since my people first arrived in this world?" Faa asked.

"Yeah," Angel said. He braced for the coming explosion, staying with the Belvedere as if he were cowed by the guards and their automatic weapons.

—*four, three*—

"Hello," Wesley answered.

"Now," Angel said softly. His voice drew Faa's attention. Suspicion darkened the gypsy leader's face. He opened his mouth to speak, but it was already too late.

The guard with the bag turned and walked away, conferring with someone on the walkie-talkie he carried. Before he had gone two steps, the bag blew up, a full two-count behind what Angel had been expecting.

The concussive blast knocked everyone from their feet. Blood and gore rained down over the nearest gypsies.

"Kill him!" Faa yelled, shoving himself back up.

The recovering guards immediately brought their weapons to bear.

Dropping to take advantage of the scant cover the

Belvedere offered, Angel filled his hands with throwing stars. Automatic gunfire raked the front of the convertible, promising days spent in a bodywork shop.

At the same moment, Gitana's band of warriors arrived. A dozen vehicles, vans and SUVs, rammed through the hurricane fence and tore across the uneven terrain. Their advance was bottlenecked by the hills of sand and gravel. In seconds, a full-fledged war had broken out on the development site.

Angel only hoped that Spike stuck to the plan.

Get up!

Snarling curses, the explosion still ringing in his ears and wondering why that deafening noise hadn't prevented him from hearing Lyanka's ghost, Spike rolled to his feet. A nearby guard looked at him in astonishment.

Come on, William. You must help save the baby. Lyanka stood over the baby and the young brunette who had held him. *Quickly! Quickly!*

"Easy for you to say," Spike groused, "you don't have a sword run through you." He stood, then kicked the gypsy in front of him in the face. Teeth scattered across the ground and the gypsy's mouth was a bloody ruin. Spike stamped down on his opponent's head before the man could rise. The gypsy's neck snapped.

Steeling himself, Spike gripped the handle of the sword and hauled the blade out of his body. Maybe the weapon couldn't kill him, but it hurt like hell. Blood-covered as it was, the grip didn't feel too sure, but he swept the sword back and attacked the nearest of the guards.

William! The baby!

The young brunette was cowering on the ground, bent over the baby in an obvious effort to protect him. Bullets chewed into the ground from several directions.

"C'mon! C'mon, now!" he yelled at the woman. "Let's get the baby out of the line of fire!"

The woman looked at him fearfully.

Spike leaned down and took up the assault rifle dropped by the man he'd dispatched with the sword. He brought the weapon to his shoulder and squeezed the trigger, sweeping out at two guards' positions. The bullets caught the men and staggered them.

Looking at the woman, Spike said, "Your name is Fred, right? Winifred Burkle?" He cut his eyes to the Anagogic demon. "And you're Doyle, right? I think I saw you last time I was in L.A."

"No," the green demon replied. "Doyle's dead. I'm Lorne."

"Great, Lorne," Spike said. "Now that we're all properly introduced, what do you say about just getting the hell out of here now while we're all in one piece?" He glanced down at the wound in his chest. "More or less of a piece."

The young woman, Fred, climbed to her feet. She kept one arm securely wrapped around the crying baby. She ran in the direction Spike indicated, around the tall gravel hill back toward the newly arrived vans and SUVs.

"Keep going in that direction," Spike ordered. "Gitana's warriors should be coming from that direction."

"All right," she replied.

Spike turned back around and sprayed Faa's men with the assault rifle. Bullets bit into his flesh, but he ignored the pain and stayed focused.

He took momentary respite behind a hill of gravel. Noting the dead man almost underfoot that he had dropped only seconds ago, Spike fleeced the corpse of extra magazines for the assault rifle.

Glancing up, he saw Angel in action. Throwing stars flew from Angel's hands with unerring accuracy. Even after all the times he'd seen Angel in combat, as Angel or as Angelus, Spike was still impressed by his prowess as a warrior. He also still thought he could take him if he had to.

Then a familiar sound drew his attention. He glanced up and watched an executive helicopter streaking for the lot.

Angel broke cover from the bullet-riddled Belvedere and ran toward the nearest gravel hill in pursuit of Chavula Faa. He paused only long enough to take the long-handled battle-ax from the car's rear seat. Bullets struck sparks from the rocks and started miniature avalanches that cascaded down the hills for a moment as the shooters tracked Angel's passage. He felt the demon take his face, adding in speed and strength. Movement ahead of him alerted him and drove him to cover just as three gunners opened fire on him as he rounded the hill.

He put his back to the gravel hill and noticed the swirl of dust that suddenly rose up from the ground. Then he heard the rhythmic chopping of helicopter blades.

The helicopter descended fast, like an attacking bird of prey, touching down just behind Faa's limousine. Faa was up and moving at once, taking advantage of his few surviving guards as he raced to the helicopter.

Auto-fire from the assault rifles kept Angel pinned down. Frustrated, he could only watch as Faa worked in relative security to take a bag from the limousine's rear. Faa stuffed the Stone he'd gotten from Angel into the bag. Light started glowing among the Stones, muted only a little by the bag he carried.

For a moment, Faa stood transfixed, evidently surprised by the reaction. Angel knew that the man didn't know how dangerous the Founding Stones were if they weren't treated properly. Faa had already pushed them into the critical situation Wesley had warned them about.

Faa slung the bag over his shoulder and ran for the waiting helicopter that had only then touched down on the ground. He was going to get away. The whirling blades stirred up clouds of dust that rolled over the landscape and obscured him.

Anger ripped through Angel. Faa had endangered Connor, had broken into the hotel and taken Fred and Lorne and his son at gunpoint. Allowing the gypsy to live after he had menaced Connor was unacceptable. Allowing Chavula Faa to get away with the Founding Stones and a way to pillage another world was impossible.

Angel turned and sprinted up the gravel hill. His feet sank into the shifting rock, losing inches but gaining feet with each stride. The three gunmen chased him with their weapons, closing quickly.

Twenty feet up the gravel hill, Angel leaped into the air and arched his body toward the three gypsies firing at him. Bullets ripped through his duster. He flipped and turned and twisted, landing among them. Lashing out with the battle-ax, he drove the wooden handle into one man's stomach and knocked the wind from him.

Another man turned and tried to bring his assault rifle to bear. Angel swept the weapon away with the ax-head, then slammed the haft into the side of the man's skull. Unconscious, the man dropped. Wheeling, Angel blocked the third man's weapon with the battle-ax. Continuing the motion, Angel brought his left leg around and back, driving his heel into the man's face and rendering the gypsy unconscious.

He turned, knowing Faa had gained precious time. Spotting the gypsy leader pulling himself

aboard the helicopter, Angel launched himself forward. Feet pounded the gravel and loose earth at his
side. He glanced over his shoulder and spotted Spike
gaining on him, wearing his own demon's face.

Angel had to stop himself from asking about his
son. "My friends?" he asked instead.

"Safe," Spike replied. "Hurry. I don't want to be
haunted forever." He put on a burst of speed, temporarily gaining a lead.

The helicopter rotor wash became more intense, a
wall of force that hammered Angel and shoved grit
into his eyes. The lights winked through the whir of
blades.

Faa ran to the helicopter and clambered into the
passenger seat beside the pilot. Angel reached him
before he could get the door shut.

"Take off!" Faa commanded. "Take off now!"

The helicopter lifted at once, digging its blades
into the sky.

Angel's hands skidded along the door, unable to
maintain a grip. He knew Spike was on the other side
of the helicopter, beating against the door with his
fists. As the landing skids came up, Angel dropped
the battle-ax and grabbed hold of the skids, rising
with the helicopter as he pulled himself up.

An assault rifle gave a full-throated roar. From the
corner of his eye through the helicopter, Angel saw
the rear gunners take deliberate aim at Spike. The
bullets chewed through the Plexiglas window and
ripped into Spike's body.

Overcome by pain, Spike slipped from the helicopter's side. Bloody smears tracked the glass where his hands had slid down.

Angel rammed his left hand through the back door window as the gunner whirled to face him. He gripped the super-heated barrel and yanked the weapon away, throwing it out over the construction area as Spike hit the ground thirty feet below. Reaching back in through the window, Angel caught the gypsy's shirt front as the man reached for a holstered sidearm. Mercilessly, he yanked the man through the window and dropped him.

Wind shoved down at Angel. He reached for Faa's door, watching as the man mouthed words and pointed at him. Even as Faa screamed the words, Angel's hand crashed through the glass and he seized the man's wrist. Angel pulled, yanking the man through the door but losing his hold on him because the door swung open more.

Angel's foot slipped on the skid as the helicopter tilted. He lost his purchase and fell, desperately managing to seize Faa's leg as the gypsy leader tried to push himself back into the aircraft. Both of them tumbled free of the helicopter, falling forty feet to the hard ground below.

Stunned for a moment, thankful that he hadn't landed on the battle-ax he'd dropped when attempting to board the helicopter, Angel forced himself to his feet.

Spike was already up, already in motion, closing in

on Faa even as the helicopter pilot guided the craft back toward the earth. Faa rose to one knee and threw out a hand. A wall of shimmering force collided with Spike, then caught Angel and swelled back over them both, knocking them backward like a child's toys for a hundred feet until they slammed up against a bulldozer.

By the time Angel could think clearly again, Faa was up and running, closing the distance between himself and the descending helicopter. Hurting, having difficulty moving, Angel stood and knew that he'd never reach the helicopter in time. He watched the helicopter blades whirl as Spike gathered himself and launched himself in pursuit.

Thinking about the helicopter blades made Angel remember how vulnerable they were. He'd seen or read that even pistol shots were known to bring helicopters down with damage to the blades. He ran forward and found the battle-ax he'd dropped, turning his steps toward the nearest gravel pile instead of in pursuit of Faa. He needed room to throw.

Raising the battle-ax to his shoulder, Angel raced up the gravel hillside, nearly falling with each step as rocks shifted out from under him. Then he was twenty feet up, looking down at the helicopter thirty feet away as Faa neared the aircraft. Guards joined him, falling into step with him. Their assault rifles blazed, driving Spike to cover. Then they turned their attention to Angel.

Without hesitation, already feeling bullets kicking

into the gravel at his feet and whistling past his head, Angel threw the battle-ax. Whirling end over end, the battle-ax reached the spinning blades before Faa reached the helicopter.

As soon as the heavy ax's trajectory took it into the path of the blades, the blades shattered. The deadly shrapnel ripped through Faa and his guards, and tore holes in the helicopter's body and Plexiglas nose.

Faa dropped like a puppet with its strings cut. Fire and smoke belched out from the helicopter's motor.

Then Gitana and her warriors were there among Faa and his guards. The surviving gypsies didn't get much mercy from Gitana's people after the bloodbath that had happened at the hotel.

Angel joined in, working on getting to the sack that contained the Founding Stones. By the time he'd worked his way to the bag, the Stones were glowing even more brightly.

Chavula's bloody corpse lay nearby, sliced into sections by the flying shrapnel. His eyes already held an unseeing stare.

"Well now," Spike said when he saw Faa, "there's a man who can't handle stress without going to pieces."

Wesley hunkered down by the glowing bag. "The Stones have already been activated by the proximity to one another. They need to be in proper alignment to open the Bridge to Journeyhome. Otherwise, they'll explode and take out a few city blocks because of all the unharnessed power."

"Then put them together," Angel said.

"I can't. I don't know the sequence or the place-ment." A look of helpless frustration filled Wesley's face.

Angel reached into the bag to try to separate the Stones. The heat was almost so hot that it burned him. He yanked his hands back.

"I can do it," Spike volunteered.

"You?" Cordelia said.

"Me," Spike insisted. He leaned forward and started to work, and as he did, Lyanka's ghost shim-mered in the air above him, letting them know she was guiding every move he made.

In seconds, the seven Founding Stones made an ancient mark on the ground. With a hollow pop, the bridge between worlds opened.

Angel stared in wonder at the idyllic lands that lay at the other end of the rainbow-colored bridge.

"Oh my God," Gitana said. "Have you ever seen anything so beautiful?"

"No," Cordelia replied.

The other end of the bridge stretched across a placid silver stream. A trail wound up between a thick forest filled with wildlife, birds, and small, furred animals.

"We can go home again," Gitana said, "to the land of our forebears."

Then a monstrous crocodile-thing broke the surface of the stream and snatched a large bird from the air. The bird squawked in fear until the crocodile-thing took it below the water.

"Or not," Cordelia suggested.

EPILOGUE

"Sleeping?"

Angel opened his eyes and looked at Cordelia standing in the bedroom door. "No. Just taking a little time with Connor."

The baby lay stretched out alongside him in his bedroom at the hotel. Angel enjoyed the warmth that his son exuded, but he was also aware that at room temperature he might feel cold to Connor.

Two days had passed since the Founding Stones had been gathered. For the time being, Gitana had decided to keep her group in the world they knew best. But they were talking about getting together with other Kalochner clans, letting them know of their true heritage, and sending exploration parties into their homeworld to see what they would find there.

"So, did you ever find out what Spike was doing here?" Cordelia asked.

"No."

"You guys worked well together against Chavula Faa. That whole sword-through-the-chest thing really bought some time."

"Yeah."

"But it wouldn't have fooled me. I would have remembered that Spike was a vampire and that the only dead vampire is a dusty vampire."

"You've probably been around more vampires than Faa has."

"Probably."

"And Faa was more interested in the seventh Stone than in making certain anyone was dead. That was what he had his guards for."

"Being around Spike, reliving Lyanka's death—maybe even seeing her ghost as Spike moved the Stones around—because I know he didn't figure that out by himself—"

"No."

"Well, that little trip down memory lane must have been hard."

"It was." Angel traced Connor's sleeping smile with a forefinger. The baby smiled a little bigger, and the expression filled Angel's heart with hope.

Cordelia joined him on the bed, lying on the other side of Connor.

Angel liked Cordelia being there. Somehow they seemed to fit together. It was . . . comfortable.

"What you were, Angel," Cordelia said in a soft voice, "you can't get away from that. You can't go back and undo those days. But you can keep reaching higher and making a better life for yourself. You already have."

"I know."

"And you've got help here, Angel. A family. Even beyond Connor." Cordelia touched Connor's hair. "You don't ever have to be alone again, and you don't have to be afraid of us finding out who you *were*, because we're dealing with who you *are*."

"There's still a lot you guys don't know."

"Doesn't matter." Cordelia smiled at Connor. "We're going to be busy raising this little guy. He'll be grown before you know it." She pushed up from the bed. "I'll leave you two alone. Let you get some real quality guy-time."

Angel watched her go. She was right about the family. He felt it more and more every day. He listened to Connor breathing soft and low beside him. Even though he didn't have to breathe, he did, matching his son's rhythm, enjoying the closeness.

He was asleep before he knew it.

Hello, William.

Spike looked across the table in the small diner and saw that Lyanka had appeared there. "I haven't seen you in a while."

I've been busy. Now that the Stones are in safe

hands, I think I'm going to be able to move on from here.

A trace of sadness touched Spike's heart. He hid the feeling with a smile, but he felt certain she could see right through him. "Me too," he said.

Lyanka arched an eyebrow. *Moving on?*

"Going back to Sunnydale. Got some unfinished business of my own to tend to."

The loan shark.

Spike shrugged. "He's just a small part of it."

I thought you owed him a large amount of money.

"I did. But by the time I sold off Arrag's van and the gadgets he had crammed in there, I got enough to square that and put back a little."

So you're going back for the Slayer?

Spike felt a little uncomfortable. "Yes."

Do you love her?

Spike chose not to answer.

Smiling, Lyanka said, *Of course you do. You always do. Just as you loved me all those years ago.* She reached out and touched his face. He felt the chill of her presence against his flesh. *There's still something very young and innocent about you, William. In spite of all the evil you've done. I'm going to miss that about you.*

Spike looked at her. He didn't want to ask the question, but he couldn't stop himself. "Did you love me?"

She smiled at him. *During those few days we had in Prague? Yes. All that I could.*

Spike felt a little better about that.

I can read your palm, you know, she offered. *Find out what may be in store for you and your Slayer.*

Closing his hand into a fist, Spike shook his head. "No thanks. Whatever's ahead, I'll wait to see it."

Lyanka looked at him. *I just came to say a final good-bye.* She leaned forward and kissed him, and her lips tasted of honey but lacked the warmth he remembered from Prague. He missed that.

Then, in the space of a drawn breath, she faded away. Her fingers slipped through his as he reached out to touch her one last time.

Impulsively, he rose and walked to the pay phone. He dropped in change and dialed Buffy's number.

"Hello," she said, and he realized again how much he loved the sound of her voice.

"It's me."

There was silence on the line for a moment before she spoke. "Look, Spike," Buffy said softly, "I'm not going to change my mind about—about us."

"I wasn't calling to ask you to. In fact, I'm not even in Sunnydale at the moment."

"Where are you?"

"Business trip. Nasty bit of business. Maybe I'll tell you about it someday. But for now, I just called to hear a friendly voice. That's all."

Buffy hesitated. "I can be your friend."

I'll start with that, Spike told himself.